ZODIAC STATION

TOM HARPER

ZODIAC STATION

HODDER &
STOUGHTON

First published in Great Britain in 2014 by Hodder & Stoughton
An Hachette UK company

1

Copyright © Tom Harper 2014

A CIP catalogue record for this title is available from the British Library

Hardback ISBN 978 1 444 73140 8
Trade Paperback ISBN 978 1 444 73141 5
Ebook ISBN 978 1 444 73143 9

Typeset in Plantin by Palimpsest Book Production Limited, Falkirk, Stirlingshire

Printed and bound by Clays Ltd, St Ives plc

Hodder & Stoughton policy is to use papers that are natural, renewable and recyclable
products and made from wood grown in sustainable forests. The logging and
manufacturing processes are expected to conform to the environmental
regulations of the country of origin.

Hodder & Stoughton Ltd
338 Euston Road
London NW1 3BH

www.hodder.co.uk

For Owen and Matthew

North Pole Adventure 388

One

USCGC *Terra Nova*
Crew: 81 Coast Guard, 33 civilians
Mission: Scientific Support
Position: Nansen Basin, Arctic Ocean

What the hell is out there?

Carl Franklin, Captain of the US Coast Guard ice-breaking cutter *Terra Nova*, stared out the wheelhouse windows. A 360° field of view – but he might as well have his nose pressed against a painted wall. The clouds had settled after the storm, fusing the sky with the air and the air with the ice to make a perfect blank. Growing up in Maine, he thought he'd seen fog, but this was like nothing else. Even the bow light wasn't much more than a rumour.

He put his hand against the cold glass, just to touch something solid. Hopefully the crew didn't notice. In the middle of the Arctic Ocean, a thousand miles of ice around them and four thousand metres of near-freezing water below the keel, he didn't want them thinking their captain was losing his grip on reality.

He rocked back on his heels, reassured by the mass of sixteen thousand tons of steel under his feet. The *Terra Nova* was state of the art, the pride of the Coast Guard: an ice-reinforced vessel capable of making a steady three knots through four-foot ice, of smashing her way to the North Pole if need be. She'd already been there twice in her short working life.

A wobbling reflection ghosted up out of the fog. Santiago, the operations officer, an Arizona Latino who'd traded his hot, landlocked state for a frozen ocean. A thing for deserts was how he explained it; a thing for desserts, they teased him back.

Franklin turned. The spooky Santiago in the window became the real deal, six foot two of seafaring muscle, slowly being promoted to fat. By the time he made admiral, Franklin thought, the doctors would be giving him a hard time on his health assessment.

'The geeks want to go play,' Santiago announced.

The geeks were the scientists, the *Terra Nova*'s cargo, and her mission. Thirty-three scientists from all over the world, measuring the water, measuring the ice, measuring the snow, measuring the air. Fifty kinds of cold, Santiago called it. It kept them happy.

'What's the ice like?' he called to the crewman hunched over the satellite chart. A tie-dye swirl of greens, oranges and reds, constantly mutating as the ice shifted.

'Shitty for fishing, sir.'

Franklin checked his watch. Ten thirty at night, but that didn't mean anything here. The sun had come up four days ago and wasn't going to set for five months. Not that you'd know, with that damned fog.

'They can have three hours.' He looked out the window again, at the blank grey void that held the ship fast. They'd be lucky to measure their own feet in that.

'Put an extra man down there on bear guard.'

What the hell is out there?

Boatswain's Mate (second class) Kyle Aaron hugged the Remington 870 to his chest and hoped he wouldn't have to use it in a hurry. The gloves made his fingers so fat he could hardly get them round the stock, never mind pull the trigger.

2

Not that the gloves kept him warm, either: the only thing he could feel in his hands was prickling cold.

He shouldered the shotgun and swung his arms to get some blood flowing. Behind him, the geeks did their thing on the ice. Some of them had put up a tripod and were using it to winch a yellow buoy down through a hole they'd bored. Others paced out survey lines, walking backwards and forwards over the snow like they were checking for litter. Aaron, who'd scraped a D in ninth-grade bio, and spent four years of high school avoiding chemistry, wondered why they did it. He stamped his feet and wished they'd hurry the fuck up.

The fog had thinned a little. A ways back, the *Terra Nova*'s red hull loomed over the ice, her white superstructure dissolving into the cloud. He could hear the rasp of the deck crew scraping off the ice, and the low throb of her engine as the propellers turned slowly to maintain position. The yellow crane arm on her foredeck dangled the gangway on to the ice. He wondered how fast the scientists could run up it if a bear came.

The ground trembled; the ice cracked and growled. The shotgun wobbled in his hands. Growing up in Florida, cold was something you only saw at the movies. If he'd ever thought about the Arctic, the sea ice, he'd imagined it would be like the local skating rink. His first transit with the *Terra Nova* had set him right. However smooth the ice wanted to be, it sat on top of an angry, heaving ocean. Signs of violence were everywhere: high ice sails, pushed up by the pressure of two plates crashing together; sudden cracks of open water, even at minus twenty, where the ice sheet had suddenly cut apart. Broken chunks of rubble, like the wreckage of a frozen civilisation; and a crust of snow that sometimes froze hard enough to walk on, and sometimes dropped you through up to your knees.

He'd joined the Coast Guard to bust drug smugglers, and

3

rescue beautiful rich women from drowning in the Gulf of Mexico. Not to freeze his ass off guarding geeks who wanted to count polar-bear shit.

The ice trembled again. He heard a howling sound, not the wind – there was none – but the agony of the ice being torn apart by the sea below. Unless it was a bear. He peered into the fog. Shadows spun inside the cloud: changing light, changing ice. Was there something else? Something moving?

If you think it's a bear, it's a bear. That's what they taught you. He lifted the gun and thought about firing a warning shot. If he was wrong, he'd have some pissed-off scientists. But let it get too close and he'd have to kill it – and you didn't make rank in the Coast Guard by shooting endangered species.

You didn't make rank by letting geeks get eaten, either. He chambered a slug. The shadows swirled like stirred paint, spots in front of his eyes. He couldn't see a fucking thing. No distance, no definition.

But one of the shadows wasn't moving like the rest. It stayed in its place, slowly swelling out of the fog. Coming towards him.

He tugged off his Gore-Tex glove. If he hadn't been wearing liners, the metal trigger would have stuck to his skin. He aimed the gun up.

If you think it's a bear, it's a bear.

The shot echoed across the open ice – maybe all the way to the North Pole. It certainly got the scientists' attention. The ones who remembered the drill ran back to the gangway, dragging equipment; others, reluctant to let a $100,000 probe sink to the bottom of the Arctic Ocean, hesitated by the borehole. Everyone was shouting.

Aaron didn't hear them. The shadow hadn't stopped moving. Now it was so close it had started to take shape. He could see legs, the bulge of a head. It didn't look right for a polar bear – too tall, too thin and too dark. Maybe a reindeer? He'd heard they could float out on the sea ice way off from land.

No one was going to chew him out for shooting a reindeer. He fired another shot into the air, scattering more scientists, then put the Remington to his shoulder and aimed at the shape in the fog. Even in the liner gloves, his fingers had got so cold they felt swollen fat. He squeezed the trigger again.

The mechanism clicked on a spent shell. He'd forgotten to chamber the next round. He pawed at the pump, ejected the shell and slammed in another round. Pulled the trigger.

It was a lousy shot. His finger wouldn't bend, so he had to jerk the trigger with his whole arm, pulling the shotgun wide. Did he miss? The bear was still coming at him. He fumbled with the pump again, but his hand was so cold he couldn't work the action. *Fuck.*

He looked up to see if he was going to die. The cloud shifted, like someone opening the drapes, and just like that he saw it clearly. Not a bear, or a deer. It was a man. Skiing over the ice in jerky, broken movements: lunging up, shuffling forward, then slumping down again, using the ski poles like crutches. He wore a red coat and black ski pants; a red fur-trimmed hood was zipped up over his face.

I nearly shot Santa Claus.

It must be one of the geeks gone off the reservation, lost his way in the fog. But the geeks didn't ski. And they wore red pants, not black.

The man stopped as if he'd skied into a brick wall, almost falling over in his bindings. He threw out his arms and flailed his ski poles frantically; maybe he tried to say something, but either his hood muffled it or his voice was too weak. Without the poles to hold him up, he lost his balance and toppled smack into the snow.

Aaron laid down the gun and ran over. There was a name

badge sewn on the jacket, *Torell*, and under it an insignia he didn't recognise. A twelve-pointed star with a roaring polar bear in the middle. Next to it, blood leaked out from a nickel-sized hole punched through the fabric, crystallising almost as soon as it hit the snow.

Oh shit.

Footsteps floundered through the snow behind him. Lieutenant Commander Santiago, the ops officer, still in his ODU pants and a jacket he'd pulled on in a hurry. He stared at the figure on the ground.

'Where in this godless white fucking hell did he come from?'

The man stirred; feeble clouds of air puffed off his lips as he tried to speak. Aaron put his head close. The fur tickled his cheek.

'What'd he say?' Santiago demanded.

Aaron looked up.

'It sounded like *Zodiac*.'

Two

USCGC Terra Nova

The *Terra Nova* had the biggest sickbay in the Coast Guard fleet, but no doctor. Just a physician's assistant, the PA, Lieutenant (JG) Carolyn Parsons. For most of the crew's problems – splinters, scalds, sprains and sore heads – that was fine. For more serious cases, she could patch in the district surgeon on the video link. If that didn't work, it was the helicopter or – worst case – a body bag and the cold-storage reefer.

But the video link was down, the helicopter had nowhere to go, and she was damned if she was going to lose her first major trauma. Even if it was more complicated than anything she'd been trained for. The manuals didn't say how to treat someone for a gunshot wound and hypothermia at the same time. Lucky the slug had gone wide, taking a bite out of his arm but missing the bone.

He lay in a steaming-hot bath she'd rigged in the corner of the sickbay; a thermometer clipped to the side read 104° Fahrenheit. A saline drip snaked down from the ceiling and fed into his arm, just below the blood-soaked gauze pad strapped to his bicep. His clothes lay in a plastic basket on the floor where she'd cut them off him, together with a few things she'd found in his pockets.

He was a big man, even bigger than Commander Santiago. He couldn't have eaten much on the ice – the only trace of food in his pockets was a Mars bar wrapper – but he was

7

still in great shape. She'd needed two crewmen to help her hoist him into the tub. He didn't fit full stretch, but lay on his side, his knees tucked up like a baby. A folded towel cushioned his head. His eyes were closed; the heat had thawed the ice in his hair and matted it flat, revealing a small scar behind his left ear. She guessed he must be about thirty.

'What's up, Doc?' Santiago ducked through the sickbay door and leaned against the cream-painted bulkhead. 'Is he gonna live?'

'Most of him.' She pointed to the patient's right foot, where hard black boils blistered the skin. 'Might need to take off a couple of toes. Too early to say just yet.'

'He'll walk funny for the rest of his life.'

'He's lucky to be alive.' She checked the thermometer and ran more hot water. 'Frostbite, hypothermia, exposure and a slug . . . Did he really ski all the way from Zodiac Station?'

'Unless he got the jacket mail order.' Santiago crossed the room and pulled down the jacket from the peg she'd hung it on. 'Imagine, you come all that way and then a Coastie puts a slug in you.'

'*Semper Paratus*.'

'To fuck you up.' He wiggled his finger through the hole in the fabric – then stiffened.

'How many times did you say he got shot?'

'Once was enough.'

'Take a look at this.' He brought the coat over and stretched it out between his hands. Just below the Zodiac Station badge, his finger poked through another hole. A broad patch stained the fabric around it a darker shade of red.

'I did a tour in Umm Qasr. If I didn't know better, I'd say that looks like the entry point for a thirty-calibre bullet.'

'Then where's the wound? If that was a bullet, it would have gone right through his heart.' Parsons pointed to the man's chest. 'No damage. Plus, there can't be anyone out there inside of a hundred miles from here.'

'Maybe the polar bears got pissed off.'

A scream, like something from a horror movie, tore through the sickbay. The man in the bath was sitting up, legs tucked against his chest and eyes wide open. Water sheeted down his bare skin, as if the ice inside him had finally melted and was flooding out through his pores.

Parsons rushed over and tried to ease him back down into the bath. 'You need to keep down, sir. If your extremities heat too fast, there's a risk of heart failure.'

He resisted. Water splashed over the side and pooled on the floor. He was too strong; even half dead he couldn't be moved against his will. Santiago came over, but she waved him back. You couldn't force this.

'Sir, if you don't stay in the water, the warm blood in your extremities will flood back to your core and stop your heart. In your condition, it probably won't start again.'

He stopped struggling. 'It hurts,' he groaned.

'Hurts like a motherfucker,' she agreed. 'That's a good thing. It means you're alive.'

She pushed his shoulders down. He didn't fight her this time; through clenched teeth, he let her add more hot water. His eyes followed the line of the IV drip up to the bag, then scanned the room. 'Where am I?'

'Aboard the Coast Guard cutter *Terra Nova*.' It didn't seem to register. She poured a cup of hot water from a flask and handed it to him. 'You're safe, Mr Torell.'

'Anderson.' His mouth could barely make the word.

'I'm sorry?'

'Anderson.' He sipped from the cup. Blood from his cracked lips clouded the water. 'My name is Thomas Anderson.'

'Your coat – we assumed . . .'

9

'The zip on mine broke.'

'Whoever Torell is, I hope he has a spare,' said Santiago.

The man called Thomas Anderson looked up over the rim of the cup. 'He's dead.'

Santiago exchanged a look with Parsons. 'You want to tell us . . . ?'

'They all are.'

'*They?*'

'Everyone at Zodiac.' He slumped back down into the bath so that the water covered his chin. Santiago reached for the phone.

'I think you need to speak to the Captain.'

Franklin met Parsons in the corridor. They'd moved the patient out of the sickbay, into one of the empty staterooms reserved for scientists.

'How's he doing, Doc?'

'Stable, sir. Temperature's back up to ninety-eight, fluids good. As long as he keeps warm, he'll be fine. He's a survivor.'

'Yes he is.' Franklin reached for the door handle, but didn't open it. 'Is there something else, Lieutenant?'

'His psychological condition, sir. I'm not qualified to assess it, but he seems pretty locked down. Experiences like what he's had, sir, it's got to screw with your mind.'

'No argument with that.'

'Chief Bondurant has CISM training, sir.' *Critical Incident Stress Management.* 'I could ask him to speak to the patient.'

Franklin turned the handle. 'When I'm done.'

Anderson lay on the bed under a small mountain of pink blankets. They'd dried him off and dressed him in regulation-issue pants and sweater; Franklin was surprised they'd found any big enough. He sat propped up on a couple of pillows, eyes open, staring unblinking at the mirror over the washstand opposite.

Franklin rapped on the open door. The gaze switched on to him like a light coming on.

As captain, he was used to commanding nearly a hundred men for months at a time, in some of the toughest waters on the planet. He didn't get many situations that made him feel uncomfortable on his own ship. But the intensity of those dark eyes, clear as a child's, was hard to take. As if the ice had distilled them down to their coldest core.

He pulled a chair from under the desk and set it next to the bed. He looked over the report that Santiago had typed up.

'How're you doing?'

'Fine.' A soft voice, hard to match with the physique. Almost shy.

'Your name's Thomas Anderson.'

'Yes.'

'Are you a US citizen?'

'English.'

'You're a long way from home.'

'We're both a long way from anywhere.'

Franklin accepted that. 'You want to tell me how you got here?'

'I was a research assistant. At Zodiac Station. It's a scientific base on the island of Utgard.'

'I know where it is. What happened?'

'An explosion. I don't know why. I was out checking instruments – there was nothing I could do.'

'When was that?'

'What day is it today?'

'Wednesday, ninth April.'

'It happened on Saturday. Four days ago.'

'You skied a hundred miles over the ice in four days? By yourself?'

'I came to get help.'

Franklin looked at Santiago's report again. 'You stated to

11

the operations officer that all other Zodiac Station personnel are dead.'

Anderson's eyes locked on Franklin's – and, again, Franklin found he had to look away. He glanced out the porthole, but there were no answers in the grey world out there.

'You're British. You want a cup of tea?'

Anderson's face thawed into a smile. 'Love one.'

Franklin went out into the corridor. Santiago was waiting for him.

'We can't raise Zodiac Station, sir. Iridium, UHF, they're not answering.'

'Who owns that place? Did you try them?'

'The Brits run it out of some place called Norwich. As in Connecticut, but in England. We put in a call – they haven't heard from Zodiac since Saturday. They said Zodiac reported comms problems a few days ago and were taking their satellite link offline for maintenance.'

'Page the XO. Rig the flight deck, and get the helo out to Zodiac ASAP to take a look around.'

Santiago hesitated. 'That's right on the edge of its range.'

'I know how far it is.'

'Yes, sir.'

'It doesn't add up. This guy Anderson skis out of the middle of nowhere with nothing but the clothes he's wearing. He says he's been out there four days, nearly died, but did you notice his beard?'

'Can't say I did.'

'Doesn't have one. You think he found a bucket of hot water to shave out there?'

'Maybe he wanted to leave a good-looking corpse.'

'Then there's this explosion at Zodiac. We need to get eyes on the ground.'

'Yes, sir.'

Santiago headed for the wheelhouse. Franklin went to the

galley and fetched a cup of tea and a mug of black coffee. Back in the cabin, Anderson was sitting up in bed, exactly where Franklin had left him, eyes fixed on the door like a dog waiting for its owner.

Franklin switched his pager to vibrate and sat down in the chair.

'Why don't you start from the beginning.'

Three

Anderson

For as long as I can remember, I've dreamed of the north. I suppose a lot of people do. That feeling you get with the first snowfall of winter, something like a cross between Christmas morning and the start of the holidays. The world's new, the rules are suspended.

I was always a solitary child. Back then, those white deserts at the top of the globe fired my sense of adventure. I read Willard Price, Jack London, Alistair MacLean. Other boys could reel off every player who ever scored for Liverpool; I could tell you about Peary and Cook, Nansen and Amundsen. I grew up, a lot of things changed but my dreams didn't. If anything, they were more urgent. The Arctic wasn't a place to prove myself, but to lose myself. Somewhere to escape to.

You know what the two most seductive words in the English language are, Captain? *New beginning*. The north's a blank page, *tabula rasa*, white space on our own private maps we can fill in all over again. Snow gives us hope that the world can be different. A glimpse of perfection.

I'd applied for a post at Zodiac twice before, but I didn't make it past the selection boards. I thought I'd missed my chance. I was working as a technician in the Sanger lab at Cambridge – not high-status work, but I was glad to have it. I have an eight-year-old son, Luke; my wife died and I look after him alone. Between him and the job I kept busy enough. But every time it snowed, I felt that familiar tug, my internal compass swinging north again.

Then I got the email from Martin Hagger. You've heard of him? Ask some of your scientists – the biologists. He's a big gun. Everyone thinks life began in the so-called primordial soup, a warm broth slopping around the tropics. Hagger's theory was that it actually evolved at the poles: that the freezing and melting of the sea ice every year acted like a giant chemistry set to turbocharge the evolution of DNA. He found some pretty convincing evidence, made the papers and everything.

I'd studied with Hagger for my master's, and the first year of my doctorate, before we parted ways. Since then, I'd kept up with his research, but we hadn't spoken in eight years. Then, one day, there it was: an email from Hagger, inviting me to come to Zodiac as his research assistant. His previous assistant had had a wisdom tooth go wrong and needed to be evacuated. His loss, my gain. I had no idea why he'd chosen me of all people, after all that time, but I didn't care. There aren't many thirty-year-old lab technicians with a PhD. This was my shot. *Tabula rasa*.

The bureaucrats who run Zodiac fought it – hated it – but Hagger forced it through. No boards, no assessment. Forty-eight hours later, I was at Heathrow.

My sister was late. Ironically, it had snowed – only a centimetre, but the roads had jammed solid. Who expects snow at the end of March? Luke and I waited in the departure hall at Terminal 3, probably the most depressing place on earth, while the crowds tramped slush through the doors and the tannoy ran non-stop with delays and cancellations. Fog steamed off the passengers; the whole place stank of damp.

Just when I thought I might miss my flight, Lorna staggered in. There wasn't much time for goodbyes. I gave Luke

15

a long, tight hug and we both tried not to cry. When I let go, he gave me the envelope he'd been clutching. I smiled when I saw the address.

'You can take it to the North Pole,' he explained.

I tucked it in my pocket and kissed him goodbye.

'Don't get eaten by the polar bears,' said Lorna.

I flew to Oslo, then to Tromsø, where I had a ham and cheese sandwich and transferred on to a small Twin Otter for the last leg to Utgard. There was no one else on the flight, just me and the pilot and a couple of tons of supplies.

I suppose you know about Utgard. It's the last place in the world, the most northerly scrap of land on the planet. Easy to miss – so easy, in fact, that no one realised it was there until the twentieth century. Most of it's covered in ice, so much that the weight has actually pushed the land below sea level. Not that there's much sea, either: for ten months of the year it's frozen solid. The only notable population is polar bears, and a couple of dozen scientists at Zodiac Station. I wouldn't like to say who's hairier.

Even from Tromsø, it took another six hours' flying. We refuelled at the base at Ny-Ålesund, where the mechanics fitted skis to the plane and the pilot changed into his cold-weather gear. He gave me a dubious look, in my jeans and the jacket I use for walking the Broads with Luke.

'They said they'll issue me clothing when I get there,' I explained.

'Then hopefully we get there,' he said. I took it as Norwegian humour.

We carried on north. I stared out the cockpit window, keen for my first sight of Utgard. Behind the clouds, dark patches swam in and out of view, like bruises forming under skin.

'Will we be able to land?' I asked. The pilot shrugged. Was that another joke?

My first view of Utgard was a swelling on the horizon,

white peaks almost impossible to tell apart from the clouds. As we got closer, they resolved themselves into mountaintops. The clouds parted on a dramatic landscape, a Toblerone rampart guarding the western approach. The island was such a small dot on the map, it was hard to believe so many mountains could fit on it. They seemed to go on for ever.

We descended between the mountains and skimmed over a white fjord. The pilot banked, turned, and suddenly I saw two rows of red flags staking out the runway like drops of blood. The plane thumped down, bounced slightly, and skied to a stop. Considering we'd landed on solid ice, it was pretty controlled. Outside, I saw a limp windsock, a clutch of oil drums and an orange Sno-Cat. Otherwise, just mountains and snow.

'Welcome to Zodiac,' said the pilot.

The cold sank its teeth into me the moment I stepped off the plane. At the foot of the ladder, I saw a woman rolling an oil drum towards me. The first thing that struck me was that she wasn't wearing a coat: just a thick knitted jumper, ski trousers, and a woolly hat with tasselled flaps covering her ears. A long blonde plait hung down her back. Her cheeks were flushed red with the cold, and the eyes that looked up at me were a cool ice-blue.

'Tom Anderson,' I introduced myself.

'You're in the way,' she shouted, though I could barely hear her. The pilot had left one of the engines running, and the propeller almost drowned her out. So much for the silence of the Arctic. I scrambled out of her way and stood on the sidelines while she and the pilot ran a hose from the fuel drum to the plane. When that was secure, the pilot climbed in the cabin while the woman reversed the Sno-Cat up to the door. The pilot began sliding out the boxes of supplies we'd brought, which she loaded into the back. They seemed to have forgotten I existed.

I wanted to savour my first sight of the Arctic, but it was hard to concentrate. The cold squeezed my skull; my ears hurt as if they'd been slapped, and the icy wind made my eyes water. The propeller racket beat against me, and every breath I took was heavy with aviation fuel. I had gloves on, but they might as well have been tissue paper.

'If you freeze to death before you sign the paperwork, the insurance doesn't pay out,' said the woman. I hadn't noticed her come over. She grabbed my arm and dragged me towards the Sno-Cat. I couldn't believe how useless I'd got so quickly: I couldn't even lift myself into the cab without a shove from behind. But the engine was on, and the heater made the cab decently warm. I didn't like to think what all those engines running non-stop must be doing to the atmosphere. At that moment, I didn't care.

The woman climbed in and circled the Sno-Cat round, while the Twin Otter executed a quick turn back down the runway. In an impossibly short distance, it lifted off and disappeared behind the mountains.

'I hope you didn't change your mind,' said the woman. I still hadn't caught her name.

'Tom Anderson,' I introduced myself again.

She nodded, and kept on driving.

'What's your name?'

'Greta.'

'How long have you been here?'

'Two years.'

'Must be tough,' I sympathised.

'I like the silence.'

I took the hint. The Sno-Cat ground and bounced its way over the snow. Round the base of an outcropping mountain, into a low valley – and suddenly there was Zodiac.

It looked like a spaceship landed on an alien planet. The main building was a low, green oblong jacked up on spindly steel legs. A white geodesic dome bulged out of the roof; the rest of it was covered with a mess of masts, aerials, satellite dishes and solar panels. Subsidiary buildings clustered around it: a mix of faded wooden huts in assorted sizes, curved-roofed Nissen huts, and bulbous orange spheres with round portholes, like deep-sea submersibles left behind by a sinking ocean. Flags fluttered from a line of red poles that staked the perimeter, a shallow semicircle down to the frozen edge of the fjord.

We pulled up outside the main building – the Platform. It was bigger than it had looked from the top of the hill, almost a hundred metres long, with a jumble of crates and boxes stored underneath. A flight of steel steps led up to the front door.

A low bang rolled down the valley as I stepped out. I glanced over my shoulder.

'Is that thunder?'

'Seismic work,' said Greta. 'They're blasting on the glacier.'

We climbed the steps. On the wall by the door, a scratched and faded plaque said *Zodiac Station*; under it, a much brighter sign added, *British South Polar Agency*. It looked like the newest thing on the base.

'Did I take a wrong turn somewhere?' I looked around, half expecting to see penguins.

'New management.'

Greta kicked a bar on the base of the door and it swung in. All the doors at Zodiac opened inwards – to stop drift snow trapping you. Inside was a small, dark boot room, and a second door opening further in.

'No shoes in the Platform,' said Greta. She turned to go.

'Wait,' I called. 'Should I introduce myself somewhere?'

The door slammed behind her.

I left my boots and coat in the vestibule and ventured through the next door. The first thing I saw on the other side was a gun rack bolted to the wall: half a dozen rifles standing upright, more spaces where others were missing. Beyond, a straight corridor ran for what seemed an eternity, dozens of doors but no windows. It reminded me, unpleasantly, of the set of the Overlook Hotel. You know, from the film *The Shining*. Stanley Kubrick directed it.

I padded down the carpeted corridor in my socks. I read the signs on the doors I passed, little squares of card that seemed to have been typed on an honest-to-goodness type-writer. *Laundry Room*; *Dark Room*; *Radio Room*; laboratories, numbered in no particular order I could work out. One said *Pool Room*, and under it someone had taped a holiday-brochure photo of an azure-blue swimming pool. I opened it, out of curiosity, but there was only a half-size pool table crammed in a windowless cupboard.

Further along, I found the door for Hagger's lab. On a sheet of A4, a red skull and crossbones warned *HIGH INFECTION RISK OF UNKNOWN DNA*. Undeterred, I knocked and when no one answered I went in. None of the doors at Zodiac have locks except the toilet (and that had broken).

Hagger's big reputation hadn't won him any favours in the room ballot. His lab was tiny, though at least there was some daylight. Two small windows looked back to the mountains behind the base, a vision of clarity against the clutter inside. Wires and tubes were draped everywhere: you had to step carefully to avoid bringing down the whole show. Somehow, he'd managed to cram a complete laboratory on to the work-benches: a mass balance, a shiny electron microscope fresh out of the box, sample bottles, Erlenmeyer flasks, and a set of green notebooks lined up against the wall. A length of yellow pipe sat in a tray of water in the fumes cupboard. A small refrigerator humming under the bench made me think of the old joke about selling fridges to Eskimos.

A hard-topped table made an island in the centre of the chaos, though you could hardly see the surface for all the stuff piled up on it. Inevitably, I knocked something off when I walked past. A stapled sheaf of paper. I bent down to pick it up, and as I glanced at it – as you do – saw my own name staring back at me.

Anderson, Sieber and Pharaoh. 'Pfu-87: A Synthetic Variant on the Pfu-polymer Enzyme and its Applications for Synthetic Genomics'.

It was my *Molecular Biology* article: the first scientific paper I ever published. It was strange to be reminded of it on Utgard. Hagger must have wanted to remind himself I'd once been a decent scientist.

'Ha. The new intruder.'

A man stood in the doorway. I hadn't heard him approach – you never did at Zodiac. He was short and, unusually for that place, clean-shaven. He had a round head with not quite enough hair to cover it, and wore one of those drab army-issue jumpers with patches on the elbows and shoulders.

'Tom Anderson,' I introduced myself. 'Martin Hagger's new assistant.'

'I didn't think you'd come to sell us double glazing. Ha.' He shook my hand. 'Quam. Base commander.'

'Pleased to meet you.'

'I hear you rather put the cat among the pigeons in Norwich, coming up like this. Very irregular.' He squinted at me. 'Still, you're here now.'

'I am.' I meant to add something like 'Thrilled to be here' or 'Glad you could have me', but somehow the phrases jammed in my head so nothing came out except a sort of hiccup. Quam looked me up and down.

'I suppose I'd better show you around.'

'It seems very quiet,' I said, as he led me on down the corridor.

'Normal, this time of year. October to February we almost shut down; just a skeleton staff. I only got here myself four weeks ago.'

I tried to imagine overwintering there: the endless darkness; the stale jokes and stale food; the long, mournful corridor and the empty rooms. You'd go insane.

'The advance party come in March to set up. The rest get here in May. After that, it's a madhouse.' He opened a door numbered *19*. 'This is where you'll be sleeping.'

I peered in, though I couldn't see much because someone had decided to put the wardrobe in front of the window. Four bunks squeezed between four walls, with a leopard-print Claudia Schiffer looking down from a poster.

'Nice to have some female company.'

'That's to hide the escape tunnel.' Quam closed the door again. 'Only you for now, but you'll have to share when the barbarian hordes invade. You won't spend much time there, anyway. Hagger will work you pretty hard, I imagine.'

A dull detonation from up on the glacier made the Platform rock slightly under my feet.

'Is he here?'

'Hagger's up at Gemini. That's our camp on the ice dome. He'll be back in a couple of hours, when the helicopter gets in. Saturday night is movie night,' he added, moving on down the corridor. 'The lab, you've seen. Toilets, surgery.' Doors opened, doors closed. 'My office, if you ever need me. Radio room.' Another cubbyhole, packed with dials, gauges and cables. Static hissed from a speaker, and an American-accented voice was saying something I couldn't make out.

'Is that for us?'

Quam shook his head. 'The Americans have a ship up north. Coast Guard ice-breaker, crew of scientists. Two hundred miles away, but it's the nearest thing to civilisation from here. Every so often we pick up their transmissions.'

He turned a knob and the sound went away. 'Did you bring a mobile phone?'

'Yes.'

'You can leave it in your suitcase. No reception here. If you go out in the field, we'll issue you a satellite phone.'

'Internet?' I looked at the antiquated computer taking up half the space in the radio room. 'If there's somewhere to connect my laptop . . . I promised my son we could Skype.'

'We've no wireless because it interferes with the instruments. You can connect to the LAN with a cable, but you'll need an account. You can use this machine with a guest account until we set you up. I'll give you a form.'

I looked doubtfully at the machine. 'Do I have to know Morse code?'

The front door banged; footsteps thudded down the corridor. A stocky man strode towards us. I'd been reading Greek myths to Luke that week: in the dim corridor, something about him made me think of a charging Minotaur.

He stopped in front of us, under one of the fluorescent lights. He had a wide face and blue eyes and a beard he must have been working on for months. On top, his fair hair was cut straight and short, sticking up in a couple of places from his hat. The slogan on the sweatshirt said, *ZODIAC STATION – HELL DOES FREEZE OVER.*

'What the fuck's going on with the supplies?' His English was Scandinavian-perfect. A Viking, not a Minotaur. He flapped a pink sheet of paper at us. 'Huh?'

Quam's chest seemed to grow slightly. 'What's the problem?'

'I ordered nitrogen. For cooling my instruments.'

I laughed. Well, it seemed funny, having to cool instruments in the high Arctic. A black look said there was nothing humorous about it. I started to stammer an explanation, something about Eskimos and fridges, but gave it up. Not a good first impression.

'And?' said Quam.

'Instead of nitrogen, they sent me two hundred litres of this TE buffer solution. Two hundred litres,' he repeated. 'I don't even know what this shit is.'

'You use it for sequencing DNA,' I said, trying to be helpful. All I got was a dirty look. 'Do they think I'm running Jurassic Park here?'

'Whose name was on the docket?' Quam asked.

The Viking screwed the flimsy pink paper in his fist. 'Mine. But I didn't order it.'

'You must have made a mistake.'

He threw the paper away. It bounced down the corridor. 'Last flight, Annabel ordered some glacier drill and got a thermal cycler instead. You need to sort this shit out, Quam, or what the hell are we all doing here?'

He would have left it at that, but Quam blocked his way. He gestured to me.

'This is Hagger's new arrival.'

'Right.' The big man gave me a look I couldn't quite de-cipher. I was starting to get a feel for how the crew at Zodiac welcomed newcomers.

'This is Fridtjof Torell. Known as Fridge.'

I offered a handshake. Torell-known-as-Fridge ignored me.

'Was there anything else?'

'No,' said Quam.

He disappeared into one of the labs.

'Atmospheric scientist,' said Quam. He opened the door at the end of the corridor. A handmade poster pinned to it said, *Your Daily Horrorscope*, decorated with grinning death's heads and a clear plastic envelope where a slip of paper could drop in.

You are about to make some bad life choices, I read.

'And this is the mess room.'

The mess reminded me of an old working men's club: brown carpet and grey walls, long tables with plastic chairs. A few sofas and armchairs, leaking their stuffing, made a sitting area in one corner around an oversized television. Faded photographs hung crookedly around the room, a few of wildlife but most of stiff-backed men with hollow eyes and frost-rimmed beards. No one could have smoked in there for years, but you could still sense the stale nicotine. The only redeeming feature was the windows, which lined three full sides of the room and gave spectacular views of the fjord and the mountains. They made me want to go outside. Perhaps that was the point.

Through a serving hatch in the interior wall, I saw a small stainless-steel kitchen. A fat man with tattooed biceps and a too-tight T-shirt gave me a wave through the hatch and turned back to the pot on the hob.

'Danny, the cook. Danny knows all the gossip.'

Quam stopped in front of two huge maps hung on the wall either side of the door. One was a topographic map of Utgard, mostly white, with Zodiac marked in the lower left-hand corner. The other showed the earth, not as you usually look at it with the equator in the middle, but as you'd see it from a spaceship hovering over the North Pole. The Arctic Ocean filled the centre, hemmed in almost continuously by the countries that bordered it. Nothing south of Shetland made it on to the map; even the southernmost tip of Greenland needed an extension.

'The Antarctic is a continent surrounded by oceans. The Arctic is an ocean surrounded by continents,' Quam said. Passable imitation of a fourth-form geography teacher.

I found Utgard, between Svalbard and Franz Josef Land and further north than either.

'What's that?' I pointed to a grey shadow shaded on the

25

map, a thousand-kilometre barb pointing down towards Finland. It covered Utgard like a bespoke rain cloud.

'That's the Grey Zone – the old disputed border between Norway and Russia. That's why Utgard's unique. In the seventies, when they agreed to disagree, both sides committed not to press their claims to the island until they'd finalised the border. When they did, a few years ago, they found the easiest compromise was to leave it as an international scientific wilderness, administered by us. Technically, we're beyond all laws and governments here.'

'Good place to commit a murder,' I said facetiously.

'Or to make a killing. The 2010 treaty also opened up the area to hydrocarbon exploration. There's a company here now prospecting for oil and gas. They can't touch the land, but anything under the seabed is fair game.' He tapped the Utgard map, halfway up the west coast at a spot labelled Echo Bay. 'You might see them around.'

I stared at the tiny blot on the map – and the vast space around it. Most of the world, and almost all its population, might as well not exist.

The tour finished back at the front door. Next to the gun rack, Quam showed me two plastic boxes nailed to the wall and labelled *In* and *Out*. The outbox bulged with paper; the in was almost empty. A vinyl-bound notebook sat on a shelf below.

'This is where you check out. Whenever you leave the base, even if it's just for a wee, you sign in and out in the field book. If you're doing fieldwork, you fill in a risk-assessment form and put it in the outbox. When you come back, you transfer it back to the in-box. Understood?'

I nodded. 'Is there anything else?'

'You'll receive a safety briefing.' I had the sense of a recorded message being switched on. 'Pay attention, learn the procedures and follow them. Up here, procedure will save your life.'

'What about clothes?'

'Greta will issue your ECW gear when she does the induction.'

'The woman who brought me here?'

'Our base mechanic, field guide, vehicle engineer . . .' He looked as though he wanted to add something else to the description. In the end, he settled for, 'She'll find you.'

I lay on my bunk and tried to trick myself into going to sleep. Twenty-four hours of airports and aeroplanes had wrecked my body clock, even before I got to the land of the endless day. Light leached around the wardrobe. I reached behind it and felt a roller blind; I fumbled with it, but the mechanism was jammed. When I tugged, it collapsed off its bracket and rolled under the wardrobe with a puff of dust. I gave up.

My eyes drifted. In the half-light, I noticed some graffiti on the wall, white letters scarred into the wood panelling at knifepoint. I sat up and squinted.

You've got it in the neck. Stick it – stick it.

I rolled over on my side, back to the wall. The words chased round my head like a song I couldn't shake. I tried to get my journal up to date, and found I could hardly remember a thing.

The door opened. Greta stood silhouetted in the corridor.

'Come and learn how to kill polar bears.'

She issued me my gear from the ECW store – a cupboard overflowing with winter clothes. ECW, it turned out, stood for Extreme Cold Weather. Insulated trousers; a thick coat with a fur-lined hood; a balaclava and face mask; Black Diamond mittens; felt-lined boots; a helmet; a heavy all-in-one suit with zips up the legs.

'Your snowmobile suit,' she explained.

She grabbed two rifles from the rack on the way out, slung

one over her shoulder and gave the other to me. The moment we went outside, I was glad of all the layers. I pulled the balaclava up over my nose as she led me to a row of parked snowmobiles. As we were walking, she pointed out the different buildings with cryptic explanations. *The shop; the summer house; optics caboose; the bang store.* Some looked as if they hadn't been opened in years.

'What's that one?' I pointed to a small wooden hut, well away from the other buildings. It stood outside the main perimeter, in the centre of its own circle of flags.

'Magnetometer.'

'How come it gets its own little patch?'

'It's sensitive. Don't take any metal inside the circle.'

I scanned the perimeter. At the far end, where piles of rocks and rubble broke the snow, the poles had been crossed against each other to make five X's standing up out of the ground.

'The Gulch,' said Greta. 'Big hole, where the glacier comes down. Don't fall in.'

'Let me guess: the insurance doesn't cover it.'

'No, it does. But you won't be there to get the money.'

We'd reached the snowmobiles. 'Do you know how to drive?' she asked.

I shook my head. She showed me a little plastic paddle on the right handlebar. 'The accelerator.' On the other handlebar, a curved metal lever stuck out like a bicycle brake. 'The brake.'

'Is that it?'

She thought for a moment. 'If you tip over, don't put your leg down. The snowmobile will crush it.'

She pulled the starter cord. If she had any more advice, the engine drowned it. I moved to get on, but she waved me away. Standing behind the snowmobile, she put her hands under the back and hoisted the rear end off the ground. She held it there a few moments, then put it down.

'The tracks freeze to the ground when it's parked,' she shouted in my ear. 'If you don't get them loose, you burn out the engine.'

She got on; I climbed on behind her. I moved to put my arms around her, like riding pillion on a motorbike, but she shrugged me off.

'You've got handles at the side.'

I hardly had time to grab them before she gunned the throttle. The snowmobile bounded forward with a pop – slowly, then quickly up to full speed once we'd left the perimeter. The wind chewed my face; belatedly, I realised I'd forgotten to put down the visor on my helmet. I let go with one hand to lower it, and nearly got pitched off my seat as the snowmobile hit a bump in the snow.

The rifle range was on a low ridge to the north of the base. There wasn't much to define it, except for the inevitable flags staking out the corners. At one end, a paper target shaped like a penguin had been stuck on to an ice wall.

Greta showed me the gun. 'This is a Ruger thirty-oh-six. You ever fire a rifle before?'

'Yes.'

She looked sceptical. 'Show me.'

I took off my mittens, chambered a round and sighted the gun on the grinning penguin. My hands were already beginning to shake in their thin gloves; I tried to imagine how much more they'd be trembling if there was a polar bear right in front of me. Not a lot of time to get off the shot.

I pulled the trigger. Twenty metres away, a white hole appeared between the penguin's eyes.

I cleared the round and gave Greta a smug look.

'Can you do it again?'

I could and I did, half an inch to the right.

'Most British scientists hate guns,' she said.

'There was a time in my life when shooting rabbits was the only way I could afford meat.'

Most people laugh when I tell them that, as if it's a joke they haven't quite worked out. They cringe when I explain it's true. They don't like to be reminded how close we all are to the survival line.

Greta acted as if it was perfectly normal. I liked her better for that.

'But you always aim for the body on a bear,' she told me. 'Too many bones in the head. And if you have to shoot it, make sure you kill it.'

I took out the magazine, made it safe and shouldered the weapon.

'If a bear comes too close, fire a warning shot. If he keeps coming, fire more – but count your shots. You don't want to be out of bullets. Also, the regulation is that you can't shoot to kill unless he's closer than ten metres.'

'Do bears know the metric system?'

I thought it was pretty funny. She just shrugged it off.

'How fast can a bear move?' I said.

'Eleven metres per second.'

'So I've got a bit less than a second to load, aim and fire the gun at a charging polar bear.'

She shrugged. 'That's the regulation.'

'Has anyone at Zodiac ever been killed?'

'Someone has to be the first.'

A throbbing noise rose behind her. A red-and-white helicopter swooped over our heads, almost low enough to touch. I watched it descend to Zodiac while Greta collected the target. A handful of people scrambled out and hurried towards the Platform. From that distance, all in their standard-issue cold-weather gear, I couldn't tell which one was Hagger.

'Movie night,' said Greta brightly.

Four

Anderson

By the time I'd struggled out of my layers, the others had already sat down for dinner. *The new intruder*, Quam had called me, and I certainly felt like it when I opened the mess door. Conversations stopped; a couple of dozen faces looked up from their food. One or two looked friendly.

There were two tables to choose from, and no free seats at either. I looked for Hagger, but didn't see him. I opted for the table where Quam and Greta were sitting.

'Room for one more?' I asked brightly.

No one moved. Fridge, the Viking I'd met in the corridor earlier, gave me a bullish look.

'Staff and PhDs only on this table. Grads and techs are over there.'

I should have accepted it. I didn't want to make enemies my first night there. But when you're as low down the pecking order as I am, you cling to what you've got.

'I've got a PhD.'

'I heard you were Hagger's lab rat.'

I stood my ground. Fridge tried to stare me down. The others mostly looked at their plates.

Except one. 'Let's show the fella a little hospitality.' An Irishman, older than the rest, stood up and ushered me into his place. 'There must be space if Martin's not here.'

Chairs squeaked on the floor as everyone shunted along

to make room. Quam, at the head of the table, made the introductions. I gave a plastic smile, forgetting the names almost as quickly as he said them.

'And Greta you know,' Quam concluded.

Danny laid a plate of food in front of me.

'Where's Martin?' I said.

'He didn't come in.' This from an athletic, trim-bearded blond with an Australian accent. The helicopter pilot, I seemed to remember.

'Is he OK?'

No one rushed to answer that one.

'Has he radioed in or anything?'

'Radio protocol is for check-ins at oh nine hundred and twenty-one hundred,' Quam said. 'He hasn't missed one yet.'

Twelve hours seemed like plenty of time for things to go wrong. 'Who's he with?'

Quam stared down the table. 'Annabel?'

I remembered Annabel from the introductions. The only other woman besides Greta: tall, Asian and almost painfully slim, in a ribbed black turtleneck and hip-hugging black trousers. Her long black hair was pulled into a glossy ponytail down her back. Among all the beards and the baggy jumpers, she looked as though she'd dropped in from the pages of *Vogue*.

'Hagger wanted to get some data up on the Helbreen,' she said.

'And?'

'I didn't stop him.'

'You mean he went alone?'

'It's a serious breach of procedure,' Quam scolded.

Annabel's cheeks flushed under the dark skin. '*I* didn't go anywhere alone.'

'It's not like Hagger ever plays by the rules,' said one of the scientists, an intense American whose beard didn't hide

33

the fact he was younger than me. He was obviously sympathetic to Annabel. Most men on that base were.

'Hagger's not the only one who has a problem with the rules,' said Fridge. He and Quam exchanged a look.

'He's fine,' said Annabel. 'He's probably fucking a polar bear.'

From the far end of the table, I heard the crash of cutlery going down hard on to a plate. I didn't see whose it was. It came from Greta's direction.

I started to wish I hadn't shotgunned my way in with the scientists. Behind me, the grad students had a party going on; our table was like open day at the Asperger's clinic. Short, dull conversations that ended as mysteriously as they began; lots of chewing; not much eye contact.

I couldn't concentrate on my food. I couldn't stop thinking about Hagger. I was relying on him, my ticket out of the wasteland where my career had stalled for nearly ten years. If anything had happened to him . . .

'You settling in OK?'

I looked up. The man opposite – the Irishman who'd taken my side in the table dispute – was waiting for my reply. The patient look on his face said it wasn't the first time he'd asked.

'A lot to take in,' he said. 'You'll get used to it. I'm Sean, by the way.' As if he'd read my mind – or the embarrassment on my face that I couldn't remember his name. 'Sean Kennedy, base doctor. Most people call me Doc, which is about as much imagination as you can expect from this lot.'

He smiled collusively. The words 'genial' and 'Irishman' have an almost magnetic coupling, and they certainly stuck to him. About forty, with salt-and-pepper hair and a squashed-up face that you'd never call handsome, but open and cheerful.

'Are you used to the cold yet?'

34

'I think I'll need all the jumpers I brought.'

'You will if you go out in the field.'

'Most of what I do is in the lab.'

'And what is it you do?'

'Molecular biology. I work on the artificial assembly of DNA.'

'Where do you do that?' He jerked a thumb out the windows, where the setting sun had turned the mountains across the fjord a peachy pink. 'In the real world, I mean.'

'I work in Cambridge.'

'That's a coincidence.' He turned to Torell. 'Fridge here's at Cambridge, too.'

Fridge gave me a suspicious look. He hadn't brushed his hair; it still stuck up like a pair of horns. 'Which college?'

I could see where this was going – and no way to get out. 'I'm at the Sanger lab.'

It didn't put him off. 'Doesn't everyone there have to be on the faculty of another institution?'

'I'm on the science staff.' My last line of defence, and it wasn't enough. He leaned forward on his elbows, tilting the table towards him.

'What exactly do you do there?'

'I'm a technician.'

If it hadn't been for the grad students, you could have heard a snowflake drop in the room.

'Well, it's great to have another biologist here,' said Kennedy brightly, as if he'd completely missed the academic pissing contest going on. Though I caught a shrewd look in his eyes that said he'd missed nothing.

'Hear hear,' said one of the men down my side of the table. He was the oldest one there, a pot-bellied man with a white beard. If it had been December, he'd have been a shoo-in for Father Christmas at the station party. 'More biologists is what we need.'

35

'Dr Ashcliffe studies polar bears,' said Kennedy.

I smiled. 'I've just learned how to shoot them.'

It was supposed to be a joke. Ashcliffe recoiled as if I'd insulted his mother; his knee banged the table, jangling the cutlery.

Don't make jokes about shooting other people's research interests, I noted.

'And not forgetting our dear leader,' said the American who earlier had leapt to Annabel's defence. He made a mock bow in Quam's direction. 'You're a biologist too, aren't you, Francis?'

'That's right,' said Quam.

I watched the others turn on him. There was a subtext here I didn't understand, but I could feel the hostility. It was like being back at school, the dread that you'd be noticed.

'Why so coy, Francis? Tell him what you specialise in.'

Quam shook his head, like a man with his neck in a noose.

'Dr Quam is the world expert on the breeding habits of penguins,' the American announced. 'Adélies, isn't it, Francis?'

Unkind laughter rippled around the table. I thought it had to be a wind-up – but Quam flushed crimson and didn't deny it.

'Our new masters at the South Polar Agency thought we needed Francis to take us in hand,' said Kennedy.

'I wondered about the sign outside,' I said.

'Bonfire of the quangos. New government thought it was an unbearable extravagance having one agency for the North Pole and one for the South, so the decree went out from Caesar Augustus that henceforth and forevermore Utgard is part of Antarctica. Isn't that right, Francis?'

Quam glowered.

'There won't be any Arctic left at all if they don't change their energy policies.' That was Torell.

'Fridge's upset they haven't turned Utgard into a wind

farm yet,' said the American. 'Or was it an organic biomass generator you wanted?'

'I'm more worried about the methane emissions from the poo barrel at Gemini,' said Ashcliffe, the polar-bear man.

'Hey Fridge, how many CFCs do you give off?'

Someone bumped my chair from behind. The students had finished and were taking their plates back to the galley.

'Movie night,' said Quam.

We cleared the table. The others settled down to watch the film – that night it was *Alien* – but I went to the radio room to Skype with Luke. I missed him badly; I wanted to be home. It wasn't the solitude – I could have handled that perfectly well, I think. It was the people there who were making me lonely.

It wasn't a great connection. The picture froze; the sound stuttered. Luke was like that, too: eager questions one moment, monosyllables the next. I asked about school, about his friends, about my sister. I tried to describe the beauty of Utgard, but he didn't look interested.

'Did you deliver my letter?' he asked.

'I will do,' I promised. I wanted to reach through the screen and hug him tight, like the days he was off school sick and we'd curl up on the sofa watching TV. But of course I couldn't.

We disconnected. I was still staring at the blank screen when Greta popped her head around the door.

'Did Hagger check in?'

I stared at the racks of equipment in front of me. They had every communications device known to man, it looked like, but nothing that meant anything to me.

'I didn't hear anything.'

She glanced at a couple of the displays, then picked up a handset and dialled a number. I heard the burr of a ringing tone down the line.

I pointed to the handset. It looked like the sort of mobile phone people carried in the mid-90s, complete with rubber aerial and real buttons. 'I thought there was no reception here.'

'Iridium,' she said. 'Satellite phone. He's not answering.' She turned it off and threw it down on the desk. I followed her back to the mess.

'Hagger didn't check in,' she announced.

'It'll unravel,' Quam said, without looking up. 'It always does.'

'He's not answering his phone.'

'Probably forgot to charge the battery.'

'He's missed the check-in.'

'It's not twenty-four hours yet.'

'He must've dropped the phone down a moulin,' said Fridge. 'Or fallen asleep in his tent.'

Greta turned for the door. 'I'm going to find him,' she announced.

That got Quam's attention. 'There's a protocol,' he said firmly. 'If Hagger misses his next scheduled check-in, we'll initiate the search-and-rescue plan.'

'If he's in trouble, another twelve hours could kill him.'

He jabbed a finger at her. 'Do you know what the biggest danger is in a situation like this? People losing their heads, trying to play the hero and getting into far worse trouble than we've got already. It'll unravel.'

Her face blazed. 'Fuck you, Francis. There's worse things than penguins out there. Who's coming with me?'

She looked around the room. Standing behind her, I could see all their faces: Quam, furious; Jensen, the pilot, bored; Annabel, indifferent. Most of the others just seemed embarrassed – or kept watching the film. On the TV, John Hurt didn't look at all well.

'I forbid it,' Quam said.

I'd only been there a few hours, and I was already desperate to leave.

'I'll come,' I said.

Five

USCGC Terra Nova

A rap on the door. A sailor entered and handed Franklin a
sheet of paper.

'Just came through from Washington, sir. Confidential.'

Franklin read it. Anderson sat up in bed, cradling the mug
in his fingers.

'Has the helicopter reached Zodiac yet?' he asked.

Franklin shook his head. 'What do you know about Bob
Eastman?'

'Eastman?' Anderson swirled the dregs of tea in his mug.
'He was at Zodiac. American, astrophysicist. He worked on
gamma radiation, or something. Has he made contact?'

'Why didn't you mention him?'

Anderson looked confused. 'I did. At dinner, he was the
one needling Quam and Fridge. I didn't know his name then.'

'Someone knows his name. And they want to know where
the hell he's got to.' Franklin folded the paper. 'What else?'

'He was good at crosswords. He had a nice smile. He ate
Cap'n Crunch for breakfast, which he smuggled up inside
his telescopes.' Anderson shrugged. 'There were some
rumours, but that was just bullshit. At Zodiac, people started
rumours just to make life interesting.'

'What rumours?'

Anderson put down his cup and slid back under the sheets.
'Can I just tell the story how it happened?'

40

Franklin checked his watch. Washington could wait. 'Be my guest.'

Anderson

In the Arctic, you never just go somewhere. By the time we'd suited up, fuelled the snowmobiles, loaded the rifles, gathered all the equipment, a full hour had passed. We even signed the exit book. The whole time, I expected Quam to come down from the Platform, threatening us with the sack or waving a gun. But the door stayed shut. Nobody wants to miss movie night.

I waited while Greta hitched low metal sledges behind our snowmobiles. Hers, she loaded with enough equipment to reach the North Pole: spare fuel, a pair of skis, a tent and three steel boxes stencilled *SURVIVAL*. Mine, she left empty.

'In case we have to bring anything back,' she said, ambiguously.

It was my first time driving a snowmobile, but that didn't count for much. The moment we passed the flag line, Greta almost disappeared over the horizon. I squeezed the accelerator until my thumb went numb. The wind blasted my visor; grains of ice rattled against it like rock salt. The sledge behind me slid around, tugging me off course. And I still could hardly keep up.

We crossed the fjord and drove up on to the ice cap. It was a magical landscape, but I didn't see much of it. I had my head down, never looking more than a few metres in front, trying to spot Greta's track and any ruts in the snow. My hands ached; I kept waiting for a rest. Each time she slowed down, my hopes lifted. But each time, it was only to navigate a bump or a slope, and then I had to gun the throttle to close the gap again.

After about an hour and a half, she finally called a halt and tossed me a Thermos from her pack. While I fumbled the cup between my mittens, she rang Zodiac on the satellite phone.

'Hagger still hasn't called in.'

We went on. Now we were on the dome, an ice sheet hundreds of metres thick that covers two-thirds of Utgard. Strange to say, it felt like driving along a beach. On my left, a chain of mountains; to my right, a flat surface stretching down to the horizon. A few lonely rocks broke the surface, trivial in that vastness, until I realised they were the tops of mountains that had been buried in the sea of ice weighing down the island. The Inuit call them nunataks.

And it never got dark. The five-month-long polar day hadn't quite dawned, but it was coming. Even when the sun got below the horizon, you knew it hadn't gone far. We travelled in a protracted twilight, dim enough to see the tail light of the snowmobile in front, light enough that I could still make out the snow on the distant mountains. A few of the brighter stars peeked through the velvet sky. In that wide, wide space, so close to the top of the world, I could almost feel the planet spinning on its axis under me.

Eventually, where the ice dome funnelled into a glacier between mountains, Greta stopped and waved me to come up behind her.

'The last place his GPS clocked in was near here,' she shouted over the idling engines. She jumped down and disconnected the sleds, then tied two lengths of rope between the snowmobiles.

'What's that for?'

'Crevasses.'

I surveyed the unbroken snow. 'Are there many around?'

'It only takes one.' She made the rope fast in an intricate

cradle of knots and carabiners. 'Keep it tight. And don't drive over the rope or you'll rip it.'

We moved down the glacier in harness. The snowmobile didn't want to go slowly: if I feathered the throttle, it would rev but not move; if I pressed harder, it suddenly popped into gear and lurched forward. It took all my concentration not to mow down the rope . . . let alone watch for crevasses . . . let alone spare any thought for Hagger. I wasn't even sure the rope would do any good. If Greta went into a crevasse, the rope would more likely pull me in on top of her than save either of us.

Greta stopped. I let go the throttle so suddenly I almost fell off.

'Is it a crevasse?' I shouted. Then I saw it. A blue snowmobile, parked where the glacier rubbed up against the mountains. Pieces of equipment were scattered over the ground around it, hard to make out in the gloom.

I got down from the snowmobile.

'Wait,' Greta called. 'Hold on to the rope. And check the snow.'

'I'll follow your track.'

'Check it,' she repeated. 'The snowmobile has better weight distribution than you do.'

I edged over the snow, one hand on the safety line, the other holding the barrel of my rifle, using the butt to probe the ground in front. A hard crust had formed on top of the snow, but that was deceptive. It squeaked under my boots like polystyrene – and, like polystyrene, it snapped under my weight. Each time it broke, my heart froze while I waited for the drop. Each time, my feet landed softly in the powder snow underneath.

Greta was prowling around, examining the equipment he'd left.

'Don't you have to worry about crevasses too?'

'Martin knew the drill.' She pointed to four fuel cans that made a rough diamond around the abandoned snowmobile. 'He marked out a safe area.'

'So where's he gone?' I looked at the snowmobile. I looked at the boxes of equipment. No sign of Hagger. A shovel stood planted in the snow beside a square pit, about a metre deep. An open Thermos stood upright on one of the boxes, lid off, cup beside it, as if Hagger had been about to pour himself a cup of tea. The water inside the Thermos had frozen solid.

'Here.' Greta bent down and lifted a red climbing rope out of the wind-blown snow. It had been tied off on Hagger's snowmobile. She followed it across the glacier.

Then she stopped. She leaned forward. The rope went taut behind her. I hurried over.

A dark cut opened in the ice, a snaking fissure going down – I couldn't see how far. Narrow enough that you didn't see it until you were nearly there; wide enough you could easily climb in. Or fall. The rope trailed down into the void.

'Martin,' I shouted. I stepped forward. My foot caught a lump of ice half buried in the snow and kicked it over the edge. Loose snow showered down after it.

'Careful.'

Greta took a head torch from her pocket. Wrapping the strap around her wrist, she shone the beam down into the gloom.

'Keep watching for bears,' she said. 'They come up quick.'

I glanced around anxiously. The sun, never far off, was circling back. The sky had started to blue. Even so, the shadows were deep enough to hide all manner of evils.

'Look at this,' said Greta, and even she couldn't keep the emotion out of her voice. She pointed the torch down, wrist trembling slightly.

The crevasse was deep, maybe eight or nine metres. The walls bent and bowed, primitive shapes that seemed pregnant with meaning. The torch beam reflected brightly off them, all the way to the bottom.

A dark shadow lay flat against the ice.

Six

It was Hagger. Neither of us doubted it. We called his name; Greta threw down the cup from the Thermos to see if he would stir. He didn't move.

'I'm going down,' she announced.

You don't just go down into a crevasse – not if you want to make it out again. Greta spent half an hour driving screws into the ice, fixing pulleys and carabiners, and running a network of ropes between them. When she'd finished, she was webbed in a harness clipped to one end of the rope; I held the other.

'Slowly,' she told me. 'I tug once, it means you stop. Two tugs, I'm down.'

Standing well back, I paid out the rope. I didn't like to think what would happen if she fell. I imagined the jerk of the rope, my feet slipping over the ice towards the edge of the hole. Would I hold on? Let go? I remembered Quam: *the biggest danger in a situation like this is people trying to play the hero.*

The rope went slack. Two tugs told me she'd got down safely. I crawled to the edge of the crevasse and peered in.

Hagger still hadn't moved. Greta knelt beside him. She took off her mitten and wriggled her bare hand under the collar of his balaclava. It stayed there a long time.

'Well?' I called.

She shook her head.

★　★　★

Hagger was still wearing his climbing harness. Greta clipped him on to the rope, then added a loop around his chest so he wouldn't spin. I lay on the ground and watched from above. Compact snow pressed hard against me; the cold seeped into my chest.

And something was digging into my ribs. I rolled over and scrabbled in the snow, expecting a pebble or a lump of ice. Instead, through my mitten, I felt something unmistakably man-made.

It was a key. A perfectly ordinary flat Yale key, attached to a teddy-bear key ring. The bear wore a T-shirt, grubby with fingerprints, that said I ♥ NY.

I stared at it and wondered how it had got there. Had it fallen out of Hagger's pocket? There are no locks at Zodiac. Why did he need a key?

I zipped it into my pocket. Greta had finished with Hagger. She climbed the second rope, and together we pulled up the body. The hardest part was getting it over the cliff. Greta chopped a ramp in the crevasse lip with her ice axe, and I hauled him over. Like landing a fish.

'He's frozen stiff,' I said. Not just the body – his coat and trousers were solid ice, as if they'd been soaked through and then frozen. How had he possibly contrived to get wet? The glaciers wouldn't start melting for months, and we were a long way from the coast.

Of course, we didn't have a body bag. We zipped Hagger into a sleeping bag from the emergency box and pulled the hood tight around his face. A tuft of his beard, frosted with ice crystals, stuck out.

The sun had come up. I felt the weariness of having seen a long night through – though really, it was only three in the morning. Greta fetched the sledges we'd left up the hill, and we strapped Hagger on the one I'd brought. *In case we have to bring anything back.*

'You take the emergency sled,' Greta said. I was grateful. I didn't fancy three hours dragging a dead man.

I pulled the starter cord and gunned the throttle. The engine roared, but the snowmobile didn't move. Maybe the weight of the sled? I added more power; I smelled smoke. Too late, I saw Greta waving angrily at me.

'You forgot to loosen the tracks,' she shouted.

I jumped off as if I'd been shot. Together, we heaved the frozen tracks off the ice. I smelled scorched metal.

'Will it be OK?'

She shrugged. 'It's a long way home.'

We followed our tracks back up the glacier. I tried to look at the ground, and not at the stiff bundle on the sledge in front. There were an awful lot of implications wrapped up in that sleeping bag, but I didn't want to think about them.

And then I couldn't. The engine note changed; I felt the power sapping. Every time I eased a fraction off the throttle, the engine stuttered as if it was about to cut out. Twice, I rescued it by jamming on the throttle again. The third time, it died.

For a heart-stopping moment, I watched Greta carry on into the distance. Then she circled round, drove back and pulled up beside me. She flipped up the snowmobile's plastic nose and peered at the engine.

'Kaput.'

The day had actually got darker since sunrise. Clouds had blown up, fed by a wind that scoured the ice dome. The moment I opened my visor, a volley of ice granules peppered my face. I didn't know exactly where we were, but I knew it was still a long way from base.

'Can you fix it?'

Ignoring me, she reached inside her coat and took out the satellite phone.

'One of the snowmobiles broke down,' she told whoever answered. 'And Hagger's dead.'

She waited, fingers drumming impatiently.

'Have you got a fix on our position?'

Evidently they had.

'We'll stay here. I'm switching off the phone to save battery.'

She tucked the phone back in her coat and starting pulling equipment off my sledge. I stood there, helpless, feeling the warmth leaching out of me.

'Can't we both go on your snowmobile?'

'It can't carry both of us and two sleds. Two people, one snowmobile and no emergency gear isn't a good equation.'

'So what's going to happen?'

'We'll put up the tent.' She undid the bag and pulled out a large red tent roll. Another blast of wind almost blew it out of her hands.

'Is it safe?'

She didn't bother to answer. We laid the tent flat on the ground and weighted it with blocks of ice and steel canisters. Several times, we nearly lost it as we raised the poles. At last, we were able to crawl in. We spread mats and sleeping bags; I massaged my jaw, trying to get feeling back.

Greta lit the stove and reboiled water from one of the Thermoses. She pulled out two orange food sachets and offered them to me.

'Chicken or fish?'

I chose chicken. Copying her, I ripped off the top and poured boiling water over the dehydrated meal. I was too hungry to wait for it to absorb: I shovelled it in too quickly, spilling it on myself like Luke did when he was a baby. Hard fragments caught in my throat. The rush of calories made me shake.

'No hurry,' Greta said. 'Too much wind for the helicopter. They won't come here for hours.'

49

'Are we going to make it?'

I could feel my chest tightening with panic. The more I fought it, the more it pushed back. Forty-eight hours ago, I'd been at home with Luke. Now I was trapped in a tent on a glacier, the wind rising, with a broken snowmobile and a dead body outside. And I was so cold.

Greta didn't offer any sympathy. 'This is a Scott tent.'

'Is that supposed to be reassuring?'

'Scott survived eight days in one of these.'

'I thought the point was he didn't survive.'

'That was on the ninth day.'

I scratched around at the bottom of my carton, trying to pick out the last bits of food. Without asking, Greta handed me another.

'Where are you from?' I asked, as I waited for the second serving to go soft.

'All over.'

I wasn't going to let her off so easily. 'You have to come from somewhere.'

She thought about that. 'My mother's Norwegian.'

That explains the looks, I thought. I almost said it, but chickened out. It would be a long wait in that tent if she took it the wrong way.

'What brought you to Zodiac?'

She rolled over on her side. 'I need some sleep.'

'Me too. But I'm not tired.'

'I'm kind of upset about Martin right now.'

'Of course.' I felt like a heel. The truth is, Hagger had made such a fleeting cameo in my life it was hard to remember he'd been there at all. In the blink of an eye, he'd gone from an email on a screen to a bundle on a sledge; I'd never even spoken to him. Whatever reason he'd had for bringing me there, I'd never find out now.

I stared at the roof of the tent. Ice crystals were beginning to form on the underside of the canvas. 'He was like a father to me.' I saw the look Greta gave me. 'For a while.'

It sounded phoney, even to me. But it was true. The memory surprised me, like an embarrassing shirt found at the back of the wardrobe – something to make you wonder who you ever were.

'As undergraduates, we were all in awe of him. So many stories went round. He was like Professor Challenger, or Indiana Jones. He overwintered in the Arctic on a wooden boat, collecting samples. They said he shot a polar bear and ate his own shoes.

'The polar-bear story's not true,' Greta said.

It occurred to me that we weren't talking about the same man. For me, Hagger was something from the past – a piece in a jigsaw I'd abandoned a long time ago. For Greta, he was now. Someone she passed in the corridor, ate with in the canteen, sat next to at their movie nights. No wonder she was taking it harder than me.

'I should have kept in touch. He was an amazing scientist. He—'

She'd stopped paying attention – still listening, but not to me. She was staring at the tent door.

I reached for the rifle. 'Is it a bear?'

She shook her head and took the gun.

'It sounds like an engine.'

I heard it too. Deeper than a snowmobile's gadfly whine – more bass, throbbing beneath the howling wind. The ice beneath us shook. Greta pulled on her boots and unzipped the tent.

The noise stopped. The shaking stopped. I heard the styrofoam squeak of footsteps crossing the snow, the crust snapping. Then that stopped, too – right outside our tent.

'It's triple-A,' an American-accented voice said. 'You want a lift?'

Seven

Anderson

A yellow Sno-Cat sat parked outside our tent. Not like the machine I'd seen at Zodiac, a relic of the 1960s; this one was low and shiny and powerful and very much of the twenty-first century. Even the snow blown over its door sills looked like it had been styled for the brochure. Three pairs of skis stuck out of a rack on the back, and three men in yellow parkas stood peering at our tent. The word 'DAR-X' was stencilled liberally on everything I could see: doors, coats, hats, skis.

'Trouble?' Even right there, the man outside the tent had to shout over the wind.

Greta nodded.

He gestured to his Sno-Cat. 'You want out?'

The tent we'd raised so laboriously came down in a hurry. We left it with the snowmobiles. Hagger came with us on his sledge, wagging behind the Sno-Cat like a tin can tied to a car. I glanced out the rear window, and thought what a strange last journey it was for him.

There were only two seats in the cab. Greta and I and the man who'd rescued us sat in the passenger cabin mounted on the back. It was almost more luxurious than the Platform back at Zodiac, complete with folding bunks, a table and even a stove. Our host – the name on his coat said *Malick*; he introduced himself as Bill – brewed up coffee. We took

                                    d cradled the mugs to
                                    . Even the mugs said

                                    e. I'd pronounced it to
                                    ploration. Oil and gas.'
                                    ent. 'Aren't there easier

                                    ed million years ago,
                                    majors figure it won't
                                    e way.'
                                    ite ice field, and tried

                                    e in global warming,'

Bill gave her a look as if she'd started to smell. 'Even a Prius needs gas.'

'Well, I'm glad you were around,' I said emphatically. 'How did you find us?'

'Your boss from Zodiac phoned Echo Bay. Said you'd had a breakdown. We were out here anyway, so we thought we'd drop by.'

Greta's eyes narrowed. 'Aren't you supposed to stick to the coast?'

Bill smiled. He smiled a lot. 'Tourism. Little R & R. We did some skiing over on the Wendel, then stopped by Vitangelsk on the way home. You been to Vitangelsk, Tom?'

'He just arrived,' said Greta. 'He hasn't been anywhere.'

'Freaky place. Old Russian mining town—'

'Soviet,' Greta corrected.

'—abandoned in the eighties when Gorby couldn't afford to keep it open. Spooky as hell. Lenin, Stalin – all the shit that came down with the Wall everyplace else, it's still there. Commie time capsule.'

'I'd like to see it,' I said.

Bill jerked his thumb out the back, where you could just see Hagger's feet bumping along behind us. 'What's the story with him?'

'He fell down a crevasse,' I said.

Bill grimaced. He was older than me, probably in his fifties, grey hair and beard, but still wiry, someone who spent a lot of time outdoors. 'Tough. We lost a guy last year.'

'How?'

'Rock fell on his head and knocked him flat. He was frozen solid before we found him. Not so far from here, actually.'

He stared out the window. 'You look at this place and you think it's some kind of winter wonderland. But it's a killer.'

I couldn't disagree.

The DAR-X camp was a few shacks and cabins sprawled around a huge gantry, on the edge of a bay on the west side of the island. Red lights flashed a warning from the top of the rig. We slept a few hours in the Sno-Cat's cabin – I could have gone much longer – until a man at the door announced that the helicopter had come.

The Platform was silent and sullen when we got back to Zodiac. I lay down on my bed, but my thoughts wouldn't let up, so I went to Hagger's lab. I had a vague idea of packing things up, but the sheer volume of equipment defeated me before I began. Outside, the sun dazzled on the snow; inside, a crippling darkness gripped me. I've had it a few times in my life, and this was as bad as any of them. I sat on a stool and stared at the mountains until I had spots in front of my eyes.

Of course I was sad for Hagger. But – I'm ashamed to say – I was also angry, and the more I thought about it, the angrier I got. He'd been my one shot at redemption, after

54

five years as a lab slave, and now he'd ruined it before I'd properly begun, because he couldn't look where he was going.

Years of injustice seethed out of me: not just what *was*, but what might have been. The papers I'd have got my name on, the conferences, the seminars. The association with Hagger would have opened so many doors – and maybe one of them would have had a proper academic job behind it. Now I was just the man who'd found the body, a footnote to a piece of academic gossip. I could imagine the conversation playing out in the senior common rooms over glasses of sherry.

Hagger fell in a crevasse. One of his old students found him, you know.

Are they sure the student didn't push him in, ha ha?

Self-pity takes a lot of concentration; I almost didn't hear the knock. I looked, and saw Dr Kennedy peering round the door.

'I thought I'd find you here. Quam wants to see you.'

I didn't move. Kennedy gave me a searching, professional look.

'Hagger's death hit you hard, I'm sure. It's a terrible thing. So . . . unlikely.'

He advanced into the room. He looked as if he was about to take my arm. I didn't want to be touched, so I got off my stool and crossed to the door, keeping the lab bench between us.

'If you need to talk about it . . .'

'I'll be fine.'

I didn't want sympathy from these people I hardly knew. Luckily, Quam wasn't the man to give it. He sat behind his computer and his papers, a silver-balled executive toy click-clacking on his desk, and waved me into the chair opposite. The picture of a bureaucrat. He looked cross. Hagger's death affected us all in different ways: for him, it was a tragedy of paperwork.

'You'll have to write it up, of course. Can't be helped – but keep it brief. There's nothing anyone could have done. Terrible accident.'

'And me?'

He looked surprised. 'The plane's coming for Hagger tomorrow. You'll go too.'

'But what about his research? There must be experiments in progress – I could finish them up. So it doesn't go to waste.' *It's what he would have wanted*, I almost said. But that would have been too trite.

Quam shook his head. There was a picture on his desk I'd just noticed – two girls, about secondary-school age. No sign of their mother, and no wedding ring on his finger. I guessed long seasons at the poles took their toll on any marriage. Not that I was in a position to judge.

'I don't think there's any profit carrying on his work. My understanding is that he'd run into a bit of a dead end.' He winced. 'Unfortunate turn of phrase. But, frankly, it's probably for the best.'

'*For the best*,' I repeated. 'Are you saying—'

'Of course not.' He rowed back in a hurry. 'Martin Hagger was a great scientist who made valuable discoveries.' The words sounded so pre-baked I thought he must be reading them off his computer screen. 'But he'd had his fifteen minutes of fame. Between you and me, he was a busted flush.'

I didn't need to hear this. 'Was there anything else?'

'That's it.' Quam smiled, as if there were no hard feelings. Then remembered something as I reached the door.

'Don't forget to return your ECW gear before you go.'

I stepped into the corridor and almost ran straight into Greta. She must have just come in from outside: her face was red, and the frost on her eyelashes had just melted, so it looked like tears. She barged through the door and slammed it behind her.

'She's upset,' said Kennedy, loitering a little further down the hallway. Clearly a psychologist.

'They're sending me home,' I said. I didn't want to talk to him, and I couldn't bear to go to my room, so I went back to the lab. Perhaps I'd find something to take with me, some crumb of Hagger's experiments I could work up into a paper. It was the least he owed me.

Quam's warning echoed in my mind. *He was a busted flush.* But that couldn't be right. Hagger had been on a roll, at the top of his game. The *Nature* paper on sea-ice evolution had catapulted him to the head of his field. And he'd been working flat out. There had to be something worth publishing.

His notebooks would be the place to start. I looked on the workbench next to the fumes cupboard, where I'd seen them all lined up the day before.

The notebooks had vanished. You could see the place where they'd been – the only clear space in the lab – but the notebooks weren't there. Instead, just a single Erlenmeyer flask, placed very deliberately, as though the empty space had bothered someone.

Who could have moved the notebooks so quickly?

I turned on Hagger's computer. Another antique: it took almost a minute for the logon window to appear. The cursor winked at me and waited for a password.

I didn't know the password. Did anyone?

Frustrated twice over, I turned to the rest of the lab. I rummaged through the drawers and the cabinets. I even looked in the fridge. It was full of water samples in sealed bags, each labelled with codes I didn't understand. In the freezer compartment, I found a foot-long tube of ice wrapped in a plastic bag with a reference number scrawled on it in black marker.

I supposed the lab would have to be cleared out, ready for the next occupant. At least it was something to do. I found some boxes and started to lay them out on the floor.

'This is bullshit.'

I jumped; I hadn't heard her come in. Greta shut the door behind her, though there was hardly room for both of us with the boxes. She looked furious.

'I thought . . . if anyone should do it, it should be me,' I said weakly.

'Quam wants to cover it up,' she announced.

'Cover what up?'

'Martin's death.'

I didn't understand. 'How could he do that?'

'Because he's scared. He's base commander, it's his responsibility. Hagger should have had a buddy with him.'

It seemed tough to blame Quam because Annabel and Hagger had broken the rules. 'Hagger's an internationally renowned scientist,' I said. 'Quam can't pretend it didn't happen.'

'He'll say it was an accident.'

'It *was* an accident.'

Greta gave me one of her impenetrable looks. 'Now you sound like Quam.'

I sat down on Hagger's stool. I was still short on sleep; my head hurt. 'Can you . . . explain?'

'Martin didn't walk into that crevasse by accident. He knew it was there. He'd rigged the ropes.'

'He could have tripped.'

'He was lying on his back.'

'Maybe the ice broke.'

'And where was his gun?'

I shook my head. 'I didn't see it.'

'At the bottom of the hole. Not slung on his back. He must have been holding it when he fell.'

Suddenly, everything fell into place. 'A polar bear. That's why he had the gun out. The bear advanced, Martin stepped back – and fell into the crevasse.'

Greta's face hardened. 'That's Quam's theory.'

'What's wrong with it?'

'There was no bear.'

'How do you know?'

'No tracks.'

'Are you sure? They'd be easy to miss.' I picked up a glass pipette from the counter and turned it over in my fingers. 'Everything was such a panic.' Not, I had to admit, that she'd been panicking.

'The first thing you look for on Utgard is bear tracks. Every time you go out, every time you stop. There were no tracks.'

'So what do you think happened?'

She looked at me like it was the most obvious thing in the world.

'Someone pushed him.'

Eight

Anderson

The pipette snapped in my hand. Broken glass scattered on the floor. Blood welled out of the cut that had opened on my finger.

'*Shit.*'

I grabbed a wad of paper from the roll near the sink and pressed it to the cut. Blood soaked it almost at once.

'You should see Doc,' said Greta.

I threw the paper away and got a fresh piece. 'It's . . . insane. There's no evidence.'

Greta's look made me forget about the cut for a moment. 'You're the scientist,' she said as she walked out the door. 'Wait,' I said. But she didn't.

I climbed down from the stool and tried to sweep up the broken glass one-handed. I couldn't find a dustpan: I had to use a piece of cardboard, trying not to step on the tiny fragments in my socks.

I paused to rearrange the tissue on my finger, and a bead of blood spattered on the floor. I stared at the Rorschach blot it made, wondering what it meant.

I didn't know anything about Greta. She seemed pretty hardheaded, but that didn't make her infallible. She'd taken a set of facts, from a confused and horrible situation, and made a leap that couldn't possibly stand up. In the jargon, she'd confused correlation with causality. Probably because she hated Quam.

Though I didn't have a better explanation. I didn't even know why Hagger had brought me there. I glanced over at the counter where his notebooks had stood. They hadn't come back.

The door opened. To my surprise, it was Greta again.

'I'm going to get the snowmobile you broke,' she announced.

Somehow, I'd been around her long enough to understand that this was an invitation.

The winds had dropped. Jensen, the pilot, flew us out in the helicopter. Greta rode up front; I sat in the back with a pile of what looked like *Titanic*-era life preservers wrapped up in a cargo net.

'Terrible thing about Hagger,' said Jensen over the intercom in my helmet.

'Yeah,' I heard Greta agree.

'Tragic accident.'

I waited for her to launch into her murder theory. Thankfully, she kept it to herself.

'What were you doing yesterday?' I asked, trying not to make it sound like I was implying anything.

'Chasing bears,' said Jensen. 'Ash was tagging.'

It took me a moment to make sense of that. I assumed Ash must be Ashcliffe, the polar-bear man who looked like Father Christmas.

'How do you tag a polar bear?'

'You shoot it with a tranquilliser dart,' said Jensen. 'If that doesn't work, you shoot it again. And make sure you're out of there before it wakes up.'

'Get many?' said Greta.

'Three.' A gust shook the helicopter; Jensen broke off to concentrate on the controls. Below, I saw the peaks sticking out of the ice cap like the funnels of sunken ships.

'Any up near the Helbreen?' Greta asked.

A defensive note came into Jensen's voice. Maybe I imagined it. 'Nope.'

'Tom thinks Martin could have been chased by a bear.'

'Maybe you saw it,' I chipped in.

'We were further over. Not many bears that far north at the moment.'

I found it odd discussing the bears so casually. To me, never having seen one, we might as well have been talking about dinosaurs.

'That took most of the day?' said Greta.

'Pretty much. We kept trying for one more. Ash buys me a beer if we get four.'

Greta peered through the canopy. 'We're getting close.'

Jensen left us in a flurry of rotors and whipped cold air. When the snow settled, it was just me and Greta, two snowmobiles and a sledge. Greta had brought some spare parts. I held open the snowmobile's nose while she knelt over it and performed surgery. As ever, the moment you stopped moving, the cold started to chip away at you. I pulled my neck-warmer up over my nose. The snow and ice stretched towards the horizon, rippled channels like a dried-up seabed. A desolate place.

'It's lucky the DAR-X people were around to pick us up,' I said.

'Mm.' Greta pulled out a piece of the engine. Oil stained the snow green. 'Lucky.'

There was an implication there, but I ignored it. The place was lonely enough without entertaining the nonsense that someone had killed Hagger in cold blood.

'Martin visited Echo Bay a couple of times,' Greta said suddenly.

That surprised me. 'How come?'

'He didn't say.'

Another conversation died before it started. But it made me think of something else.

'How well did you know him?'

Greta unscrewed a Thermos and poured hot water over the engine. Steam hissed off the cold metal. 'Can you pass me the five-eighths-inch spanner.'

'You were good friends?'

'That's the three-quarter-inch. Read the number on the handle.'

I filed the question under 'Save for Later' and found the right spanner. 'Did he ever say why he brought me here?'

'He thought you could explain something. "Tom Anderson will know," he said.'

'What does that mean? Know what?'

'He wasn't talking to me.'

'Who, then?'

'Himself.'

She pulled the starter cord and the engine exploded back to life. I dropped the nose cone and she latched it shut.

'You want to go?' she asked.

'Where?'

'The crevasse. It's only a few kilometres.'

I hesitated.

'What are you afraid of?'

'Bears,' I said, straight-faced.

The crevasse looked different now. In the twilight that passed for night, it had been a dull grey hole. Today, in the sunshine, it came alive. The walls glowed a cool blue, like a swimming pool sparkling in the light. Greta held me a few metres back.

'Do you see any bear prints?'

'I wouldn't know what to look for.'

She took off her glove and pressed the heel of her hand

into the snow, making a rounded kidney shape. Spreading her fingers, she poked five holes just in front of it for the toes.

'That. But bigger, like a soup plate.'

I didn't see any. 'Couldn't the wind have covered them?'

'You see your prints?'

I did. Softened by the wind and half filled with blown snow, but still clear enough from the day before.

'A bear weighs up to a thousand kilos. He makes a deeper print than you.'

I did a slow scan of the snow, right the way around Hagger's safe area.

'Point taken.'

Greta advanced to the crevasse. I followed – and almost walked straight into a hole. Not a natural hole: an almost perfect cube cut out of the snow and ice, straight-sided, flat-bottomed, about a metre and a half deep. I'd seen it the day before, with a shovel standing next to it. The shovel had blown over in the night.

'What's that?'

Greta barely looked at it. 'Snow pit. To measure layers in the glacier.'

'Martin's work was on sea ice, not glaciers.' Notwithstanding the glacier core I'd seen in the freezer in his lab.

'He said he'd come to get samples.'

'Isn't there a glaciologist at Zodiac who does that?'

'Dr Kobayashi.'

I remembered her. Annabel, the only other woman on base. Slimmer, taller and – some would say – more attractive than Greta. Perhaps that explained the sourness that had crept into Greta's voice.

Greta knelt and scrabbled in the loose snow, about ten feet back from the crevasse. Her hand came up holding a black mitten.

'He dropped his gloves.'

'Why?'

'Stand here,' Greta told me, pointing at a spot on the ground next to where she'd found the mitten. 'Now take a step back.'

Feeling silly, I did what she told me.

'You see your footprints.'

'Yes.'

'And the ones next to it?'

Now that she said it, I did. Side by side with mine, softened by the wind and slightly longer.

'Those are Hagger's.'

I took her word for it.

'What do you see?'

Even with the outline eroded, I could make out the heel and the toe. Pointing the opposite way to me.

'He walked away from the cliff.'

Greta gave an impatient sigh. 'Really?'

I thought about it for a moment – and reached the obvious conclusion. 'He was walking backwards.'

'You think it's a good idea to walk backwards in a crevasse field?'

'He would have had to go backwards to climb down into the crevasse.'

'Yeah,' she agreed. 'Except he wasn't clipped on to the rope.'

Greta walked to the edge. 'Martin was roping up. He put the harness on. Then someone came. They threatened him. Martin backed off; he was scared enough to get out his gun. He took off his gloves so he could pull the trigger. But he'd gone too far.'

I came up beside her and looked down into the crevasse. At the bottom, I could just see the impression in the snow where Hagger had landed. The abandoned rifle lay a few feet away.

Had he really been chased to his death by someone from Zodiac?

'It's too sick to think about,' I said out loud.

Greta's look made me cringe.

'Is that what they taught you in science school? Don't ask difficult questions?'

'I don't even know what questions I'm supposed to ask.'

She started to walk back to the snowmobile. 'Who's got big feet?' she called over her shoulder.

'What's that supposed to mean?'

She stopped and pointed. In a clean patch of snow, I could see another set of footprints. Bigger than mine; bigger than Hagger's. They tracked Hagger towards the crevasse – then stopped, a couple of metres back from the edge. Probably about the time Hagger realised there was nothing under him but air.

'Who's got big feet?' I repeated. I traced the tracks in the snow, wondering how far they'd lead me. About ten metres, where a jumble of broken rocks marked the edge of the glacier. Another dead end.

I put my hand in my pocket and felt a lump, the key I'd found by the edge of the crevasse. I took it out for Greta to see and explained where I'd found it.

'It must have fallen out of Martin's pocket, I suppose.'

'I never saw him with a key.'

'How else—'

She pointed to the large footprints. 'Maybe his.'

That was a nasty thought. I dangled it away from me, like something picked out of a blocked drain. No clue to say who it might have belonged to. I ♥ NY didn't mean much. I mean, who hasn't been to New York?

I put it away and looked back at the footprints.

'Shouldn't we take some photographs? Something to show Quam?'

'You trust Quam?' Greta had got her backpack off the snowmobile seat and zipped it open. She pulled out a fat coil of rope and a webbing harness, which she tossed to me.

'What's this for?'

She shook out the rope and tied it around the snowmobile's cowling. She handed me the other end and nodded to the crevasse.

I backed away. 'I've never done anything like this.'

'Then you should learn.' She snapped a carabiner at me like a crab's claw. 'If something happens, you need me up top to get you out.'

The light changed as she lowered me in, like slipping into a lagoon. An intense, sapphire blue that soothed my eyes after the stark white landscape. I couldn't stop looking at it. The ice walls swam in sinuous shapes, curves and hollows that no human mind could have conceived.

I shuddered as my feet touched down on the snow at the bottom. For a moment, I felt very clearly that I was standing in Hagger's grave. My senses came alive, fluid roared in my ears and the ice seemed to tremble, as if the walls were colliding to crush me.

Greta's face appeared above me. Small, a long way off.

'Are you OK?'

'Fine.' I put out my arm and pressed my gloved hand against the wall, just to be sure. The ice was cool and adamant. One day, it would move and close up Hagger's grave. But not now.

I walked along the crevasse floor, the rope paying out behind me. It wasn't long, maybe twenty or thirty metres, curving in a shallow crescent so that from one end you couldn't see the other. The only marks in the snow were my own footprints. Whatever Hagger had planned to find here, he hadn't had a chance to look.

They call Utgard the last place on earth. For me, buried in ice, freezing cold, at the end of a crevasse where a man had died, I felt like the last man on earth. The blue walls no longer bathed me: they drowned me. There was nothing here.

But as I turned to go back, something caught my eye. A strange formation at the bottom of the cliff, flat grey against the blue-gloss ice. Spindly columns poking out of the snow like the teeth of a comb. Ivory smooth. I reached out to touch them.

And gasped as I realised what they were. The sound echoed off the ice, back and forth, as if I was in the throat of an enormous beast.

A beast who ate bones. That was what they were. Bones. I saw it the moment I touched them. Limbs and a ribcage, so small that for a ghastly moment I thought it might be a child's. Then I got hold of my senses.

Greta's face appeared again at the top of the crevasse, dark against the sky.

'Find something?'

'There are bones down here. A polar-bear cub.' I didn't look too closely, but that was all it could be. Definitely not a bird, and no way a seal could have come this far from the sea. 'The body's completely decomposed.'

'Bodies don't decompose on Utgard.'

'They must be ancient, then.' Perhaps that explained the size, some prehistoric creature that had dropped dead thousands of years ago – millions, maybe – and been swallowed by the ice. Preserved perfectly, museum-fresh; only revealed this year when the crevasse split open.

And Hagger had died here. A gruesome coincidence, I insisted, trying to shut up the superstitious voices in my head. Still terrifying.

'Is that what Martin came for?' she asked.

I looked around. Only my footprints.

'Martin never came down here.' That wasn't quite accurate. 'Not when he was alive.'

'Anything else?' She jerked her head towards the snowmobiles. 'It's a long drive back.'

I left the bones in their icy grave. And this time, I remembered to free the snowmobile tracks from the ice before I started the engine.

Nine

Anderson

Nobody enjoyed dinner that night. Hagger's death made for a brittle mood. People shuffled food around their plates and didn't make eye contact. Across the table, Fridge gnawed the meat off a chicken drumstick. I tried not to think about the bones in the crevasse.

Quam got the evening off to a bad start. As soon as the food was served, he stood up and tapped his glass with a fork. He had to wait, awkwardly, while the conversations grudgingly wound down.

'I want to say a few words – since you're all here.' He wiped his mouth with his napkin. 'Martin Hagger's death is a tragedy. He was a great scientist, a respected colleague, and a good friend.'

That morning, he'd told me Hagger was a busted flush. Glancing around the table, I didn't see much evidence of good friends. Most of them looked hostile – or just bored. I couldn't tell if it was Hagger they didn't care for, or Quam.

'The important thing is, we don't let this get in the way of what we're all doing. The best tribute to Martin Hagger will be carrying on our valuable science here at Zodiac.'

I think I snorted out loud. Fridge, across the table, gave me a funny look. I could have told him that Quam had forbidden me from carrying on the *valuable science* that Hagger had been doing – but I refrained.

Quam pulled out a piece of paper. 'I'd like to read a few words. I'm sure they'll be familiar to most of you, but I think they capture something. By Captain Robert Scott.'

'Penguin shagger,' someone said.

Quam ran the paper between finger and thumb to smooth the crease.

'"I do not regret this journey. We took risks, we knew we took them."' He coughed. It's fair to say, he wasn't a natural public speaker.

'"Things have come out against us, and therefore we have no cause for complaint."'

'Easy for you to say,' muttered a voice behind me. But most of the room had settled into a respectful hush. Even on the Platform – heated, insulated, Internetted and well fed – we knew the line between life and death up there was fragile and transparent as a window pane.

Quam raised his glass. 'To Martin Hagger. We'll miss him.'

The rest of us shuffled to our feet and mumbled Hagger's name. 'We'll miss him.'

'And the grant money he brought in.'

Eastman's voice cut through the toast, loud and meant to be heard. Quam's face went bright red.

'That's in poor taste.'

'It's true, isn't it?'

'I won't dignify—'

'And it wasn't just the grant money,' piled in Fridge. 'Hagger brought in all kinds of extra funding for you.'

'If you're insinuating . . .'

It was fascinating, watching the scientists tear into their base commander like a pack of wolves. Far more than just professional rivalry. I leaned back and watched the sport. The only person who ignored it completely was Annabel. She sat up, finishing-school straight, dismantling her chicken with small, precise cuts.

'Let's cut the bullshit,' said Eastman. 'We're all sad Hagger's dead. But hands up who actually liked the guy.'

It was obscene to play along – but I put up my hand. I owed Hagger that much. Down the table, I saw Greta's and Jensen's arms up too. Kennedy, Ashcliffe the polar-bear hunter and Quam followed suit more slowly, reluctant to get drawn in. Fridge's and Eastman's hands stayed down. Annabel kept eating.

Someone killed him. Even after our trip to the crevasse, I only half believed it. But that didn't mean I trusted these people. Was it really possible? Three of them clearly had enough against Hagger they couldn't even pretend to have liked him. But then if you'd killed him, you'd probably hide your motive a bit better. Or double-bluff. Or . . .

If I thought like that, I'd tie myself in knots until I doubted everything. Meanwhile, Quam was still standing. 'I think an apology's in order.'

Like a lot of Americans, Eastman had a naturally theatrical presence. He looked around the table and gave a small bow. 'I'm sorry if I embarrassed your British, uh, sensibilities.' Heavy with sarcasm. 'But let's not pretend this was something it's not. He's not a martyr to science. He died; it was an accident. Move on.'

'If it was an accident,' I said. I thought nobody heard me.

Eastman checked his watch. 'Isn't it time to get the mag reading?'

The others suddenly took a keen interest in their half-empty plates. I was too slow; I caught his eye.

'Anderson's the rookie – he should go.'

'He's going home tomorrow,' Quam pointed out.

'Then this is his only chance.'

I wasn't going to be haggled over. I stood. 'What do I have to do?'

'There's a logbook in the mag hut. Write down the number

on the readout, and the time. Wait ten minutes, do it again. That's it.'

I was glad to get out, even with all the fiddle of layering up again. I took a gun from the rack by the door – already second nature – and clomped down the steel steps. The cold air pinched my nose dry; my eyes watered. I'd forgotten my neck-warmer, and by the time I was halfway across the base my chin stung as if I had lockjaw. That was the thing with Zodiac. No slack.

I stopped at the flag line, where the ring that surrounded the magnetometer hut met the base perimeter. A sign warned me, *NO METAL OBJECTS BEYOND THIS POINT*.

I didn't see anywhere to put the gun. After a moment's thought, I laid it down on the snow. Strange to say, I felt incomplete without it, like taking off a wedding ring. Walking across the circle of snow to the hut, the immensity of my surroundings pressed in on me. Twilight had fallen; a few stars were bright enough to show in the sky. I checked the shadows for signs of danger, ready to run back for the gun if I saw anything that looked like a bear.

The hut was a simple, one-room wooden cabin, almost colder than the air outside. A wooden table stood in the centre, two grey boxes on top of it like outmoded stereo components. The logbook lay beside them, a battered exercise book with a pencil hanging off it on a piece of string.

I wiped a layer of frost off the readout and studied it. A thin digital line scribbled up and down the screen, recording infinitesimal oscillations in something I couldn't even imagine. I looked for an obvious number to write down, and didn't see it.

In the chill quiet, the steps in the snow sounded as loud as bubblegum popping. I looked at the door; I listened. The steps came closer. Two legs, or four?

There was no lock on the hut, and my gun was back at

the flag line. Could a polar bear open a door? Could he fit through? I'd thought the bear warnings were just talk, a fairy tale to frighten new arrivals. But human beings are uniquely bad at judging risk. The longer something doesn't happen, the more confident we become it won't. We don't see the sand running out of the glass.

The door swung in. I almost whimpered with relief when I saw it was Dr Kennedy, bundled up in a snowmobile suit and a loud tartan scarf.

'I hope I didn't scare you.'

'Were you worried I'd screw up the measurements?'

Kennedy shut the door and tipped back his hood. 'I wanted a word in private. About Hagger.'

'OK.'

'I probably shouldn't tell you this . . .' Kennedy rummaged in his suit and produced a bottle. He offered it to me. 'Medicinal supplies.'

I took a slug and gave it back.

'Jameson's,' said Kennedy. 'Just the thing.'

'What did you want to tell me about Martin?'

He screwed the cap back on the bottle. 'You know he overwintered here?'

I didn't. Overwintering was a hard assignment, a job for grad students or people who couldn't get any other foot on the ladder. Darkness, solitude and endless instrument readings. I'd applied for it twice.

'Why?'

'To get some work done. There were experiments that hadn't gone the right way, he wanted time to sort it out.' He fiddled with the bottle. 'He was quite down about it, poor fellow.'

'Four months of night would do that to anyone.'

The cap came off. Kennedy offered me the bottle again. 'Not just in the usual way. He came to see me. As a patient, I mean.'

74

'He was depressed?'

'Clinically. Mirtazapine helped, but he was very low. Of course, he's not the first person Zodiac's brought down. Fridge says most people have to be half mad to come here in the first place. As I say, I probably shouldn't tell you this. Patient confidentiality. Not that that applies, any more.'

'And you think . . .' I struggled to say the word aloud. 'Suicide?'

Kennedy nodded. 'Sad.'

'Did it seem especially bad these last few days?'

'That's a funny thing. The day before he died was the happiest I'd seen him in months. Very excited. But that might have been a sign. You know how it goes with depression, up and down. The higher you go, the further you fall.'

Automatically, he offered me the bottle again. Automatically, I took it. I could feel the whiskey softening my thinking, lowering my defences.

'Why are you telling me this?'

'What you said at supper, about it not being an accident. I thought you'd guessed.'

I took it he hadn't heard Greta's theory. I didn't put it to him. I didn't want to be the next one getting happy pills on his couch.

'The point is, we don't want it taken the wrong way. You know there's a lot of pressure on Zodiac's funding. Some people think the reason we were packed off to the South Polar people was so they can shut us down.'

'Is that Quam's agenda?'

'No.' Emphatic. 'Quam's in charge of Zodiac, he wants to see it do well. If it goes, he'll be out of a job with the rest of us. But he's under a lot of pressure from Norwich.'

'What's that got to do with Hagger?'

'Quam's worried there'll be a witch hunt. It's no secret he made mistakes. He should never have let Hagger go out on

75

his own – especially in the condition he was in. But if they use that as an excuse to shut down Zodiac, it's a travesty.'

He put the bottle back in his pocket. I think it was empty.

'They'll debrief you when you go home tomorrow. You'll have first bite. What you say becomes the first draft of history.'

'You want me to tell them Hagger committed suicide?'

'It's the truth. Almost certainly.'

He'd said what he had to say. He pulled up his hood and opened the door, then remembered something. He came back to the table.

'Don't forget to take the mag readings.' He tapped a dial to the right of the main readout. 'It's that one you want.'

I wrote down the numbers. *Wait ten minutes, do it again*, Eastman had said. I waited and shivered. The glow from the whiskey had worn off; I could feel the heat escaping through my pores. I tried a few jumping jacks, but worried I'd knock the instruments off the table.

I stared at the columns of numbers in the book and wondered if anyone ever did anything with them, or if they just accumulated. Everyone took turns: you could read the rota like the strata of an ice core in the different handwriting, the initials scrawled in the margins beside the observations. As much a record of human presence as of the vagaries of the magnetosphere.

MH. Martin Hagger. He'd stood in this frigid hut just like me, swinging his arms to keep warm, watching the clock count ten slow minutes before he could go back inside. He'd probably stood in the exact same spot.

For the first time, I really felt his loss. More than carrying his body, or clearing out his lab, the simple act of occupying the same space, only time between us, brought me closer to him than I'd been in years.

Why did you fall? I asked him.

I liked Kennedy; I wanted to believe him. I didn't like

Quam, but at a stretch I'd have taken his polar-bear theory. I'm a scientist. At science school, as Greta would put it, you're taught the simplest explanation is the best. Occam's razor.

But you can't change the data. Whatever pressure Hagger had been under, whatever black cloud, I didn't think he'd roped himself up in that harness just to throw himself in. And Greta had convinced me the polar-bear theory didn't hold up.

What happened to the notebooks?
Why did he have his gun out?
Why did he bring me here?

Questions chased around my head like snow devils blown by the wind, and in the end it all came back to the same place. In twenty-four hours I'd be in the slush and drizzle at Heathrow, and Utgard would be a bad dream. I'd tell the bureaucrats that Hagger's suicide was an unavoidable tragedy. Perhaps Quam would write me a reference.

Ten minutes were up. I wrote down the number, noted the time and signed my initials. One more layer accumulated in this freezing room.

Outside, my eyes struggled to adjust. Hemmed in by mountains, the twilight was darker here than it had been up on the ice dome. The red eyes on the radio masts blinked their warnings. Slivers of yellow light showed behind the gaps in the blinds on the Platform. I'd read some experiments that had been done here in winter, measuring exposure to artificial light. Apparently, there wasn't even enough to convince the body's clock to wake up.

I hurried back towards the flag line. Then stopped. Above the drone of the generator, I'd heard the snap of the snow crust cracking underfoot.

'Who's there?' I called.

No answer.

'Dr Kennedy?'

I couldn't tell where the sound had come from. I couldn't see anything. In the jumble of rocks and buildings there were plenty of places to hide.

I started running, back to where I'd left the gun. I reached the flag line – but the gun wasn't there. Had I missed it? I'd followed my footprints.

A few yards away, a figure reared up from behind a cache of oil drums. Something flew out of the gloom – I barely saw it – and hit me bang in the face. I screamed and dropped to the ground.

Wet snow trickled down my nose and on to my lips. Eastman advanced from behind the barrels, one arm cocked back holding a snowball. He grinned, and pitched it at me like a baseball. I tried to roll out of the way but it smacked me on my ear.

'Gotcha.'

Ten

Anderson

I overslept. No one came to wake me, and the light creeping round the wardrobe wasn't enough to break into my dreams. When I did open my eyes, and found my watch, I stared at the dial almost incapable of understanding time. I'd missed breakfast. If I wasn't quick, I'd miss the plane.

I threw my clothes into the bag. There wasn't much to pack. I'd just about finished when there was a rap at the door.

'Plane's cancelled,' said Quam. 'Bad weather.'

I peered at the crack around the window. The sun was shining; I couldn't hear any wind.

'At the other end,' he elaborated. 'You live to fight another day.'

I gave up on packing and padded along the corridor to the galley. Danny the cook was there, elbow-deep in washing-up.

'Any chance of some breakfast?'

He heated oil in a pan, and soon the galley was filled with the smell of bacon and eggs. He was a big man, with the sort of gentleness that comes from total confidence in your own strength. The sort of gentleness that could turn ferocious in the wrong circumstances. I never saw him wear more than a T-shirt; I don't think he ever left the building.

He handed me the plate, and a steaming mug of coffee.

Mid-morning, the mess was empty; I'd have felt ridiculous sitting there on my own. I gestured to the island in the middle of the galley.

'Do you mind if I . . . ?'

'Pull up a pew.'

I tucked into my breakfast while he started on the washing-up. The food tasted like heaven. As he pottered around the kitchen, I remembered what Quam had said. *Danny knows all the gossip.*

'Tell me,' I said. 'At dinner last night – when Eastman was making a scene. There were three of them who didn't put their hands up. Eastman, Fridge and Annabel Kobayashi.'

'Yeah.'

'What did they have against him?'

Danny took an enormous pot out of the sink and rubbed it with a dishcloth. 'Fridge and Hagger, they used to be good mates, but then it went wrong. They had some bust-ups. Slanging matches you could hear through the whole station.'

'What about?'

'Science stuff. Fridge thought Hagger had nicked some of his work.'

I found that hard to believe. Fridge was an atmospheric scientist, nothing to do with microbiology.

'As for Eastman,' Danny continued, 'well, that's easy enough. You know he's CIA.'

I almost laughed – but that would have been a mistake. Danny was deadly serious. 'How do you know?'

'In the kitchen all day – you hear things. All those aerials and satellites – says he's working on astronomy or something, but that's just cover, innit.'

'Is it?'

'They pay three million pounds a year for this dump. You think anyone spends that on polar bears? Look at the map. When Russia launches its nukes, they're coming straight over our heads on their way to the States. This whole place, it's one big spook station.'

'Like an early-warning station?'

'That's right. So that when it all kicks off, they're ready. The old mining tunnels up in the north? They're kitting them out as some sort of bunker. When the ice caps melt and sea levels rise, this is where they'll hole up.'

I felt dizzy. 'The CIA?'

'The Illuminati. The CIA are the frontmen, but it's the Illuminati who really call the shots.'

'You think so?'

'Logical. The bees are dying out. When society collapses because there's no more crops, they'll need a safe place to sit it out. Nowhere's further off the edge of the planet than Utgard.'

Now I wasn't sure if we were talking about a nuclear holocaust, or climate change, or some other environmental catastrophe. 'Next you'll be telling me there's a spaceship buried under the ice.'

He gave me a measured look. 'More likely it's a meteorite carrying alien DNA. Between you and me, I think Dr Hagger might have been on to it. That's why they got to him – to shut him up.'

'Well, he did do work on DNA,' I allowed, 'but—'

'Exactly. You've seen the sign on the door – "High infection risk of unknown DNA". What else could it be?'

There was no point trying to explain that the only risk of contamination in Hagger's lab was that someone would mix up his samples. 'I'll try to avoid any alien DNA,' I promised.

Danny's knives gleamed as he snapped them on to a magnetic strip on the wall. 'Truth to tell, they'll probably come for you next.'

'You think so?' I looked over my shoulder. All I saw was the empty dining room.

'You're Hagger's assistant – who knows what he told you. It's probably best you're leaving.'

'Not until tomorrow.'

'Then watch your back,' said Danny darkly. 'They're already on to you. Probably gave you some bollocks excuse about the plane needing a part, or the weather or something.'

I scraped up the last few bits of yolk from my plate and licked them off the knife. Clearly, it was nonsense. But I wasn't able to laugh it off as much as I'd have liked.

I carried my plate over to the sink. 'And Annabel? What was her beef with Hagger?'

'He was shagging her.'

I thought of Annabel – aloof, unattainable, slicing up her food like a surgeon with a scalpel. I tried to imagine her falling for Hagger. I'd have been more ready to believe she was part of the Illuminati conspiracy.

'When?'

'Last summer. Then she turned up here this season and found someone else had been keeping his bed warm over the winter.'

'One of the grad students?'

A sly shake of his head. 'Students only got here last week.'

I was about to ask who – and then I realised I knew. It came down to a shortlist of one.

'Greta?'

The pan went up on the shelf with a clatter. 'Well, he wasn't gay, was he?'

Danny had given me so much to think about I didn't know where to begin. Eastman and the Illuminati, I discounted. Fridge and the stolen data didn't make any sense. And Annabel's affair with Hagger seemed almost as far-fetched – though, on reflection, I could just about believe it. More than one pretty young student had found herself in Hagger's office after hours; three of them had married him.

But *Greta*?

I was still thinking about it when I ran into Fridge coming down the corridor in his cold-weather gear.

'Where are you going?'

'Gemini. Jensen's flying me up. Annabel has some samples for me.'

I had a day to kill, and I didn't want to spend it hanging around the base. And I was suddenly interested in seeing more of Fridge and Annabel.

'Got room for one more?'

Camp Gemini was a few tents and three of the round red huts on the top of the ice dome. I saw them as we flew in, spread over the ice cap like oversized snooker balls. A rough flag line marked out the boundary; inside were four snow-mobiles, a couple of sledges and a lot of equipment boxes. A weather station stood on a steel truss at the edge of the camp. The anemometer rattled around, and the wind made the guy ropes moan. I hoped it wouldn't be too windy for Jensen to fly us back.

Annabel came and met us. Out here, with the high sun full on the snow, she looked dazzling. Even her ECW kit looked tailored. Her trousers hugged her long legs, stretching when she knelt to examine something. Her red parka was cinched in at the waist, her hair swept under her hat to show a slim neck and elfin face, covered with a chic pair of sunglasses. No wonder Hagger fell for her; no wonder she was furious when he dumped her. I felt aggrieved on her behalf.

She pointed to a pile of plastic cool boxes – the sort of thing you'd use for beer at a barbecue.

'You need help lifting?'

Fridge nodded at me. 'Tom's the muscle.'

The coolers weren't big, but even with two of us I struggled to carry them. After the first two, I had to stop to catch my breath. Cold air rasped my lungs and made me cough.

'What's inside?'

'Popsicles,' Fridge said with a grin. He snapped the catches and opened one up. Inside, I saw stacks of long cylinders: ice cores, milky white, about ten centimetres thick and wrapped in plastic. Each one had a reference number scrawled in marker pen.

'What happens to these at Zodiac?'

'We've got a cold store – a hole, basically – dug into the ice. Better than a freezer. I do some preliminary work at Zodiac, and when the plane comes, we send them back to Norwich for more analysis.'

It didn't sound as if Hagger's lab freezer was part of the workflow. I wondered how one of the cores had ended up there, and if that had anything to do with the data Fridge had accused Hagger of stealing – if Danny was right about that.

We loaded the last box. Jensen still had some refuelling to do; Fridge and I retreated out of range of the propellers, watching Annabel's team take ice cores. Like most science, it involved a lot of waiting. A steel cable spun lazily from a tripod. Somewhere on the end of it, deep inside the ice, it turned a hollow drill bit, cutting out the glacier like coring an apple. I kept expecting something to come out, but it never did.

Fridge cleared his throat. 'Last night. Eastman's game. It was wrong I didn't put my hand up. Martin deserved better.'

I made a no-hard-feelings gesture. 'I heard you were friends.'

'From way back. We both were at McMurdo in the eighties. In the south.'

Almost everywhere on the planet is south of Utgard. It took me a moment to work out that he meant Antarctica.

'So what happened here?'

'It was dumb. We disagreed over an interpretation of the data.'

'Data?'

'We detected high methane levels in the first-year sea ice. I thought it was atmospheric; Martin thought it had a biological origin.' He saw the look on my face and cracked a rueful smile. 'Stupid, right?'

I didn't comment. Fridge stared out at the white plateau around us. 'This place – you think it's going to be perfect space. Mind-expanding. But actually, it just boxes you in.'

He broke off as Jensen came over from the helicopter. 'Ready to go?'

'Problem with the weight,' said Jensen. 'Annabel drilled too much bloody ice. I've only got room for one.'

'I'll stay,' I volunteered.

I watched the helicopter lift off, whipping up the snow as if someone had shaken a snow globe. When it had disappeared behind the mountains, I wandered over to the drill rig.

'Anything I can do?'

Annabel looked round. 'How much do you know about glaciers?'

'I'm a fast learner.'

'Then let me give you Glaciology 101. Glaciers are ice, but they're made of snow. Snow falls, and because it's so cold here it doesn't melt. As it piles up, year after year, the weight of the new snow above compresses the old snow and changes its crystal structure to ice. Each year, another layer forms.'

'OK.'

'Now, the important thing about glaciers is that although they're frozen, they don't stand still. They're fluid. The ice is

85

actually flowing very slowly, moving outwards under its own weight.'

I looked at my feet. The ground seemed solid enough.

'Imagine pressing down on a balloon. The more pressure you apply on top, the wider it spreads out at the sides. That spreading is why glaciers move forward.'

'Got it.'

'But because it's spreading, the layers of ice don't go anywhere. They just stretch out and get thinner – like the balloon. So in the centre, you can drill down and extract cores that sample every snowfall that's ever happened on this glacier, one on top of the other. You can read them like tree rings. Fridge, for example, can analyse the air trapped inside the ice and tell you what the weather was like four thousand years ago.'

'Core up,' called one of the students on the drill. The cable stopped turning and started to reel in. The winch whined like a dentist's drill; it took a long time to come up.

'We're about three hundred metres down right now,' Annabel said.

A grooved steel pipe emerged on the end of the rope. Two of the students swung it out and laid it on a work table. They wore white clean-room suits; with the ECW clothing bulking them out underneath, they looked like abominable snowmen. They slid a cloudy cylinder of ice out of the tube and on to a sheet of plastic. They handled it delicately, like the fuse of a bomb. But they must have done something wrong: halfway out, the core cracked in two. Chunks of ice splintered off and dropped into the snow.

Annabel swore. 'Brittle ice. It's under so much pressure down there, when it comes to the surface it expands too quickly and cracks.'

While the students tried to extract the stump of the core, Annabel picked up the pieces that had fallen in the snow and dropped them into two of the Thermos cups. A small bottle of vodka appeared from inside her jacket.

'Nothing like a glacier martini.' The ice hissed and popped as the vodka covered it. 'What you're hearing is four-thousand-year-old air. It gets trapped when the snow falls; as the snow compresses into ice, the air gets frozen into it.'

I sniffed the cup. 'Is it safe?'

'Probably cleaner than what you're breathing now.' She laughed. 'Fridge would kill me if he knew we were wasting it.'

I downed the vodka and felt the cold spreading through my stomach. 'I heard he disagreed with Martin over some data.'

'That was a different project – sea ice, over on the west side. Fridge was getting some anomalous readings so he asked Hagger what he thought.'

'And didn't like the answer.'

'Hagger was a shit,' she said suddenly. She tossed back the last of her drink. 'He used people, and then he forgot them.'

The vodka had made me less cautious than usual. 'Why did you let him go off on his own that day?'

'I had work to do here.'

'Couldn't you have sent one of your grad students?'

'He wanted to go on his own.'

'Didn't you care about the risks?'

A blush rose in Annabel's cheeks. Behind her sunglasses, I felt her gaze harden.

'I've got eight weeks on Utgard, and it's costing my funding body two hundred pounds every hour I'm here. We work eighteen-hour days, seven days a week, freezing our arses off. And if you think that makes me sound like a workaholic bitch, Martin was just the same. He wanted to get the work done. I respected that.'

I backed off. 'I'm sorry. I'm just trying to understand.'

'There's nothing *to* understand.' She pointed to the drill rig. 'I can tell you how much snow fell four thousand years ago, and Fridge can tell you if it was barbecue weather that year. But why Martin broke his neck on the Helbreen . . .' She shook her head. 'The data isn't there.'

I remembered the sample I'd seen in Hagger's freezer. 'Did you do any ice coring on the Helbreen?'

'Last summer. Nothing this year.'

'But his work was on sea ice. Didn't you think it was odd he wanted to go to a glacier?'

'If I thought about every odd thing that people do at Zodiac, I'd never even get dressed in the morning.' A gust of wind blew the cups off the packing crate. She pulled up her hood.

'Would you like to be useful?'

I couldn't very well say no. She handed me a spade and pointed me to one of her students, knee-deep in a hole.

'Help Pierre dig out the snow pit.'

It was hot work, but I didn't mind. Soon, I took off my coat and worked in my jumper, hat and gloves. I remembered how I'd seen Greta doing the same thing when I arrived at Zodiac, and how I'd thought she must be some kind of Inuit. Perhaps I was evolving.

We dug adjacent holes, separated by a thin snow wall that got taller as the holes got deeper. We talked as we worked. Pierre was a master's student from Quebec, a lanky young man with a wide grin and a bandana tied over his head. He'd been here two weeks, had one more to go.

'Looks like Annabel keeps you busy,' I said.

'Yeah.'

'Two days ago, when Martin Hagger—'

'That was too bad. He was a nice guy.'

'Did anyone from here go and check up on him?'

'Like, down to the Helbreen?'

'Yeah.'

'I don't think so. We were all busy coring. Dr Kobayashi was away for a few hours checking the ablation poles, but that was it.'

He checked my side of the pit. 'That's deep enough.'

We squared off the two holes until the sides and floor were flat, taking extra care around the thin wall that divided them. Pierre put down his spade.

'You wanna see something neat?'

He went off and came back with a square sheet of plywood. He laid it so that it half covered the hole I'd dug.

'Get in.'

I slid in the gap between the snow and the board. Pierre wriggled in beside me – there was just enough room for both of us. He reached up and slid the board back until it completely covered the top of the hole.

'You see?'

It was breathtaking. Sunlight shone through the thin wall that divided the two pits and lit up the snow, making it glow a perfect holy blue, like a Chagall window. Like the crevasse, only more concentrated in the tiny space. The different snow layers made stripes of light: pale powder blue where it hadn't compacted, vivid neon where it had.

'It's a time machine,' said Pierre. 'The darker bands are summer snowfall. The lighter ones are winter. Wind blows more air into them so they're less dense.'

I sat there and traced the layers, winter and summer, year after year. I counted back: the summer Luke was born; my winter wedding with Louise; the September I started my PhD. I'd gone back as far as the summer I finished primary school before the layers got too thin for me to tell them apart. My life didn't feel like much compared with the vastness of the snow quietly piling up here.

A rap on the wooden board told me someone else wanted to admire the view. We lifted it up and scrambled out of the hole, being careful not to touch the thin wall. The sun outside dazzled me; I fumbled with my sunglasses before I went blind. The wind cut through my jumper like a razor.

I put on my coat and went to join the others. They were taking a break over by a folding table. Pierre snapped me off a piece of chocolate and gave me a hot cup of tea. It went stone cold in the time I took to drink it.

'At fifty below, you can throw boiling water in the air and it freezes before it lands,' said one of the students.

'We should try it,' said Pierre. 'It's supposed to get cold by the weekend. Big storm coming in.'

'Send me a link to the video,' I said. 'I'll be gone by then.'

Hard to imagine I'd be watching *Dr Who* with Luke in the living room. I looked over at our snow pit and thought of the light inside, the blue cathedral of the crevasse. I'd miss that. Other things, not so much.

There'd been a snow pit where Hagger died, I remembered. Except—

The idea hit me so hard I started to tremble. I grabbed Pierre's arm.

'Is that how you always dig snow pits? One covered, one open?'

'Pretty much. Why?'

Some of the others had started to drift back to work. I ran to the coring rig and found Annabel. 'The place where Hagger died – the Helbreen. How far is it from here?'

'About thirty kilometres.'

'I need to go there. Now.'

'You don't know the way.'

I could see she didn't think I was serious. I ran over to a snowmobile and yanked on the starter cord. It was harder than it looked.

'What the hell do you think you're doing?'

'I'm going to the Helbreen.'

'You'll kill yourself.'

'Then you'd better come with me.' *Or else* . . . 'You don't want someone else going off there without a buddy.'

The glacier was exactly as we'd left it: the jerrycans marking out the safe area, the yawning blue crevasse beyond. And the snow pit, half filled now with drifting snow. I jumped in and kicked against the walls. One stubbed my toe, so did the next, but the third disintegrated in a blizzard of collapsing snow. A ceiling appeared, a wooden board that had been covered by the drifts, making a small square cave. A red backpack lay on the ground.

I pulled off my mittens and unzipped the bag. There wasn't much inside: a bar of chocolate, a Thermos (frozen solid), a topographic map, a pen and a green notebook.

I opened the notebook. My hands were already going numb – the thin liners were no match for the icy wind – but this was too important. I turned the pages, searching for any clue to what Hagger had been doing.

It looked like any other lab notebook. Neat columns of figures, measurements, interspersed with scrawled calculations and cryptic half-sentences. *Sulphite calibration* (double underlined); *Ratkowsky growth rate profile*; *Concentration of X*. Without careful reading, I couldn't guess what it all meant. I could barely read the handwriting.

'I need a wee,' said Annabel. She went off behind a pile of moraine boulders at the edge of the glacier. I turned my back and kept reading.

A loose sheet of paper stuck out between the pages. I pulled it out and smoothed it against the notebook's cover. It was a printout. Easier to read, but that was no help understanding it. Just a string of numbers, no spaces, zeros and ones and twos in an apparently random order: *1100121101012* . . . Some sort of data set, I supposed.

A gust of wind lifted the paper. I snatched for it, but my fingers were clumsy with cold. It blew out of the notebook and fluttered across the glacier, white against white. In a split second, I could hardly see it.

I wasn't going to lose it before I knew what it meant. I scrambled out of the pit and ran after it, floundering through the snow, skidding where the wind had scoured out patches of ice. Behind me, Annabel was shouting something, but with my hood up and the wind roaring around me, I didn't make out the words.

The paper blew up against a rocky outcrop and stopped. I grabbed it, but my fingers wouldn't move. I clapped it between my hands to lift it, then just about managed to stuff it into my coat pocket. I had to get my mittens back on.

Annabel was still shouting. I looked around to see what she wanted, and realised how far I'd come. Well beyond the safe area. Perhaps that's what she was trying to tell me.

'I'm coming,' I called, and stepped forward.

Something cracked. The ground gave way under me. I felt a sickening emptiness as I fell. I remember thinking, *This is how a snowflake feels*.

Snow lands soft as a feather. I didn't. I hit my head, and the white world went black.

Eleven

USCGC Terra Nova

The vibrating pager skittered across the tabletop like a beetle. The captain's hand trapped it right before it went over the edge. He read the screen and stood.

'Give me a minute.'

Anderson, half buried under the pink blanket, gave a lean smile. 'I just reached the most exciting part.'

'Yeah. But the helicopter's coming in.'

The smile vanished. 'Any survivors?'

'That's what I'm going to find out.'

Franklin closed the door behind him. Santiago was waiting in the corridor.

'You get anything, boss?'

'Long story. What's the word from the boarding party?'

'ETA five minutes. They said to have a couple of stretchers ready. And to open up the cold locker.'

They climbed the stairs towards the wheelhouse. There were ten decks on the *Terra Nova*, and wherever you happened to be, the chances were that what you wanted would be on a different deck. A floating StairMaster. The crew were the fittest in the Coast Guard.

Santiago's voice dropped. 'We've been doing some checking up on this guy. There's a few wrinkles.'

'Like?' They went past the wipe board where the science

schedule was written up. Sailing in the Arctic, things changed so often the geeks called it the Board of Lies.

'For starters, he doesn't have a PhD like he claimed. He got kicked out of school before he finished – some big scandal. An experiment went wrong, he'd faked the paperwork, they cut him loose.'

'You figure all that out yourself, Ops?'

Santiago grinned. 'I got one of the geeks to help me out.'

They came out on the bridge. Franklin crossed to the rear windows and looked down on the flight deck. Snow was blowing over the side, covering the deck as quickly as the crew could sweep it back. He scanned for the helicopter. Couldn't even find the sky.

'There, sir.'

Santiago pointed. A dim light had appeared, blinking in the fog like a distant lighthouse. It grew brighter. Rotor blades chopped a hole in the fog.

'"At length did cross an Albatross,"' Franklin murmured. '"Through the fog it came."'

'What's that, sir?'

'Poetry, Commander. You wouldn't like it.'

'Is it gonna be on the test?'

The helicopter swam out of the fog and towards the deck. In the Navy, they'd drop a wire to the deck and winch the helicopter in. But everyone knew the Navy were pussies. The Coast Guard liked to keep their birds free-range. As it passed the wheelhouse, Franklin could see the pilot only a few yards away, concentrating like hell.

The helicopter touched down, bounced on its wheels and settled. The deck crew raced to secure it; Parsons and her team ran out from where they'd been sheltering and slid open the door. Two stretchers came out, covered in foil blankets that flapped and crinkled in the wind. Then came the bodies. Franklin counted eleven. Last of all, Lieutenant Klein, the first officer, who had led the mission. He looked none too steady on his feet, though the crew had done a good job clearing the ice.

'Tell Klein to see me in my quarters. And send someone to make sure Anderson stays in his cabin. I don't want him seeing this.'

Tim Klein, *Terra Nova*'s first lieutenant, sat in the easy chair opposite Franklin. His family were Marines, three generations; it had been a minor family scandal when he went into the Coast Guard. But he still had the posture. He sat ramrod straight, but angled about ten degrees forward, gripping the coffee cup two-handed. He still couldn't stop it shaking.

'It was real bad, sir. First they burned, then they froze.'

'There was a fire?'

'More like an explosion. The main building was jacked up on stilts. Something blew a hole right out of it: whole thing collapsed and burned. Like a car bomb, or a missile strike.'

He stared at his reflection in the cabin window. 'You wouldn't think it could burn so much in this cold.'

Franklin waited for Klein's thoughts to settle, and made a mental note to arrange some CISM counselling for him with the Chief.

'Any idea what caused it?'

'There were some gas tanks – but they were a ways from the Platform.' He knitted his fingers together around the cup and frowned. 'To be honest, sir, it looked like high explosive.'

'It's plausible. Anderson – the guy from the ice – he said they did seismic blasting on the glaciers there. Something could have gone wrong.'

'Yeah.' Klein was looking at Franklin, but his eyes were seeing something else. 'We found these, too.'

He held out his palm. Three copper bullet casings gleamed. 'There was blood on the snow nearby.'

'Did you get anything from the survivors?'

'They weren't in a position to talk. Frankly, they were lucky to be alive.' His voice shook. 'There were a lot of bodies, sir. We brought back the ones we could fit, but there's more we'll have to go back for.'

'There's no hurry, Lieutenant.'

'Thank you, sir.'

A knock at the door; Santiago came in. Klein looked grateful for the intrusion.

'The Brits emailed photos of their Zodiac people. We've identified three of the bodies so far – the rest got burned too bad.' He handed Franklin the printout, three of the photos circled in red marker. 'Stuart Jensen. Daniel MacGregor. Francis Quam.'

Franklin scanned the rest of the pictures. 'Where's Anderson?'

'They didn't have him on file.'

'Makes sense – he said he went there in a hurry. So who are the survivors?'

Santiago pointed. 'These two, sir. Bob Eastman and Sean Kennedy.'

'Can they talk?'

'Eastman had it worse – he's still out. Doc has him rigged up in the sickbay. But Kennedy's OK. Well, conscious. She's moved him to one of the staterooms to keep him comfortable.'

'Then let's go see what he has to tell us.' Franklin touched Klein on the shoulder. 'You've done good work, Lieutenant. Get some rest.'

It was strange meeting a man you'd just been hearing about. Stranger still when he was bandaged up like a mummy, one eye and his mouth about all you could see. Kennedy was taller and thinner than Franklin had imagined him. As much as he could tell.

He held up the bottle he'd brought from his cabin. 'I thought you might like this. Scotch – not Irish. It's the best we could do.'

Kennedy struggled to prop himself up.

'It's kind of you, Captain.' His voice was hoarse, the Irish accent almost buried in the rasp. 'And I don't want you to think badly of the Irish, now – but I don't drink.'

'Really?'

'A disgrace, to be sure.'

Franklin was about to say more, but decided against it. 'My apologies.'

He put the whisky on the table and took the seat beside the bed. Santiago loitered by the door.

'Are you able to talk? I don't want to—'

Kennedy shook his head – as much as the bandages would allow. 'I'm better than I look. On the outside, anyway.'

'How did you . . . ?'

'Survive?' Kennedy lapsed into a fit of coughing. 'The luck of the Irish. Bob Eastman and I had just gone out when the explosion happened. That was what saved us. From the fire, of course – and from the cold. We had our ECW gear on, you see; none of the others did. We did what we could for them, but in that climate . . .'

He slumped back. 'The ones that didn't burn froze to death.'

'I'm sorry,' said Franklin. It sounded inadequate; it always did.

Kennedy put out his hand. 'Perhaps I will have that drink after all.'

Franklin splashed some whisky in a plastic cup. He thought about taking some for himself, and decided against it. He had to stay sharp.

'I'm trying to figure out what happened at Zodiac. There are folks back in Britain and Stateside who are asking a lot of questions. If there's anything you can tell me . . .'

97

'I've spent the last five days asking myself these questions. I don't know why it happened.'

'I understand. But maybe if you go through what happened those last few days before the explosion, you'll remember something.'

Kennedy's good eye flickered towards Santiago. 'I don't want to take up your time, Captain. You're a busy man, you've a ship to run.'

'Just give me a second.'

He took Santiago into the corridor.

'Keep an eye on Eastman. Tell the Doc I want to speak to him the minute he comes round. And keep tabs on Anderson, too.'

'You think something's up?'

'Something very bad happened at Zodiac. Until we know what it is, I don't want to risk it affecting my ship.'

Back in the cabin, Kennedy had put his whisky down on the table, almost untouched.

'I'll tell you what I can.'

Twelve

Kennedy

The dirty secret to being the doctor at a place like Zodiac is you don't actually have much to do. Especially outside the summer season. You've got maybe two dozen people, mostly young and fit, all screened for every disease under the sun before they set foot there. I had a surgery kitted out like a small hospital, a dispensary to make a pharmacist weep with envy – and all they ever needed was a few paracetamol on Sunday mornings after movie night.

But you've got to keep busy. Some of my predecessors dabbled in science; others painted, or wrote the novel they'd always meant to get round to. I'm a fossil man, myself: Utgard's stuffed full of them. But there're always odd little jobs coming up that need to be done. Because the scientists have no time, they usually land on the doctor.

Now, there's an outfit in America called Planet Climate Action. Don't let the name fool you: it's actually a front for oil companies, car companies, utilities, anyone who wants to burn fossil fuels like there's no tomorrow. They'd been getting hold of some of our data and leaking it so as to make us look bad. Quam, the base commander, had it in his head that someone at Zodiac was helping them. He asked me to find out about it.

To tell the truth, I hadn't got very far. To leak the data, you'd have to understand it, and the climate expert at Zodiac was Fridge Torell. Well, he's the biggest global-warming fanatic there is: Greenpeace, Friends of the Earth, WWF, he carries so many cards they don't fit in his wallet. Scientists guard their results like a pot of gold at the best of times. It was inconceivable Fridge would give away his own data to undermine the cause.

Then Martin Hagger died – fell in a crevasse. Tragic. I knew, from some private conversations, that he'd been under pressure with work, things not going his way. I thought it had got too much for him. But then I started to wonder.

I know it sounds ridiculous, that someone would be killed for a few numbers on a graph. But there's a lot of money chasing round the Arctic. Ice caps are melting; places that have been out of bounds for fifty thousand years are suddenly opening up. Just when we thought we had the planet all parcelled out, it turns out there's a bit more to grab. People get foolish when they think they can have something for nothing. And if fools and money are involved, anything can happen.

Hagger had an assistant, fellow named Tom Anderson. Quiet, gentle and desperately unlucky: he landed at Zodiac the day Hagger died. I spoke to him once or twice, liked him at the time. There was a sorrow in him, but dignified, you know? Life had dealt him a rough hand, and he was trying to play it the best he could. He was supposed to have gone home already, but the plane got delayed – often happens – so he went up to spend the day at Camp Gemini, on the ice dome. Then Annabel Kobayashi and Jensen the pilot carried him into my medical room on a stretcher. He was out cold.

'He fell in a moulin,' Dr Kobayashi explained.

Well, you couldn't make it up. First Hagger, now his assistant. A moulin – perhaps you know this, Captain? – is a hole in the glacier that the meltwater bores out in summer.

They tunnel under the ice; some of them go on for miles. Anderson did better than his boss – he was alive, at least – but he'd banged his head hard. I gave him Mannitol to ease the swelling, and put him on halothane to keep him under.

'Is he going to make it?' Jensen asked.

There was no point lying. 'You can't tell with head injuries. He could be right as rain tomorrow morning – or he might never wake up.'

Of course, I wondered if it could be coincidence. 'What happened?'

'Didn't see,' Annabel said. 'I'd gone for a wee behind the moraine. When I came back, he wasn't there. I found him at the bottom of a moulin. *Stupid*,' she added fiercely. 'He shouldn't have left the safe area. I marked all the moulins at the end of last season. Martin must have taken the pole down.'

The emotion surprised me. Annabel wasn't what you'd call a demonstrative person. Around Zodiac, they called her the Ice Queen. If she'd been shaken up, I didn't like to think how the others were taking it.

The doctor at Zodiac has a tricky role. He's confessor, counsellor, friend – and psychologist. If people start cracking up, it's his job to nip it in the bud. It happens more often than you'd think. Or perhaps you think it would happen all the time in a place like Zodiac.

Annabel slipped a bag off her shoulder, a standard-issue Zodiac field pack. She unzipped it and took out a green notebook, with a sheet of paper pressed between the pages. It was damp and creased and made no sense at all. Just a page full of numbers – zeros, ones and twos, like some kind of Sudoku for idiots.

'This was Hagger's. Anderson found it in a snow pit just before he fell.'

'Did he say what was so important?'

'No.'

I glanced through the rest of the notebook. 'You'd best leave this here.'

'I think—'

'Obviously it meant something to Anderson. If I put it where he can see it, it might help him come round.'

Annabel gave me a look – but we doctors are trained to sound convincing. It might even have been true. A head injury's a funny thing, poorly understood.

I shooed the others out of my office. Once I'd satisfied myself Anderson's condition was stable, I turned my attention to the notebook. An idea had struck me, and was building nicely into a theory. There hadn't been a fatal accident at Zodiac in twenty years. Now we'd nearly had two in three days: Hagger and his assistant. It couldn't be coincidence. I'd seen Anderson poking around Hagger's lab. I wondered what he'd found. Or been trying to hide.

And if you started to think about it, you might ask a few more questions about Anderson. Starting with how he came to be at Zodiac in the first place. Most personnel are selected a year in advance, there's rigorous screening and months of training. Anderson swanned in on forty-eight hours' notice, didn't even bring a proper coat. The story they put about was he'd come to replace Hagger's old assistant, South African fellow named Kevin, who'd had to go home with a wisdom-tooth infection. But the doctor at Zodiac is also the dentist, and I can tell you that boy's teeth were sound as a drum. The truth is, Hagger decided he wanted Anderson, and when Quam said he didn't have funding for two assistants, he packed off the unfortunate Kevin and replaced him. So you could say I was curious to see what Hagger had in his notebook.

Unfortunately, I couldn't make head nor tail of it. Lots of

numbers, some equations and pretty graphs, and precious few words to explain what they might be. Lots of cryptic little notes like *Check SO ions* and *Concentration of X* and *Where is X coming from?* A hand-drawn map of Utgard scattered with little x's like a treasure map.

But there were a few sentences I could read. And one of them made me very anxious to talk to Fridge Torell.

I found him up a mast on the edge of the base, cracking ice off some instruments as he hung on to the steel frame. It's tricky work: if your skin touches the metal, it bonds like cement. Most scientists would leave it to their students, or the techs, but Fridge is a hands-on sort of fellow.

'I need to ask you something,' I called up. 'About Hagger.'

An icicle, two feet long and sharp as a knife, dropped off the mast and stuck quivering in the snow. I took a step back.

Fridge clambered down and dropped the last few feet on to the snow.

'Nothing works in this fucking place,' he complained.

'Data link down again?'

'It's up – but all I'm getting is garbage.' He made karate-chopping motions with his hands to get the circulation going. 'Some kind of interference screwing with it.'

I showed him the notebook. 'Anderson found this. It belonged to Hagger.'

He shouldered the rifle he'd left leaning against the base of the tower. 'Can't Anderson help you?'

'Anderson's in a coma.'

'Shit. How did that happen?'

I told him. 'The last thing he did was find this notebook. I thought there might be something in it that could explain why Hagger died.'

I could tell the kind of look Fridge was giving me from behind his sunglasses. 'Quam said it was a polar bear.'

'There are different theories about that,' I said, non-committally.

'So what do you want to know?'

'Can we go somewhere private?'

He thought a minute, then nodded to a hut near the flag line. 'How about Star Command?'

Star Command was one of those prefab red pods that we used all over the place at Zodiac. This one was fitted with a sliding roof, and a Buzz Lightyear figure nailed above the door. Someone had stretched out his arms so that he approximated a crucifix. In winter, the caboose housed telescopes and aurora cameras – hence the name. With summer coming on, the telescopes had been packed away and the caboose was empty. Or should have been.

Fridge kicked open the door and stuck his head in. 'Who put these here?'

Three machines sat on a table against the far wall. From a distance, they looked like fancy photocopiers. I went over and wiped a layer of frost off the front of one.

'"Life Technologies",' I read.

Fridge examined them. 'I think they're some kind of DNA machines.'

'Who could they have belonged to?'

'Hagger was the only guy who could have used this. Unless Quam thought he could sequence penguin DNA.'

We both laughed. I laid the notebook flat on the table.

'I'm not a biologist,' Fridge warned. 'I don't know how much I can help.'

'It's not the science.' My heartbeat quickened as I turned the pages. Suddenly, I was very conscious that I was at the very edge of the station, and that Fridge had a hunting rifle slung on his back. My cold fingers fumbled the pages as I found the one I wanted.

It was near the front. *Echo Bay – CH4 concentrations*, said the heading. There were some numbers underneath, and a simple graph. And under that, one brief sentence in the margin.

Fridge will kill me.

Thirteen

Kennedy

'Care to explain that, Fridge?'

I hoped I sounded more confident than I felt. Fridge stepped back, lifted his hand. I watched him like a hawk. I wished I'd brought a flare pistol, even one of those little flash-bang pens we use for scaring the bears.

He lifted his sunglasses and rubbed his eyes. 'CH_4 is methane.'

'That's not the bit that wants explaining.'

He sat down on a steel box. Without the sunglasses, he looked more wrung out than I did. He hunched over, staring at the page in the book.

'A little while ago, we started getting big spikes in the methane readings. Not in the upper atmosphere – right down here on the ground.' He showed me a hand-drawn graph in the notebook, swooping up like a ski jump. 'You see? Atmospheric methane concentrations have been rising for a hundred years, but on a gradual slope. This is off the scale.'

He saw the look on my face. 'How well do you remember high-school chemistry?'

I shook my head. 'Bad teacher.'

'Methane is the main ingredient in natural gas, like you probably use for cooking back home. Governments want you to believe it's a clean fuel – which it is, next to coal or oil.

Burning methane produces carbon dioxide – CO_2, climate enemy number one – but not as much as the other fuels.'

'Is this relevant?'

'But methane is a greenhouse gas in its own right also. It traps heat sixty times more efficiently than CO_2. Now, there's not so much methane in the atmosphere as CO_2, and it doesn't last so long, so it doesn't get the bad headlines. But if we emit too much of it, we'll all fry.'

'And Martin found the level is going up?'

'*I* found the level is going up,' he corrected me. 'I showed the results to Martin to get his opinion. If I was going to publish data that far off the curve, I needed to be sure it was right. And I also needed to make a guess where it was coming from.'

I nodded, to show that I followed.

'Normally, methane is created by bacteria working in warm dark places. Swamps and intestines are two of the better-known culprits.' He gestured out the window. 'Not a lot of swamps on Utgard. And even if the Platform stinks when Danny cooks beans, we don't fart that much. So what was making the readings go crazy?'

'Am I supposed to guess?'

'Have you ever heard of methane clathrate? It's methane that's trapped in a lattice of ice crystals – so much that if you get a piece, you can literally set the ice on fire. It needs to be kept cold and under pressure, so the bottom of the Arctic Ocean suits it fine. There's probably more methane in clathrates in the seabed than all the other fossil fuels on earth put together. And if the sea warms up, then the ice melts and all that methane trapped inside squirts up into the atmosphere.'

'So that's what was happening?'

'That was my hypothesis. Well, the ocean *is* warming, and some of the gas *is* coming up. There are known methane plumes off the west coast of Svalbard, not so far from here. But Svalbard's atypical – it's warmed by the Gulf Stream. If I could show it was happening this far north, that would be big news.'

We seemed to have drifted a long way from the point of discussion. 'What did Martin say?'

The look on Fridge's face said I'd hit the mark. 'He told me a secret. He said DAR-X had asked him to examine some water samples. I didn't know. Some bug was corroding their equipment, they thought a microbiologist could help – and somewhere in the process he found out what's really going on at Echo Bay.'

'Aren't they drilling for oil?'

'That's what they tell people. In reality, they're trying to mine methane clathrate. The methane I detected was coming from their well.'

'And Hagger told you that?'

'I wrote it all up. Some of the best work I ever did. If DAR-X pull this off, every oil and gas company in the world is going to come here. They've spent twenty years in Alaska trying to get into the ANWR wildlife reserve – here, there's twice as much gas and nothing to stop them. But if one well can leak enough methane to skew the data, think what a thousand of them will do. I had to tell the world.

'Then Quam brought me into his office. He'd found out what I was doing; he forbade me from publishing.'

'*Forbade* you?'

'What Hagger had told me was commercially sensitive information. When DAR-X brought Hagger in, they insisted on a non-disclosure agreement. Except they didn't get it from Hagger: Quam signed it on behalf of the whole of Zodiac. If I published, DAR-X could sue and have everything shut down. Not only that, the contract said we'd be personally liable. Maybe that wouldn't have held up in court – but you can be damn sure it would cost a lot to find out. You think an oil company's going to run out of money before a bunch of scientists do?'

From the corner of my eye, I thought I saw a movement outside the window. Probably someone going to check a reading – but just then I was ready to suspect anything.

'You know what "clathrate" means? "Cage" – from the Latin. The ice structure forms a cage around the methane molecules. Well, Hagger had me caged up good. I withdrew the paper and I sat on the data.'

'You must have been pretty furious with Hagger.'

Fridge laughed – a bleak, cold sound in that bleak, cold room.

'You really don't get it, do you? We're operating on a scale people like you and Quam can't imagine. People talk about how the dinosaurs got toasted by a meteorite. But two hundred and fifty million years ago, before the dinosaurs, ninety per cent of all life on earth was wiped out because an undersea volcano warmed up the sea floor and released several billion tons of methane into the atmosphere. The biggest extinction event of all time.

'Or, if you want something more recent, take what happened at Storegga, eight thousand years ago. Thirty-three hundred cubic kilometres of seabed collapsed because temperature changes destabilised the clathrates. You know what happens when that much material starts moving underwater? A tsunami that makes what happened to Japan and Indonesia look like a kid in a bathtub.'

He shut the notebook and tossed it back to me.

'I didn't kill Hagger. First, because I didn't; second, because I wouldn't; and third, even if I would have, I didn't have to. We're fucking with this planet so bad, pretty soon we'll all be history.'

Fourteen

Kennedy

I wanted to get to DAR-X. As luck would have it, my chance came the next morning. Danny had baked them a cake as a thank-you for rescuing Greta and Tom Anderson from the ice cap. Jensen was going to fly it down; I volunteered to go too.

I can see the look on your face. You think we were mad to fly a cake a hundred kilometres, a cake made with liquid eggs and powdered milk at that. But Utgard's frontier country; it's the little courtesies that make life bearable. People put a lot of effort into them. Sometimes they might even save your life.

'Make sure you're back by seventeen hundred,' Quam told me. 'The plane's coming. We'll need you to load up Anderson.'

I didn't like the thought of Anderson flying, and I told him so.

'Anderson should be in a hospital,' he lectured me. 'We don't have the facilities to treat him here.'

I didn't agree. Whatever benefit he'd get from a hospital, it didn't balance out the risk of putting him on a plane. Anderson was stable, and his signs were encouraging. I'd started to hope there'd be no lasting damage. But I wasn't the base commander.

So I climbed in the helicopter with a big Tupperware container full of cake. Bob Eastman came too He's an astrophysicist; he'd been getting electrical interference with his instruments and wanted to see if it could have come from the DAR-X equipment.

'What's your theory?' he asked, as soon as we were airborne.

'My theory?'

'Hagger – Anderson. You don't think it's a coincidence?'

'What else?'

'Well for one, Danny's pretty sure it was the Freemasons. He's just trying to figure out if they did it off their own bat, or if it was for their alien overlords.'

Danny, the cook, is the nicest man in the world. But he has the most extraordinary world view, and he isn't backward about sharing it.

'I asked him once why he stays at Zodiac if it's so full of Illuminati types,' Eastman said. 'You know what he said? "If you can't beat 'em, join 'em." You think he really believes that shit?'

'Sometimes it's comforting to believe you're helpless before a higher power.'

Eastman chuckled. 'Maybe it's the frickin' aliens messing with my instruments.'

I said Utgard is frontier country. If so, Echo Bay was the pioneer camp, deep in Indian territory. The only permanent structure was the drill rig, a ten-storey steel gantry erected on the ice in the bay. Thick hawsers tied it down like a ship's rigging; yellow plastic pipes snaked out of a hole in the ice. Beside it, steam rose from three enormous black silos clustered behind a chain-link fence. Everything else was strictly temporary: canvas tents, a few shipping containers and some corrugated-iron huts. Even those looked like they were being dismantled.

The man in charge was a big Texan called Bill Malick. I half imagined he'd be wearing a ten-gallon hat, but of course it was too cold for that. I presented him with the cake and said a few nice words about how grateful we were. Jensen took photographs for the blog as Eastman and Malick posed with a knife and cut it on top of an oil drum, out in the snow. It's the sort of thing the comms people in Norwich love.

'No one's gonna realise the fucking cake's frozen,' said Malick. He took me inside their mess quarters, a wooden Portakabin that was the most solid building there, and gave me coffee. Eastman disappeared to talk to their radio engineer.

I pointed out the window to the huge drill rig in the bay. 'Hit the gusher yet?'

'That's commercially sensitive information.' He smiled. 'Not that I don't trust you, you understand.'

I thought about what Fridge had told me. 'You really think there's oil under Utgard?'

'That's what they pay me to find out.'

'Or is it natural gas you hope to find?'

He never stopped smiling – but the smile was a hard one. 'You looking to buy shares?'

I made an imaginary money-rubbing gesture with my fingers. 'They don't pay me enough.'

He saluted me with his cup of coffee. 'Amen. I guess they didn't pay your guy Hagger enough, either.'

'They surely didn't,' I agreed.

'You ever figure out the whole story with that?'

I gave him a sharp look. But all Texans are poker players, and his face gave nothing away.

'We're hoping it was just an accident,' I said carefully.

'But . . . ?'

'You were up on the Helbreen that day.'

He put his cup down with a bang. 'Are you . . . ?'

'I wondered if you'd seen anything,' I said. Innocence itself. 'Hagger was an experienced fellow. We're trying to learn lessons.'

That was plausible. With someone like Quam in charge, lessons must always be learned. Measures taken, safeguards put in place. Even if the lesson is: *Don't step into a feckin' great crevasse.*

Malick leaned back. 'Even the most experienced guys, it only takes one bad move. We had a crew chief, Earl, he'd worked twenty years at Prudhoe Bay. He was up north last September, poking around the old Soviet harbour. Took off his coat because I guess he was sweating, piece of debris fell on his head and that was it. Must've only been out five minutes, but the coat blew away and he froze to death. We never even found the coat.' He swirled his coffee. 'It's easy, dying in a place like this.'

In his Texas drawl, it sounded like a line from a country and western song.

'What took you up that end of the island on Saturday?'

'R & R. Project's nearly done, we're going home this weekend. Figured we'd get some skiing done before we leave.'

'On the Helbreen?'

'Further down – in the Adventhal. On the way back, we stopped by Vitangelsk, the Commie ghost town. One of our guys was near there a couple of weeks ago, said he saw lights at night.'

He saw my expression. 'I know, right? One too many beers.'

'Did you find any nasties?'

'Stalin's ghost singing the Internationale.' He laughed. 'Just snow and crap. Same as everyplace else on this island.'

Eastman still hadn't come back. Malick upended his mug and drained the last of his coffee, then put it down with a conclusive thud. He looked ready to go.

'I heard Martin Hagger did some work for you,' I said, as casually as I could.

Malick nodded. 'Water quality. It wasn't a big deal. Something under the ice was corroding our pipes. We asked if there was anyone at Zodiac who could take a look at it, and your boss sent Hagger.'

'Did he find anything out?'

'He ran some samples. Apparently it was a bug, some kind of plankton or something. Waters are getting warmer here, sea-ice cover's thinning. He said it makes sense something new would evolve to take advantage.'

I glanced out the window again at the drill rig. If Fridge had told the truth, it wasn't oil flowing through those yellow pipes. *Commercially sensitive information.* But would you kill for that?

Malick followed my gaze. 'I know what you're thinking.'

'Really?'

'Melting icebergs and baby seals and all the rest of that Sierra Club shit. You think this job's easy? Tell someone you work in oil exploration, it's like you're telling them you got rabies. Tell them you're prospecting in the Arctic, and they want to put a bullet in you. They act like we're up here drowning polar bear cubs in barrels of oil.'

'You don't deny the planet's changing.'

Malick wiped a smear of cake icing off his beard. 'Have you been up in the mountains? Seen any of the old mines?' I nodded. 'You know what they used to dig there?'

'I heard it was coal?'

'And you know what coal is, right? It's dead trees. Same way, if we find oil here it'll be dead plants from two hundred million years ago. You see any swamps and forests here now?'

'Of course not.'

'This planet's always changing. I've been in a cave a hundred feet under a glacier, and seen a leaf fossil printed on a rock. There were trees here before the glaciers, and when it's gone maybe they'll grow back. You think at the end of the last ice age, when those hairy-assed Neanderthals looked out their cave one day and saw the ice had gone, they blamed each other for making the glaciers melt, or started a Save the Mammoth campaign? Hell no. They got off their cold butts and started to hunt.'

We'd stayed so long they felt obliged to give us lunch. Eastman and Malick talked about something called March Madness, which I gathered was to do with basketball. Some team called the Huskies had been doing well, which gave rise to some obvious topical jokes. I smiled along, and considered what I knew.

Hagger had obviously had plenty of opportunity to give information to DAR-X. From what I knew of his work, it involved plenty of chemistry, so he surely could have understood the data. And then DAR-X had been near the Helbreen glacier, probably the only people at that end of the island, when he died.

That still didn't explain how they could have got to Anderson. But all I had for what happened to him was Annabel's word. Annabel and Hagger had been close – that was common knowledge. And she should have been his partner the day he died. Could they both have been in on it?

I worked on the theory. Annabel and Hagger had been passing secrets to DAR-X – but then he got cold feet and wanted to stop. That was why she'd been so cross with him when she came back this season. The two of them went to the Helbreen to rendezvous with DAR-X, he threatened to expose them, and she pushed him into the crevasse. Then took out Anderson for good measure.

I didn't want it to be true. I didn't want to think the worst of them. But that's the problem with Zodiac. All the thoughts that anchor you in real life, the routines and the friendships, go out the window. Nature abhors a vacuum: something has to evolve to fill the gap. And often it isn't very nice.

★   ★   ★

We had one stop to make on the way home. There's an old hut at Seal Point, about sixty kilometres up the coast from Zodiac on the east side. They built it in 1953 for the International Polar Year; four unlucky scientists spent thirteen months there recording the weather. Legend has it when the relief party came, three of them were living in an igloo eating seal meat, and one was holed up in the cabin with his rifle.

After that, the hut was abandoned. But a few years ago, the base commander of the day decided to refurbish it as a holiday cottage for scientists who wanted a break. I've sent one or two people there myself, when I thought they needed to get off the Platform. It's a picture-postcard place: little red cabin nestled in a hollow, tin chimney poking out of the roof and snow-capped mountains behind. All that spoils the scene is the barbed wire strung around the windows. You need it to keep out the bears.

We'd come to drop off emergency supplies. Jensen and Eastman left a couple of fuel drums in the cache, while I went inside to check the first-aid box for anything that had expired. It's a strange feeling, being the first person in a place that hasn't been touched in months. All the windows were shuttered, though sunlight wormed around the cracks creating a sort of amber twilight. Just the one room. Two bunks on each wall – the lower ones doubled as benches for the table that folded down between them. A tall cast-iron stove, vintage 1953, stood in the corner like one of those Victorian grave markers, next to a cupboard. On the wall, a woman crouched in her bra and knickers and made come-hither eyes at me. She must have been cold, wearing so little. She'd been torn from a magazine, though she still looked good. I think it was Cat Deeley.

A tin of corned beef lay open on the table, spoon lolling inside it, as if someone had been here moments ago and just popped out. I could smell smoke in the air.

I stepped over the threshold – and almost fell on my arse. A thin slick of ice covered the floor. I suppose snow must have blown in, melted when they lit the stove, and then froze again.

I found the medicine box in the cupboard and went through it, checking the contents against the list, filtering the out-of-date stuff. A couple of the morphine bottles were missing, which worried me. Probably an oversight, but I made a note to tell Quam. You don't want people shooting up out there.

I finished, but the smoke smell still bothered me. The biggest risk at Zodiac is fire. You wouldn't think it, surrounded by ice and snow, but it's so dry that once fire takes hold it doesn't let go. Well, we found that out, as you know.

I opened the stove, just in case. You're supposed to sweep it out before you go, but this was full of ash. Fine, white and spindly: they'd been burning paper, not coal or wood. They must have left in a hurry. A few fragments hadn't burned properly.

I reached in. The feathery ashes crumbled under my touch. My hand came out grey with soot, clutching a charred corner of green cardboard. It looked like the cover of the notebook Anderson found up on the glacier.

Fifteen

Kennedy

'You all set?'

I spun round as if I'd been caught stealing from the church box. It was only Eastman.

'We're done with the fuel dump.' He saw my hand covered in ash. 'Did you start a fire?'

'Just checking for safety.' I clanged the stove door shut. 'We'd better get back. The plane'll be coming soon.'

I slipped the cardboard fragment in my coat pocket and hoped Eastman hadn't seen it. Paranoia was in full flow: I sat tight in the helicopter, silent with my thoughts, while Eastman and Jensen chattered away. Below us, the helicopter's shadow chased over the frozen ocean, rippling on the bumpy surface. I thought about the vast pressures seething under the ice, crushing and pulling in every direction, and those little wrinkles that were the only outward sign.

The moment we landed, I hurried to the medical room. Anderson lay on the bed, still out, fogging the mask with his breath. I was surprised how relieved I felt. If someone had tried to kill him once, what was to say they wouldn't try again.

I opened the drawer where I'd put Hagger's notebook. And – nothing. It sat exactly where I'd left it: green cover, graphs, all the pages. I had to touch it to be sure it was real.

So what got burned?

I compared it to the fragment of green card I'd rescued from the stove. No question, they came from the same batch. Same colour, same thickness.

Hagger might have had more than one notebook. I might even have seen them, lined up against the wall in his lab. I went down and put my head round the door. If there had ever been notebooks there, they were gone now. A big glass flask sat where I remembered them, as if trying to fill the space.

I went to the front door and examined the field log. It was a long shot, and it didn't come off. No one had helpfully signed out that they were going to the cabin to destroy Hagger's research. Just the usual comings and goings. The thing with the cabin is, anyone could go there without being noticed. An hour or so by snowmobile, a quick blaze and then home.

As I said before, bad thoughts grow like weeds. Each time the Platform creaked in the wind, I jumped like a schoolgirl. Back in the medical room, I popped a diazepam to calm myself down. I don't often self-medicate – but I was trembling badly; my heart was threatening to run off with me. I locked the notebook in the cabinet where I keep the hard stuff. I was about to add the piece from the cabin, when something made me give it one last look.

I squinted at it, and as it caught the light I saw tiny indentations. Writing. Grey pencil on green card, hard to make out under the muck from the furnace. I blew off the soot, trying not to smudge it any more, and angled the card to the light.

Does Ash know where it's going?

'Is he ready?'

Greta had come in without me noticing. It happened a lot, that sort of thing – it's how Zodiac was. No locks on the doors, not even the medical room. I looked to see if Greta had seen what I'd been doing. If she had, she didn't comment. She never gave anything away.

'Plane's coming,' she said. 'Help me move him?'

We wrapped him up the best we could manage and stretchered him down the steps. The Sno-Cat was waiting, engine running to keep the cab warm. We loaded Anderson in the back; Hagger's body went strapped to a sled behind it, wrapped up in a body bag I'd found at the back of a cupboard. Greta drove as carefully as she could, but the old beast wasn't built for a soft ride. A couple of times, I almost had to throw myself on top of Anderson to keep him from hitting the ceiling.

The plane was already there. We loaded the two men on-board – Anderson in the front, Hagger in the hold – and waved it off. Soon, it was just a speck in the clouds.

USCGC Terra Nova

'Wait a minute.' Franklin had been standing, pacing the room while Kennedy talked. 'You're telling me that Anderson was shipped home from Zodiac?'

'You sound surprised, Captain. Find the body, did you?'

'We . . .' Franklin gathered his thoughts. 'No. Not yet. But we had, uh, indications he was still on Utgard.'

Behind the bandages, Kennedy's mouth tightened. 'Did you, now? I can jump to the end of my story, if you like.'

Franklin checked his pager. Still nothing on Eastman. Under his feet, he could feel the familiar rise and fall as the *Terra Nova*'s bow rode up on the ice, then crushed down through it. They were making good headway.

'You go on.'

Quam met me when I got back to the Platform. 'Is he away safely?'

I tugged off my mittens and fiddled with my boots. 'Away – yes. Safe . . .' I shrugged. 'If anything happens to him, it's on your conscience.'

'It's for the best. He can get the care he needs, and we can get on with the job.' He touched me awkwardly on the shoulder. 'You know I'm right, Sean.'

I excused myself. I know I shouldn't speak ill of the dead, but I didn't enjoy his company. He knew his status, and wanted you to know it too. I didn't mind that so much – a base commander *should* keep his distance, or he's courting trouble – but he made an exception for me. Treated me like some kind of confidant, as though we shared something we didn't. To tell the truth, it made me slightly sick.

I'd just got back into the medical room and was starting to clear up when Greta came in.

'Anderson had a kid,' she said. 'Has anyone told him?'

'I wouldn't know . . .'

'Anderson Skyped him from the radio room. Guest account. You can log in and get the details.'

'Go for it,' I told her.

She didn't move. 'If his dad's in a coma, he should hear it from a doctor.'

'Anderson will be in England in twenty-four hours. No point worrying the boy.'

'Maybe he should be worried.'

Our eyes met; I understood what she was getting at. She wanted him prepared in case the worst happened.

'He'll be fine,' I insisted.

'Are you sure?'

I headed to the radio room and logged in to the computer,

opened Skype and found the last conversation. I clicked the button and waited, hoping he wouldn't answer.

The screen came alive. A boy, probably about eight years old, with an eager smile that flicked off when he saw my face.

'Who are you?'

'My name is Dr Kennedy.' I cleared my throat. For all the courses they give you on your bedside manner, nobody ever covers how to break bad news over the Internet to a boy you've never met. 'I'm the doctor at Zodiac Station, where your daddy's been working.'

He stared at me.

'I'm just calling to let you know there's been a little accident. Your daddy fell and banged his head. He's coming home. He's fine.'

He stared at me.

'He's going to be fine,' I said. Repeating myself. 'He's just hurt himself a little bit.'

He glanced over his shoulder. In the background, I heard a woman's voice calling, 'Is that Daddy?'

The boy shook his head. A moment later, a harassed-looking woman appeared over his shoulder, peering closely at the camera. 'Who is this?'

'My name's Sean Kennedy. I'm the doctor—'

Over my head, one of the radios crackled.

'Why are you talking to my nephew?'

'*Zodiac Station, this is Tango Oscar two niner.*'

I looked up, trying to work out where the interruption was coming from.

'Daddy's hurt,' the boy told the woman.

'Is Tom all right?' The woman leaned in so close her face filled the screen. 'What's happened?'

'*Zodiac Station, please come in.*' Even squawking through the radio, I could hear panic in the voice. '*We have an emergency situation.*'

'Is this some kind of joke?'

Greta pushed in to the tiny room. She must have been listening outside. She grabbed a microphone.

'What's your status, Tango Oscar two niner?'

'Zodiac Station, we have a critical equipment malfunction.'

'We'll call you back,' I told the woman.

'Can you make it to Longyearbyen?' Greta asked.

'Negative, Zodiac. Longyearbyen is out of range. We're returning to Utgard. Please stand by for emergency landing.'

'Is Daddy OK?' said a forlorn voice from the computer.

We all gathered at the airstrip. Even Danny came, squeezed into a parka he'd borrowed from Fridge. The only one that fit. Greta ransacked the base for every fire extinguisher she could find and loaded them in the back of the Sno-Cat.

Eastman manned the radio, though there wasn't much chat – just occasional terse position updates. I guessed the pilot had better things to worry about. Across the runway, Fridge climbed a ladder and smashed ice off the windsock. The moment he freed it, it started snapping and jerking like an angry dog.

'Bad crosswind,' said Greta, as you might talk about the weather with the postman.

Behind the runway, you could see plumes of snow lifting off the mountains. The wind cut through us, freezing any skin it touched. Quam's right: everyone loves the drama of a rescue, and the biggest danger is often to the rescuers. I made them all get back in the Sno-Cat – everyone except Greta and Quam – until the plane was on approach. I pulled the hood of my parka over my hat, and Velcroed the flaps over my jaw. The world shrank, blurred at the edges by the fur trim on the hood whipping in the wind.

Bundled up like that, I didn't hear the plane. Greta did. She tugged my arm; a moment later, Eastman waved from the Sno-Cat's cabin. I scanned the southern sky with my binoculars. The clouds hid the plane and the wind made my eyes tear: by the time I found it, it was nearly on top of us.

Something was badly wrong. The plane bounced around the sky like a kite. One propeller wasn't turning at all. I kept waiting for it to stabilise, to flatten out into its approach. If anything, it got worse. It looked as though the pilot had no control at all.

The others got out of the Sno-Cat and spread out along the runway clutching fire extinguishers. Fridge sat on a snowmobile, engine running.

It came over the shore – too fast, it seemed to me. The wind whistled off the glacier – heavy, katabatic wind, the weight of cold air pushing down from the high ground. A gust hit the plane. It jerked back then dropped forward.

It was too close to the ground. The front ski tip hit the snow, tore off and got left behind. The plane bellyflopped on to the runway and skidded across, white clouds billowing behind. Could have been smoke or snow. Greta jumped on the back of the snowmobile; Fridge gunned the engine and raced after it. The rest of us followed, struggling with the heavy fire extinguishers. I thought I heard Quam shouting at us to stay back, that it was too dangerous, but no one paid any attention.

It takes a lot to stop a plane sliding over what's effectively an ice rink. It reached the end of the groomed ski way, past the marker flags, and kept going. Snow mounded up around the nose; suddenly, the plane slewed around ninety degrees. The wings shook so hard I thought they'd snap off. The propeller churned snow into a blizzard.

The Twin Otter shuddered to a halt. One propeller spun in the wind, the other engine poured out smoke. Fridge jumped off the snowmobile and started dousing the engine.

Greta ran to the fuselage door and tore it open.

The rest of us had finally caught up. We let rip with our fire extinguishers until the plane was so doused with foam it looked as if we'd buried it in a snowdrift. In retrospect, it's a shame we were so enthusiastic.

Quam arrived, flapping his arms, trying to shoo us back. I ducked away, and ran round the other side. The door was open, lying flat in the snow. I crawled in and looked around.

It was a mess. Boxes and bits of kit had been thrown about as though a tornado had hit. Smoke and snow blew through the cabin. I smelled kerosene from somewhere near my feet.

Anderson was the only untouched thing in that chaos. He lay on the stretcher where I'd loaded him up a couple of hours earlier, arms folded across his chest like a dead man.

Sixteen

USCGC Terra Nova

'But he made it.'

Franklin stood in the centre of the cabin, staring down at Kennedy. The mummified face looked right back. If there was any expression there, the bandages hid it pretty well.

'Is there something you want to tell me, Captain?'

No point bluffing. 'Anderson's on this ship. He's hurt, but he's alive. We picked him up off the ice a few hours ago. He's the one who told us about the fire at Zodiac.'

Kennedy reached out and scrabbled for the water on the side table. He nearly knocked it over.

'Let me.' Franklin tipped the plastic cup to Kennedy's lips. The water slurped and gurgled in his throat.

'Have you got someone watching him?'

'Yeah.'

'And would he be carrying a gun?'

'You think—'

Kennedy gripped Franklin's wrist. Water slopped over the cup's edge and soaked the bandages.

'If Anderson's on-board, you'll need all the protection you've got.'

'Was he responsible . . . ?'

Kennedy released his grip. 'Have you spoken to Bob Eastman yet?'

'He's still unconscious.'

'He knows more than me.'

Franklin refilled the cup at the washstand faucet and put it back beside the bed. He picked up the stateroom phone and put in a call to Santiago, on the bridge. Then he sat down.

'Just tell me it how it happened.'

Kennedy

I opened the Twin Otter's door, just as I described. Up front, I could see Trond, the pilot, slumped down in his seat. His harness had broken – we found it later several metres from the aircraft. He had a cut to his head, but he was OK. With a little help from Greta, he was able to walk away.

Anderson lay on his stretcher – untouched. At the risk of offending his guardian angel, I'll take some of the credit for that. I'd worried so much about the flight, I'd wrapped him up like a china doll. I checked his vital signs – all good. The only thing that had come off in the crash was the gas-supply mask. I left it off. If he'd survived that, perhaps he was ready to wake up.

I'm making light of it now, because no one was badly hurt. At the time, we were all shaken, especially the students. Back at the Platform, they gathered in the mess: lots of tears and hugging and cups of tea. I wandered around dispensing comfort and chocolate. When they weren't looking, I popped another diazepam. Works better than tea, for me.

In between, I shuttled back to check on my patients. As I went past the radio room, I saw Greta sitting in front of the computer talking to someone. I assumed it must be Anderson's kid – she never called anyone normally. God only knows what she said to him.

Anderson was still asleep in the medical room; Trond was

127

awake, but I'd made him lie down in a bunk to be sure he hadn't any internal damage.

'What happened?' I asked him, shining a light in his pupil.

'Fuel leak.' He grimaced. 'I don't know how. Everything was checked in Tromsø before we left.'

'Could you have hit something when you took off? A piece of gravel? A lump of ice?'

'I doubt it.' He winced as I changed the dressing on his forehead. 'But the aircraft is old. Perhaps a seal had broken, or one of the tubes came loose.'

'Accidents happen,' I said. If you're a doctor, you learn to talk in clichés.

'Yeah,' he said heavily. Almost as if he didn't believe me.

There'd been one other person on the plane – though he didn't much care. When Trond and Anderson were settled, Greta and I drove out to the wreck and fetched in Hagger. There was something grotesque in the way he'd been carted around since he died – sledges, Sno-Cats, crashed planes and still not at rest. Like something out of Faulkner.

There was no telling how much longer he'd have to wait for his eternal peace. The South Pole gang only keep one plane to service Zodiac; the rest are in Antarctica. They'd need a few days, at least, to dig up a replacement, and even then they'd want to take out the wounded first. So I put him on ice.

The cold store's a spooky place. The ice cover around the base itself isn't deep enough, so they put it in a glacier just over the hill. As you know, the glacier moves, so every season they have to build a new one. They dig a trench about two metres deep in the ice, cut some steps down to it, then roof it with plywood. As soon as the first snow falls, the plywood's covered and frozen into the glacier. The room underneath stays chilled steady at ten below, no need for electricity. And if you run out of space, you can just carve out more room from the side walls, like the ancients quarrying out catacombs as they filled up with the dead.

As I say, it's a spooky place. The snow accumulates, the cave sinks deeper and the stairs get longer. The roof sags under the weight. The only light comes from a few bare bulbs strung from the ceiling; the shadows loom large, especially down the side tunnels. Samples wrapped in plastic rustle as you go past, and it seems to go on for ever.

I loaded Hagger on to the dolly and pushed him to the far end. The body bag I'd put him in was a brittle thing, probably twenty years old, and all that banging about in the crash had torn big holes in it. You could see him inside.

I sliced it off with a box cutter. Underneath, he was still wearing the clothes he'd had on when he died – right down to his glove liners. I hadn't examined the body properly when Greta and Tom brought him in. Checked the pulse, signed the certificate. Again, I noticed the clothes were stiff and heavy with ice, as if they'd been drenched and then frozen. If he'd been working on sea ice and fallen through, I could have understood it – but he'd been halfway up a glacier.

Down in the dark, something offended me about those clothes. I unzipped the coat, pulled off the hat and worked his hands free of the gloves. It was ridiculous, sentimental, but I thought he deserved a more traditional pose. I lifted his arm and tried to fold it across his chest.

The arm was frozen solid. I bent it as delicately as possible, terrified of snapping it. Too gingerly: it slipped out of my grip. I lifted it again, and as it came into the light I saw the palm of his hand.

It was covered in blood.

I would have screamed, if it hadn't been for the diazepam. The drug numbed me better than the cold. Instead, I examined the body with narcotic detachment. Hagger had died of a fall; there'd been no puncture wounds. So where could the blood have come from?

It wasn't blood. Shining my head torch on his hands, I could see the stain was too pink for that. Even in the poor light, it made a shocking splash of colour on his pale skin.

'Have you started robbing graves now?'

Annabel's voice was enough to lower the temperature in that room another couple of degrees. I turned slowly. She stood at the bottom of the stairs, framed by the blue light seeping through the ice.

'The plane shook him about. I'm tidying him up.'

She advanced down the long tunnel. Her breath made icy clouds under the lamps. She stopped at a metal rack full of ice cores and started checking the labels.

'I had a month's worth of ice on that flight. Now all it's good for is cocktails.'

'And was that the most important thing on the plane, do you think?'

She didn't rise to the bait. 'You can't fix the ice cores with paracetamol and a sticky plaster. But . . .' she pulled out a semicircular tube of ice '. . . we back it up. We split the cores down the middle with a table saw, so if there's any doubt about the lab sample, we can double-check against the original.'

She counted them off, then swore. 'One of them's missing.'

'I didn't take it,' I said reflexively. Probably sounded guilty as sin. I glanced at the body behind me. I thought how grudges stack up. 'Could Hagger have taken it?'

'The one that's missing is a deep core, right from the glacier bed. Martin wouldn't have been interested.'

'Hagger's got something on his hands,' I said. I twisted the arm so she could see his palm. 'Do you know what that is?'

She gave it a quick glance. 'Do you?'

I did. But I wanted her to say it. 'Some kind of stain.'

'It's Rhodamine B. Fluorescent dye. We use it to measure flow through the glaciers. It's so concentrated, you can pour fifty mil into the top of a glacier, and a few hours later you'll find it coming out the bottom.'

She played with the end of her hair. 'It stains like hell if you spill it.'

'Who else uses it on Utgard?'

'My students.'

I let his hand drop and stood. 'Any thoughts how Hagger got it on himself?'

'We haven't used it here since last summer. Rhodamine's only any good in the ablation season – i.e., when there's meltwater.'

I wondered if it had anything to do with the water that had soaked Hagger's clothes. I decided it was time to be blunt.

'What have you got on your hands, Annabel? Blood, maybe?'

She stared at me in disbelief. 'God, you're melodramatic. And mean.'

'You were supposed to be Hagger's partner on Saturday. You were alone with Tom Anderson when he fell in the moulin.' Without really thinking about it, I'd started to move towards her. Annabel took a step back.

'Do you think I didn't think of that? I've seen the way everyone looks at me. For what it's worth, I was as shocked about Anderson as anyone. I had to pull him out of that hole. As for Martin . . .'

'As for Martin . . .' I prompted.

'He was an arrogant shit. But that doesn't make him worse than any other man on this base.'

'Present company excluded.'

'Do you really think . . . ?' She laughed, as if the whole

idea was too ridiculous to contemplate. 'Maybe I should be flattered you think I'm such a stone-cold bitch I could do it. I suppose you've invented a motive.'

'Revenge.'

'For what?' I made a you-know sort of gesture with my eyes. '*That*?' Another incredulous laugh. 'He was a fifty-something man with three divorces, receding hair and a career going down the toilet. Life was getting its own revenge on him.'

'Then how do you explain the dye on his hands?'

'I can't.'

She held my gaze, defiant across the frozen room. The light flickered; the roof seemed to sag in. Suddenly, what had felt so certain a minute ago melted away.

'Did you have any more mud to throw? Or have you finished?'

I mumbled something. She advanced towards me so that her face glowed yellow in the light.

'Do you think this is easy? I'm the only woman scientist on a station full of men. Technically, I'm sure you're all brilliant, but socially you're hairy Neanderthals who haven't emerged from the last ice age yet. Everyone here looks at me like I'm a fucking piece of steak they want to get their paws on.'

She moved to go, then thought of one more thing.

'You know why you want to believe that I killed Hagger? Because the idea that a woman would kill a man for love flatters your egos. It makes you think you're worth something.'

Seventeen

Kennedy

I hadn't finished breakfast next morning when Quam called me into his office. He sat behind his desk, fingers working a rubber band fit to snap.

'What the hell do you think you're doing?' he demanded.

'I was hoping to finish my cornflakes.'

'You know damn well what I'm talking about. I've had reports – from more than one of my staff – that you're putting it about Hagger was murdered.'

'You asked me to find out who was leaking data to DAR-X. I'm pretty sure it was Hagger. He even did a little unofficial work for them on the side.'

'Hagger's project had nothing to do with that.' The rubber band was wound so tight it had cut off the blood to his fingertip. 'I authorised it myself.'

'And they were up by the glacier the day Hagger died.'

'So were half the Zodiac personnel, for God's sakes. You can't be suggesting that DAR-X would do . . . *that*.'

'No one ever accused oil companies of playing by the rules.'

I didn't mention Annabel. I guessed she'd already told Quam what I thought of her.

'This has to stop,' Quam said. 'We're all living close to the edge. Hagger, Anderson, now the crash. More major incidents in a week than we've had in twenty years.'

'Still, it's three,' I said flippantly.

'Three what?'

'Bad things come in threes. Maybe that's the end of it.'

Quam didn't see the funny side. 'One man's dead, two more nearly followed him. With the Twin Otter gone we're cut off, probably for at least a week. If you ratchet up this paranoia any more, someone's going to crack.'

'Don't you see the connection?' I insisted. 'First Hagger, then his assistant – and then the plane they were both on. The leak in the fuel tank – you think that was an accident too?'

'Hagger was a busted flush. Shall I tell you a secret? His reputation, the big *Nature* paper – all built on lies. No one can replicate it, you know why? Because he doped his samples.'

'He couldn't have,' I protested.

'They emailed last week. They're retracting the paper. We can't have that kind of fraud here: the funding bodies would hit the roof. I told him to his face I was sending him home.'

That set me back. I knew he'd been having trouble with his work, but this was something else. A third of scientific articles, even the peer-reviewed ones, turn out to be wrong, but no one ever says anything. They're swept under the carpet and forgotten. For a major journal to publicly disown a paper is almost unheard of. Even the fellows who faked cold fusion back in the eighties didn't have that happen to them.

'You sacked Hagger?'

'That very morning.' He stretched the broken rubber band. There was a nick in it: I could see it would snap again soon.

'You think I'm proud of it?' he said. 'If anyone's responsible for his horrible death, it's me. I must have driven him to it.'

'I still think we should look into it. If Hagger committed suicide, it doesn't explain Anderson. Or the plane, or—'

'Enough!' Quam stood. His face had gone as red as his fingertip, as though someone had wound a rubber band around his neck. 'You've got to stop spreading these rumours – I'm ordering you. You can't go around making people think there's some kind of murderer on the loose.'

Too late, he realised the door was open. Danny stood there, a dishcloth draped around his neck and his eyes wide. He'd started to shuffle back into the corridor, but Quam's furious gaze brought him to a guilty stop.

'Just wondered if Doc had finished his breakfast,' he mumbled.

I'd lost my appetite. But back in the medical room, Anderson had woken up. He sat on the little bed, staring around like an abductee taking his first look at the spaceship. His face was grey, his hair was a mess, and five days of beard growth made him look like a tramp.

'Where am I?'

'Wednesday morning. And still at Zodiac.'

He rubbed the back of his head. 'I'm not sure . . .'

'Some short-term memory loss is normal. You mustn't fret about it. It'll come back in good time.'

'I need to talk to Luke.' He glanced at the clock on the wall, panic spreading. 'He'll be at school.'

'Greta's spoken to him. He knows you're OK.'

'Right.' He lay back, wincing as his head touched the pillow. I put two paracetamol in a cup and popped it on the table next to his bed. He stared at the ceiling.

There was something I was dying to know. 'Up on the Helbreen – when you fell. Do you remember that?'

'I didn't fall.' Behind those eyes, the clouds parted. 'Someone came at me.'

'There wasn't anyone there,' I told him. 'Except Annabel.'

He frowned. 'She'd gone behind the rocks. For a wee. Someone hit me from behind.'

All my suspicions about Annabel came back in a flash – her and Hagger, her and Anderson. But I couldn't make myself believe it. She'd brought Anderson back to Zodiac, after all. Rescued him. If she'd really wanted to kill him, she'd gone about it all wrong.

'You fell in a moulin,' I corrected him. 'Didn't watch where you were going – banged your head.'

'Someone hit me from behind.' His eyes narrowed, focused on something far away.

'Must have been a dream. You've been asleep for two days, head stuffed full of bumps and drugs. It's normal you're a little confused.' I got my ophthalmoscope and shone the light in his eyes to check for concussion.

'I found a notebook,' Anderson said. 'I was reading it.'

So much for short-term memory loss. I wondered what to do. I still wasn't sure if Anderson was on the level. At that stage, I didn't trust anyone.

If you ratchet up this paranoia any more, someone's going to crack. Maybe Quam was right. My body was already starting to tell me it wanted another diazepam.

I opened my cabinet. As I took out the notebook, I saw the burnt corner of the other notebook I'd found at the cabin. *Does Ash know where it's going?* I hid it under the prescriptions book.

'I had a flick through. Couldn't make much sense of it,' I said casually.

He turned a couple of pages and raised an eyebrow. '"Fridge will kill me,"' he read aloud.

'A figure of speech. Martin did some work for DAR-X. Fridge thought that was sleeping with the enemy.'

'And all this about "X". "Concentration of X", "dispersal of X" . . . Do you know what "X" is?'

'I was hoping you could tell me.'

I thought about what Quam had said. *Hagger was a busted flush.* Did it make any difference what he'd written in his notebook – or was it all fiction?

I excused myself to check on the pilot, Trond. Halfway down the corridor, I ran into Jensen.

'Can I have a word, Doc?' I nodded. 'In private?'

'Of course.'

There was no privacy in the medical room; we went to the pool room. It used to be a store cupboard, but one winter some bored technician made a half-size pool table out of old packing crates and crowbarred it in. The cues were flagpoles that had been machined down; the felt from old boot liners. I can't imagine where he found the balls.

There was barely room for two people to stand either side of it, let alone to wield a cue. But it was tolerably private, and no one ever went in there outside the annual pool tournament. I leaned against the door to keep it shut, while Jensen spun a ball on the table.

'There's a rumour going around,' he said. 'Hagger – they're saying it wasn't an accident.'

I didn't need to ask how the rumour had started. If Danny had heard me in Quam's office, everyone on Utgard would know by now. Eastman's instruments had probably picked it up from space.

'Ask Quam,' I told him.

'Do you know who'd have done it?'

'No.'

With a flick of his wrist, he sent the ball rolling towards one of the pockets.

'I think I do.'

137

The ball dropped in the pocket. Lost in my thoughts, I almost missed what Jensen had said: I was too busy thinking about Annabel and Anderson and Fridge and Quam.

Then it registered.

'You know who killed Hagger?' I said stupidly.

'That day – when Hagger died. I said I was flying Dr Ashcliffe all day looking for polar bears.'

I nodded.

'It's not true. Not all true. We were out there, but we didn't have much luck. Mid-morning, he told me to drop him off. He thought he'd have a better chance watching and waiting on the ground.'

'Where was that?'

'The Russian mining town. Vitangelsk. I went off by myself, restocked a few of the fuel depots.'

'How long were you gone?'

'Two hours. Maybe three.'

'Can you check the flight log?'

He picked at the felt on the table. 'Ash said I should write it up as if we'd been flying all day.' He saw the look I was giving him. 'It didn't hurt anyone. The company bills the scientists for the time they book. They have to pay even if they don't use it.'

'You falsified the flight log? To hide the fact that Ash was on his own all afternoon?' Vitangelsk is the other side of the mountain from the Helbreen; no distance at all. Ashcliffe could have skied it easily. If DAR-X hadn't given him a lift.

Jensen looked miserable. 'I didn't think it mattered.'

'Hagger died that afternoon,' I reminded him.

'Jesus, you think I don't know? But we all heard it was an accident. I didn't think it could've been anything else, until today.'

I backtracked. 'How did Ash seem when you picked him up.'

'That's the thing. He looked pretty shaken up, said he'd had a close encounter with a bear.'

'A bear?'

'But that's not all.' Jensen glanced at the door and leaned over the pool table. 'He had blood on his coat.'

Eighteen

Kennedy

Does Ash know where it's going? Suddenly the words in the notebook took on a whole new meaning. I'd thought so hard about Fridge and Annabel, I'd never really considered him.

'He had blood on him?'

'Big smear, right along the sleeve.'

'You didn't wonder—'

'He said he'd had a nosebleed.' Jensen caught my eye; despite the situation, we both laughed. 'Well, the air's pretty dry up here.'

I thought about Hagger's body in the deep freeze. I hadn't seen any wounds on him. Even so . . .

'Where's Ash now?'

The field logbook said Ash had checked out an hour ago, headed out on the sea ice in the fjord. Going to confront him didn't exactly fit with Quam's instructions to let this go, but that didn't bother me. I wanted the truth.

'You'll have to come too,' I told Jensen. 'I need you to back up what you told me.'

He edged away a fraction. I wondered if he was having second thoughts.

'Eastman's booked to fly in half an hour. Up to Vitangelsk. I'll be gone most of the day.'

I made a quick decision. I hadn't completely forgotten

Quam: if I was going to accuse Ash of anything, I needed all the evidence I could get. He'd been at Vitangelsk that day; so had DAR-X. What if they'd left something behind?

'I'll come too.'

Jensen glanced nervously towards the medical room. 'Shouldn't you be taking care of your patients?'

'Some painkillers will see them right.'

I filled some Thermoses with hot water from the kitchen. On the mess door, the Daily Horrorscope had been updated: *Your plane is going down and your parachute is on fire.* Sometimes it could be quite witty, but I thought that was in poor taste. You know, I still have no idea who wrote them. Never saw anyone put them up.

One day at school, in biology, they showed us a human skull. I've never forgotten the shock of it, the hollow cavity that had once been stuffed with life. Vitangelsk was a bit like that. The Russians had built it overlooking a snowy valley, tiers of barrack dormitories staring out from the face of the mountain. As we flew closer, you could see the sunken roofs and all the broken windows. Steel gantries teetered over the scene, waiting to fall. To the west, a line of wooden pylons stalked across the long ridge that led to the mine. They'd been part of the cableway that carried buckets of coal from the mine to the processing facility at Vitangelsk.

Eastman leaned over and tapped me on the shoulder. 'Can you believe anyone ever came here to mine coal?' I shook my head. 'I mean, they can't make that pay in West Virginia. How the fuck did they ever expect to turn a cent here?'

'I don't suppose it was about the coal,' I said.

'I'll tell you a story I heard. During the Cold War, the CIA was one hundred per cent positive there had to be more to this place than coal. Uranium mining, or rare earths, or else the mine shafts were really launch silos for nukes. They spent millions trying to infiltrate this place: spy satellites, Blackbirds, never got anywhere. Soon as the Ruskies pulled out, a big-shot team from Langley arrived to pull it apart. You know what they found?'

I let him have his punchline.

'A coal mine.'

I laughed with him. 'I suppose it was nationalism. Staking their claim.'

'Right. Governments see a place like this, pure and virginal. What do they want to do? Fuck it in the ass. You know, the only reason they let us do science here is because they haven't figured out how to make money off of it. We're just the hold music. Soon as they think of something better, we're outta here.'

The depressing thing is, he was probably right. 'Doesn't that worry you – as a scientist?'

He laughed. 'I'm not like Fridge. I never made the mistake of thinking what I'm doing is worth a damn.'

We made a quick drop at the edge of town, scrambling out the door, wincing as the rotors pummelled us with icy air, racing away to get behind a cluster of rocks. Jensen gave us a thumbs up from the cockpit and took off in a swirl of snow.

We trudged up a gully that had once been a road, between the dead buildings. After the helicopter racket, the silence took on an almost physical dimension, oppressive with its weight. I couldn't shake the feeling that someone might be watching. The old barracks loomed over us, the paint almost stripped away. In the faded murals that survived, the ghosts of happy workers traipsed through flowery meadows, enjoying picnics and cuddling children.

I thought of the men – they must have been men – who'd

walked past those murals every day on their way to hack open the mines. Did the pictures remind them of home? Or just harden their hearts?

'What are you looking for here?' I asked Eastman.

'I still haven't figured out the interference I'm getting. I thought maybe there could be some old electrical equipment, generators or something, giving off some kind of a signal.'

I pointed up. Over our heads, a skein of cables and wires drooped between the buildings like some enormous spiderweb.

'There must have been something.'

'Once upon a time.'

We climbed a snow bank that had been a flight of steps and came out in the old central square. A brick building with a rusty hammer and sickle above the door stood on the uphill side – the most permanent place in town. In front of it, in the centre of the square, a tall man stood striding forward on top of a granite plinth. I'm sure the sculptor meant it to look purposeful; to me he seemed to be stepping off a cliff. I couldn't read the inscription, but I recognised the face from the history books: the bald head and iconic beard; the bulging forehead; the twisted lip and sneer of cold command. Lenin.

'"Look upon my works, ye Mighty, and despair,"' I murmured. I wanted to touch him, though the sculptor had made sure I could only reach his foot. So much for the brotherhood of man. Even through my mitten, I felt the deep cold seared into the metal. I almost felt sorry for him. Not even a hundred years ago, his name had shaken the world. Now his empire was broken windows and snow gathering in empty doorways.

'You think in a hundred years people will look at our statues and pity us?'

'They'll probably have smashed all the statues because they're so pissed at the way we trashed the planet.'

143

It sounded like the sort of thing Fridge would have said. 'I thought you were an optimist.'

Eastman grinned. With his shaved head and trim beard, there was a touch of Lenin about him I hadn't noticed before.

'I'm a fatalist. Same difference.'

He pointed up the mountain. 'I think they kept most of the technical stuff up top. I should check it out.'

I hadn't told him about Ashcliffe. I was keen to do some exploring on my own. 'I'll stay down here.' I tapped the bulge under my jacket. 'I've got the VHF.'

'Don't go too far.' He stretched his arms and made a whoo-whooing noise. 'Never know who'll turn up in a ghost town.'

Once Eastman had disappeared, I got out my GPS and tried to read the map on the tiny screen. The Soviets had sunk mines all along the valley, with Vitangelsk more or less in the middle. To the west, the valley wound down to the coast; east, it continued another few miles until it ran into another mountain, the last bulwark against the eastern ice dome. Go around that mountain, and you'd eventually come out on the Helbreen.

I put the GPS away and looked around. For a ghost town, Vitangelsk had seen a lot of traffic of late. There were footprints and ski tracks everywhere. Flying in, I'd seen a corrugated Sno-Cat track approaching from the south, and what looked like a couple of snowmobile trails heading east.

One set of prints looked fresher than the rest. Big and heavy, putting me in mind of a Yeti. Easy to follow, so I did: along the street, round a corner, and up to the front door of one of the barracks. I say front door, though the door was long gone. All that survived was splinters in the frame. But someone had trampled the snow flat all around.

I looked at the footprints again. Fresh-ish – but not so

much you expected to see the owner come whistling round the corner. Still, I hesitated.

Will you be running away from ghosts, Dr Kennedy? I asked myself.

Angry with myself for being so foolish, I went inside.

In a queer way, it reminded me of the Zodiac Platform. A long corridor, lined with doors and the remnants of doors. So dark, I couldn't see the far end. Snow had blown in, gathering in little piles by the door frames.

Now, I don't believe in ghosts – but I don't read ghost stories either, if you get my drift. Still, I'd come that far: I made myself go on. Just so I could satisfy myself I'd done it. I looked in a couple of the rooms and found what you'd expect: broken bunks, mattresses with the stuffing knocked out, some Soviet pornography pinned to the walls. Surprisingly tasteful.

You'd think that would have calmed me down, finding nothing. But the longer I stayed there, the more desperate I was to go. Each step, I had to swallow a little more panic.

One more room, I told myself. Just to prove I was bigger than my fears.

I was in such a hurry to go, my head was almost out the door before I'd looked in. But something made me look again.

This room wasn't like the others. The snow had been swept out, and the broken furniture cleared. It had been replaced by a mattress, a sleeping bag, an oil lamp, a pile of books and a few tins of baked beans.

I checked the dates on the beans. They didn't expire for a couple of years – and I didn't think the Soviet Union had imported Heinz. The books were well read, but relatively new to judge from the covers, all in English. Milton's *Paradise Lost*; Watson's *The Double Helix*; one of Stieg Larsson's. Eclectic tastes.

Paradise Lost still had a bookmark in it. Feeling like a thief, I opened to the page. Two lines had been underlined in pencil.

> *Did I request thee, Maker, from my clay*
> *To mould me man, did I solicit thee . . .*

A crack ripped open the silence. Probably just an icicle falling off the roof, or a piece of wood the frost had got to. But it was too much for me. The next thing I knew, I was outside in the snow, blinking at the daylight.

'Bob?' I called.

No answer.

I walked on, mostly to get away from that place. A little distance gave me some perspective. DAR-X had been up here – they'd probably bunked there for the night and left some things behind. Nothing sinister. Who knew oilmen read Milton?

The more I thought it over, the more I convinced myself I'd come on a fool's errand. Hagger, Ashcliffe, the whole lot: my mind playing tricks. If what Quam had said that morning was true, Hagger had every reason to kill himself. He'd been depressed enough, God knows. As for Anderson, he had no one to blame for his bump but himself. And the plane was probably just bad luck.

Lost in thought, I'd reached the edge of town. Ahead of me, the old pylons marched across the side of the valley, clinging to the precipice like spiders. Bleached telegraph poles knocked together into A-frames, with platforms at the top like ancient siege towers. They still had the cables running between them, and a few rusting coal buckets dangling below. I wouldn't like to be standing underneath one of those when it gave out.

I'd just started back towards the square when a movement caught my eye. A flash of yellow darting between two buildings. Too bright to be a bear.

'Bob?' I called, but it couldn't be him. He'd been wearing a red coat, same as me.

A cold wind blew down the alley. I unshouldered the rifle, though I kept the safety on – and my mittens. I didn't want any accidents. Holding the Ruger like a cowboy, I edged around the corner. In the virgin snow between the buildings, I saw footprints coming out the end of one barracks and disappearing into the next.

I pulled off my mittens and aimed the rifle at the door. 'Who's there?'

No answer. One-handed, I pulled down the zip of my coat and reached for the VHF radio strapped across my chest. I toggled the button.

'Bob?'

Static. The buildings must have blocked the signal. I climbed the shaky steps and pushed on the door with the gun barrel. It swung in slowly, opening up on a long dark corridor that ran the length of the building. Dim doorways lined the sides. At the far end, a square of blue light showed an open door.

I didn't go in. So many rooms just right for hiding, or he could nip out the other door and circle round behind me. I toggled the radio again. Still only static.

I backed off, keeping the rifle towards the barracks, until I was far enough away that I could see the front and the side of the building. I swept the rifle from side to side, though my hands were so cold I doubt I could have pulled the trigger.

I lifted my hat off my ears so I could hear better, twitching my head this way and that. Terrified I'd miss something, terrified what I might find. I heard footsteps in the snow; someone was running. He must have gone through the barracks and out the far door. I listened a moment longer. The footsteps retreated. He was getting away.

I ran along the front of the building, floundering through

the snow. The thing about Utgard is that there's so little snowfall, the actual cover can be very thin – or three feet deep where the wind's blown it into drifts. It makes for treacherous footing. Whether it was a rock, or a piece of Soviet mining equipment they'd left behind, or a piece of shingle fallen off a building, I have no idea. All I know is that my boot caught something in the snow and pitched me forward.

I fell, winded. The gun flew out of my numb hands, skidded away across the snow and disappeared in the crawl space under the barracks.

No way was I going to go in to look for it. I picked myself up and ran on. I came around the corner of the barracks, giving it a wide berth in case he was waiting to jump out at me. He didn't jump; he wasn't there. He'd vanished.

I ran another few metres, out on to the mountainside. The footsteps led towards an outcropping of rock, near the base of a cableway tower. I paused. Did he have a gun? Did he know I didn't?

I had to get hold of Eastman. I lifted my hand to the radio – but I never pressed the button.

Off to my right – down the slope, away from the rocks – the snow started to move, rising up like a cloud.

Then it opened its mouth and roared.

Nineteen

Kennedy

Perhaps you've seen polar bears on TV. Kings of the Arctic, majestic lives lived to a David Attenborough commentary. Reality isn't quite like that. For starters, unless you've a paparazzi-length lens, you never get so close as you do on TV. The bears I've seen on Utgard were all miles off, mostly dots on the horizon. Generally, it's best to keep it that way.

This one, I could see the breath coming in clouds out of his nostrils; the pricked-back ears; the way his shaggy coat wobbled when he moved, like a blanket thrown over his bones. He must have been sleeping. He leaned down on his front paws and arced his back like a cat, then shook himself vigorously. A cloud of snow flew off his fur.

I had no gun. Somewhere in one of my coat pockets, I had a flare pen, but that's a fiddly piece of kit. You have to screw in the flare like a fountain-pen cartridge, then flick a tiny plastic catch. I doubted the bear would wait for all that.

He looked at me. I glanced back at the town, but it was a good way off. Even if I made it into the barracks, I've heard of bears breaking in locked doors. And the doors at Vitangelsk wouldn't keep out a kitten.

'Bob!' I shouted, hoping Eastman would hear me.

The bear craned forward, sniffing the air.

There was only one place to go. Up the hill, one of the old towers that had supported the cableway loomed over me.

It looked as if one good kick would send it crashing down the mountain, but I didn't have a choice. I ran for it.

It was like running in a bad dream, the sort of running where your feet feel tied together and your legs are made of treacle. The snow didn't help. I didn't dare look back. I reached the bottom of the tower and flung myself up the ladder. Not a proper ladder, just thin crosspieces nailed on to one of the legs. Too small for a bear to climb – I hoped. My feet slipped; I struggled to get a grip. One rung snapped off in my hand, and I nearly wrenched my arm out of its socket grabbing on to the pylon. I held on, kept climbing.

I reached the platform at the top. Icy, but at least the wood was solid. I knelt, gripping the wooden struts, and peered down.

The bear prowled around the base of the tower, sniffing and growling. Suddenly, it reared up on its hind legs and threw itself against the pylon. The whole structure shook.

I unzipped my coat. My fingers were fat and clumsy with cold. I tapped the VHF radio strapped to my chest.

'Bob? Are you there?'

A gunshot shattered the frozen air. The bear dropped back on to its feet and looked around.

A man in a yellow parka advanced from the cluster of buildings. With his hood up and a ski mask covering his face, I couldn't tell who it was. A big man – carrying what looked like my rifle. He aimed it in the air and fired again.

'Careful,' I called. The bullet had come dangerously close to me.

The bear growled and stepped back, head down, swaying on his haunches. Fight or flight – it was impossible to know what he'd choose. Perhaps he didn't know himself.

Another shot made up his mind. As if he'd never been interested in the first place, he turned and loped off.

I would have cheered – but something had stung my face.

A splinter, gouged out by the bullet that had just hit the woodwork. Flowing blood warmed the frozen skin on my cheek.

I leaned over the platform edge. 'Look out,' I warned. 'You nearly hit me.'

He put the rifle to his shoulder and sighted it – straight at my head. I rolled away, just as the bullet passed through where I'd been a second earlier and buried itself in the top of the A-frame. It almost did for me anyway: dodging it on the icy platform, I nearly went over the edge. I grabbed for the posts and just managed to hang on, my legs dangling into space. If he'd been quicker with the next round, he'd have had me.

He wants to kill me.

I don't know if you've ever been in a situation where you had to face that? It's a hell of a thing to realise. All the good things you've tried to do in your life, everything you thought was right and important and moral, none of it matters a damn. You're on your own, and the only question is, can you do what it takes to save yourself? To tell the truth, it's surprisingly liberating. If you survive it.

The odds didn't look good. He had a gun; I was stuck on an icy platform ten metres up. But you see the world differently when you don't have a choice – like a cornered animal.

A little way from the platform, one of the old coal cars dangled from the cableway, like a mine car without wheels. Probably two metres away – two metres of space with nothing underneath except a long drop on to ice, and a man waiting there to kill me. In normal circumstances, I'd never have dreamed of trying to make it. I didn't even know if the cable would hold, or the rusting arm that the car hung on. But these were pretty far from normal circumstances.

I got to my feet, crouching so he wouldn't get a clear shot. The gap yawned in front of me, hypnotising me. I remembered

151

something I'd read about basketball, that the mistake most people make is to focus on where they might miss, rather than on the hoop itself. I stared at the coal car, concentrating like mad. It still looked a long way off.

Our minds are fickle things. Even on the highest diving board, there's a moment your attention wanders and you forget the big drop you're so frightened of. That's the moment to go.

I jumped.

In a perfect world, I'd have worn something more flexible than a heavy coat and thick trousers; I wouldn't have had such stiff legs, or numb hands. But then, in a perfect world I'd not have been there. All I could count on was the adrenalin charging me up, and the focus that comes when there's no alternative.

I slammed into the side of the car and just managed to hook my arms over the edge. It was like trying to clamber into a boat without capsizing it. The more I pulled, the more it tried to tip me out. My legs kicked air; the rusted metal scraped holes in my jacket. Too late, I realised the whole contraption was designed to swing ninety degrees to tip out the coal.

But twenty-five years out in the cold had gummed it shut. I pressed my arms against the rim, heaved – and was stuck. The radio on my chest had caught on the lip. I heaved some more. Velcro tore; the radio came loose and fell. I popped up like a cork, wriggled forward and somersaulted over the edge with a thud. The car swayed; I waited for something to snap.

It held.

The whole manoeuvre had taken a matter of seconds. Too quick for my enemy to get off a shot, but not by much. I heard the shot and the impact almost simultaneously. The coal car rang like a bell, trembling all around me, but the metal – good, Soviet steel – turned the bullet away.

The sound died. Cowering in the bottom of the coal car, all I could see was the sky, and three cables dissecting it. The bullet's echo rang in my ears, mingling with the moan of the wind in the wires.

Had he run out of bullets? I counted back in my head. There might have been five shots – I couldn't think straight enough to be sure – or there could have been four.

Five would be good news. Four was a problem.

Do ya feel lucky? Clint Eastwood enquired.

The metal under me shivered again. Not the hard clang of an impact, but a steady vibration. Tremors were coming through the wire, down into the bucket. Feet climbing the ladder up the pylon.

What could I do to stop him? If he tried to jump, we'd probably both tip out. My hands were so numb now I couldn't have held a football. Second-degree frostbite, the doctor in my head diagnosed, though at that moment it was a long way down my list of concerns.

The tremors stopped. I had to look. I raised my head over the edge of the bucket – and there he was. The wind puffed out his parka so he seemed more massive than ever, a yellow monster with black eyes, crouching to spring at me.

We stared at each other. If we'd both reached out, we'd almost have touched, but even that close I couldn't see anything of his face. The hood, goggles and ski mask hid it completely.

'Who are you?' I shouted. I don't know if he heard. The wind whipped my voice away from me.

He spread his arms against the posts of the pylon and leaned back, ready to throw himself at me. Then paused. I saw him look around, checking something.

I'm not a brave man. That face – the mirrored goggles, the slit mouth and what he wanted to do to me – I couldn't look at it. I must have closed my eyes. From down on the snow, I heard the radio squawking. Eastman at last – but too late, and nobody to answer it.

The vibrations started again. Not the hard impact I'd expected; the gentle knock of fcct on a ladder. I opened my eyes.

He'd gone. The vibrations faded, until I couldn't feel them at all. Only the coal car rocking gently in the wind.

I lifted my head as high as I dared and strained to listen. I thought I heard footsteps, crunching quickly through the snow. Then silence.

I still didn't dare look. I imagined him waiting behind a rock, my own gun trained on the coal car, ready to shoot the minute I put my head above the parapet. *Four shots or five?* The first thing Greta teaches you at Zodiac is to count your shots, but it's harder when it's your own gun being shot *at you*. And what if he had his own weapon?

More footsteps, punching through the dry snow at a run. I huddled lower in the coal car.

'Doc?'

Eastman's voice. I was shivering so badly I could hardly haul myself over the edge of the coal bucket. I pulled myself up, resting my chin on my sleeve so that the steel didn't freeze to my skin.

Down below, through the wooden girders, I saw Eastman in his red coat. He had his back to me, walking towards the town.

'*Here*,' I called. My teeth were chattering so hard I could barely speak. I cursed myself for dropping the radio. I tried again – louder, but still not enough to carry.

Eastman turned. Hope soared; I waved like an idiot. But he was looking at the ground, and it's hard to see ten metres up when you've a fur hood around your eyes. He turned away again.

In a fury, I thumped my frozen hand against the coal car.

The metal rang: a low, mournful noise like a funeral bell. This would be my coffin. Frozen in the dry air, I wouldn't rot: I'd stay preserved for centuries, maybe until global warming made coal mining economical again and some future miner got the shock of his life when he dumped the first shovelful of coal in the bucket.

I pounded on the steel. I kicked and thumped. The coal car swayed. Eastman was almost behind the barracks now. When he vanished, that would be that. The angels could sing, and Francis Quam would write an empty note to my daughter in Dublin.

They say low frequencies can travel for miles. I don't know how far my banging went, but it was far enough. Eastman heard. He turned, and this time – glory be – he looked up. I waved a limp arm at him, saw him start to run. I slumped down in the car.

Shock, cold, adrenalin, terror – I had it all. I could hardly hold on for him to climb the ladder. At last his face appeared over my steel horizon.

'What the hell are you doing in there?'

Twenty

Kennedy

Eastman stood where the monster had been a few minutes before, so close we could almost touch. But those last two metres were a problem. I couldn't jump back to the pylon – the coal car wasn't a stable platform, even if I'd had the strength – and the idea of me swinging along the cable like a monkey was laughable, if I'd been in the mood for humour.

Quam liked to say that in a place like the Arctic, procedure will save your life. Ever so pompous, but it's true. Procedure says that any party in the field has to carry a survival pack, and in that pack there'll be a thirty-metre length of nylon rope. Eastman fetched the pack and found the rope.

'Can you tie it round yourself?'

I shook my head. I hadn't stopped shaking since he got there. He frowned.

'OK.'

He tied a carabiner to the rope end, so I could clip it around me without having to knot it, and tossed it to me. He looped the rope over the steel hawser, wrapped a couple of turns around one of the wooden posts, and lowered me to the ground. Not gentle, but I was in no state to care. I almost kissed the ground when I landed.

He dragged me to the nearest building and found a room where the walls were tolerably intact. It wasn't any warmer than outside, but he shoved me into the bivvy bag and got the MSR stove going. We didn't speak. For now, the priority was survival. The blood coming back in my hands made me cry out in pain: they'd look pretty ugly in a week or so. At least I had feeling.

Eastman warmed some chocolate between his hands for me, and chipped icicles off the building outside. While they melted, he made me a cup of sweet tea with water from our Thermos. The heat from the cup sent tremors through my hands; when I sipped it, I thought my teeth would explode. I forced it down.

'You picked one hell of a time to play hide and go seek,' Eastman said.

I told him everything that had happened. I didn't think he'd believe me – with a cup of tea in my hand, I hardly believed it myself – but he never challenged me. I was grateful for that. If anything, he seemed slightly distracted. He kept glancing at the door. Perhaps he was worried the gunman would come back. I certainly was. Each time the ice popped and cracked in the pot, I imagined a heavy footstep on the stairs, that faceless man approaching through the rotten building.

'DAR-X wear yellow jackets,' Eastman said when I'd finished.

'I thought of that too.'

'You didn't recognise him? From when we visited Echo Bay?'

'There wasn't much to go on.'

The water had finally melted and boiled. He made me another cup of tea, then poured the remainder into two of the dehydrated meal packs.

'I called Jensen. He was heading back to Zodiac. He has to refuel, then he'll come right out. Should be a couple of hours.'

I lay back in the bivvy bag. A blissful glow had started warming through me. If I closed my eyes I saw euphoric white light.

Don't go to sleep, I warned myself. The gunman was still out there. So, for that matter, was the bear. I forced my eyes open.

Across the room, Eastman was giving me a crooked look.

'What?'

'There's another option, of course.'

'Another option for what?'

'There's how many people on this island? A couple dozen, maybe thirty if you count the students? That guy who just tried to kill you, he's still around. Do you want to go back to Zodiac, wait until he finds us again?'

Extraordinary question. 'I want to go back to Zodiac so I can get away from him.'

'Or do we try and get him where we know he's at?' Eastman leaned forward, a predatory set to his jaw.

'*Get him?*' I repeated. 'I'm not John Wayne.'

Eastman picked up his rifle and squinted down the sight. 'We'll be ready for him.'

'And what makes you so sure he'll come back?'

A bright white grin. Wolfish, you might say, if wolves had access to modern orthodontics.

'Because you're still alive.'

And that seemed like a fine reason to go home. Quit while I was ahead. It's a thin line you walk in the Arctic at the best of times, and I'd very nearly gone over the edge. I needed food, warmth and rest. Then there was the matter of my patients, Anderson and Trond, who needed my care back at base.

But I'd spent days blundering around, and it had nearly killed me. The figure on the cableway terrified me, true, but running away wouldn't cure that. The only way to escape – really, truly escape – was to get answers.

Eastman called Jensen on the satphone and said we were spending the night. 'Tell Quam we've got high winds at Vitangelsk. We'll let you know when it's safe.'

I heard Jensen's surprise through the speaker. It must have been a calm day at Zodiac.

'Just tell him,' Eastman said, and rang off.

'Do you trust Jensen?' I asked.

'What do you mean?'

I hesitated. I'd spoken without thinking – but now that I had, I wanted to go on. I was too tired for games. And Eastman had saved my life.

'Someone at Zodiac's been leaking information to the oil companies,' I began. 'Whoever it is, I think that person killed Hagger – either because he was in on it, or because he found out.'

It was the first time I'd mentioned the possibility of Hagger's murder to him. He didn't look shocked, not even surprised. He must have been thinking along the same lines.

'Are you sure?'

'Hagger was moonlighting for DAR-X,' I went on. 'They were up here the day he died, and then they kindly helped bring in his body.'

'So they were in the same place. Why would they go for Hagger?'

'You know, it's not oil they're drilling at Echo Bay. It's something called methane . . .' I stumbled over the word '. . . clathrate. So bad, it'll make oil and gas look like eco fuels.'

'Who told you that?'

I decided to leave Fridge out of it. 'Hagger found out. I don't know who else knows. It might be a secret worth keeping.'

Eastman took a silver hip flask out of his coat. 'JD. You want some?'

I demurred. He took a long swig. 'If you're right – and it sounds kind of crazy to me – then Hagger must have been acting alone. He was the only one of our guys up this end of the island that day.'

'He wasn't.' I sat up in the bivvy bag and leaned forward. 'Ash was, too. Jensen dropped him off right here in Vitangelsk.'

For the first time, I sensed he might be taking me seriously. 'Jensen kept that quiet.'

'Ash warned him he'd get in trouble if he told.'

Eastman put away the flask and picked up the rifle. Working quickly, hardly looking, he unclipped the magazine and ejected the cartridges.

'You think the guy on the cableway could have been Ash?'

I'd wondered. 'He seemed too big. It was hard to get a good look.'

'Maybe we'll get a better view tonight.' Eastman reloaded the magazine, pressing the bullets down one by one with his thumb. He snapped it back into the rifle and chambered a round.

'I'll keep watch. You get some rest.'

As well as the rifle, he kept a flare pistol strapped to his thigh – a snub black thing that looked like a child's toy. He loaded a flare into the pistol but left it broken open. He put it on the floor next to me.

'For you. Just in case.'

I didn't sleep well. My hands ached like an old lady's; even in the bivvy bag, I couldn't stop shivering. With my eyes open, the room seemed dark and dim; when I closed them, the night seemed far too bright. Every creak in the building had my imagination working overtime. And every time I started to drift off, the man in the yellow parka reared up in my mind's eye like a bear, killing my dreams before they began.

But I must have fallen asleep – or I wouldn't have woken up. Eastman was shaking my arm. The first thing I saw was the rifle on his shoulder.

I glanced at my watch: 4 a.m.

'What is it?'

'Come and see.'

I'd slept fully clothed. I pulled on my boots and gloves, and followed Eastman out the door. Even that close to the twenty-four-hour day, some primitive part of my circadian clock picked out the signs of morning: the empty streets, the dewy silence.

I was fooling myself. A ghost town's streets are always empty, and there hasn't been dew on Utgard for about ten million years. In the distance, I heard a faint drone like a buzzing fly.

We tramped over the crisp snow to the edge of town. The noise got louder. On my left, the pylons marched away across the ridge. Down the slope, the sun gleamed off a lone snowmobile racing up the valley from the south.

We crouched behind the snow that had drifted against the barracks. Eastman handed me his binoculars and pointed. 'Is that the guy?'

Through the binoculars, the snowmobile jumped into focus. I could even read the manufacturer's name: Polaris, the same as we used at Zodiac. A hunched figure in a red suit straddled it, though the glare on his visor hid his face.

'He looks too small,' I said. But fear grows in memory. Perhaps I'd misremembered him.

Eastman took a turn with the binoculars. 'He's hammering that thing.'

We ducked lower. I expected the snowmobile to turn towards

Vitangelsk – there was nowhere else to go – but instead it carried straight on, to the end of the valley and up towards the ridge. The engine whined as it fought the steep slope.

Eastman lay flat on the snow bank. I lay beside him, and watched the snowmobile crawl on up. It swerved this way and that, either to avoid obstacles I couldn't see, or perhaps because the driver was looking for something.

Eastman gave me the binoculars again. I needed a moment to pick out the snowmobile; when I did, it had stopped, just below the line of the cableway.

The driver got off, walking in that stiff, bandy-legged way you do when you've been riding a snowmobile for hours. He must have come from Zodiac. The snowmobile suit, the machine, the rifle on his back – they were all standard-issue equipment.

Could it be the man from yesterday? Why would he have gone back, got a snowmobile, changed his clothes? But who else would come here at this time of morning?

He lifted off his helmet and put it on the seat. He had his back to me, and his balaclava hid his hair. I waited for him to turn around.

'Can you see who it is?' Eastman reached for the glasses, but I kept hold of them. I had to know.

And then the man disappeared. One moment he was a bright red blot against the snowfield. The next, he'd vanished.

Even with the naked eye, Eastman could see he'd gone.

'Did he see us?'

I shrugged. 'He must have gone behind a rock. Or down a gully.' I scanned the hillside with the binoculars. All I saw was snow, and the abandoned snowmobile.

'If we can't see him . . .' Eastman climbed over the snow bank and started galloping across the hillside. After a moment, and checking I had the flare gun in my pocket, I followed.

At that altitude, the wind had scoured most of the snow

off the rocks, but the slope made it heavy going. After a hundred yards, I was puffing; after two hundred, the cold air rasping my lungs made me want to vomit. In the clear air, I could see the snowmobile pin sharp, but it never seemed to get any closer.

Eastman got there first. I caught him up a minute or so later. He pointed to the Zodiac number stencilled on the snowmobile's cowling.

'Definitely one of ours.'

Footprints led away towards a rocky overhang. Orange-brown marks discoloured the snow like a rash. It could have been lichen – there are types that grow in snow and spread like stains – but these weren't like that. They looked like blood.

Under the overhang, a dark hole opened in the mountainside. Sunk in a hollow, angled away from Vitangelsk, invisible until you were virtually in it. Snow had collected by the entrance, and I could see footsteps leading in, as well as the corrugations of an old snowmobile track. And more of the stains, thicker and bloodier than before.

Eastman aimed the rifle at the cave. I cocked the flare gun.

'Who's there?' Eastman shouted. I hoped he was as confident as he sounded.

Silence. Then a shuffling noise from inside the cave, the clatter of stones. I had a vision of some primal monster woken from sleep, Yeats's rough beast slouching towards Bethlehem. Or maybe nothing so fanciful. Bears live in caves, after all.

A figure appeared in the blue light around the entrance. He looked shorter than the man who'd chased me up the pylon. I couldn't see a gun, but I wasn't taking any chances. I gripped the flare pistol tighter.

He pulled off his balaclava and rubbed his eyes. He stepped into daylight, arms half-raised in a bemused way, as if he couldn't believe there was really a gun pointing at him. With his red suit, black boots, white beard and pot belly, he looked like nothing so much as Father Christmas.

The pistol shook in my hand.

'Ash?'

Twenty-one

Kennedy

Ash sat on a rock and rubbed snow out of his beard. If it surprised him to have two colleagues pointing guns at him at four in the morning, here on the upper edge of nowhere, he kept it to himself. Perhaps he expected it.

'How did you guess?' he said. No pretending.

'Jensen told us he dropped you off here. We worked the rest out ourselves.'

'I thought he might. I could see he wasn't happy, not after what happened to Hagger.'

A pause.

'You killed him,' said Eastman.

Ash closed his eyes and nodded silently.

'Why?' I wanted to know.

'I had no choice. He came at me, I had to protect myself.'

'Why?' I repeated. Eastman cut me off.

'What about DAR-X? They were there too?'

'They'd been around. I saw their Sno-Cat. I don't think they saw me.'

'And then you went back and pretended nothing had happened.'

He shrugged. 'What else could I do? It would have been the end of my career if I'd confessed I shot him.'

That gave me a jolt – like a spelling mistake that jars you out of a book.

'What are we talking about?' I said.

Ash looked puzzled 'What are we talking about?'

'Martin Hagger,' said Eastman. 'And why you killed him.'

Ash blinked. He looked slowly between me and Eastman, started to say something, then shook his head. Strange to say, he was smiling.

'You think I killed Hagger?'

'You just admitted it,' said Eastman.

Ash stood and turned towards the cave. Eastman's rifle twitched, but it didn't seem to bother him any more.

'I'll show you.'

Eastman and I followed Ash in with our head torches. The cave was just high enough to stand in, if you stooped. Perhaps it had been an attempt at a mineshaft; if so, they hadn't got very far. A few metres in I could see a corrugated-iron wall blocking off the passage, with a heap of snow blown against its base.

Except the wall wasn't corrugated iron. As my torch caught it, I saw colours, writing. Pictures of broccoli and tomatoes, spaghetti letters and smiling beans.

It was cans. Tin cans, all stacked up as you might find them at Aldi. Soups, vegetables, baked beans, spaghetti hoops – the whole fifty-seven varieties. So many, they walled off the back of the cave.

'You been stealing from the kitchen?' Eastman asked.

Ash looked as if he was about to cry. He shook his head and pointed to the floor. Then I understood.

The wall wasn't corrugated iron – and the wind-blown snow at its base wasn't snow.

Too soft; more yellow than white. As I shone the torch beam down, I made out two legs, the crease of a floppy tail. Further forward, I could see an outflung paw and a black nose resting on it. Much smaller than the bear that had chased me the day before. Just a cub.

Eastman got it a second before me. 'Jesus Christ, Ash. You shot a baby polar bear?'

'When did it happen?' I asked.

'The day Hagger died.'

'Why didn't you tell us?'

'I'm a zoologist. What do you think would happen to my career if it came out I'd shot a polar bear cub. I might as well take up whaling.'

'But you said it was in self-defence.'

'As if they'd care about the details.'

Eastman wiped his face. Out of the sun, the sweat he'd built up running had started to freeze. He was shivering.

'I think some detail here would be good.'

Our torches were fading, the batteries sapped by the cold. In the failing light, the bear carcass seemed to swell up before my eyes.

'Let's get out.'

We went back to the snowmobile and shared a cup of hot water from Ash's Thermos. Eastman hammered a chocolate bar until it snapped.

'I don't know what Jensen told you,' Ash said. His eyes kept darting back towards the cave. 'We'd flown around all morning looking for bears, no luck. Then Zodiac called – they wanted him back for something. I couldn't afford a wasted day, so I had him drop me off here. I'd heard a rumour there might be a bear near Vitangelsk.'

He scratched the back of his head. 'It's like all these things – the wood for the trees. I was so busy looking for a bear, I didn't see the one that *was* there. But he saw me. He must have been watching for a while: they're used to being patient.

'I found the cave. I thought there might be a bear denning inside, so I took a peek. No bear, but I saw those strange

167

tins at the back. I went in, looked around. Couldn't understand what so much food was doing there.

'I went back out. That was when I saw the bear. Juvenile, probably a year old, but with my eyes not used to the daylight, rearing up, he looked like death incarnate. No time to think. I just fired.'

He wiped his mitten across his cheek, where a tear had fallen.

'I shot him right in the heart, just the way they teach you. Greta would have been so proud.'

Another tear appeared. He jerked his head angrily, trying to shake it away. There's not many sights as pathetic as seeing an old man cry.

'It was him or you. We'd all have done the same,' I said.

'Would you?' He stared at me. 'Maybe I could have done it differently. He wasn't charging, just making a display. Trying it on. Maybe a warning shot would have scared him off.'

'A polar bear that had you trapped with your back to the cave?'

'That's not the point. It's not what might have happened; it's what I *did*. One of those moments when you don't have time to think, to intellectualise it or worry what other people will say. That's when you find out who you really are.'

'What you are is alive,' said Eastman, impatiently. Ash gave him a cold look.

'There are more important things.'

'Not in my world.'

'I'm sorry.' I didn't know what else to say.

Ash shrugged. 'It's better now. The secret was murdering me. Now I know what to do.'

'Yeah?' said Eastman.

'I'll tell Quam I'm quitting. I won't tell him why – unless either of you gentlemen feels the need to disclose it. I shan't blame you.'

'I can give you a medical note,' I offered. Ten minutes ago, I'd been ready to shoot him. Now I had nothing but pity.

Eastman looked back across the valley to Vitangelsk. 'Did you come here yesterday?' he asked.

'I was at Zodiac all day. Then Anderson mentioned you'd radioed in, that you'd found a bear here. I thought . . .' His gaze drifted back to the cave. 'That's why I came.'

'We did see a bear,' I told him. 'Very much alive – and all grown up.'

'Maybe your little dead guy's momma,' suggested Eastman.

Ash winced. So did I. There was still a bear out there – quite possibly an angry bear nursing a grudge. And worse. If Ash wasn't the man who'd shot at me on the tower – and you couldn't possibly think so, looking at that poor broken man – then *he* was still out there too. I looked around the desolate valley, the black cliffs too steep for snow. Plenty of places for someone to hide, to watch us. I listened so hard, the silence sang in my ears.

I exchanged a look with Eastman. After a cold, sleepless night, and then this bizarre episode, I just wanted to go home.

'Let's get out of here,' he said.

It was only when we were in the helicopter, safely on the way back, that I wondered what all those cans of food had been doing there.

USCGC Terra Nova

The door opened. A sailor poked his head around the door.

'Ops said you wanted to know when the other guy woke up?'

Franklin stood. His legs had started to go to sleep from

sitting listening so long. On the bed, he could see Kennedy's one good eye watching from behind the mummy mask.

'Eastman?'

'He's ready to talk.'

Twenty-two

USCGC Terra Nova

No one had imagined a scenario like this. The *Terra Nova* had four body bags aboard – the same ones that had been issued when she was first outfitted. The bodies coming out of the helicopter now were wrapped in black trash bags, laid out on the deck like so much garbage. The crew handling them looked like they wanted to puke.

Santiago met Franklin by the flight-deck door.

'Helo just made her second run. Everyone's accounted for – except two.' He showed Franklin the printout. The pages were heavily creased and damp with melted snow; most of the photos had red X's scored through them.

'This one, Fridtjof Torell, and her, Greta Nystrom. Both missing.'

'She was the base mechanic,' said Franklin. Again, it felt strange to confront a photograph of someone he'd already imagined. The woman in the picture looked like a ski instructor, or one of those round-the-world solo yachtswomen: hair in braids, tanned skin, and a natural glow that said she spent a lot of time outdoors. Her tight-lipped expression only made her look like she was pissed off with the photographer.

'When are the Brits going to arrive?'

'Gonna be a while. They launched a plane from Longyearbyen, a Dornier 228, the only thing they could find. But they had to abort the landing. They said the runway at Zodiac had gotten too chewed up.'

'That makes sense.'

Santiago followed the captain down the stairs towards the sickbay. 'There's one other thing, sir. Flying back, the pilot says he got a signal on the emergency channel. A locator beacon.'

Franklin stopped on the stairs. 'A beacon?'

'He couldn't be sure. Reception's shitty, and he said it was faint. I figure it was probably sunspots.'

'You seen any sun around, Ops?'

Santiago acknowledged the point.

'There's no way Anderson walked to where we found him alone. He must have had help.'

'You've got a suspicious mind, Captain.'

'Everything about this situation gets weirder and weirder.

'Maybe the new guy can explain some stuff.'

Bob Eastman lay in the sickbay, on the bed where Anderson had been the night before. His shaved skull looked too big for his shoulders; his beard had grown wild. His hands were wrapped, like a boxer ready for a bout. An oxygen tube snaked into his nostrils, and two more tubes plugged into his arm. He looked helpless – except for his eyes, which never stopped moving. Franklin wondered if he was suffering from some kind of post-traumatic syndrome. Who could blame him?

The eyes locked on to Franklin as he approached.

'Do you have secure communications? I need to talk to Washington.'

Franklin held up his hands in a 'Stop' gesture. 'Before you make any calls, let's get a few things straightened out.'

'I have to—'

'My ship, Dr Eastman. My rules. You want to tell me what this is about?'

Eastman leaned over as far as the tubes and bandages would allow.

'Hagger used to say, everyone who comes to Zodiac has a secret. He called it Fort Zinderneuf – like in that old movie about the French Foreign Legion. You want to guess my secret, Captain?'

Franklin considered it. He hadn't made captain by taking half-assed guesses. As the man who'd won most of the late-night poker games at the Coast Guard Academy , he hated to show his cards. But the nature of command, and of gambling, was that sometimes you had to make a leap.

'You work for the CIA?'

The eyes opened wider. 'Who told you that?'

'Kennedy.'

'Bullshit.' Colour was coming back into Eastman's voice. 'I spent five days locked in a caboose with Kennedy. He doesn't know jack.'

'Am I wrong?'

Eastman sank back. 'I'm an atmospheric scientist. But . . .' He paused. 'You know, you're trained so hard to keep the secret, I don't even know the right way to say it. Let's say I work two jobs. One full-time, one part-time.'

The cook had it right. 'Just so we're clear, we're talking about the CIA?'

'NSA. They've had a bug in their ass about Utgard since the Cold War. When they found out I got a place at Zodiac, they asked me to feed back anything interesting. The Russians have been developing – this is classified, by the way, but what the hell – they've been developing a new radar. SAR – synthetic aperture radar. It can spot a boat the size of a Honda Civic from space.'

'Not a lot of boats around here,' Franklin said. 'Anyhow, I thought they could read golf balls from space twenty years ago.'

'You can see what the hell you like – if you know where to point the camera. What this does is tell you where *everything* is. All over the world, anywhere and everywhere. Now, that creates a shitload of data, and that data's no use stored up on a satellite. You need a base station on earth to download it to. The reason everybody loves Utgard is that it's in a sweet spot. Any orbit, any time, you can download data there.'

'And you thought they were using Zodiac for that?'

'Nuh-uh. Zodiac's clean. But there was another outfit on the island.'

'DAR-X. The oil exploration company.'

'You're up with the news, Captain.'

'I've been speaking with Dr Kennedy.'

'Kennedy's an ass. He didn't have a clue what was going on right in front of him. You know, the only reason he rocked up at Zodiac was because he was about to be sued for medical malpractice. Drinking on the job. You know how drunk you have to be before the Irish kick you out?'

'He seemed sober to me.'

'He cleaned himself up. To be fair to the guy, I never saw him touch a drop at Zodiac. Anyhow, DAR-X are a front. They're just doing the exploration. The actual contract goes to a company registered in the Bahamas, which is owned by a shell outfit in Liechtenstein, which is controlled by an outfit in Cyprus – which gets its cash and its orders from the Russian national oil company.'

'Is that common knowledge?'

'They go out of their way to make sure people don't know. Way out of their way, if you catch my drift. I don't know how long it took our guys to pin them down.'

'I thought the Cold War was over.'

'Do they teach reality at the Coast Guard Academy? Russia these days, it's like one of those stores where they've changed the name tags and the shelf stackers are now called Customer Fulfilment Associates. They're still the same, and you know exactly what they are really. Instead of our nukes against their nukes, we play Amoco v. Rosneft. We don't want truth, justice and the American way; and they don't care about the brotherhood of the proletariat. It's proven reserves and barrels per day.'

'You said this was about satellites and radars.'

'It's all the same play. A few years back, people who said the Arctic would be ice-free by the end of the century were called crazies. Then serious folks thought it might be 2050. Then 2030. Now best guess is the end of this decade, and some people think that's too conservative. It's coming, faster than we think, and when there's no ice left then everything's up for grabs. The land, the oil, and the sea routes. As long as Walmart wants cheap crap stamped "Made in China", they'll need ships to bring it to us, and the shortest way to get cheap crap from Shenzhen to New York is across the Arctic Ocean. And the fuel they save, steaming across the melted Arctic? They'll count that towards their CSR greenwash, and brag how they're cutting down CO_2 emissions.'

'You almost sound like you're sympathetic.'

'Don't be cute, Captain. Take a look at yourself – you're a long way from Kansas here. You want to believe that's because the United States Coast Guard gives a shit about polar bears? I'm guessing that strapped to the bottom of this tub, you've got the most expensive sonar Uncle Sam can afford, colouring in the seabed. So that when this place looks like Galveston with all the supertankers and container ships and drill rigs, our subs can keep an eye on them without crashing into an uncharted undersea mountain. But all that won't be worth a nickel if the Russians get this satellite radar working. They'll own the whole enchilada.'

His mouth had gone so dry he was croaking like a raven. He sucked water from a tube and glared at Franklin.

'The Cold War didn't go away, they just monetised it. And if history teaches anything worth a damn, it's that the only thing countries really go to war for is cash. That's why they sent me to Zodiac.'

There weren't any chairs in the sickbay. Franklin leaned against a bulkhead, and folded his arms across his chest.

'Why don't you tell me about it?'

Twenty-three

Eastman

I said DAR-X are a front and that's true – but they're a real oil company. My job was to get close to them, so I could find out if they were working on the satellite thing. So I started leaking them some confidential data from Zodiac, stuff they could use to undermine the global-warming mafia.

Don't give me that look, Captain. It was for the greater good. What I do, science-wise – the reason the NSA approached me – is pointing antennas at space. And I was getting some screwy readings. You go to the Arctic because it's pristine, no cellphones or TV or garage-door openers clogging the signal. But from the noise I was getting, I might as well have parked my telescope next door to Verizon. So I knew something was going down. If the Russians get that radar, they'll have total mastery of the seas. You think that compares to whether our kids might need more sunscreen in a hundred years?

DAR-X had their base at Echo Bay, about halfway up the west coast. I went there to take a look round, didn't find anything. They had a big drill rig that could have been used for an antenna, but it looked real enough. Rumour was they're not drilling for oil, some kind of natural gas instead, but I don't know.

There's a million places you could hide an antenna on Utgard and nobody'd see it except the bears. But you can't just stick that thing in the middle of a snowfield. You need infrastructure, power, a way of getting the data back to Echo Bay. So when I heard that DAR-X had been hanging out at the old Commie ghost town at Vitangelsk, I decided to check it out.

Kennedy tagged along: he had some theory about Hagger, the guy who fell in a crevasse. Not that I thought that was irrelevant – far from it. I figured Hagger most likely found something out about DAR-X, or the radar, or the Russians, and paid the price. I won't pretend it didn't freak me out. I'm not James Bond. At the same time, it made me feel Hagger must have gotten close to something. And I was going to find it.

Kennedy thought Hagger'd been murdered by a jealous scientist. Like I say, he didn't have a clue. But then, none of us did at that stage.

I left Kennedy in the main square at Vitangelsk, next to the statue of Lenin, and climbed towards the top end of town. If you ever want to see the hypocrisy of the Communist system, take a look at Vitangelsk. It's built up the side of a mountain: the workers lived in wooden barracks at the bottom, the managers in brick houses higher up, and everything that really mattered – the machinery, the stores, the processing plant – was up top, along with the power station. I don't know how much coal they had to burn just so they could mine more of it, but it must have been a ton. You could still see the power cables stretched from roof to roof, down the mountain and right around the town, a total spiderweb.

When the Soviet Union collapsed, the Commies left Vitangelsk so fast they didn't even bother to pack. Everything's kept perfectly in the deep freeze: you can still see papers on the desks and rubber stamps with the hammer and sickle; beer and cookies and bread and pickles, still in mint condition. Hard hats, overalls and pickaxes hanging on pegs at the mine head where the guys finished their last shift. Like Lenin's tomb, if you've ever been to Moscow. It's hard not to look over your shoulder and wonder if they're coming back.

The moment I got there, I knew I had to be close. I got out my spectrum analyser and did an RF sweep, checking all available frequencies. When I got to the C band, the satellite wavelength, it went off the scale.

There's maybe thirty or forty buildings in Vitangelsk – too many to explore each one. But if you're going to mount a satellite dish, the best place is on the roof. I was at the top of the town. I figured if I could get on top of one of the buildings there, I'd have a good view right the way down.

I got on to the roof of the old machine shop. From above, even that Soviet ruin looked almost quaint. Snow-covered roofs descending the mountain, the frosted power cables running like icicles between them. If someone had lit a fire, you could have imagined you were in a Disney movie.

I got out my binoculars and scanned the town. Nothing. No satellite dish, no masts, not even a TV antenna. No sign of Kennedy, either.

I walked across the roof to check the other side. Should have watched where I was going. My toe snagged something just under the snow and threw me forward. I stumbled a couple of steps, threw out my arms and bellyflopped on to the roof a few inches shy of the edge. I lay there a moment, sick with adrenalin and what had almost happened.

When I picked myself up, I looked back to see what I'd tripped on. A black rubber cable lay in the snow. Where my boot had rubbed off the ice, it looked about a hundred years newer than anything else in town.

I tugged. It didn't give more than a couple of inches. I

followed it through the snow. It ran all the way to the edge of the roof, where a steel clamp held it in place. But that wasn't the end of it. It carried on, across the street and down on to the roof of the next building.

I found the binoculars where I'd dropped them and brushed off the snow. Focusing on the cable, I followed it over the next building, then the next. I lost it there, until I realised it had hung a right and was headed cross-town, where it disappeared behind a smokestack.

'Holy shit.'

The wires I'd seen from the street didn't go inside the buildings, like power cables should have. They ran across the roofs, building to building, making a single vast loop around the town. They weren't power cables; they made an antenna, as big as the town, and you'd never see it because it was all around you. With that thing, you could probably hear what they were saying on Mars.

Now I knew where to look, I found other cables connected to it, running to the centre of the circle. They all seemed to come together someplace by the main square.

I ran back there. I hadn't seen it when I was there before. Now I knew what to look for, I got it straight away. More cables, maybe a dozen in total, running in from every side of town and coming together on the old HQ building like the spokes of a wheel.

The door was an old piece of wood that cracked open with one good kick. Inside, it looked like the staff had gone for lunch and forgotten to lock up: chairs fallen over, papers blown in the corners, an old calendar from 1991 hanging crooked on the wall. I think if you'd looked, you'd have found old coffee frozen in the bottom of the mug.

But I figured what I wanted was upstairs. I chased up the first flight – and stopped.

I was in the right place. A heavy-duty steel trapdoor had

been laid across so you couldn't go up. A padlock, shiny with grease, made sure of it.

At that moment, I wanted to be on the other side of that door more than I'd ever wanted anything. I got the rifle out and put the muzzle against the lock. I almost pulled the trigger. But I've seen that Master Lock commercial (though this was a Yale); I didn't want to risk a ricochet. I'd have to come back with the right equipment.

I was still looking at the lock, wondering if bolt cutters would do the job, when I heard the first gunshot. I'll tell you, my first thought wasn't Kennedy: I was certain the Russians had arrived. But I hadn't heard anyone coming, no snow-mobiles or helicopters buzzing around.

I heard another shot. The echo scrambled the sound so much I couldn't tell where it came from; not so close I needed to duck, at least. It sounded like one of our Rugers. I've spent enough time on the range at Zodiac to know the sound.

Was it Kennedy shooting? If so, he was more than likely to blow his own head off. But the procedure at Zodiac is that if you hear your buddy shooting, you assume it's a bear and go help. As Quam liked to say, procedure can save your life. He was wrong about a lot of things, but he got that right. Plus, I'd get a rocket up my ass if anything happened to Doc.

I ran down the stairs and out into the street, just quick enough to hear another shot. Then two more, almost on top of each other, but I couldn't get a fix on them with all the buildings around. I followed Doc's prints heading downhill.

The shooting had stopped. Normally, you'd assume that meant the bear had gone away – but this was pretty fucking far from normal. And I'd counted five shots. Kennedy must have been out of ammo. I tweaked the radio again, but no answer. Between the buildings and the massive antenna hanging over my head, I didn't expect anything.

I searched everywhere. He'd traipsed around like a tourist,

which made it harder; sometimes I lost the track when he'd gone inside a building. Finally, I came out on the edge of town, where the cableway heads off toward Mine 8. He'd definitely come this way: I could see his trail. And someone else's, too, long strides that looked like they'd been chasing after him. Now I was really starting to freak out.

With so many prints pounding up the snow, I almost missed the bear tracks. But there's nothing else like them on Utgard. Strange to say, the sight made me breathe easier. If a bear had got Kennedy, there'd be blood, and I didn't see any. And I'd rather find a bear than Russians.

I had a flare pistol in a side holster, like always when I'm in the field. I took it out and loaded a cartridge. We carry the rifles because you can kill the bear if you have to, but a flare pistol's much better for scaring them off before it gets to that.

The bear tracks headed out of town. I found broken snow where he must have sat down a while, near the base of one of the cableway towers, and more tracks going off across the mountain. Nearby, copper cartridges shone on the ground.

He used up all his ammo. But where did he go then? I still didn't see any blood. Another set of footprints led away up the hill. Reasonably fresh, but they looked too big to be Kennedy's. Probably one of the DAR-X guys who'd been here earlier.

I'd just about given up when I heard a low clang, like someone pounding on a bucket. I thought it must be some old machinery knocking in the wind. I started back towards town, figuring I must have missed something. The clanging kept going. If anything, it sounded louder.

Just before I hit town, I looked back. Christ knows, but he was a lucky s.o.b. I saw his arm sticking out of the coal car and realised what it was. I climbed the ladder and saw him huddled in the bottom.

'What the fuck are you doing in there?'

★   ★   ★

I got him down. It was a hell of a job, and the story he told about how he got there was crazier still. Chased by a bear, then by a guy with a gun. He wanted to go home – frostbite had nearly crippled him – but I talked him out of it. I was too close. I'd found the antenna; then this gunman – he had to be DAR-X – had almost killed Kennedy. If he came back, I wanted answers.

You've heard this part? I won't repeat it. Long story short, we froze our asses off all night jumping at shadows, thought we'd found something, and all we got was a sad old man and a dead bear. I mean, can you believe it? Guy shoots a polar bear and he goes around like the fucking Tell-Tale Heart. And Kennedy's feeling like an idiot, because he more or less accused Ash of murdering Hagger.

I didn't tell them what I'd found. I didn't know who I could trust. But as we lifted off in the helicopter, I knew I had to get back to find out what the hell that antenna was receiving. And where it was going to.

Twenty-four

Eastman

Flying into Zodiac, we could see the wrecked Twin Otter at the end of the runway. Christ knew how long before they got it out: might be a hundred years.

I was busting to get back to Vitangelsk right away. I grabbed some coffee and cereal from the mess, then found Greta in the shop. She kept that place like your granddad's basement: tools hanging on nails on the walls, hardware spilling out of plastic boxes, smell of oil and fried metal in the air. She was working on a busted snowmobile, stripped down to her tank top, hair braided back.

'You look good,' I told her.

She gave me a look like she could care less.

'Do you have any bolt cutters I could borrow?'

She took a heavy-duty pair of long-handled bolt cutters off a peg on the wall and gave them to me. You could break into Fort Knox with those things.

But I wasn't taking a chance. 'You don't have something like a portable gas-cutting torch too, do you?'

Her eyes narrowed. She didn't say anything – but for some reason I felt I had to explain myself.

'One of the struts buckled on my radio telescope. Crushed the cable; I need to get it out.'

'I can help.'

Was that a straight offer? Or was she calling my bluff?

'I'm good.'

'Be quick. There's a storm coming.'

'*All staff,*' said the speaker on the wall.

I'd spent a night in the cold, no sleep: I was twitchy as hell. The voice coming out of the speaker almost made me jump into Greta's arms.

'*All staff, please report to the mess for an urgent briefing,*' Quam said over the intercom.

The Horrorscope on the door said *Your future is stormy.* Inside, everyone was sitting on the couches – like movie night, only without the entertainment. Anderson had gotten out of bed, I noticed, though Trond the pilot wasn't there. Ash sat on the end nearest Quam. I wondered if this was about him.

'I have an announcement to make,' Quam said. Guy couldn't open his mouth without telling you he was a pompous ass. 'Following a consultation with Norwich, it's been decided that all Zodiac personnel will be confined to base until further notice.'

The room erupted. Quam looked surprised, though he was an idiot if he hadn't seen it coming. He took a step back, pressed up against the TV like a prisoner facing the firing squad.

'Did the penguins make that decision?' someone asked sarcastically.

Quam held up his hand for silence, like an elementary-school teacher with a rowdy class. It was a while before everyone quieted down enough for him to speak.

'We can't afford any more accidents. With the Twin Otter out of commission, we're terribly exposed. If anything else happened, there'd be no way to get us out.'

I didn't think that would improve morale any. I kept quiet, and watched the others. They'd started shouting again. Ashcliffe said something like 'health and safety gone mad';

Annabel was listing all the people who funded her research. Show-off.

'I've got instruments collecting data up on the mountain,' said Fridge. 'Am I supposed to forget about that?'

'Use the data link.'

'The data link is fucked.'

'What about Gemini?' Annabel said.

'Gemini's off-limits.'

'My funding body pays a fortune to keep me here so I can do science.'

'Violating this policy will put you in breach of the contracts you signed,' Quam said. He sounded desperate.

'So what?' Fridge demanded. 'You can't send us home. Will you throw us out into the snow like fucking Captain Oates?'

'That would be a breach of contract,' Ash said. Heavy with sarcasm. He must have forgotten he was going home anyway.

I raised my hand. Quam pointed to me, grateful for that gesture of respect.

'Did the assholes in Norwich consider that someone's more likely to end up dead if we're all locked in together like this?'

'*Enough!*' Quam thumped the TV so hard I thought he'd broken it. Then he really would've had a mutiny. 'I didn't make this policy, but we all have to stick with it. For our own protection.'

'Who do we need protecting from?' Anderson asked. If Quam heard that, he ignored it.

'As a positive,' said Quam, breathing hard, 'I'd like to announce that this Saturday will be Thing Night.'

That earned him an ironic cheer. Everybody loves Thing Night.

★ ★ ★

Quam went and shut himself in his office. I guess he was regretting not fitting locks. I sat down in my room and thought about what had happened.

Kennedy's story was crazy, but it wasn't the craziest thing that had happened at Zodiac that week. If he wanted to lie, there were easier ways to do it than almost freezing to death in a mining car. And I'd seen the extra set of footprints around the tower. I wished I'd have followed them.

So who was the guy in the yellow parka? He had to be DAR-X, protecting whatever they had locked in the HQ building where all those wires led. I had to get back there.

Of course, I wasn't allowed off base, but I wouldn't let Quam's BS regulations stop me. And while I was going off the reservation, I might as well kill a few birds.

I got out my laptop and wrote an email to a colleague of mine, physicist at Rutgers called Guy Roache.

Getting some interesting results from my probe at Vitangelsk. Levels ~ 1400.

In case you're wondering, there actually is a physicist at Rutgers called Guy Roache. Except, he spells his name without an 'e'. The email address I used was a good-looking fake set up by my buddies at Fort Meade. The messages went all the way to New Jersey, then bounced right back to Echo Bay to set up a meet with Bill Malick. Vitangelsk was the place, 14:00 was the time. The tilde meant 'today'.

You're probably thinking it's kind of dumb. But we had to be careful. Rumour at Zodiac was that Quam used his administrator privileges to read other people's mail. If he'd caught me giving out data, he'd have had me on the first plane out of there.

Not that that was a problem now, with the Twin Otter trashed.

★   ★   ★

I still wanted to know what Hagger could've found up there. For starters, it might explain some things I needed to know. For another thing, it might have gotten him killed. If I was going to meet Malick in Vitangelsk, I had to be prepared.

I let myself in to Hagger's lab and found someone already there. Anderson was on a stool, squinting into a microscope. A green notebook lay open on the bench beside him. Beside that, like he'd just taken it out of his pocket, lay a key on a teddy-bear key ring.

'Feeling OK?' I asked, like I'd come to see how he was doing. I tried not to stare at the key too obviously.

'Better, thanks.' He smiled. 'It's very strange, missing two days of your life. You go around the whole time with that feeling you've forgotten to turn off the gas.'

'And back at work already.' Edging closer, I could see it was a Yale key. And under the microscope, he had a section of yellow tube that looked like the pipes at Echo Bay.

'I'm trying to tidy up a few things Hagger left behind.'

'Whatcha got?'

'Nothing I can understand.' He picked up the notebook and pulled a loose-leaf sheet from between the pages. A computer printout, covered in a grid of zeros, ones and twos. 'This, for example. I can't make head nor tail of it.'

I'd wondered what Hagger did with that. I thought about telling the truth, and couldn't see any reason why not.

'It's mine,' I said. 'I gave it to Hagger. I was getting interference with my instruments. One day, I was playing around with frequencies trying to figure it out and I picked up this fragment. Nothing else, just a series of numbers. I showed it to a few people at Zodiac to see if it had anything to do with their work. Hagger didn't know, but he was interested. He liked crossword puzzles; said he'd see if he could do something with it.'

Anderson looked it over. 'The twos are what make it odd.'

Smart cookie. 'That's what we thought. Zeros and ones could just be any kind of binary, what you'd expect. The twos make no sense.'

'And this is all you managed to get?'

'Yeah.' I gave him back the paper; it was only a copy. 'Did you ever find out what Hagger wanted up on the Helbreen? I mean, his major work was on sea ice, right?'

'It's possible Hagger had traced some sort of chemical in the sea ice. He thought it might be coming off the glacier in meltwater.'

I dismissed that. It might have been what he was looking for, but it wasn't what got him killed. 'Nothing about DAR-X in the notebook?'

'That was a different project.' He slid off the stool so I could take a look through the microscope. 'Some micro-organism in the water was corroding their pipes. They asked Hagger to analyse it.'

I was more interested in the pipe than the bugs in the water. I hoped I'd find something inside it, fibre optics or antenna cable. So far as I could see, it was just a hollow tube.

'How about that key?' I asked. Casual as I could. 'Last I heard, we didn't have any locks at Zodiac.'

A strange look crossed his face, like he wished I hadn't seen it. I could see him thinking about what to tell me.

'I found it where Hagger died, by the crevasse. It must have fallen out of his pocket.'

That got my attention – if it was true. 'Did Hagger have a filing cabinet, or a desk drawer he kept locked?'

He waved his hand around the lab. 'I've looked everywhere. As you say, there aren't any locks at Zodiac.'

'No secrets among friends,' I said cheerfully.

'Maybe it was his house key and he forgot it was in his pocket.'

'Maybe he had a secret liquor cabinet chilling in the glacier.'

We both laughed.

'I have to go,' I said. 'Need to check my emails. Let me know if you find anything.'

'Right away,' he promised.

I could tell he wanted me to leave, so I didn't linger. I went straight out in the corridor. Of course, I left the door open a tad. The corridor's so dark, you wouldn't really see someone watching you through the crack.

As soon as I was gone, Anderson took the key off the bench and hid it in a drawer. I guess he wished he could have locked it away safe – but there are no locks at Zodiac. Nothing to stop a guy going into a lab at night and taking something out of a drawer.

Back in my room, the reply had come in from Malick.

I'm in meetings all day, but hopefully can get to it tomorrow.
Levels >1400 definitely something worth talking about.

He couldn't make it until tomorrow. I remembered what Greta had said and called up the weather forecast. It didn't look good. A polar low was heading our way from Greenland: I could see the comma cloud coming together on the satellite, the long tail starting to turn. Those things move almost as fast as a hurricane. When it hit, it was going to get ugly.

But I had to get back to Vitangelsk, and see if the key fitted the lock.

Twenty-five

Eastman

I could have just snuck off, and taken Quam's shit later. But if anyone noticed me gone, I didn't want them sending out search parties with a storm coming in. So, next morning, I spun him a line.

'One of the struts buckled on my radio telescope,' I told him. If you're going to lie, lie consistently. 'If I don't get it fixed before the storm comes, the whole thing could go.'

Of course he said no. 'Safety is paramount.'

'I've just been shortlisted for a million-dollar grant from the NO double A. You want me to tell them I can't bring it to Zodiac because my instruments got trashed in a storm?'

Everyone has weaknesses. Quam's were more transparent than most. Mention a grant, you could almost see the dollar signs ring up in his eyes.

'Everyone has experiments running out there.'

'So don't tell them. I won't sign out; I'll check in directly with you on the satphone. No one has to know.'

'But you can't go on your own.'

I pointed out the window, to the upper slopes of the mountain behind us. Clouds dashed over it.

'I'm not going far.'

Quam played with the Newton's cradle executive-toy thing he had on his desk – the classic bureaucrat's move. I tell you, Captain, only the fucking Brits would send a vanilla

191

guy like that to run a place like Utgard. Maybe he was good at cricket.

'Don't let the others see you,' he said.

Just as I was leaving, I pretended I'd thought of something else.

'Don't worry if I'm out for a while. If the weather goes south too soon, I'll stay in the caboose up there.'

I thought he'd complain. Perhaps he wanted to, but didn't have the strength. He slouched in his chair as if something had snapped inside of him.

'Please don't let anything happen to you. It's my job, if anything else happens.'

'It's my life,' I pointed out.

I didn't much care about the storm. If it got too bad, I could hole up in one of the buildings at Vitangelsk until it passed. I made sure I packed fuel for the MSR, and plenty of food. Plus a few pieces of equipment from my lab that had nothing to do with survival.

The hardest part was getting away. There's no quiet way to drive a snowmobile. In the end, I had to disengage the drive belt, and push the thing around the base of the hill like a broken-down car. If anyone heard it from there, they could think what they liked. I opened up the throttle, turned on my iPod and let rip.

Was I scared? Not really. At that speed, you feel invincible. The clouds built their castles in the sky; the wind cried against my helmet. The flat light smoothed the terrain so you couldn't see the bumps, but I didn't care. I was riding the storm.

I got to Vitangelsk early. I parked my snowmobile in the square and made a circuit of the town, to be sure there wasn't anyone waiting. If you think a frozen ghost town is freaky, wait until you've been in a frozen ghost town with a storm building. Down the valley, I could see dark clouds gathering out over the ocean. The moment I took my helmet off, the ice in the air stung me so bad I had to put it back on. But with my ears covered, I couldn't hear a thing. I took it off again. I should have brought goggles, but all I had was my sunglasses. When I put them on, the dark day got darker. Every shadow was rendered deep black, every building looked like the House on Haunted Hill. Even the fucking snow looked dark.

I didn't see anyone else in town. That didn't mean they didn't see me. I kept looking over my shoulder as I went back to the HQ building. The moment I was through the door, I took off my sunglasses and got to work.

The padlock was still there. A Yale lock, just like I remembered. I had Greta's bolt cutters with me, but first I wanted to try something. I took out the key I'd borrowed from Anderson's lab and pushed it in the lock.

It fitted. I twisted and it turned, smooth as butter, no hint of rust or age. The hasp popped open and the lock dropped into my hand. I stared at it like it had fallen from outer space.

'And what in hell were you doing with that key, Dr Hagger?' I asked aloud.

I put my shoulder against the steel trapdoor and heaved. It resisted a second, but only because of the weight. Nothing wrong with the hinges. The door swung up and clicked into the upright position.

'Anyone home?' I called. All I heard back was the wind howling around the outside of the building.

I took off my hat and hooked it on the rifle muzzle, then pushed it up through the hatch. A dumb trick – I probably got it from an old war movie. Anyhow, nothing happened. Either there wasn't anyone there, or they'd seen the same movie.

Leading with the rifle, I put my head through the hatch.

Even in the cold, my forehead prickled with sweat; my heart was going about a million miles an hour. I'd never felt so naked and so alive.

Above the first floor, the whole building had been gutted out. No internal walls, no floors, not even a roof. Just a brick shaft, three storeys high and open to the sky. Over my head, out of reach, eight cables came through the walls from different directions and met together in a long steel needle suspended in mid-air, pointing straight at outer space. A couple inches of snow covered the floor, but there was none on the wires. Someone made sure they got dusted off pretty regularly, it looked like.

I closed the trapdoor behind me, so that no one could sneak up. I checked the lock was in my pocket: I didn't want to get locked in. Then I examined the antenna.

Keeping equipment in any kind of shape up there is tough. I should know. But this was pristine: all the cables tight, the metal buffed. A single wire hung down from the needle to a cleat in the floor, then ran across into a black box bolted on to the wall.

I went over and checked it out. Nothing on the outside to say what it did, not even a light to show if the power was on. A black box in every sense of the word. The only opening was the socket where the cable plugged in.

I squinted at the plug. It looked like a regular RF. The same kind I use to connect my instruments.

I took off my pack and got out my laptop. It wouldn't boot, so I popped the battery and stuck it down my shorts for five minutes. Meanwhile, I found the interface cable I use when I'm in the field and connected it to the laptop. I put in the warmed-up battery and started the computer.

'Here goes nothing.'

I yanked out the cable from the box. Somewhere on Utgard, if someone was watching satellite TV, I'd just ruined his show.

I didn't waste time. Even weatherised, the battery doesn't last much more than fifteen minutes in that cold. I connected the RF plug to the laptop, and opened a software transceiver program I use. I dialled it in to the C-band frequencies and hit record. I didn't bother with transforms or other graphical shit: I just wanted to grab it as fast as I could.

The battery was dying in front of my eyes. When it hit ten per cent, I saved the file and shut down. Then I plugged the cable back in the black box. Didn't want to piss off whoever the signal belonged to. With luck, they'd think it was the storm screwing with the transmission.

Or maybe they were closer than I'd thought. Before I'd even zipped my bag, I heard a creak on the stairs. I forgot the pack and grabbed my rifle. More creaks – definitely someone coming up. He stopped, just the other side of the trapdoor. I aimed the rifle.

The steel door squeaked. A gloved hand pushed it up until it latched open.

'If you take another step, I'm going to blow your head off,' I warned.

I heard him stop. Then, a rustling sound as he unzipped his coat. A hundred crazy scenarios played out in my head. What if he had a grenade? Or a bomb? Or—

A head popped up like a rabbit through the hatch. I was so wired, I almost pulled the trigger right there.

'Jesus, Bob,' said Malick. 'I thought you wanted to see me.'

Twenty-six

Eastman

He lifted himself through the hatch. He noticed I hadn't moved the gun.

'What is this?'

'You tell me.' I nodded at the antenna hanging in the space above us like a giant spider. 'In fact, there's a few conversations we need to have.'

He looked up, and did a pretty good job of making himself seem surprised. 'What the hell is that thing?'

'You tell me,' I said again.

'I swear on my mother's grave, I never saw it in my life.'

'Yeah?'

He chuckled. 'Truth to tell, Mom's alive and well, doing just fine in Fort Lauderdale. But you get the point.'

I didn't smile. 'I'm not sure that I do.'

'I only came here because you asked me, Bob. If you want to show me whatever fancy toy you've got here, you go right ahead. But don't make out like I should know what the hell you're talking about.'

'It's not my toy. It's a satellite antenna – and I want you to tell me what you're doing with it.'

He shrugged. 'I'm in the oil business.'

'Really? I heard you have something called methane clathrates coming out of that well.'

He didn't argue the point. 'Either way, DAR-X isn't exactly

196

AT&T. We've got Iridium and UHF at Echo Bay, and that does us fine. We're not searching for E.T. in our spare time.'

'You expect me to believe that.'

He managed to make himself look genuinely hurt. 'As a matter of fact, Bob, yeah, I do.'

I pitched him the change-up. 'Tell me about Martin Hagger.'

He looked confused. 'Your guy who fell down the crevasse?'

'Who was doing a special project for you. Why did you need to get rid of him?'

Malick just stared at me. Big Texas oilmen don't go down easy, but he looked floored.

I switched up again. 'Were you here two days ago, Bill? Any of your people chasing us? Our doc almost got himself killed, running away from some guy in a yellow parka shooting at him.'

The fear I'd felt was flowing out now. Strength and weakness, it's the same thing, they just run in opposite directions depending on which way the switch is flipped. I had the gun; I could make him do what I wanted. I jabbed it at him in case he'd forgotten.

'I can account for every one of my guys. None of them's been up here since the weekend. Show's over; we're breaking down the camp. Heading home tomorrow.'

That surprised me, if it was true. Maybe now they had this thing up, they could leave it to run itself.

'Can we rewind?' said Malick. 'I came here because you said you had some data for me.'

'I lied.' I'll admit it, I enjoyed saying that. Something about a gun that strips away the bullshit. 'I just had to get you here.'

'So you could show me this space needle?'

'So you could tell me what it's about.'

He looked at me like I was crazy.

'What the hell are you on? Yeah, we're drilling for

methane at Echo Bay. Yeah, we were having problems with the pipes and Hagger looked into it. All above board. Why he died, and what that has to do with this great big radio you've found – maybe you can tell me.'

'You know who you're working for?'

'I work for DAR-X.'

'I mean, who's paying you.'

'Some company out of the Bahamas. Why are you looking at me like that? They've got the concession, they've got the permits, they've got the paperwork. We're just the contractors. The only reason we keep quiet about the methane is to stop Greenpeace getting on our asses. You saw what they did to Shell in Alaska.'

'The guys you're working for are Russians, Bill. I guess you know that. And they don't give a damn about gas or oil, do they?'

'They do when I give them my progress reports.'

I nodded my head up at the giant web above us. 'This is what it's all about.'

He shrugged. 'If I even knew what it was, I could tell you why you're wrong.'

We stared each other down, like two gunslingers in a stand-off. Except, I was the only guy with a gun. And you know what?

I had no clue what the hell to do with it.

Like I said before, I'm a scientist, not Jack Bauer. I couldn't waterboard the guy, or hook electrodes on his balls. I'd counted on the gun to scare him into confessing. Now what?

I almost shot him out of sheer frustration. That's what power can do: overload you.

'This place has a good, strong door,' Malick said. 'There a lock?'

I nodded.

'Not when I arrived. How'd you get through?'

'I found the key.'

'Uh-huh.'

I didn't like the way he was looking at me. The gun in my hand felt solid and dangerous. 'Don't try to imply—'

'Jesus, Bob, listen to yourself. You asked for this meet. You chose the place. If I was what you say I am, you think I'd have come in here, no gun, no backup? You're the guy with the gun. You're the guy with the key. Tell me, if the cops showed up now, who'd look like the bad guy?'

'Hagger had the key.' I wished I hadn't have said it. 'But—'

He knew where I was going and cut me off. 'I didn't give it to him, if that's what you think.' Leaning forward, on the attack. 'Hagger worked for you guys.'

'You too,' I reminded him.

'One small job. For you, he was full-time.'

When you're looking down the barrel of a gun, it's easy to ignore what the other guy's saying. But I had just enough sense in me to hear it. What if DAR-X was a decoy? What if the Russians sent them up here, not to run the radar program, but to double bluff us. We'd be so busy looking at them, we'd never guess the real bad guys were right under our noses. Inside Zodiac.

I put the gun down. Losing it made me physically nauseous, like when you're so hungry you want to puke. My hand hovered over it, in case Malick made a move

He gave me a fake smile that was supposed to reassure me. 'Now. You want to tell me what this is about?'

For a minute, I just stared at him. But either he was lying, in which case he knew already; or he was being truthful, and he could maybe help me. I told him in three sentences: the Russians, the satellite radar, the base station.

'Well I'll be goddamned,' Malick said, like a guy who's just found his wife in bed with his pastor. He looked up at the needle pointing into space over our heads, the taut wires holding it in mid-air. 'That's why we had radio trouble.'

He pulled off his heavy mittens and wiped his nose. He noticed the wire that ran down into the black box on the wall.

'Where does that go?' he asked.

I gave it a glance. Not for more than a second – but that was all he needed. You don't make it in the oil industry, not in places like Athabasca and Prudhoe Bay, if you can't handle yourself. He shot out his arm. Before I even knew it, he had his hand on the rifle barrel and was twisting it away.

My grip was too slack. I snatched, but he had it before I could grab hold. He took a step back, reversed the weapon and pointed it at me just too fast for me to wrestle it back off of him. His finger danced on the trigger, warning me.

Now I understood why he took off his mittens.

'I really hate having a gun pointed at me.' He squinted down the barrel, right at my chest. 'Right now, I'm sure you appreciate that.'

Oh fuck! Panic raced through me. I realised how cold I'd gotten. I'd been standing still in that room a long time. I was shaking.

'You're a good liar,' I told him. 'You played me just right.'

He shook his head. 'I don't know shit about this radar thing. But you . . .' A jab of the rifle. 'You seem real familiar with it.'

My mind raced. It sounds dumb, but I had to know how much I could believe him. Was he one of the bad guys? Or just pissed off because I pointed a gun at him?

'I only know what I told you.' I couldn't take my eyes off that gun. 'Please. You have to believe me.'

I hated myself for begging. I didn't think it made me sound any more truthful, either.

'I'm keeping an open mind. And a slug in the chamber.'

He nodded toward the loose cable that hung down from the needle, though the gun never left me. 'Where does that go?'

'I don't know.'

'Let's go see.'

We went down through the hatch and outside, round the side of the building. Malick followed me all the way with the rifle. Now we knew what we were looking for, we saw it right away. A black cable coming out the brick and down the wall, like a TV antenna. Hiding in plain sight. It vanished under the snow.

'You gonna tell me you don't have a clue where that goes?' Malick said.

I looked him in the eye. White pearls of frost beaded his eyebrows.

'I know why you don't trust me. I get it. But if neither of us has anything to do with this, we're on the same side. We can figure it out together.'

'That'd be fine.' He gestured with the gun. 'So long as you go first and keep your hands where I can see them.'

Every snowmobile carries a shovel with the emergency pack in case we have to dig a snow shelter. I fetched it, and dug away the surface where the cable went under the snow. A few inches down, it had already hardened to ice, but I could see the cable running below it like a vein. I scraped away more snow, peeling back the line. It pointed up the hill, towards the coal-processing buildings on the top level.

'I checked there yesterday.'

'Maybe you missed something.'

We tracked the cable under the ice, pausing every ten feet or so to check we had it right. It went pretty straight, not hard to follow. Up the hill, and into a big corrugated-iron barn on the north-east edge of town.

'This is where the coal came in,' I said, to break the silence. Any silence is awkward when there's a gun pointed at you

– and this was a freaky place. The front of the building faced away, out to the cableway towers that went across the mountainside to the mine. Around the barn, elevated tunnels and rusted gantries led off to satellite buildings; cranes drooped from the sky and icicles hung off of the rails. The whole thing made a hell of a tangle, plenty of steel waiting to collapse on your head. Plenty of places for someone to watch.

A beating noise broke the cold silence. I spun around, trying to see where it came from. Snow fell from one of the gantries. A white bird flew into the sky, almost invisible against the grey. Probably a ptarmigan. Behind me, Malick had the gun raised like a hunter. If he'd been faster, he could have had it for dinner.

He saw me watching him and swung the gun back down to cover me. 'Don't get any cute ideas.'

I put up my hands. 'I'm as scared as you are.'

He didn't argue the point.

We picked our way over the crap on the ground to the big barn. There was no entrance at ground level, just a creaky flight of stairs going up the side of the building to a door. They hadn't put a lock on this one. Or a handle.

'Open it,' Malick told me.

He was behind me, a couple of steps down. If I'd been Jackie Chan, I could maybe have knocked the rifle out of his hands and kicked him down the stairs. But that shit's only for the movies. And tell the truth, I was more interested in finding where that cable went to. So long as Malick wanted that, we were on the same team.

It's a weird thing to say about a guy with a gun at your back, but I was starting to trust him. I believed he didn't know about the radar. Sure, he could have been pretending, but why bother? Now all I had to do was stay alive long enough to convince him he could trust me too.

I put my shoulder against the door and pushed. The only

thing holding it shut was ice; it creaked like Scotch tape being peeled off. I opened it an inch, paused, then kicked it in and jumped inside.

The metal stairs outside clanged as Malick ran after me. But I wasn't trying to get away from him. I just didn't want a bullet in my face the moment I stepped through the door. Not that my Delta Force impression would've fooled anyone.

There wasn't a sound. And – so far as I could see through the gloom – no one there.

I was in a long corrugated-iron shed, thick plank floor, no windows, but open at one end where the cableway brought the coal buckets in from the mine. It gave enough light to see by. A few of the buckets still hung off of the cables. In the centre of the room, I saw a rusted mess of gears and axles, and a huge flat wheel at head height that used to drive the cableway.

I didn't see anything that looked like what we wanted. A computer, I guess I was looking for. I listened out – a machine like that needs power – but I didn't hear anything electric. Now we were in, I couldn't even see where the cable we'd followed from the antenna came through.

I went further in, carefully, stepping on the cross-beams where I could see them through the cracks in the planks. A couple inches of snow had blown in through the front, though it didn't reach this far back. Neither did much light. I almost caught myself on a pointed iron hook someone had left hanging from the roof on a chain.

I was just past the big wheel when Malick spoke behind me, sharp and cold.

'Don't take another step.'

What a fucking idiot I was. I'd believed him. I'd let him bring me into a dark corner, no fuss, where no one would find me for five hundred years. I hated myself. I threw up my hands. Like that was going to save me.

'There's a hole right in front of you,' said Malick. 'You nearly fell in.'

I nearly fell in anyways. That spike of terror flipped, the bottom dropped out of me and I almost collapsed. He'd only been trying to warn me. I hated myself all over again.

I could see it now, four sides sloping down to darkness. A giant hopper head – where they tipped out the coal, I guess. God knows where I'd have landed if I'd have fallen in it. A black hole.

Except it wasn't. You probably know, in physics nothing escapes from a black hole. But something got out of this one. A black cable that came up the side and ran over the edge, dodging between the warped floorboards as it headed towards the centre of the room.

'I got it,' I said, forgetting that thirty seconds ago I thought he was going to kill me. I followed it back, sweeping aside drifted snow, until I reached the motor. The cable disappeared somewhere inside.

Malick came over. We both stared, trying to find the line in the rusted machinery. 'It sure as hell isn't connected to that.'

We'd forgotten the rifle. Malick didn't point it at me, and I didn't think about getting it off of him. All we wanted was an answer.

'It's gotta go somewhere,' Malick said, frustrated. He knelt down and peered through the tangled metal. 'I should get my flashlight. It's back at the snowmobile.'

I didn't answer. My eyes ran over it, every nook and cranny. The cable had to come out somewhere. Unless we'd missed something. My eyes drifted upwards.

And then I got it.

'I know where it goes,' I said.

Malick gave me a quick look. 'You see it?'

'No.' Without explaining, I ran to the end of the room and

looked out the opening. The clouds raced in and the wind pushed me back; even so, the snow dazzled me after the darkness. I dropped my sunglasses on to my nose.

I didn't really need them. I knew what was there without having to look.

A row of wooden towers, marching across the side of the mountain towards the mine.

And strung between them, a cable.

Twenty-seven

Eastman

Of all the places you think you'll hear a cellphone, an abandoned coal plant on a frozen island at the end of the world is probably the last. For a moment, I thought the ringing must be the bell for the start of a shift, that a dead-eyed crew of Soviet miners would file through the door, pickaxes on their shoulders and lamps glowing over their faces.

Malick unzipped his coat and took out his Iridium phone. 'Yeah?' He listened. 'I'll get back right away.'

He pulled the phone away to hang up, then remembered something.

'Wednesday afternoon,' he said into the phone, 'when we were packing up. Everyone was there, right? No one off base?'

I didn't hear the answer.

'No one unaccounted for?'

He listened, nodded a couple of times, grunted and hung up.

'That was my crew chief. I checked, and he had eyes on every one of our guys Wednesday afternoon. Whoever chased your doc, it wasn't us.'

He zipped the phone back into his pocket. 'Now I gotta head out.'

A quarter-hour earlier, he had a gun at my back. Now, I didn't want him to leave.

'What about the mine?'

'Gotta get back before the storm hits. As soon as it's over, chopper's coming to fly us home.'

'We have to find out—'

'Not my problem. If there's some Russians in there, or some Nazis who didn't hear the war ended, or a bunch of extraterrestrials trying to phone home, that's your deal. Although,' he added, looking at the sky, 'don't take too long.'

We walked down the steps and back towards the snow-mobiles in the main square. The buildings around us looked deader than ever.

'You ever hear of an outfit called Luxor Life Sciences?' Malick said suddenly.

Meant nothing to me.

'They came here a couple years back, just when we set up Echo Bay. A guy and a girl. He was called Richie, don't remember her name, but she had a great pair of tits. Scientists, both of them, looking for a place to build a gene bank.'

I didn't hear him right. 'A what?'

'Somewhere to keep DNA. So that when the whole world looks like this' – he waved at the skeleton buildings around us – 'and there's only eight survivors, and humanity's family tree looks like a twig, we can spice up the mix some. That, or make us some new cows and horses, like Jurassic Park.'

'Like that's going to happen.'

'Right. And if it does, we'll be too busy chewing sticks and wiping our asses with our hands to think about sailing to Utgard for takeout DNA. But they had some money for it, so they came to check us out. All you need for a gene bank, turns out, is someplace dry and cold and no neighbours to look in when you're not home.'

'Say, a mine on an Arctic island?'

'They came up and down this valley a bunch of times. Must have been at Mine Eight, too.'

'Luxor Life Sciences,' I repeated, making a mental note of it. 'They ever do anything with it?'

'Poured some concrete, brought in some equipment. Then they never came back. Guess they found somewhere else to keep their goop.'

'Anyone at Zodiac help them?'

'Don't know. DNA, all that biology stuff. That would've been Hagger, right?'

'Right.'

We'd reached the snowmobiles. Malick strapped on his helmet and started the engine.

'You've still got my gun,' I said.

He slipped it off his shoulder and looked at it, as if he'd forgotten. He thought for a moment, then handed it back to me.

'Guess you just might need it.'

I waited after he'd gone, trying to process everything that had happened in the last hour. I knew I didn't have long. From up on the hillside, you could see all the way down the valley, right to the sea ice. Black clouds bigged up the horizon, and the wind was getting nasty. I wondered if I should go back now.

I couldn't. If I turned around, I could see the cable stretched across the mountainside, past that cave where we'd found all those cans of food, right the way to where the valley ended.

No wonder the guy in the yellow parka had got antsy when Kennedy started sniffing around the cable towers.

I started up the snowmobile. The slope was too steep to follow the cableway: I had to drive right down into the valley, then back up the other side. The mountain peak hid the mine, but I aimed for where the towers pointed. Up and up, the engine fighting the slope, until I came around a corner into a little valley. The towers were so close now I could touch them as I drove by; the noise echoed back off the valley walls like gunfire. And at the top of the valley, perched on the mountain face like some Blofeld secret hideout, was the mine.

I guess no one became a Soviet miner for the life expectancy. I guess they didn't have much choice. Uncle Joe said, 'Get in the hole,' and they said, 'How low do we go?' Maybe it made a nice change from Siberia, I don't know. But even with all that, the mine didn't look like the sort of place you'd want to come to risk your life. The whole thing was built of wood, bleached planks peeling away like even the buildings wanted out. The sheds were built one on top of the other, with chutes and tunnels connecting them Rube Goldberg-style, running down from the mine to the cableway. No murals on the walls here to pep up the workers, just big metal letters on the front building: *MINE 8*. I guess that was all they needed to know.

I made a quick search of the buildings, working my way up to the top. The place was emptier than Vitangelsk. I didn't waste time looking for the cable: I knew where it was going.

Beyond the buildings, where the mountain got so steep you couldn't see the top, was the mine head. You couldn't miss it: a massive concrete retaining wall, six feet thick and twenty feet high, propping up the mountainside. A run-down wooden shack leaned against the base, like the frill of a skirt.

I climbed the wooden steps. There was no lock on the shack door, which surprised me. I was about to let myself in when something on the snow caught my eye. Utgard's so pristine, any trash stands out a mile. I picked it up: a clear plastic bottle, smaller than a soda. The label said *Rhodamine B*.

I put it in my pocket for later and went inside. Straight away, it reminded me of the boot room at Zodiac: hooks on the walls, shelves for boots and gloves. I could almost imagine those Commie miners coming off shift, downing tools and getting dressed to go out into the cold, joking about vodka and women.

The back of the shack was the concrete wall, with a slab of something covering the mouth of the mine. In the bad light, I thought it must be plywood – until I touched it. Even through my mitt, I could feel the cold, even colder than the air. I looked closer.

It was a steel door, surrounded by a steel frame riveted into the concrete. No lock, no keyhole, not even a handle. This one was strictly exit-only. Greta's bolt cutters wouldn't get me through there. Even oxyacetylene gear might not do it. Whoever put those doors on, they didn't want visitors.

I stared a while, until the wind rattling the shack walls reminded me I better go. Quam would have a conniption if I didn't get back.

The day had gotten so dark it turned the ground grey, flat and featureless. Getting home, avoiding the bumps and lumps (and maybe worse) would be a bitch. But if I looked, I could see some not so old footprints breaking up the snow where they'd come out of the shack. I followed them until they stopped at a big dent in the snow near where I'd parked. About right for a snowmobile. And, if you looked, there was the track the snowmobile had made down the mountain, not far from where I'd come up.

I saddled up my snowmobile and followed the line to see where it went – straight back to Zodiac.

Twenty-eight

Eastman

I made it about five minutes in front of the storm. Sky so black, I needed my headlight; wind blowing the ground snow into blizzards that reached halfway back to the clouds. It almost ripped me off the stairs before I could get through the door.

Annabel saw me the minute I got in. So much for sneaking back.

'Aren't you supposed to be locked in here with the rest of us?'

'Nice to see you too.'

I pulled the empty bottle out of my pocket and tossed it to her. 'You recognise this?'

'Have you been stealing my dye bottles? There's no alcohol in them, you know.'

'I found it up at Mine Eight, near Vitangelsk.'

She shrugged. 'Not guilty.'

Interesting. 'Sure?'

'There's no glacier up there.' She looked at my snowmobile suit, covered in a fine frosting of blown snow. 'You've come a long way. I hope Quam doesn't find out.'

I took off the suit and clipped my rifle in the gun rack. Part of me wondered if I shouldn't hold on to it.

'I've been on a snipe hunt,' I told her. 'Rare Arctic bird, very hard to catch. It's endangered, actually.'

'Aren't we all?' she said.

★   ★   ★

With everyone locked up, you couldn't move an inch without running into someone. Halfway down the hall, I met Greta coming out of the radio room.

'How's your leg?' she asked.

I didn't know what she was talking about. I slapped my thigh; I must have looked like some kind of idiot. 'Leg's fine.'

'Your telescope. The strut.'

'Right.' The lie was so old I'd forgotten it. 'All fixed. Thanks.'

At the best of times, Greta has a way of looking at you like you don't exist. Just then, I was certain she saw straight through me.

'Can I have my bolt cutters back?'

'I'll drop them by the shop when the storm's over.'

'Quam wants you.'

I bet he did. Quam's the kid who jerks off, then lies awake all night praying his dick won't fall off. Ever since I left, he'd have been wishing he hadn't let me go, worrying how it would look if I got buried by an avalanche or eaten by a bear.

'I'll say "hi" when I have the chance.'

I went into my lab before anyone else could grab me. I had a lot to do – but most of all I needed to think. I sat at my desk, listening to the wind howl through the masts above my room. It snapped off pieces of ice and scattered them on the roof, right over my head. It made a sound like a kid tipping out a box of Legos.

There's an innocent explanation for everything, if you shut your eyes tight enough. But I wasn't after innocent explanations.

I started with what happened to Kennedy and the big guy in the yellow coat who chased him up the cableway tower. I believed Malick when he said it couldn't have been one of his people. He was as surprised as me: the antenna, the mine, the cableway. If he was one of the bad guys, he could have shot me when he had the chance. Or let me break my leg falling down a coal hopper in the cableway station.

It had to be someone at Zodiac.

It wasn't me or Kennedy. After the scene in the cave, Ash crying over a dead bear, I doubted it was him. That left Quam, Fridge, Annabel, Greta and Jensen.

I wrote them all down on a sheet of paper, thought a minute, then put Anderson on the list. He said he'd been in bed all day, but had anyone seen him? Unlikely he'd have made it out, with his head so banged up, but unlikely isn't impossible.

After another minute, I drew a line connecting Anderson and Greta. I remembered the way they'd both raced off the day he arrived. They'd found Hagger's body, no doubt about that. But was he dead when they got there?

I added Hagger's name, off to one side, and put a line between him and Anderson. Then another one between Hagger and Greta. Everyone knew he'd been screwing her.

I'd made a triangle. I sat back and wondered what it meant. Loose ice jittered across the roof. I began to wish I hadn't asked Greta for the bolt cutters. Had she guessed why I wanted them? Did Anderson know who'd taken his key?

I got out my laptop and opened up the sample I'd grabbed from the antenna. I ran it through some software, cleaning it up and zooming in. Even in that short clip, there was a hell of a lot of data going through the pipe. It took some work, but I had the tools, and the closer I looked the more

I recognised repeat patterns in the signal. That gave me an idea what I was looking for.

1010211201020012010201110212.

I was back where I began. The same pattern I'd snatched out of the air before. Now I knew where it went to, at least. I ought to compare it with the original intercept. Except, I'd left that with Tom Anderson.

I stared at the triangle on my paper again. Hagger – Greta – Anderson. Why did Anderson come here? Why did it all go to shit the moment he arrived?

I wrote down another name, *Luxor Life Sciences*, and drew a dotted line connecting it to Hagger. Biology – biologist. After a minute's thinking, I added a question mark next to the line.

Companies leave records. I opened my browser and searched for Luxor Life Sciences. The storm made the connection run slow, like the dark ages of dial-up. I clocked it at nearly two minutes before the search results came up.

None of them looked like the magic bullet. No corporate website or Wikipedia entry. I clicked on one of the links at random, then stood. I could get a cup of coffee while it loaded.

Something hit the roof so hard, the whole room shook. I ducked. I heard more thuds, ringing on the steel roof like footsteps. Some monster piece of ice must have broken off of something.

The screen flashed. ERROR – THE CONNECTION WAS LOST.

I hit 'reload'. After a long wait, the machine flashed up the same message again. I tried my email. Couldn't connect. That bump must have knocked out the communications antenna.

Fuck.

'Bad day?'

Kennedy came in and sat down on my spare chair. He was holding a piece of paper.

'Where have you been all day?' he said. He sounded pissy. Jesus, it was like being thirteen again.

'Did something come up?'

'I should say so. Anderson worked out Hagger's password. He checked his email.'

That might be something I could use. 'And . . . ?'

He handed me a printout. 'We found this.'

The header said it was to Hagger, from some guy at Cambridge University. Not that you can always trust an email address. The subject said, bold letters, *URGENT –* NATURE – *RETRACTION*.

'Read it,' said Kennedy.

Dear Martin,
In view of our friendship, I'm writing to you in confidence.
Whatever you've done, I want to offer you the chance to withdraw
the paper voluntarily. If not, I will write to Nature *and insist*
they retract it.

There was a whole lot more, which I scanned. All I saw was science stuff: chemicals, concentrations, shit I haven't thought about since AP Chem. The point seemed to be that Hagger had faked the data on a big research paper.

'I don't get it,' I told Kennedy. If Hagger was a fraud, that wasn't irrelevant. But it wasn't a smoking gun, either.

'The time-stamp.' He pointed to the top of the page. 'This came in at eleven o'clock on Saturday morning.' He dragged me down the corridor to the front door and flipped open the field log. 'You see?'

I read what he wanted to show me. 'Hagger left the base at nine a.m. So, he never saw the email. So what?'

215

Kennedy hustled me into the pool room. 'I spoke to Quam two days ago. He knew about all this, Hagger's problems, the retraction.'

'Wasn't it common knowledge?'

'That Hagger had been having problems with his data, yes. But a wholesale retraction from the world's most prestigious journal? That's a whole different kettle of fish. And look at the message. He says he's writing in confidence.'

'You know what academics mean when they say "in confidence". It means they didn't post it on their blog. Anyhow, Quam has the administrator password for the whole Zodiac network. He can read anyone's emails.'

'That's it!' Kennedy thumped the side of the pool table, like I'd just answered the million-dollar question.

'You want to explain?'

'When I saw Quam on Wednesday, he told me about the retraction. But he also said he'd brought it up with Hagger. "I told him to his face I was sending him home." Those were his exact words. "*I told him to his face.*"'

He was looking at me like he expected the light bulb, like he'd given me everything I needed.

'Tell me in words of one syllable.'

'The email came in at eleven a.m. Quam read it, using his master password, and was so shocked he confronted Hagger about it.'

I got it. 'Except Hagger had already gone up to the glacier.'

'And never came back.'

I stared at him over the pool table, spinning a ball in place. A heavy gust of wind hit the outside wall. The Platform shivered.

But it wasn't so cut and dried. 'Quam was around that afternoon. There's no way he could have gotten up to the Helbreen and back again in time. Not without the helicopter. And Jensen was out all day.'

Our eyes met. Jensen had already lied once about what he did that day, we both knew it. What if he hadn't come completely clean?

'We need to talk to Jensen.'

Twenty-nine

Eastman

First, we checked the logbook again. It had been a busy morning, last Saturday, but not so busy you'd lose track. A few lines down from when Hagger left, there was Quam, signing to go check a seal colony at Nansen Bay. *Out: 11:30. In: 14:00.*

'Enough time to get to the Helbreen, if he had the helicopter.'

I found Jensen in the mess, helping the others get ready for Thing Night. With so much time on their hands, they'd really gone to town. Someone had taken a bucket of dry ice from one of the labs to make fog, which they were testing out. They'd even made a cardboard cut-out of the Thing himself and painted it nice and lifelike, seven feet tall and green skin. It looked a lot like a recycled Frankenstein's monster.

'You think Quam will make us watch the John Carpenter version?' I heard Fridge say. Several people laughed like they'd been thinking the same thing.

I guess you've seen *The Thing*, Captain? The John Carpenter one from the early eighties, probably. It's about a badass alien that crash-lands in Antarctica. It eats the staff at a science station one by one, then takes their shape, so you can never tell who to trust. But it's a remake. The original was an old Howard Hawks black and white movie, and that one's set in the Arctic.

There's also a crappy remake from a few years back, but

no one cares about that. To be honest, I prefer the John Carpenter one. It's in colour, the effects are better, you get Kurt Russell, and snow looks like snow whatever caption they put on the screen. They filmed it in Alaska, for Chrissakes. But saying that at Zodiac is like coming to Fenway Park in a Yankee cap. They take it seriously. Thing Night's the biggest party of the year, and it's got to be the Arctic Thing.

I circled the room slowly so I wouldn't look like I was targeting Jensen. By the fireplace, I found Greta up a ladder hanging a tinfoil spaceship from the ceiling.

'The Internet's down,' I told her.

She nodded. 'You can go out and fix it.'

I took a look at the weather readout on the monitor in the corner. The wind speed clocked in at a hundred kilometres an hour. Not a good time to go crawling around rooftops.

'I'm good. I have my emergency porno stash.'

I moved on. Jensen was in the corner, surrounded by the female students. He was an attractive guy: surfer looks, sexy accent and a cool occupation. The closest thing to a rock star we had at Zodiac.

'Kennedy wants a word,' I said cheerfully. 'Something to do with Trond.'

He looked sad to be dragged off, but he didn't argue. I followed him out, slow enough so I didn't *look* like I was following him, and came into the medical room just in time to hear Jensen saying, 'Bob said something about Trond?'

'Trond's fine.' I stepped in and closed the door. 'Tell us about Quam.'

Jensen moved for the door. I leaned against it and crossed my arms over my chest.

'That day Hagger died. You were flying Ash around looking for polar bears.'

Jensen looked from me to Kennedy, like a man who's heard footsteps in a dark alley. 'That'd be right.'

'And you left Ash at Vitangelsk for a couple of hours.'

'Yeah, I told you. What—'

'Where'd you go?'

'Checking fuel caches.'

It was what he'd said last time. I didn't really think about it then; I should have seen the lie right away.

'How much does one of those fuel drums weigh? Three hundred and some pounds? Lot of weight for one man to cart around.'

He didn't say anything. Like all pilots, he was cocky as hell, but not then.

'You came back here and picked up Quam.' I didn't make it a question. 'You flew him to the Helbreen to speak with Hagger. The only thing I want to know is, did you help him push Hagger in the crevasse, or did he do it himself?'

'That's absurd.'

'Then why don't you tell us something that makes sense?'

No answer. He looked at me, and he looked at Kennedy. He ran his fingers back through his hair. I just kept staring at him.

'What do you want me to say?'

'We just need to get it clear,' said Kennedy. Irish accent: he was made to be the good cop. He offered Jensen a breath mint. Nice touch.

'Quam called in straight after I dropped Ash. He wanted to find Hagger on the Helbreen. I took him up and they had a conversation.'

'Did you hear what they said?'

'I stayed in the helicopter.'

'And afterwards?'

'Quam came back. I brought him home. Then I went to pick up Ash.'

'Was Hagger alive when Quam left?'

Jensen sucked on the mint. 'I don't know.'

'Did you see him?'

'Look, I had plenty to do. If I'd known Hagger wouldn't come back, I'd have paid more attention. Taken a picture or something.'

'So you didn't see Hagger alive after Quam had finished?' Kennedy said.

Jensen looked between us again – trapped. 'To be honest? I can't say a hundred per cent.'

'But you're not certain you did see him?'

He shook his head.

'Then why didn't you say anything?'

'Soon as we knew what happened – when Greta called in – Quam got me into his office. He said he knew it was awkward, but he didn't want to explain himself because it would start rumours. He said that if the truth came out, why he had to go, that it would make Hagger look bad, and he didn't want anyone speaking ill of the dead.'

'Anything else?'

'He said if I said anything, he'd get a new pilot.'

'How did he seem when you flew back? In himself, I mean?' That was Kennedy.

'Tense. But that wasn't unusual. You know how Quam is.'

'The stick's so far up his ass it almost comes out his mouth,' I agreed.

Jensen risked a smile. 'You could say.'

'Nothing else?'

He thought about it some. 'Nothing. If there had been, I'm sure I'd have said something.'

'I'm sure you would have.'

'I mean, I knew it was suspicious.'

'Of course.'

'I'm not even sure I didn't see Hagger still there. When we

left. I might have done. That's why I wouldn't have said anything.'

I could see his conscience rewriting history. I wouldn't get anything else reliable from him. I stepped aside from the door.

'That's helpful, thanks.'

Jensen almost tore off the handle he was so happy to escape. Then he paused, troubled.

'You really think Quam could've . . . ?'

I shook my head and smiled. 'Not at all.'

'But he must have done it.' Kennedy barely waited until the door was shut. 'Everything fits.'

I could have punched his fat face. 'Shut up,' I told him. 'If this is right, you think we want to be talking about it ten feet from Quam's office?'

Kennedy flushed. 'Is anywhere safe?'

I looked at my watch. 'It's nine p.m.'

'Is that relevant?'

'Let's go get a mag reading.'

The mag hut is maybe a hundred-yard walk. It took us ten minutes to get dressed; by the end of it, we looked like spacemen. Hat, hood, goggles, face mask. We didn't take rifles. We couldn't have brought them in the mag hut, and if we put them down we'd never find them again. I figured polar bears are too smart to be out in a storm like that.

I checked the weather screen by the door. The temperature was -40°. The wind speed read zero, which was a lie. I could hear it through the door, howling like a dog.

'It busted the anemometer.'

'That's encouraging.' Kennedy pulled up his face mask so it covered his nose a bit more. 'Shall we?'

I opened the door. You remember the scene in *Alien* where she blows the monster out of the airlock into outer space? It was like that. The wind roared like it was sucking the life off of the planet. Damn near carried us away before we got down the steps. Ice crystals peppered my goggles. I thought I'd covered up pretty good, but the wind cut through cracks I didn't know I'd left. Fine snow filled the inside of my goggles and froze my eyeballs.

We roped ourselves together and followed the flag line towards the mag hut. In theory, it was daylight; in practice, you could barely see the next marker. When I looked back to check Kennedy was still with me, I saw the lights on the Platform glowing, blurry pools that looked a million miles away.

You're in the Coast Guard, Captain, so maybe you've seen a man go overboard in a storm. That's how it felt. The noise, the force, the feeling your body is fighting every second just to stay in place, forget moving forward. Sometimes you'd be walking across scoured ice; the next, knee-deep in a snowdrift. Without the flag line, we could have kept walking till we hit the North Pole.

It was just as well we didn't bring the rifles. I never saw the perimeter, just the mag hut like a dark shadow in the storm. We wrestled the door open and collapsed inside.

'What do you have to do to get some privacy around here?' I was shouting, still tuned to the storm. Not that anyone would hear.

Kennedy pulled off his hat, and shook the snow off his suit. 'Jesus.'

I took the readings while he warmed his hands and stamped his feet.

'One thing I don't understand,' said Kennedy.

'That's an understatement.'

'If it's been Quam all along, why did he ask me to find out who was telling our secrets? I mean, he might have thought I wasn't up to much, wouldn't get anywhere, but still. He didn't have to say anything.'

I didn't know what he was talking about. 'What secrets?'

'The climate data, the person who was spilling beans to DAR-X. Remember, I told you in Vitangelsk? It was Quam who wanted me to find out who it was.' He clapped his hands together and winced. 'Maybe it was just as well I didn't. That must have been what did for Hagger.'

I almost laughed. Fuck-a-doodle-doo. We'd all been running around chasing our tails.

'I don't think this has anything to do with DAR-X,' I said carefully. 'Or with our data. It's bigger than that.'

How much to tell him? 'There's a secret facility by Vitangelsk, inside Mine Eight. Some kind of Russian military radar.'

Kennedy stared at me like I'd announced I was Jesus Christ. 'How do you know that?'

'I can't tell you.'

'You sound like Danny.'

'This isn't some crazy conspiracy theory. That guy who chased you at Vitangelsk – did you make him up?'

Kennedy puffed out his cheeks, then blew a long breath like a puff of smoke. It made me want a cigarette. And I quit three years ago.

'I thought DAR-X were running it,' I continued. 'Now I'm certain there's someone here at Zodiac.'

'Francis Quam.'

'That's the way it looks,' I agreed.

'So what about Hagger?'

'I haven't figured him out yet,' I admitted. 'Either he was part of it and threatened to expose Quam, or he found out something he shouldn't have. Either way, Quam got shot of him.'

'That explains the notebooks,' Kennedy said.

'What notebooks?'

'On Tuesday, when we went to the cabin. Do you remember

that I looked in the stove? I didn't tell you then, but what I found was the charred remains of Hagger's notebooks. Someone took them there to get rid of them.'

'Any idea who?'

'I looked in the field log. Everyone comes and goes, but no one's been to the cabin. Or admitted to it. I'm afraid that doesn't do us much good.'

I thought through my list of names, all the lines connecting them.

'How do you think Tom Anderson fits?'

'Quam didn't want him here,' said Kennedy thoughtfully. 'He and Hagger had the most tremendous row about it last week.'

I gave him a stern look. 'Were you spying?'

Kennedy squirmed. 'I couldn't help overhearing.'

'Forget it. I heard it too.' The whole base had heard it. 'So Hagger knew something. Quam thought he might tell Anderson, so he tried to stop Anderson coming here. When that didn't work out, he killed Hagger.'

'That explains why Hagger was up on the glacier near Vitangelsk when he should have been working on sea ice. But what about the faked data?'

My brain was working overtime, like I'd drunk three cups of coffee on top of a NoDoz. 'How's this? Hagger and Quam were in this together, working for the Russians. Hagger faked his data so he would get the funding to come to Zodiac. But he did it in a dumb way, and someone figured it out. Quam got pissed off, because Hagger had drawn suspicion on them; he went up to the Helbreen to bitch Hagger out. Someone lost their temper, there was shoving, and Hagger bit the dust.'

'So what do we do now? Confront Quam?'

'We don't have enough evidence.'

'But Jensen—'

'Proves nothing. Quam can bluff that out. You have any

idea how dangerous he is? If he thinks we've figured him out, he'll disappear us down the nearest ravine.' I flexed my fingers. Even inside the mittens, they'd begun to go numb. 'We need proof.'

'How?'

I grinned. 'I'll break into his office tonight.'

Kennedy looked unhappy, but it was only a mild case of morals. Hell, it's not even breaking in if there isn't a lock.

'And you keep an eye on Anderson. Either he's one unlucky son of a bitch – or he's more dangerous than we can imagine.'

I turned for the door. 'Let's get back to the Platform. It's too fucking cold out here.'

Outside, the storm hadn't died down any. The second I opened the door, I got a face full of ice. We were straight into the wind now, and it cut right through to the bone. Forget the flag line, or the lights on the Platform. The visibility was so bad I could barely see Doc six feet in front of me. I had to hope like hell he could see where he was going.

It felt like it took for ever. At first, I assumed it was the wind and the cold and hating every second. But even then, we should have made it eventually. Looking ahead, I couldn't even see the Platform lights.

I tugged on the rope. Doc stopped and waited for me to catch him up.

'Are we going the right way?' I had to pull aside his hood and put my mouth almost against his ear so he could hear me over the roar of the wind.

He shrugged, and pointed to the marker post just in front of him. *Still on track.*

OK. We went on, heads down, faces frozen, not even bothering to wipe off the snow that gathered in the creases on our coats. I started to think about all the guys who went out in the snow and nearly died, Victorian explorers who thought a tweed suit and a pocket watch were all you needed for polar expeditions. Was this how they died? Walking on, bent lower and lower, until finally they collapsed face first and never got up? Not one of my life's ambitions.

The rope went tight so fast it almost knocked me on my ass. Before I could wonder what the hell Doc was playing at, I was being pulled forward, jogging over the ice in a crab run I couldn't control.

I didn't know what was happening, but I knew I had to stop it before we both got killed. I kicked my heels into the snow, trying to get a hold. Couldn't. The rope pulled me on, my feet skidding over the snow like I was skiing. Ahead, through the chaos in the air, I could see a dark scar cutting across the ground, and the rope dropping into it.

The gulch. The crack at the edge of the glacier. I could just about see some of the warning poles whipping about in the storm. How the hell did we get here?

It was too close. The rope wasn't long enough, and I was going too fast. I pulled off my mittens and reached for the knot around my waist, scrabbling to undo it. Kennedy was screwed either way, but maybe I could save myself.

With so much tension, the knot was never going to come undone. Normally, I carry a penknife in my pants pocket, but I'd taken it out to go to the mag hut. I was fucked. I wondered whether if I landed on top of Kennedy, he'd break my fall.

You know what saved me? The wind. An Arctic storm blowing fifty knots in your face is one hell of a brake. It slowed me down enough that I could dig my heels into the snow. I leaned back almost forty-five degrees. The wind, Kennedy's weight on the rope, friction and gravity came into perfect equilibrium. I was weightless.

I'd stopped.

Then the hard work began. Inch by inch, I hauled myself

back. The first three steps almost broke my back; each time I lifted my foot, I thought I'd lose it completely and go right over the edge. But it got easier. Once he stopped falling, Kennedy'd managed to get his feet against the ice wall to brace himself. As I pulled, he was able to walk up, taking some of the weight. The wind kept pushing me, so hard that when Kennedy finally made it up I lost my balance and sat down hard on a bare sheet of ice.

The rope went slack. A dark figure staggered out of the storm, covered all over in snow like fucking Bigfoot. He crouched beside me.

'That's the last time I let you go first,' I shouted at him.

He shook his head. 'I followed the flag line.'

He was right. I'd seen it too, the red poles every ten feet, all the way from the mag hut.

'Someone moved the poles.' It was the only explanation. Someone had actually tried to kill us. It was a hell of a thought.

If he thinks we've figured him out, he'll disappear us down the nearest ravine. Christ, I didn't mean it that literally.

And if I didn't get off my ass and out of that storm soon, he'd have succeeded. My hands were already ice, and God knows where I'd dropped my gloves. They were probably halfway to Siberia by now. Pulling out Kennedy had cost me most of my strength: even in my ECW gear, I couldn't stop shivering. In those conditions, that gives you less than five minutes.

I stuck my hands in my coat pockets. At least it kept the wind off of them. Kennedy put his arm around me, and together we stumbled our way back along the flag line. If it led straight from the mag hut to the gulch, I had a pretty good idea where the Platform ought to be. Soon, off to our right, I saw a dim glow. We broke towards it. The lights got brighter. Now I could see the steel legs, rigid in the chaos. Best goddam sight I ever saw in my life.

I just managed to get up the stairs, kick the bar to open the door and fall inside the vestibule. I couldn't even get my gear off. Kennedy had to unzip me and pull off my coat. His hands were shaking almost as bad as mine.

'Jesus,' he said. 'Did someone just try to kill us?'

'Look on the bright side.' Hunched over on the bench, I looked around the boot room. A few of the other coats were still wet with melted snow: Quam's, Greta's and Fridge's. Anderson's wasn't there at all. A lot of people to be out on a shitty night like that.

'At least if they're trying to kill us, we have to be on the right track.'

Thirty

Eastman

It fries your brain when you wake in the night and it's daylight outside. Humans are tropical mammals; we like some darkness in our lives. Spending summer in the Arctic is like being dumped on the bright side of the moon.

Not that there was a whole lot of daylight that morning. The storm had died down, but it was still blowing strong. I could hear it moaning through the antennas. It's lucky I don't believe in ghosts.

After we came in from the mag hut, after I defrosted my hands, I'd gone in to the mess. Some of the others had gone to bed, most were still decorating for Thing Night, listening to music and drinking a few beers. Quam was in his office.

There was no point asking if anyone had gone out while we were in the mag hut. People had been coming and going all evening. Whoever did it, I didn't want to alert him.

I worried Kennedy might say something. He looked as if he was about to flip out. But he went off into his medical room, and when he came back he seemed a whole lot calmer. Soon after, we both went to bed, though it took me a long time to get to sleep.

I got out of my bed at 3 a.m. and walked down the corridor to Quam's office. Maybe I should have felt nervous, or guilty: the truth is, I was juiced. Quam had tried to kill me – I was certain it had to be him – and I wanted to nail him. Forget the radar, the Russians, the mine and all that. This was personal.

But I wasn't so mad I got dumb. I got to the office, had my hand on the handle, when I heard a noise from inside. *Tick, tack, tick, tack.* A metallic sound, so regular I could have convinced myself it was a clock or some piece of machinery playing up.

Except I'd seen Quam's desk, and that executive toy he kept next to his computer monitor. Newton's cradle: you swing a ball from one end, and the ball at the other end kicks up. The conservation of momentum, Newton's laws, if you want the technical explanation.

Now, I have a PhD in physics, so I can explain Newton's laws pretty good. In a closed system, momentum is never gained or lost. In other words, if you set one of those toys off in outer space, it would keep going for ever.

But Utgard's not outer space. Not quite. Gravity and air resistance mean the balls eventually slow down and stop. Unless there's someone to keep them going.

I backed away. There was no light coming under the door. Maybe he'd gone to bed right before I got up.

Tick, tack, tick, tack.

I listened in the dark. The balls got slower. *Tick . . . tack . . .* Slower, and stopped.

I counted ten, then reached for the door handle again. But right before I touched it, the noise began again, firm and hard.

Newton's first law says that if something's stopped, it stays stopped unless an external force is applied. Quam had to be in there, sitting in the dark, listening to the balls clack just like me. What else was he doing there? Waiting? For what?

Suddenly, I heard another noise. A chair scraping back from a desk. I didn't have time to get back to my room. I

231

ducked across the corridor and slipped inside Fridge's lab opposite, leaving the door open a crack so I could see.

Quam stepped out. In the dim light, he looked a hundred years old. Shoulders slumped, face lined. He had a slip of paper in his hand.

He walked up the corridor and stopped outside the mess door. I thought he'd go in – maybe he had the munchies – but he didn't. He just stood there, doing something with the paper. Then he turned around and went back into his office. The chair squeaked, and a moment later the *tick tack* of the toy reset again. Just in case the laws of physics had changed while he was away.

I snuck out of Fridge's lab and headed for the mess. It was a dumb thing to do, with Quam right there. He could have come out again any moment. But I had to know if he'd done what I thought he had.

On the door, the Daily Horrorscope had changed. Guessing who wrote those things was one of our favourite games at Zodiac, but in all those conversations I don't think anyone ever suspected Quam. Now that I knew, I kind of wished I didn't.

There wasn't much light, but I could read what he'd put up.

The storm is just beginning.

Thirty-one

Eastman

Everyone makes it to breakfast on Saturday. It's waffle day. Somewhere along the line, someone had too much time on his hands and spent the winter making an old-fashioned, cast-iron waffle maker. Every Saturday, Danny wheels it out with little plastic cups of batter, and everyone stands in line to make their own. It even stamps a little Z for Zodiac in the centre of the waffle.

Now, I like waffles as much as the next guy. But that morning, I hardly tasted it. Knowing someone in that room had tried to get me to walk into the gulch the night before kind of put me off my breakfast. I kept on sliding down in my chair, like my body wanted me to keep my head down. I stared at the others: sticky fingers, syrup dribbling down their chins. Some of them caught me, gave me looks that said I was some kind of freak.

I'm the only one here who has a clue, I said back, in my head.

No one was happy. For some of those people, a season at Zodiac was the high point of their careers. Instead of using it, they were sat there wasting tens of thousands of dollars a day doing squat. But you know what really pissed them off, the one word you heard over and over when you listened in on their conversations? *Internet.* That's what was driving them crazy: twenty-some people trapped on the Platform, and no

Internet. Do you blame them? Captain Scott took a lot of shit, but he never had his web access cut off.

Kennedy joined me at my table. He always poured his syrup so neatly over the waffle. Mine was drowning in it.

'Did you find anything last night?' he asked, looking so guilty he might as well have put it on Facebook.

'Quam was in there all night.' He hadn't showed up at breakfast. I wondered if he was still in there, tick-tacking his Newton toy, or if he'd gone to bed.

I looked out the window. The weather was still ugly. Snow devils whipped across the ice; clouds covered the mountain peaks. From my table, I could see the mag hut, and the flag line leading to it. Or where the flag line had been. The poles lay scattered on the ground like someone had been through with a giant lawnmower.

'Terrible storm damage,' I said sarcastically.

'The Internet's still down, too,' Doc said.

'I know.' I swabbed up some more syrup with a piece of my waffle. Maybe it was because I was sitting under the tinfoil spaceship Greta'd hung for Thing Night – or maybe because someone had tried to kill me – but I felt kind of paranoid.

'You look anxious,' said Doc. 'Would you like something for it?'

I shook my head. Those pills dull your brain; I had to stay sharp. Keep my wits. I didn't know when, but I knew for sure they'd come for me again. And I was going to be ready.

I strolled down the corridor and knocked on Hagger's lab. The red skull smiled at me from the door. *HIGH INFECTION RISK OF UNKNOWN DNA*. No one answered, so I let myself in. I dropped the key I'd taken back in one of the drawers, and buried it under some pipettes and tubing, the kind of place it might have gotten lost. Then I had a look around.

The yellow pipe Anderson had been looking at sat in the

234

corner in a tray. The pipe looked pretty ragged, peppered with holes like someone had blasted it with a shotgun. Maybe Malick's story, the bug munching on his drill rig, had something in it. Hard to see what that had to do with Mine 8. Maybe nothing.

Anderson arrives, Hagger dies. Couldn't be coincidence. I wished I could have had a look at the notebook, but I didn't find it. Nothing in the fridge except a can of Coke. Nothing on the benchtops except instruments, and a paper printed off from about ten years ago. Anderson, Sieber and Pharaoh, 'Pfu-87: A Synthetic Variant on the Pfu-polymer Enzyme and . . .' *blah blah blah . . .*

The door crashed open. There's only one person who bangs a door that hard at Zodiac. I turned around and saw Greta behind me. All dressed up in her coat and snow pants, and the cutesy hat with the strings down the side.

'How you doing?' I asked – mainly because I could see she looked furious.

'If one more person tells me that the Internet's down . . .'

'The Internet's down.'

She made a kind of growling noise. Without really thinking about it, I found myself backing off a couple of paces.

'I was looking for Tom,' I said.

'He's working in Star Command.'

'I didn't know he was interested in astronomy?'

She gave me one of those Greta looks that says it's none of your business and she could care less anyhow.

'Help me fix the Internet? You're the radio man.'

'Sure thing.'

You're the radio man. What did she mean by that? Maybe nothing. Or maybe she was thinking of that big antenna strung across Vitangelsk, and the cable carrying the signal to Mine 8. Her face, like always, could have meant anything.

★   ★   ★

I got on my gear and headed for the laundry room. The temperature dropped about fifty degrees the moment I went in. There's a hatch in the ceiling that opens on to the roof. It stood wide open, with a ladder going up and Greta's boots on the top rung.

'Shut the door,' she told me.

'Already have.'

I climbed up after her and clipped in to the safety rope she'd fixed. The storm was still kicking around, and the roof was an ice rink.

'Safety is job number one,' I said, wriggling into the harness. Hard to do when you're wearing three pairs of pants.

'Too many accidents,' Greta agreed.

'Quam must be shitting bricks.'

That got me one of her twitchy half-smiles. Though I never knew with those if it was what I'd said, or if there was something else completely going on inside her head, and the smile just happened to pop out at the same time. Often, with Greta, I felt like *I* was the joke.

I'd been at Zodiac a month and I still hadn't worked her out. She wasn't gorgeous, exactly, but she had something that meant she stuck in your mind. Like a lyric in a song that makes no sense, you spend hours trying to think what it means. Oftentimes, I found myself wondering what it would be like to fuck her. And it's not what you're thinking. Like I said, I'd only been there a month.

'You think Quam seems stressed out at the moment?' I tried.

Dumb question. 'Always.'

We crawled across the roof to the main satellite dish that gave the Internet hook-up. You didn't have to be a mechanic, or even the 'radio guy', to see what had gone wrong. The dish was dinged up like someone had taken a hammer to it. Worse, the feedhorn hung off of its bracket like a broken arm.

'You won't get that working any time soon,' I said.

'There's a spare in the store.'

I didn't really hear her. The feedhorn's mounted on a big steel bar bolted right through the back of the dish. I was trying to imagine how big a piece of ice you'd need to break it like that. I remembered the noises coming through my office roof the night before. Almost like footsteps.

'We need to shut down all comms to do the installation,' Greta said.

I rubbed my eyes with my mitt. No comms. No plane. One by one, our links to the outside world were getting cut off.

Greta must have thought the same thing. She nodded to the safety rope.

'Better hold on tight.'

We unscrewed the broken dish and lowered it to the ground. Between us, we carried it to the shop. Halfway there, she turned and looked back. Her nose wrinkled up.

'Those oil drums shouldn't be so close to the Platform. It's a fire risk.'

'Not a big risk at twenty below.'

'I'll move them.'

'Can we do it later? This dish is killing my arms.'

Inside the shop, everything was shipshape in that obsessive Greta way. Weirdly, it reminded me of being in a church: the light coming in through the windows, the dust in the air, the smell of burning. The broken-down snowmobile under the tarp could have been a coffin set out for last respects.

We laid the dish in a corner. Greta went to the store to dig out the backup; while I waited, I eyed up the tools on the wall. She had everything there. A couple of big sledgehammers, for example, that could make a nasty dent in a piece of steel.

Maybe I was crazy. I'd heard the wind outside last night. If anyone had gone out on that roof, he'd have been blown into the mountainside at a hundred miles an hour. You couldn't stand up, never mind swing a hammer.

Even if you wore a safety line? Greta had looked pretty nimble up on the roof just then.

She came out of the store empty-handed. As much as you could ever tell, she seemed puzzled.

'No joy?'

'It's not there.'

I guess I didn't look too surprised. 'You know how pissy this is going to make everyone,' I warned her.

She rolled her eyes. 'Don't even tell me.'

She stepped towards the door – and found me blocking her way. I wanted to get some things straight while I had her alone.

'Tell me,' I said. 'You knew Hagger as well as anyone.'

She gave me an *Oh, please* look.

'Did he ever say why he brought Tom Anderson up here?'

'Ask Tom.'

I didn't like her tone. 'I'm asking you.'

I was standing closer to her than I'd realised. In the sunlight, I could see the tiny soft hairs on her cheek. I had a powerful, stupid urge to kiss her.

'You and Tom seemed to hit it off pretty fast,' I said. 'Soon as he gets here, you're racing off together. Maybe you wanted to trade Hagger in for a younger model. Maybe Hagger got in the way, and Anderson got rid of him.'

'Fuck you.'

Something inside of me snapped. I only meant to grab her, but suddenly, not even thinking, I was kissing her, pressing my mouth against hers. She struggled, but I had her pinned against the wall. And I was hard.

I tasted blood in my mouth. The bitch bit my lip. I pulled

238

back, ready to slap her. That was what she wanted. Before I knew it, she'd grabbed a crescent wrench from its hook on the wall and swung it against my elbow. Christ, it hurt.

Greta was breathing hard, her cheeks red.

'Is that what you did to the satellite dish?' I gasped. I wanted to hit her back, but there wasn't anything in reach. And she was holding that wrench like a morning star.

'Get out,' she said.

Truth is, I was so hopped up on adrenalin, I didn't know what I'd do next. If I'd slap her, or get her down on the floor and fuck her, or what. I stared her in the face.

'If you ever do that again, I'll feed your balls to a seal,' she said.

I left.

I knelt down in the snow outside. My legs were trembling; I wanted to puke. I blamed it on the pain in my elbow. I didn't know what came over me in there. She was dangerous.

I rubbed snow on my face to cool off. I took some breaths. It felt like a jackhammer was pounding against my skull, harder and harder, until I clocked it was coming up from the sky. A helicopter flew over the station: big, ugly-looking thing with a double-bubble nose. Must be DAR-X heading home. Too high to see if Malick was in there waving.

I went over to Star Command. The crucified Buzz Lightyear smiled down at me as I reached the caboose. I went in without knocking. Anderson was inside, still wearing his coat and hat, looking at a readout on a monitor. Three machines that looked like laser printers sat on a tabletop, humming and clicking.

'What's going on?' My voice sounded loud and fake, even to me. Did he look guilty – or just surprised someone had burst in on him? I admit, everyone looked guilty to me that day. Someone had to be.

Anderson waved a plastic Baggie at me. All I saw inside was water. 'Analysing Hagger's samples.'

'I heard they were bullshit. He doped the data.'

He didn't ask how I knew. 'I don't think he did. If you look at the notebooks, he knew the samples were dodgy but he didn't know why. That's what he was looking for.'

I didn't buy that for a second. Hagger knew exactly what he was doing. I pointed to one of the machines.

'What's that?'

'A mass spectrometer. It gives you the mass of the elements in a sample, so you can guess what's in it.'

'And this one?'

'DNA sequencer.'

'I didn't know we had those here.'

'Hagger must have set them up.'

Far away from where anybody could see them. They looked good, but who knew what was inside them. 'Do they work?'

'Perfectly.'

Was he covering for Hagger? Time to show a little more leg. I pulled out the sheet of paper and showed it to him.

'I got another reading on that interference. Looks like it's coming from near Vitangelsk.' I watched him like a hawk as I fed him the bait. If it meant anything, he hid it well.

'Up by Mine Eight,' I threw in.

He read the numbers. 'It's the same as before.'

'If only we could unlock it,' I deadpanned. 'You know, with a key.'

His eyes flicked up at me. Only for a second, but my senses were white-hot and I caught it. He knew. He fucking *knew*.

'Why did Hagger bring you here?' I asked

I thought he didn't hear me – the DNA sequencer had started to spit out some data, and he was copying them down in his notebook. A string of letters, G's, C's, A's and T's, repeating themselves in random combos. Not so different from the numbers coming through the antenna, if you thought about it.

'Have you ever been to New York?' he asked.

'Sure. Empire State Building, NBC tour, all that shit. Why, you want some tips?'

Just then, Kennedy walked in.

'Quam's gone out to check one of the bear cameras.'

It was all I needed to hear.

Thirty-two

Eastman

I was in that office so fast, the balls on the Newton cradle were still swinging. *Tick, tack.* For once, my luck was in: he'd forgotten to log out of his computer. His email sat wide open on the monitor.

I sat on the edge of his chair and scrolled through his in-box, the messages that had come through before the Internet went down. For such an anal guy, he didn't file as much as he should. It was all in there together, and with everything that had been happening, there was a lot of traffic. Stuff from the honchos at Norwich HQ, from his ex-wife, from the flight contractors. I read through it as fast as I could.

Please update your Health and Safety report, in light of recent events, as a matter of urgency.

The BSPA Twin Otter has been delayed in Port Stanley by mechanical failure and will not now be available until next Wednesday.

The consultation on Zodiac Station's function in the new Polar Research Funding framework will conclude in June. Please ensure your submission is completed by then.

Will you be home in August? I've got to go to a conference in Copenhagen, and it would be helpful if you could take the girls.

Please demonstrate how your research program fulfils Value for

242

Money criteria, in conjunction with the new Delivering Excellence in Research initiative.

There was £500 missing from your child support payments this month.

If he had to deal with that bullshit all day every day, no wonder he was so tense. And reading between the lines, it looked like money was a problem – maybe his job was even on the line.

I checked my watch. Fifteen minutes down – and there was no telling when Quam might come back. Reading through everything was like picking up pebbles looking for diamonds.

I had to try smarter. I found the search box and tried a couple of terms. *Vitangelsk. Mine 8. Radar.* Not really that smart: a six-year-old would have known to use code words. And another five minutes gone.

I listened out. All personnel were still confined to base, so the Platform was loud with noise: talking, laughing, footsteps. No chance of picking out Quam when he came.

The last message I'd read was still open on screen.

There was £500 missing from your child support payments this month.

Nothing relevant – but it got me thinking. First, I thought how much it would suck to have Quam as your dad. Then I wondered if he was short of cash – and what he might do for money.

I put a new term into the search. A single character: £. It brought up a bunch of results, but not as many as you'd think. There's no money on Utgard.

I scanned through them. Mostly budget stuff, a few questions about maintenance. And then this:

We have received a grant of £100,000 from Luxor Life Sciences Corporation in respect of work at Zodiac. Please advise which fund to credit.

I thanked God and Bill Malick that I'd been paying attention. *They came here a couple years back, just when we set up Echo Bay . . . looking for a place to build a gene bank.* They'd looked around Mine 8. And here they were paying an awful lot of money to Quam.

'What the hell?'

Time was up. Quam stood in the doorway, like he'd just walked in on me fucking his daughter. He looked terrible. I'm not judging – I mean, most of us at Zodiac looked like Deadheads – but Quam was usually so pristine. He combed, he shaved. Now, he had red-rimmed eyes, crazy hair and stubble like an axe-murderer.

And a face so red I expected to see a fuse sticking out his head. He slammed the door, crossed the room, and would probably have hauled me out of his chair by my collar if I hadn't have jumped up.

'What do you think you're doing here?'

No point trying to bluff. 'Why don't you tell me what *you've* been doing here?' I said. Adrenalin had me pumped; I was feeding off of his anger.

'I beg your pardon.'

'Luxor Life Sciences mean anything to you. Huh?' I emphasised it with a jab of my finger that almost took his eye out. 'They've damn sure been paying you enough.'

'I don't know what you're talking about.'

'Bullshit you don't. What about Mine Eight? And Hagger – you want to tell me what you did to him?'

'Are you trying to imply—'

'Shall I get Jensen in here? He had a hell of a story to tell me, how you called him in to fly you to the Helbreen last

Saturday. He said you came back alive. He wasn't so sure about Hagger.'

All the colour drained out of his face. 'What Hagger did threatened everything we'd achieved at Zodiac. I had to stop him before he ruined everything.'

'So you killed him.'

His whole body shook. '*No.*'

'And then you took his notebooks up to the cabin and burned them to cover the tracks.'

He didn't try to deny that one. 'How do you know?'

'Because I'm smarter than you, Quam. I've been up to Mine Eight; I've seen the antenna at Vitangelsk. Did you think you could keep all that secret for ever?'

He didn't have anything to say to that. Couldn't even look me in the eye. He stared past me, at the Newton's cradle on the table. His fingers twitched, like he couldn't stand that it had stopped, he had to set it going again.

I picked it up and slammed it on the floor. The frame cracked; the balls came loose and scattered across the room like a pinball machine. Quam flew at me, but I was quicker. I grabbed his wrists and twisted so hard his eyes watered. Damn, it felt good.

'How long have you been working for the Russians?'

'Russians?'

'Did Hagger find out? Or maybe he was part of it and got cold feet?'

'Hagger had nothing to do with it.'

We were both shouting – and the walls at Zodiac are made of spit and toilet paper. I tried to bring my voice down before someone came in.

'How about Anderson and Greta? Were they helping?'

It didn't quiet him down any. 'You're mad,' he shouted. 'Russians, radars, murders . . . you've read too many spy novels.'

'What was in those notebooks you burned?'

He scratched the stubble on his cheek. The skin underneath was chafed raw, like he'd been doing it a lot.

'Hagger was a fraud. His results, his samples, everything. I did him a favour.'

'Bullshit.'

'I had to protect Zodiac. Do you know how badly Norwich want to shut us down? This would have been the perfect excuse. Scandal, questions in the press, demands to do something.'

'Very convenient.' I pointed to the email on the screen. 'How about Luxor Life Sciences?'

'They gave us a grant.'

'I bet they did. Did they also tell you to take out anyone who poked into what was happening up at Vitangelsk?'

'I don't . . .' He was struggling to speak. He sat down hard in his chair. 'I don't know who they are. They're planning to do something with Mine Eight but they haven't got all the funding. They asked me to keep an eye on things.'

'Is that why you snoop on other people's emails?'

He had the audacity to look hurt. 'That's for morale. If anyone's not happy here, I have to be the first to know about it.' He tapped the papers on his desk. 'It's all in the contract.'

'And when you found out Hagger had been looking around there . . .'

Again, that blank look. 'Hagger never went near Vitangelsk.'

'It's around the corner from the Helbreen glacier.'

'With a bloody great mountain in between.'

He started to get out of his chair, saw me square up and thought again.

'The only time Luxor Sciences said anything about Hagger was after he died. They suggested removing his notebooks.'

'I bet they did.'

'To protect our funding,' he protested. 'They didn't want the scandal to ruin Zodiac.'

'And how did they know all about that so fast? Did you tell them?'

'No.' He scratched his beard again. '*No.*'

Quite suddenly, he dropped his head on the desk and started crying.

'Jesus,' I said in disgust.

'Get out,' he screamed. 'Get out, get out, *get out!*'

There was no way I could shut him up – not unless I clocked him. And if he kept on, someone would walk in in a minute, and then it would take one hell of an explanation. His word against mine – and mine was full of murders, Russians, secret radars and spies. They'd have locked me up in two minutes.

So I left him, weeping on to his desk like it was the end of the world.

Thirty-three

Eastman

It was weird, stepping out of his office. Like waking up after a bad dream. I could hear Danny in the galley cooking lunch; students laughing and joking in the mess. Through the end windows, I could see a bunch of people playing soccer in the snow. They looked like they were having a good time.

I had nothing in common with them.

I went into the bathroom, leaned on the sink and took some deep breaths. I stared at myself in the mirror. You don't do that too often at Zodiac; I barely recognised myself. My beard had grown full, and my eyes seemed to have shrunk into my head. It reminded me of those old photos you see, guys who got stranded on the ice and had to survive a winter eating their boots. You wonder how they managed when they finally got back to civilisation. One of them shot himself in a hotel room, I seem to remember.

Was Zodiac changing me? For sure. First Greta, then Quam: something was coming out of me that hadn't been there before. In a place like Utgard, you freeze hard without even knowing it. Maybe I should have popped one of Kennedy's chill pills.

'Gotta stay sharp,' I told the man in the mirror.

Gotta stay sharp, he mouthed back at me.

What to do now? The showdown with Quam should have locked everything in place. Instead, I felt less certain than ever.

He admitted going up to see Hagger on the Helbreen.

He admitted burning the notebooks.

He admitted taking money from Luxor.

So why wasn't I more sure that he'd killed Hagger and sold us out to the Russians? Was it his sob-story act? Was I that gullible?

And how were we supposed to rub along, now that I'd effectively accused him of espionage and murder? Did we just show up to dinner together and act like it never happened? Or should I go all *Mutiny on the Bounty* and try and relieve him of his command?

If I did that, who'd be with me?

I picked up a satphone and rang a number in Washington DC. It was against protocol, but only a little. It was also 5 a.m. on the Eastern seaboard, but those guys are open all hours.

'I need to find out about a company called Luxor Life Sciences,' I told them. 'Our Internet went down, so call me back on this satphone.'

I didn't tell them why I wanted it. You never know who's listening – especially if down the road they happen to have an antenna as big as a small town. Plus, the guys I was speaking to get paid to figure out that stuff.

You know what's crazy? After all that, I spent the afternoon catching up on work. It had to get done some time – and I was way behind. Human beings are weird that way: we go through the wildest experiences, then you drop us back in the cage and we go right back on to the hamster wheel.

You remember that tsunami that hit Japan a few years back, the one that knocked out the nuclear reactor? I saw a TV documentary about it, just before I left the States. There was a guy in it: lost his home, his job, his mom, everything. And you know what pissed him off the most? He'd spent the

249

whole afternoon before it hit washing his goddam car. That's what he couldn't get over.

I laughed at him, then, but now I know how he felt. If we could see what was coming, we'd all do things differently.

About five of eight, I went along to the mess for Thing Night. No sign of Quam, or Anderson. Or Greta or Fridge. In fact, the whole thing felt kind of flat. Usually, Thing Night happens in July, when Zodiac's crawling with people. I guess Quam moved it forward to improve morale. Instead, it probably made everyone more depressed over how lame it was.

But people made an effort. Jensen had stuck some badges on his flight overalls so he looked like an air force pilot; Ash had put on a Frankenstein mask and taped drinking straws on to his fingers for claws. He kept complaining he couldn't hold his drink properly. Danny had tied his hair in a samurai-style topknot, like the cook in the movie who never gets a line; he kept bringing out trays of cookies shaped like UFOs, and miniature green jello shots that smelled of gin.

I sat down next to Kennedy. He'd trimmed his beard into a mad-scientist goatee and powdered it white, and put on a jacket and tie. Which, if you're in 1949, is apparently what you wear at the North Pole.

'Where's Quam gone?' I whispered to him.

'I haven't seen him all day.'

The old RKO logo came on screen, the radio mast blaring out from the top of the world. Kind of appropriate, under the circumstances. Everyone got quiet and gripped their drinks.

I should explain that watching the movie isn't the point; the point is to drink. The two main characters are Dr Carrington and Captain Hendry. The rules of the game are that every time someone says 'Doctor', anyone with a PhD drinks. When they say 'Captain', the others drink. And when there's a reference to 'science', or some bogus piece of pseudo-science, everyone drinks.

Every time someone came back from the bathroom, I looked over my shoulder to see if it was Quam.

A phone rang. After just long enough to make me look like an ass, I realised it was my Iridium. I pushed out through the crowd and took it in the hall.

'We checked up on Luxor Life Sciences,' said a voice. Those guys don't do introductions. 'Nothing funny, no connection to any known Russian organisations. Only flag that came up is the founder died in mysterious circumstances. Plane crash, body never found. British biologist called Richie Pharaoh.'

I remembered Malick had said the guy's name was Richie. But Pharaoh sounded familiar, too; I couldn't think where from.

'There is one link to Zodiac,' the voice went on. 'Pharaoh used to be a professor in the UK, at Cambridge University. One of his PhD students was a guy called Tom Anderson.'

I went so quiet they heard it in Washington. 'You still there?'

'I got it,' I said. 'Get me some background on Anderson, any links to the Russians, anything suspicious.'

I hung up.

Anderson wasn't watching the movie. I checked his room and his lab: nada. But there was the paper I'd seen that morning: *Anderson, Sieber and Pharaoh*. I could have kicked myself for not checking on Luxor Sciences earlier.

Maybe he was still in Star Command. I checked the boot room. His coat and boots were gone. So were Greta's. I opened the door and stuck my head out.

The temperature had dropped after the storm. Cold air pinched my nostrils and made my ears burn. Up on the Lucia glacier, against the black sky, I saw a flashing orange light. I caught it just in time to see the old Tucker Sno-Cat bounce over the ridge and disappear.

Fuck. On the off chance, I checked the field log to see if he'd signed out. Amazingly, he had: I guess protocol dies hard.

If I'd had any last doubts, they vanished when I saw what they'd written. *Anderson, Nystrom. Out: 8:30 p.m. Destination: Helbreen glacier.*

I ran back to the mess and found Kennedy. In the movie, they'd just reached the bit where Captain Hendry and Dr Carrington fight over whether they should kill the alien or try to talk to it.

'There are no enemies in science, only phenomena to be studied,' said the doctor on screen.

'To science,' everyone cheered. Luckily, Kennedy was on Coke. Probably the only sober man in the room.

'Come with me,' I told him.

The time it takes to get dressed at Zodiac, I thought I'd burst with impatience. Kennedy was even slower. I stood in his room, watching him pull on his two pairs of long johns and his pants, buttoning his shirt, finding the right sweaters.

'You don't need all that,' I said.

Kennedy ignored me. And you know what? He was right. You take shortcuts up there, you die. Anyhow, a snowmobile can outrun the Sno-Cat, easy. We'd catch them up.

It must have been twenty minutes before we'd got ready. In the mess, I could hear everyone shouting along with the movie's last line. '*Watch the skies! Watch the skies!*'

We grabbed a couple of rifles and ran down the steps to the snowmobile park. Predictably, just when I needed to go fast everything went to shit. I flipped the choke, pulled the starter cord but nothing happened.

I patted my pockets. 'Goddam it,' I said.

'What?'
'I forgot my satphone.'
'You'd better get it,' said Kennedy.
And then the Platform exploded.

Thirty-four

USCGC Terra Nova

Franklin was on his feet. He crossed to the phone on the wall and dialled Santiago.

'You still got the guard on Anderson's room?'

'Affirmative, Captain.'

'Page him to tell him I'm coming.'

On the bed, Eastman had sat up. His hungry, hollow face stared at Franklin like the grim reaper.

'Anderson's here?'

'We found him on the ice.'

'You locked him up?'

'He's secure.'

'I hope you chained him down.'

'I'm going to check on him now.'

Eastman swung his legs off the bed and stood up. The blankets fell in a heap on the floor. 'I want to see that cocksucker.'

Franklin pointed to the IV drip. 'He's going nowhere. You need to take it easy.'

'Fuck easy.' Grimacing, Eastman ripped off the Elastoplast strip and pulled the needle out of his arm. Blood welled out of the hole but he didn't seem to notice. The tube dangled limp, oozing fluid on the floor.

'He's a spy who damn near murdered every man on Zodiac to cover his tracks. You bet your ass I'm coming.'

★   ★   ★

Franklin didn't like to think how many regulations he was breaking, bringing a hypothermia patient through his ship in bare feet and a smock. Then again, if it turned out he'd unwittingly harboured a mass murderer working for the Russians, he wasn't going to be short of explaining to do.

'Did you find Greta?' Eastman must barely have been able to stand upright, but he never dropped a step back.

'Not yet. It was one in a million Anderson found us.'

'Bullshit. You really think that? You were his way out. Heroic survivor, walking across the ice. No one left to spill his secret. He knew exactly where you were. If you search, you'll probably find he ditched that Sno-Cat a half-mile from your boat. Unless he drove it into a hole in the ice.'

'What about Greta?'

'Maybe he killed her too. No witnesses.'

'My pilot reported he'd heard something that sounded like an emergency beacon out on the ice. I sent a crew to take a look. Could be Greta.'

'I hope you sent them armed.'

Eastman put his arm to his mouth and sucked off some blood from the IV hole. Franklin waited for him at the bottom of the next flight of stairs. Suddenly, his pager started buzzing. Before he could look at it, someone burst through the door on the deck above and came sliding down the stairs three at a time.

Only one man aboard the *Terra Nova* hit the stairs that hard.

'Ops?'

Santiago came around the corner, swinging himself on the rail for maximum velocity. He stopped a couple of inches short of the Captain, breathing hard.

'What is it?'

'Anderson's gone.'

255

Thirty-five

USCGC Terra Nova

The crewman sat on the bed with red welts burned around his wrists. White threads stuck to his cheek where Santiago had ripped off the surgical tape that Anderson had used to gag him. None too gently, Franklin guessed.

'He said he needed the head.' The crewman rubbed the back of his head and winced. 'Next thing I knew, I was tied to the chair with my own belt.'

'He can't have gotten off the ship.' Franklin looked out the porthole, almost by reflex, as if he expected to see Anderson running by. 'Get the Doc up here to check that bump on your head, and pipe General Emergency. I'm going to the wheelhouse.'

Word spread fast on the *Terra Nova*. All his officers were already on the bridge, waiting for him. Glad it wasn't them who had to take the PA.

'All hands, this is the Captain. We have an escaped detainee aboard our ship. His name is Tom Anderson. He may be armed and he is certainly dangerous. I'm initiating a lock-down, and a search of the ship as per our evacuation drill. Use extreme caution.'

He paused, then added: 'If you can hear this, Tom Anderson, I advise you to surrender yourself. You cannot escape.'

He hung up the mic and turned to Santiago.

'Get the helo airborne and fly a SAR pattern centred on the ship.'

'You think Anderson could have run for it?'

Franklin shrugged. 'He got here, didn't he?'

The wheelhouse emptied. Franklin sat down in his chair, staring out the windows at the panorama of ice. Anyone who made captain had learned to listen to his ship: even up here, he could hear the urgency of his order spreading through the *Terra Nova*. A faster rhythm, the vibrations of doors slamming and boots running. He could pick them out like an astronomer reading the stars through the fluctuations of radio waves. And all the while, beneath everything, the sawtooth rise and fall of the prow obliterating the ice.

'There's a good lead ahead,' said the bosun's mate on ice watch. 'We should be able to get some speed up soon.'

Franklin nodded. He looked at Eastman. 'What happened then? After the explosion?'

Eastman shivered. One of the crew brought him a space blanket and wrapped it over his shoulders, a silver cloak that made him look like some alien overlord.

'They lit up Zodiac like the fourth of July. Oil barrels packed underneath, and all the blast cord we used for seismic work. With everyone packed into the mess for Thing Night, no one had a chance. Even if they'd survived, all the ECW clothing burned up in the Platform. So did the radios, the Iridium phones. Anderson took care of everything. If Kennedy and I hadn't gone out when we did, no one would ever have known.'

'Shit.' What else could you say?

'A disaster like that ought to be impossible. We keep emergency supplies cached all around the base – food, clothing, radios. That was the first thing we looked for, even while the Platform was still burning. All gone. Anderson must have cleaned them out.'

'Survivors?'

'The Platform was burning so hot, you couldn't get within fifty feet of it. Fuel drums exploding, throwing off pieces of metal – rip your head off. One cut Kennedy's arm. No one could have survived.'

He stared at Franklin, like it was the most important thing in the world.

'No one could have survived.'

'Got it.'

'I don't know what bad things you've done in your life, Captain, but if you ever die and go to hell, it can't be worse than that. The Platform burning, the snow in the smoke. Me and Kennedy running around like chickens, digging up the caches, one after the next, finding everything gone. We must have spent a half-hour trying to get the snow-mobiles started before we figured out Anderson had taken out the spark plugs. At that point, we were pretty fucking sure we were gonna die. And not quick, like the others, but slow, hungry and cold.'

The space blanket crinkled and rustled.

'The weirdest thing was, it all happened in broad daylight. You think bad things happen at night, and maybe the sun'll come up and things'll get better. We didn't even have that.'

He took a cup of coffee that someone had poured him.

'Anderson came back with his Russian friends. A couple of snowmobiles – they must have stashed them someplace else. Looking for survivors, I guess. Me and Kennedy hid in the mag hut, only place that was intact.'

He stared into the cup of coffee. 'I thought we were dead when Anderson opened that door.'

'He found you?'

'If I hadn't busted my leg, I'd have launched myself at him. Instead, I just huddled in the corner. I swear he looked right at me.

'Then he went away. It's dark in there, and bright outside; maybe he didn't see. We heard some shots—'

'My crew found a shell casing.'

'Then there was some shouting. I don't know what that was about. After a while, I heard a snowmobile start up. I dragged myself to the door and peeked out, saw someone heading out on to the ice. Big guy.'

'Not Anderson? He's big.'

'Not like this guy. I don't know where Anderson had gone, couldn't see him. After that, nothing happened for a while. I almost went out, but I didn't like the fact I hadn't seen Anderson or Greta leave. And I was right. After an hour, something like that, I heard the Sno-Cat come back. Greta poked around a little – didn't find us – and then she rode off on the second snowmobile, following the tracks.'

'Any clue where they were going?'

'My guess? Evac. The Russians must have a ship someplace near here, maybe one of their nuclear-powered ice-breakers, and they'd gone to rendezvous with it.'

Franklin glanced at Santiago.

'Nothing on the instruments.'

'So you saw Greta and this other guy leave. How about Anderson?'

'Yeah.' Eastman scratched his beard. 'I thought about that a lot. Best I can come up with is he jumped on the snow-mobile somewhere I couldn't see him. I didn't exactly have a widescreen view, shitting my pants behind that door.'

'But you survived.'

'What saved us was their stupidity. The one thing they forgot. Went to all that trouble to sabotage the snowmobiles, then forgot they'd parked the Sno-Cat right in back of us. I mean, how stupid can you get. Not a lot of gas, but enough to run the heater a couple of times a day. And he'd left survival gear: food, sleeping bags, even a box of matches for the stove.

'We holed up in the cab and sat there right up until we heard your helicopter flying in.' He bared his teeth. 'You know how boring being terrified can get? If I ever play another hand of gin rummy, I'll slice my fucking wrists.'

A light blinked by the phone. Franklin let Santiago take it. When he turned around, he didn't look happy.

'XO says they finished searching the ship. No trace of Anderson.'

'That's impossible.'

'There's a mustang suit missing from the locker. Also, they found a rescue line tied off on the deck rail.'

Franklin got out of his chair and walked to the back of the wheelhouse. He looked out astern, at the blue scar the ship had left behind in the ice.

'What's our speed, Helmsman?'

'Four knots, sir.'

'Anyone here think a guy can jump off a moving vessel, surf a piece of broken ice and get on to the main pack without falling in?'

No one answered. Franklin found a pair of binoculars and looked through them. Staring at all that ice and cloud, you couldn't even be sure you had the focus right.

'Might be trying to fake us out,' Santiago suggested. 'Get us chasing ice while he sits tight in the lifeboat with a bottle of Scotch.'

'You think anyone on this ship would have missed an open bottle of Scotch?'

'You think we could have missed a guy built like a linebacker?'

'Look again.'

He sat back down, lost in thought. The phone rang. He snatched it before Santiago could pick it up.

'You got him?'

'It's the radio room, sir.'

'Go ahead.'

'The helo just called in. They found something on the ice.'

'Patch them through.'

A click, and the sound changed. Static, throbbing rotors, and the pilot's voice coming through the cold air.

'No sign of Anderson, but we got that radio beacon. Fifteen miles north of your position.'

'Is the ice stable? Are you able to land?'

'Yes, sir. We set down and had a look. Signal's coming from inside of a tent.'

'Anderson?' The minute he said it, he knew that couldn't be right. No way could he have gone that far across the ice so fast.

'I . . .' A flare of static. '. . . ought to come . . . see for yourself, Captain. And bring the Doc.'

Thirty-six

USCGC Terra Nova

The ice fled away below the helicopter – and however much they covered, there was always more. Hard to believe in global warming when you saw a sight like that, though Franklin had served on enough Arctic deployments that he wasn't fooled. Every year, a little less ice. A lot less, some years. If it kept up, the *Terra Nova* would be the last Coast Guard ship of her kind.

Out the window, a speck of colour broke the infinite whiteness. A drop in the ocean – but his eye picked it out. As the helicopter flew nearer, it separated in two, like an amoeba. A bright red Scott tent, pitched in the shadow of a huge ice ridge, and in front of it a black snowmobile.

'Hell of a place to go camping,' said Santiago.

The ice hardly stirred as the helicopter touched down. Concrete solid. Franklin remembered a class at the academy, some guy in World War Two who'd calculated how thick ice needed to be to hold a given weight. At two inches, it would hold a man; ten inches, a truck. What he was standing on now was probably a good couple of feet. Still.

The tent door opened and an ensign came out, waddling over the ice in his bulky mustang suit. They must all look like a group of old-school comic-book astronauts, Franklin thought. All they needed were the fishbowl helmets.

'Nothing's changed, sir.'

As they passed the snowmobiles, Franklin noticed someone had rubbed a hole in the frost that covered the gauges.

'Out of gas,' the ensign explained.

'Of all the luck,' said Santiago. 'There's a Mobil two miles up the road.'

They reached the tent and hesitated, unsure who should go first.

'Take a look,' the ensign said.

The first thing that hit Franklin when he crawled in was the colour. Soft, opium red after the whiteness outside. A survival bag lay on a mat on the floor, surrounded by candy-bar wrappers. Two heads stuck out, a man and a woman spooning side by side fully clothed, straining the close-fitting bag almost to breaking. A strand of blonde hair escaped from under the woman's hat; the man wore a beard that couldn't be much more than a week old.

'Are they . . . ?'

The ensign had stuck his head through the door behind him. 'Hanging in there. Passed out. I thought it was better to let them rest.' A sheepish look. 'In case, you know, they weren't happy to see us.'

Franklin fished out the battered sheet of paper and studied it. The photographs had never been great. Now, emailed, printed, handled and frozen, they looked more like master-pieces of impressionism. Even so.

'That's got to be Greta Nystrom.'

He looked at the man next to her. 'But there's no way that's Fridtjof Torell.'

He unzipped the sleeping bag. The man still wore his coat underneath, the white Zodiac Station insignia half covered by his arm. Above it, a name stitched into the Gore-Tex, dim in the tent's red gloom. *Anderson.*

A little dizzy, Franklin pulled apart the Velcro fastenings that held the coat together. No zip – it had broken. He opened the coat and reached inside to feel a pulse. Weak, but not gone yet.

As he pulled out his arm, he felt something hard on the inside of the coat. A notebook bulging out of the inside pocket. Two notebooks, in fact, a green one and a brown one, and an envelope sandwiched between them that dropped on to the tent floor when he pulled them out. Still sealed, addressed in the loopy writing kids use when they're trying hard.

He ducked out of the tent and showed it to Santiago. 'You believe this?'

Santiago read the address. 'Is that what this is about? Santa Claus?'

Franklin ripped a hole in the envelope, then paused, embarrassed. Santiago smirked at him.

'Worried the real Santa's gonna know you did a bad thing?'

Franklin slit it open with his finger and unfolded the letter inside. He read it quickly.

'Kid wants an Xbox game and a new bike. Must be British – he says "thank you" at the end.'

'Show it to Eastman?' Santiago suggested. 'Could be a Russian code.'

'You're a cynical bastard, Ops. No presents for you.'

'So my mom always told me.'

Putting the letter aside, Franklin gave Santiago the green notebook and took the brown one for himself. They flicked through.

'Get anything, Ops?'

'If I remember the eighth grade right, sir, I'd say this looks like science. Maybe we can have the geeks check that out.' Santiago looked at his captain. 'You OK, boss?'

Franklin was staring at the brown notebook as if he'd been hit with a two-by-four.

'A ham sandwich,' he murmured to himself.

'Come again, sir?'

He pulled his hood back, as if he needed more space around him. 'This one's some kind of journal.'

Phrases swam off the page.

Laid over in Tromsø – had a ham sandwich at the airport.

Quam calls me 'the new intruder'.

Why did Hagger bring me here?

If he reads this, he'll kill me.

'Did he write his name and phone number in the front?'

Franklin went back to the very beginning and read the first line.

For as long as I can remember, I've dreamed of the north.

Thirty-seven

It's not often you wake up to find you've been unconscious for two days. And survived a plane crash. And that someone wants to kill you.

I lay on the bed, staring at the grey ceiling, as pieces of memory fell into place. Each one was a minor revelation. I had no framework, no preconceptions at all. Just curiosity, like a tourist flipping through the guidebook of an unfamiliar city.

Heathrow Airport.

Zodiac Station.

Martin Hagger.

A crevasse.

The last piece I remembered was myself. Like looking up from the guidebook and finding the city all around you: suddenly, abstract facts meant something. I shuddered; I think I must have cried out loud in terror. It's a frightening thing, remembering who you are.

I touched my neck and felt hair, stubble grown just long enough to lose its abrasive edge. I touched my head and felt a bandage.

I heard a door click open, and twisted my head round to see. Which was a mistake: someone had left a red-hot coal in my skull that rocked around when I moved.

Through the tears, I saw a man walk in, wearing a grey polo neck and corduroy trousers.

Dr Kennedy, my mental guidebook informed me.

'How are we this morning?' He certainly talked like a doctor.

'Where am I?'

'Wednesday morning. And still at Zodiac.'

Zodiac. Lying on the ground, ice crystals cold against the back of my neck. Awash with pain. A figure standing over me. A rock raised to strike.

I rubbed the back of my head. Gingerly. 'I don't know . . .'

'Some short-term memory loss is quite normal,' he said. As if that was reassuring. 'It'll come back in time.'

Another piece of the jigsaw dropped into place – and another surge of panic. How could I have forgotten—

'I need to talk to Luke.' I struggled up, fighting the pain in my head. The clock on the wall said ten past ten. 'He'll be at school.'

'Greta's spoken to him,' Kennedy said. 'He knows you're OK.'

Greta. Another piece, though I couldn't fit it into the main picture straight away. I lay back while he fiddled around putting some pills in a cup. I took them gratefully with a glass of water. I hadn't realised how thirsty I was.

I caught him watching me. The panic tightened my chest. In that situation, you're so vulnerable: anyone could tell you anything.

'Do you remember the fall?' he asked.

All my memories felt fake, like slide pictures in one of those old plastic View-Master things, clicking round as you squeeze the button. *Click.* Standing on the ice, reading a notebook. *Click.* An explosion in my skull; sinking to my knees. *Click.* A man standing over me, so big he blotted out the sun. Arm raised. *Click.* Leaning forward, face buried in his hood, watching me. A start as if he recognised me.

Click. White light.

'I didn't fall,' I said. Experimentally, testing a hypothesis, but saying the words felt right. 'Someone came at me.'

He tried to tell me there hadn't been anyone else there except Annabel.

'She'd gone behind the rocks.' *I need a wee.* 'Someone hit me from behind.'

'You fell in a moulin,' he told me. But there was a long pause before he said it. He didn't look well. His face was grey; his hands were twitching.

'Someone hit me,' I repeated. Saying it again to affirm the memory. The View-Master slides had upgraded to video, strictly VHS, like the old tapes you find at the back of a cupboard. Skipping and jerking; bars of static raining down the screen.

Kennedy checked my pupils and tried to tell me it was all a dream. His face came so close, his beard rubbed my cheek as he peered into my eye. Shining the light through me, as if I was the View-Master and he could see the pictures inside. I could smell mouthwash on his breath.

'I found a notebook,' I remembered.

An unhappy look crossed Kennedy's face. As if there were things he didn't want me to remember. The panic inside me went up a notch. I wished I hadn't swallowed those pills quite so readily.

He went over to the side and opened a cabinet. I couldn't see him much – I didn't want to move my head again – but I had the sense he'd deliberately turned his back on me. There seemed to be a lot of fumbling going on inside the cabinet.

I heard it snap shut. Kennedy reappeared and handed me a green notebook. The moment I touched it, I remembered a bright cave, light so blue I wanted to drink it. A backpack inside.

On the inside cover, I read a handwritten sentence, all

capitalised. *SOME SAY THE WORLD WILL BEGIN IN FIRE, SOME SAY IN ICE.*

Robert Frost, my guidebook said. Strange, the things you remember.

I flipped through slowly. Pulling each page into focus hurt my head; trying to understand it was worse. As much as I knew anything for sure, it looked like a standard lab notebook. Lists of samples with places and dates, hand-drawn graphs and equations. And, not far in, a line that almost made me fall off the bed.

'"Fridge wants to kill me,"' I read aloud.

'A figure of speech.' Kennedy smacked his hand to his mouth and swallowed something. 'Martin did some work for DAR-X. Fridge thought that was sleeping with the enemy. Fridge is a bit of an eco-warrior,' he explained, in case I'd forgotten. Which I had.

'And what's "X"?' I asked. I saw it on every page: *Concentration of X, dispersal of X, flow of X.* The punctuation – sharp exclamation points, heavy question marks – emphasised his frustration.

'I was hoping you could tell me.' Kennedy glanced at the clock on the wall. 'If you're feeling up to it, see if you can make anything of the notebook while I have a look at Trond. Good to give your brain something to work on,' he added as he went out.

'Who's Trond?' I asked. But he'd already gone.

Greta came in. A second later, I realised I'd known her name without thinking about it. That felt like progress.

'You woke up.'

'I'm starting to wish I hadn't.'

'What do you remember?'

'I don't know how much there is to forget.'

'Do you remember the plane crash?'

269

'Very funny.'

'It's not a joke.' Briefly – she doesn't have any other way of talking – she told me how they'd loaded me on to the Twin Otter to fly me home, how it had turned around with mechanical problems, and how it had crash-landed. 'You were lucky you survived.'

'Jesus.' I lay down on the bed. Sweat soaked my cheeks.

'Kennedy said you spoke to Luke. To tell him what happened.'

'Somebody had to.'

'I'm glad you did.'

'He said he was staying with his aunt.'

She said it the way she said everything: every word a nail to be hammered in straight. But I heard the question. Or maybe I imagined it, from hearing it so often before.

'His mother's dead. In a plane crash, not long after he was born. That's why, when you told me about the plane . . .' I pulled up the sheet and wiped sweat off my face. 'Both parents – what kind of desperate coincidence would that be?' I forced myself to calm down. 'Anyway, I'm alive.'

'It sucks about your wife.'

Interesting reaction. 'Most people say they're sorry.'

'I'm sorry.'

She was teasing me, I think, but not unkindly.

'We'd already split up.' Three years from falling in love to divorce, via marriage, a baby, an affair and a scandal. And her PhD. We packed a lot in, in those days. We were young.

I looked at Greta for some sort of signal to go on. She was staring into space, face fixed in an expression of furious concentration.

With a shock, I remembered another piece of the puzzle. Her and Hagger. There was I, wallowing in pity for something that had happened seven years ago; her wounds were still wide open. She didn't want to hear about me.

270

Greta and Hagger. An image flashed through my mind: glass snapping, blood on my fingers. Greta had been there, I knew now. She'd said—

'Hagger's death wasn't an accident.'

She gave me a cool once-over. 'What do you think?'

'How about the plane crash?'

'They said it was the fuel tank.'

'And?'

'I filled the tank. It was fine.'

'You think someone was trying to cut us off? So no one could leave?'

'Or they didn't want you to make it.'

It was just as well I was lying down. Blood pounded in my skull, each spurt a jolt of pain. Strong enough to rupture the thin bone where I'd banged my head and spray all over the medical room's clean white walls.

'Someone at Zodiac?'

It was a silly question, and Greta's expression let me know it.

'Why would anyone want to kill me?' I ransacked my memories, pulling them out frantically like clothes from a cupboard and leaving them scattered over the floor. Nothing fitted. I looked at Greta. 'What have I forgotten?'

'What did you know?'

Not nearly enough. 'Was my bag on the plane?'

'It's in your room.'

I leaned up, wincing. 'Could you do me a favour? There should be a brown hardback notebook inside. Can you bring it?'

She came back two minutes later. As she handed me the notebook, an envelope tucked inside it fell out. It slid off the bed before I could grab it.

'I'll get that,' I said. But Greta had already bent down to pick it up. She read the address on the envelope and gave me a funny look.

'Aren't you too old to believe in Santa?'

I shrugged. 'A man's got to believe in something.'

I took the letter off her. *Father Christmas, The North Pole,* the address said.

'Luke gave it to me. I think he expects me to hand-deliver it.'

'We're five hundred miles from the pole.'

I pulled a face. 'Next you'll be saying Father Christmas doesn't exist.'

'Of course he does. But the elves drowned because of global warming.'

'Who's going to make the presents?'

Greta flicked back one of her braids. 'That's what happens when you fuck the planet. No presents.'

Abruptly, she checked her watch and headed for the door. No apology, no goodbye. That's Greta.

'Where do I start?' I asked.

She didn't stop, but she said something as she walked out. It sounded like, 'Trust no one.'

Thirty-eight

Kennedy came back.

'I've got to go up to Vitangelsk with Eastman,' he said. 'Can't be helped.' He got two pill containers out of a cabinet and put them on the side. 'Paracetamol. Take two every four hours to keep the pain away. And this one's diazepam. Memory loss, coming out of a coma, it can all be a bit stressful. If you feel panicky, diazepam will calm you down a treat. And don't overexert yourself,' he added.

'Next time, I'm going private,' I said. But he was out too quick to hear.

I picked up the pill jar and put it right against my eye. The plastic showed me a fisheyed, amber world. A dangerously distorted place.

The panic and the pain were almost unbearable. I twisted off the cap and looked down the barrel of the jar. Four white pills, lonely at the bottom. Obviously I wasn't the only one at Zodiac feeling stressed out.

Why would anyone want to kill me?

I hurled the jar away from me. It rolled across the benchtop, spilling a couple of the pills. Kennedy hadn't said anything about staying in bed. I got up, clenching my teeth against the pain, and went to my room to get dressed. One of the things I'd been happy to forget is how depressing that room is. I didn't stay longer than I had to. I went to the mess to get a cup of tea.

Mid-morning, Zodiac's a quiet place – like a resort hotel on the day the guests change over. I could hear Danny in the kitchen washing up, a stereo playing somewhere. Everyone else was in the field. I settled into a chair by the window with my journal and Hagger's lab book.

Someone said, I can't remember who, that everyone who keeps a journal secretly hopes someone else will read it. Like a murderer wanting the police to catch him – however much you pretend you're writing for you alone, your most intimate thoughts, you can't let go the hope that one day, someone will care and *know who you were*.

I never thought of my journal that way. I started it when Luke was small, because I was terrified at how much I was already forgetting. If I did think someone else might read it one day, I never imagined that the someone would be me. But there I was, reading through what I'd written, like a technician reloading data on to a computer that's crashed. It felt strange. Even things I'd written just a couple of days ago didn't feel like me any more. We put so much faith in words, but they're flimsy, inadequate things. Even what I'm writing right now, if I read it back next week, it won't seem the same.

But this morning, it was enough to jog a few memories. By the time I'd reread it, the only thing missing was an explanation.

Why did Hagger bring me here? I wrote that on Sunday. And, the question I hadn't written, but which might as well have been at the top of every page: *Why did he die?*

I put down my journal, grabbed myself another cup of tea and opened Hagger's notebook. Maybe that would have some answers.

I saw the quote on the inside cover again.

Some Say The World Began In Fire, Some Say In Ice.

I was pretty sure the quote was wrong. In the Robert Frost poem, the world's supposed to *end* in fire (or ice). His colleagues would say it was typical of Hagger's ego to rewrite a great poet, but I got the joke.

It's never easy reading someone else's lab book: it's much more private than a diary. After all, there's always a chance someone someday might be interested in the diary. Hagger's lab book was mostly an assortment of graphs and tables, like a PowerPoint presentation with the interesting bits cut out. No context, just lists of numbers that looked like sample labels to me, and probably like a phone directory to anyone else.

But even the numbers couldn't completely stifle Hagger's personality. He hung around in the margins and the blank spaces, shouting from the sidelines even after he was dead.

Where is it coming from?

Why Why Why? (Double underlined.)

Maybe Anderson?

And, a couple of pages in, the line I'd read in the sickbay. *Fridge will kill me.*

'Feeling better?'

You could have predicted who it would be. Fridge, still dressed in his ECW trousers. Not holding a fire axe or pointing a gun at me, just giving me his friendly Viking smile.

I remembered (or did I?) the man standing over me on the glacier. Fist raised to strike. Could it have been Fridge? He seemed familiar, but all my memories felt like half-truths that morning.

I snapped the notebook shut. Then I decided to go on the attack.

'There's something I'm trying to understand.' I opened the notebook again and spun it around so he could see.

The smile vanished. I looked him in the eye, trying to squeeze out the truth. Maybe I'm not much of an interrogator.

'I wish he hadn't written that.'

'It's awkward,' I agreed.

'Kennedy already asked me about this. I shared some

confidential results with Hagger; he got Quam on my ass saying I couldn't publish.'

I spun the notebook back so it faced me. Above the smoking-gun sentence was a table labelled *Me Concentrations, Echo Bay*.

'Methane,' I guessed. 'Something to do with the DAR-X drill site?'

Fridge didn't contradict me.

'Methane gets produced by the breakdown of oil in water.'

He gave me a grudging nod of respect. 'Can do. Or, hypothetically, if you're pretending to pump oil, but actually drilling for methane clathrates in the seabed.'

'Hypothetically?'

'Hypothetically unless you want to be sued for violating commercial secrecy.'

'Was Hagger's work commercially secret?'

Fridge shook his head wearily. 'He didn't even care about the methane. He just found it out by accident.'

'What was he looking for?'

'Bugs,' said Fridge. 'Bugs in the water. Something corroding DAR-X's pipes. Hagger found a bug in the water munching them.'

'What sort of bugs?'

He shrugged. 'You should talk to K-Mart.'

I looked out the windows, confused. 'Where's K-Mart?'

'The guy you replaced, Hagger's old assistant. Kevin Maart, so we called him K-Mart. He must have helped Hagger.'

The room was filling up with students drifting in for lunch. I could smell lasagne, and I was ravenous.

Fridge gave an odd laugh. 'But maybe K-Mart didn't know anything. If he had, Hagger wouldn't have brought you.'

I ate quickly and messily. It's hard to linger over a meal when you're staring round the room wondering if someone could really want to kill you. Hard to keep the soup on your spoon if your hand won't stop trembling.

Afterwards, I stopped off in Quam's office and asked him if he knew how I could contact Kevin Maart.

'I can't tell you that.' Every time he speaks, he makes you feel you've done something wrong. 'Data protection.'

I told him I just wanted to check out a couple of things that Hagger had been working on. That seemed to upset him even more. He set his perpetual-motion toy going, staring at it as if he could glimpse something profound in the spaces between the swinging balls.

'You're supposed to rest. If it weren't for these . . .' *click* '. . . regrettable . . .' *clack* '. . . circumstances, you wouldn't even be here.'

'I thought I might make myself useful.'

'Don't. Just . . .' *click* '. . . keep out of trouble.'

There were a lot of things I'd have liked to ask him. Like: *Who killed Hagger?* Or, given how fidgety Hagger's research made him: *What happened to his notebooks?* But I didn't think bringing any of that up would count as keeping out of trouble.

'Did you ever set me up a login account on the network?' I asked.

His eyes narrowed, as if I'd asked for his PIN. 'Didn't get round to it.' He was trying to sound casual, though that was a stretch. 'Now you're leaving, you don't need it.'

'I'll be around for a few days yet.'

He acted as if he hadn't heard me. 'How's your head?'

'Better, thanks,' I said, through gritted teeth. 'But about the login account . . .' I relaxed into the chair with an appreciative sigh. The sound of a man who might be there some time. Quam took the hint. He got a piece of paper from his desk and slid it across to me.

'Fill this in and get it back to me.'

★   ★   ★

277

Quam's martinet routine annoyed me – especially as data protection's a rather anachronistic concept these days, given what governments get up to. I went to the radio room, logged in to the guest computer and googled Kevin Maart. I found his home page at Cambridge, his publications record. Rather more impressive than mine, to be honest: if we ever run into each other, I'd be embarrassed to say I took his job. It also gave a phone number, and an email address: kevin.maart@ zodiacstation.org.uk.

He wouldn't be checking that any time soon. Obviously he hadn't updated it yet. I wrote an email anyway, just in case. It amused me to think of it travelling halfway around the world, and pinging into the room next door.

I took one of the Iridium phones from the charging shelf and rang the number on the website. Quam would hit the roof, no doubt, at the cost of it.

A receptionist answered. 'Kevin Maart's away in the field,' she told me.

'He flew home a week ago.'

'He hasn't been back in the office.'

Strike two. I asked if she had a mobile number for him. Perhaps she did, but of course, she couldn't give that out. Data protection.

I took the notebook back to Hagger's lab to see if I could make more sense of it in context. I looked in the fridge and found the samples he'd left there: forty-three of them, clear plastic bags filled with water, each numbered and dated with a white sticky label. Also, I noticed, each one had a round dot coloured in on the label, either red or green.

I turned through the notebook until I found a list of samples whose reference numbers matched the bags. Beside each one, he'd written down where he'd taken it. *Helbreen. Helbreensfjord. Echo Bay. Nansen Bay. Luciafjord. Konigsfjord.*

Some of those places I knew; most of them I didn't. I went to the bookshelves in the mess and rummaged through the thrillers and potboilers until I found a survey map of Utgard. I spread it out on Hagger's lab table. It had been made in the sixties, but I didn't suppose Utgard had changed much. I worked my way over it, marking the location of each of Hagger's samples with pencil X's. It reminded me of being home with Luke, drawing treasure maps together.

As soon as I'd finished, it was easy to see where Hagger had been. A row of X's ran down the west side of the island, with a cluster in Echo Bay and another up at the Helbreensfjord, where the glacier met the sea. More sporadic samples made a dotted line along the coast, north to the tip of the island, and as far south as Zodiac, where they grouped in another cluster. A single spur branched off up the Helbreen glacier, regularly spaced X's until they reached more or less the place where Hagger had died, with a couple more on the other side of the mountain, near a place labelled Mine 8.

I found green and red marker pens in one of Hagger's drawers. Cross-referencing the samples and the notebook, I circled my X's on the map red or green, whichever colour Hagger had marked the bags. I also wrote in the dates. Then I stood back and examined my work.

The red circles made a bone shape, with clusters at Echo Bay and at Helbreensfjord, and a thinner stretch along the stretch of coast connecting them. North of the line, and south down to Zodiac, they turned green.

He'd been sampling for something in the ice, or the seawater beneath. From the numbers in the lab book, it looked as though red meant positive and green meant negative. Transferred to the map, that meant that the substance appeared in the water either at Echo Bay or at the Helbreen, flowed along the coast, then vanished.

It might have been flowing in from the glacier's run-off.

But all the circles on the Helbreen were green. Could it be something the oil company was emitting from Echo Bay?

I studied the dates next to the circles. He'd started last October near Zodiac, taking samples along the shore and out in the fjord. All green. November, December, January: he hadn't gone far, but he'd stuck at it, picking up a couple of samples every week. What drove him? He didn't have to be here. Why suffer months of darkness and freezing temperatures when he could have been at home in Cambridge sipping port in the SCR? Tracing my finger over the samples, I could almost feel his frustration as January slipped into February and everything stayed green. The samples became less frequent.

Then, in the middle of March, he suddenly turned up in Echo Bay. Nine samples that week alone, all ringed bright red. Nothing the next week; then the samples started marching north along the coast until they reached the tip of the island, where they went green again.

Whatever was in the water, he'd tracked it from Echo Bay to the Helbreen. Overshot, then circled back the next week to take a dozen more samples at the mouth of the glacier. All red. The week after, he carried on up the Helbreen, almost to its head on the big ice dome. Green again. The week before I arrived, said the dates. The week before he died.

'And what did he find in the water?' I asked the map.

My head was hurting. I went to the medical room and took two of Kennedy's paracetamol. Then I stared at the map some more. Inevitably, I found myself focusing on Echo Bay.

The notebook didn't give any clues to what Hagger had found in the water. The ubiquitous X, but he never named it. After my chat with Fridge, methane was an obvious candidate. But I'd read all the way through the lab book: apart from Echo Bay, he'd never tested any of the other samples for methane. And if that was it, he'd have labelled it for what it was.

I had the samples; I could always test them myself. But there are a million ways to test a water sample. Spectral analysis, gas chromatography, chemical analysis, DNA tests . . . You have to have some idea what you're looking for. Otherwise, it's needle-and-haystack territory.

But I did have one idea. Hagger found some bug in the water munching on DAR-X's pipes, Fridge had said. And bugs aren't that hard to find. Not if you have an electron microscope sitting on the bench.

I took some water from the Echo Bay sample and strained it through a polycarbonate filter, then stained the residue with fluorescamine dye. The fact that Hagger had all the equipment to hand gave me confidence. Then I popped the sample under the microscope.

A mass of blurry chaos appeared when I put my eye to the microscope, like snow on a television set. I turned the knob and it came into focus. That hardly changed the picture. That single drop was full of life: scores, if not hundreds of tiny organisms, twitching and swarming. Even under magnification, they didn't look much clearer than grains of rice.

Back home, I could have extracted DNA to find out what they were. Here, I didn't have that option. From the notebook, it looked as though Hagger had – he must have sent it back to the UK – but the tests hadn't been conclusive. In his notes, he referred to the organisms as *Gelidibacter incognita*.

A quick lit search confirmed that *Gelidibacter* is a genus of bacteria that grows in ice and cold water; the *incognita*, I presumed, was for this unknown species. Why Hagger should have been so excited about it, I can't guess. Even if it's never been described before, it's not exactly a new flavour of Coke he discovered. Dip a bucket in your local pond and you'll probably find an uncategorised bacterium if you look hard enough.

I spent a couple of hours working with the microscope, checking each sample. Simple, repetitive work: exactly what I'd come here to escape from. Back home, I'd be checking the clock, looking forward to getting out to collect Luke from school. Now, I was happy to lose myself in it. It distracted me from the thought that someone might want to kill me.

At the end of it, I had some pretty conclusive results. The twelve samples from Echo Bay all contained the bugs. None of the others did, not even the ones from the Helbreensfjord. Whatever red meant, it wasn't that.

That's the bit I hate about science. You have a lovely hypothesis, so self-evident you know it must be true. And then it isn't.

Thirty-nine

Anderson's Journal – Wednesday

I filled in Quam's form for the network account. There was a long section on how to choose a secure password: between nine and fourteen characters, containing two numbers and a capital letter (but no punctuation); not a recognisable word, certainly not a significant date. An acronym for a memorable sentence, suitably jazzed up with said aforementioned capitals and numbers, would be advisable. Writing that must have warmed his bureaucratic heart. Complete with the absurdity that after you'd ticked all those boxes, plus the one that said you would never divulge the password to anyone or write it down anywhere under any circumstances, you wrote it down on a piece of paper and gave it to Quam.

He wasn't in his office, so I left it on his desk. Folded three times, with *CONFIDENTIAL* scrawled over it. I didn't suppose he'd notice the irony.

It occurred to me he must know Hagger's password, too. No point asking him: I could imagine the delight he'd take in preaching the gospel of data protection all over again. I thought about rummaging through his desk – surely he'd keep it on file. But footsteps in the hall made me think better of it.

I went to my room and lay on my bunk, more to avoid the pain in my head than because I was tired. It was hard to believe I'd slept for three days. Without Kennedy's sedative, my mind wouldn't shut up. Graphs and numbers floated in front of my eyes, even when I closed them. All scientists have a stubborn streak: we have to put the jigsaw together. Louise used to say that on a bad day, we're all borderline Asperger's.

Thinking of Louise reminded me how much I missed Luke. I went back to the radio room and tried to Skype him.

'He's playing with a friend,' Lorna said.

'Is he OK?'

'Not really. I promised you'd buy him a mountain bike when you get back.'

She asked me how I was, about the fall and the crash, but I didn't want to talk about it. Didn't have anything to say. It's hard to explain you've been in a plane crash that was a total non-event.

'Don't forget to post his letter,' she said at the end. 'He keeps asking about it.'

The air in the radio room was stale, and I hadn't been outside (conscious) in three days. I dressed up in my ECW gear, zipped the letter in the inside pocket and headed for the door. On the way, I ran into Fridge. Apparently, high winds at Vitangelsk meant that Kennedy and Eastman couldn't get back tonight.

'Eastman said Doc got chased by a polar bear,' Fridge told me. I laughed, then realised it was no joke.

'I'd better take a rifle.'

I'd been desperate to leave the Platform. But as soon as I was outside, all I wanted was to scuttle back in again, like Plato's prisoner who can't stand the light outside of the cave. On the Platform, I could hide from the danger I felt around me. Out here, I was a butterfly on a card. Not forgetting the cold. I'd forgotten how bad it is: my eyes watered, my nose pinched tight. The pain in the back of my head spread all over.

284

My plan was to get on to the fjord and bury the letter, persuade myself that the current might carry it up to the North Pole one day. That's what I could tell Luke, anyway. Under the snow, I barely noticed the shoreline, but I felt the change underfoot. Hard sea ice, scoured by the wind. Walking across it was like walking across a desert, so wide and flat it makes you dizzy. Mountains framed the fjord on either side, but straight ahead there was nothing except a shimmering line between sky-blue ice and ice-blue sky. And, at the join, a dark figure, a nomad on the horizon.

What if it's him? screamed the danger signal in my head. I couldn't tell who it was, no more detail than a Lowry man, but that didn't get in the way of a good old-fashioned panic. Whoever pushed Hagger over the crevasse, whoever stole the notebooks, whoever hit me over the head and sabotaged the plane: what if it was him?

I almost ran back. Then I got a grip on myself. I shifted the rifle on my shoulder, angled so it was pointing almost ahead, and carried on.

It seemed to take for ever to reach him. Out there, you lose all sense of distance. He was standing very still, staring across to the far side of the fjord with a pair of binoculars. A neat round hole punctured the ice by his feet. Blood smeared the ice around it.

'Fishing?' I asked, pointing at the hole.

Ash turned abruptly. 'It's you,' he said, as if I'd done something wrong. 'I thought you were blotto.'

'I've woken up.'

'Hah.' He turned back to his binoculars. I tried to follow his gaze. All I saw was snow.

'Is there anything out there?'

'Bear.' Manners overtook him; he handed me the binoculars. 'Just to the right of that big boulder.'

A shiver went through me as I put the binoculars to my

eyes, though I still couldn't see it. All the training, all the warnings and briefings, they'd never sunk in to the point I really believed they were real. Now it was out there, a few hundred yards away.

Ash guided my arm until I was pointing in the right direction. Even with the binoculars, I had to look hard to make out his features: the black nose, the legs with their awkward, lumbering gait.

'It's a big one,' said Ash.

Whether the bear caught my scent, or a movement, or a glint from the binoculars, I don't know. But he stopped, turned his head and stared straight at me. Another shiver. Suddenly, half a mile didn't seem nearly far enough.

I was glad I'd remembered to bring a rifle, and said so. Ash shuddered as if I'd stepped on his grave. Having devoted his life to the bears, I suppose the thought of shooting one was abhorrent.

'My first bear,' I said.

'You're lucky. Don't get many down here these days.'

I wasn't surprised. I'd seen the pictures in the *Guardian*, bear cubs marooned on shrinking ice floes waiting to drown.

'I wonder if there'll be any left at all by the time my son grows up.'

'That's the paradox,' said Ash. 'Sea ice is melting faster than ever, earth's boiling like a kettle, but here on Utgard the bears are thriving.'

'I thought you said you don't see them much any more.'

'We don't see them *here* – because they've all gone north. The seal population up in the north-west has exploded in the last couple of years. I haven't seen them this healthy in twenty years. And where the seals go, the bears follow.'

'Why would that be?' I wondered aloud.

Ash shrugged. 'My theory? There's a current that comes down the west coast. I think that's warming, so everything in

286

the food chain, from krill to seals, is thriving. Eventually, it'll kill them if they can't adapt. But for the moment, they're in clover.'

I thought of the micro-organisms teeming in the samples from Echo Bay. I thought of the neat row of red-ringed X's flowing along the west coast on my map, until they stopped in Echo Bay.

'We're on the west coast,' I pointed out. 'Shouldn't the current bring them here, too?'

With the toe of his boot, Ash scraped a rough egg shape in the snow. 'That's Utgard.' He made a mark in the bottom, and another halfway up the left-hand side. 'Zodiac. Echo Bay.' Digging in his heel, he drew a line that started just above the top of the egg, ran along the left side as far as Echo Bay, then spun away at a right angle.

'The Stokke current. It—' He broke off as he realised I was laughing. I couldn't help it. 'What?'

'Stokke's a make of pram.' I remembered the yummy mummies at the baby groups when Luke was small, swapping notes on their state-of-the-art baby kit. Space-age designs that looked nothing like Luke's third-hand relic. I'd hung around on the fringes, the only father there, like the shy boy at a school disco.

'This Stokke was a polar explorer. Anyway, the current brings cold water down from the far north. But at Echo Bay, it meets the very tail end of the Gulf Stream coming up from the south and gets deflected out west, towards Greenland. That's why it doesn't reach here.'

I stared at the diagram he'd drawn. It was crude, but I'd spent so long looking at the map in Hagger's lab I could visualise it easily.

'So this current goes past the Helbreensfjord.'

'That's right. In summer, ice from the Helbreen calves off and floats down to Echo Bay. Played havoc with the rig there last year, I heard.'

He took the binoculars back off me and scanned the horizon.

'He's gone. Let's go in.'

We trudged back over the flat, frozen fjord. Across the ice, Zodiac looked a long way away, a Matchbox model dwarfed by the mountains.

Two Englishmen, even in a frozen wilderness at the end of the earth, will always end up talking about the weather.

'Nice day,' said Ash. And it was. White snow, blue sky and pure light crystallising everything.

'Hard to believe Eastman and Kennedy are trapped in Vitangelsk by the wind,' I said.

Ash gave me a look. 'I didn't know they'd gone up there.'

He sounded unhappy about it.

'They radioed in. Apparently, they found a bear.'

I couldn't see his face, between the hood and the beard and the icicles hanging off his eyebrows, but he seemed to tighten up at the news.

'A bear? At Vitangelsk?'

'I thought you'd be interested.'

We carried on, two lone figures on a crystal plain. I glanced back one more time, in case the bear had decided to follow us, but of course I couldn't see him.

When I got back to the Platform, I realised I'd forgotten to post Luke's letter.

Forty

Anderson's Journal – Thursday

Woken at 4 a.m. by footsteps in the corridor. I lay in bed, wishing there were locks on the doors. Wishing I'd borrowed one of the rifles from the rack. Being trapped at Zodiac with someone who might want to kill me is bad enough. The fact that he's got full access to a well-stocked gun cabinet at the end of the hall terrifies me.

The footsteps passed my room and headed towards the front door. Towards the gun rack. I heard the boot-room door squeak open – but not shut. He was trying not to wake anybody. Maybe he didn't want to make himself unpopular.

I slipped out of my bunk and poked my head round the door. Moving suddenly, in case anyone was there.

The corridor was empty, the boot-room door shut.

I walked to the end of the corridor. Zodiac at 4 a.m.'s a ghostly place: full daylight leaching through the windows, but not a soul to be seen. As if the aliens came and abducted everyone except you. The only sound was a soft wind sighing through the aerials on the roof. It seemed to have risen since yesterday evening.

Just as I got to the boot room, the outer door closed with an unmistakable thud, and the click of the latch. I heard footsteps descending the metal stairs outside.

I checked the rack on the wall. All the guns were there.

The snarl of the engine broke the silence so suddenly I

jumped. The sound of a cold snowmobile being pulled to life. Once, twice, and then the steady roar of the running engine.

I hurried through the boot room and opened the main door. The cold hit me like a concrete wall and made my eyes water. Through the tears, I saw a red brake light disappearing off towards the Lucia glacier, a dark figure hunched over the controls. With his back to me, wrapped up in the snowmobile suit and helmet, he could have been my twin brother and I wouldn't have recognised him.

I retreated inside before the cold killed me, telling myself it was probably nothing. One of the students who'd drawn the short straw, checking some remote set of frozen instruments. I'd ask at breakfast and—

At the far end of the corridor, near the mess, a door opened. Someone stepped out, checking the corridor both ways as if he was crossing a road. No time for me to hide.

He approached. I tensed, full fight-or-flight mode, but it was only Quam. Not sure why I say 'only' – being base commander didn't put him above suspicion.

'Early to be up,' he said, in the sort of too friendly voice headmasters use just before they reach for the cane.

'I needed the loo.'

He nodded, and didn't ask why I hadn't used the toilet opposite my room.

'Head OK?'

'Better, thanks.'

'Good.'

He seemed nervous, shifting on his feet, drumming his fingers in mid-air. Like a man with something on his mind. Maybe a guilty secret.

Suddenly, I really didn't want to be alone in that long, long corridor with him. I stared at the rows of doors, willing someone to come out. I tried to step past him, muttering about getting back to bed. Quam shifted his weight a little, not so much as to be obvious, but enough to block my way.

'You've got a son, it says on your file.'

'Luke. He's eight.'

'You must miss him.'

I nodded, and balled my fists. Maybe it was paranoia, but I couldn't get it out of my head he was making a threat.

Maybe not. 'I've got two daughters,' he said. 'I don't see them often.'

'It's a long way,' I sympathised.

'We come out here, we fight every day. Do you ever wonder if it's worth it?'

'It's science, I suppose.'

'You haven't been here long.' His chin jerked up; he looked at me as if he'd only just noticed me. 'Still, you know what we have in common?'

'Insomnia?'

'This island's trying to kill both of us.'

There's not much I could say to that. 'I'd better get some sleep.'

He shook his head, as if he'd been thinking about something quite different. 'Of course.'

A gust of wind shook the Platform. Quam pressed his hand against the wall, bracing himself. 'Wind's getting up. There's a storm coming.'

'You're blocking my way,' I said politely.

Greta came to the lab after breakfast. She was carrying one of the heavy red ECW coats in her arms.

'Going out?'

She unfolded it and held it up so I could see. On the left breast, above the Zodiac badge, she'd embroidered my name. For a woman who spends her life welding snow-mobiles and shovelling snow, she does a surprisingly dainty stitch.

'You shouldn't have.'

'Now we own you.'

I put it on. I stroked my fingertip over the corrugations of the thread. I suppose she did it for everyone; probably, it was just one more job ticked off on a list. But I felt ridiculously grateful, almost weepy. As if I belonged.

'I might not be around long enough to make use of it.'

She didn't comment one way or the other.

Wearing that coat indoors, I'd already started to sweat. I stuck my hands in the pockets. Deep and padded, but I felt something hard at the bottom. I pulled it out. A teddy bear in a grubby I ♥ NY T-shirt, with a ring in its head and a key.

'You found it. By the crevasse,' she reminded me.

'Did I find out what it opens?'

'There aren't any locks on Utgard.'

The conversation came back. Me: *It must have fallen out of Martin's pocket.*

And Greta, pointing to the footprints that had chased Hagger to the brink. *Or maybe his.*

I put it on the bench to think about.

Later

Eastman and Kennedy are back from Vitangelsk. After being in a coma for two days, it's good to have a doctor around. Both of them dropped in to see me, either side of a rather contentious staff meeting.

Kennedy came first. I was already up and poking around the lab. He asked how I was, though I could as easily have asked him. He looked terrible. Raccoon rings round his eyes, hair askew (not that any of us looked like much), and his face that shade of grey T-shirts go when they've been through the wash too often.

'Rough night?' I asked as he shone a torch in my eyes. 'The bear must have been quite a shock.'

He almost took my eye out with the torch. 'The bear?' he repeated, as if it was something I wasn't supposed to know.

'I heard you had a close encounter with a polar bear yesterday.'

'That.' He nodded, as if he'd only just remembered. I wouldn't have thought it was the sort of thing you forgot so quickly. 'Yes.'

He made me stand on one leg, touch my toes, count backwards from thirteen.

'Keeping busy?' he said, pointing to the map I'd left out on the table.

'Trying to tidy up some of Hagger's loose ends.' He'd seen the cluster of X's at Echo Bay; there was no point trying to hide it.

'I thought Anderson's last assistant might be able to fill me in. Kevin Maart.'

'K-Mart.' Kennedy chuckled. 'South African, mad as pants. He used to wander around the Platform in his flip-flops. Hated the cold.'

'I heard he left because of a wisdom tooth.'

Kennedy fiddled with a pen. 'That's right.'

'Quam won't give me his email address. I thought maybe you might have contact information. For emergencies, or whatever.' I gave him a smile, to show I didn't mean to impose. Kennedy didn't return it.

'I'll see what I can do,' he said. And left quickly.

★   ★   ★

I went back to the map and pencilled in a line that charted the current Ash had told me about. Where the current flowed on the west coast, between the Helbreensfjord and Echo Bay, the whole food chain was exploding, Ash said. But these little creatures, *Gelidibacter incognita*, were localised in Echo Bay.

I flipped through the notebook until I found a graph labelled 'Propagation rates – Echo Bay'. It wasn't hard to interpret: it swung up like a ski jump. Whatever was propagating, they were breeding like rabbits. I assumed it was the microorganisms I'd seen under the microscope.

But the bugs weren't in the upstream samples. That meant they weren't floating down from anywhere: they were growing in Echo Bay.

Why?

Not my question: Hagger's. Scrawled under the chart, heavily underscored.

I tried to think logically about what Hagger would have done. I stared at the graph. The time series across the bottom was measured in hours – terrifyingly fast.

I flipped over the page. On the back were two more graphs. One was a copy of the previous page, the vertiginous swoop up as the bugs replicated like crazy. But underneath, a second graph on the same scale painted a different picture: just a flat line across the page tapering towards zero.

Sometimes they thrived, sometimes they died.

The two charts were labelled X-positive and X-negative.

What is X?

Again, Hagger's question. I didn't know either. It must have something to do with the red and green dots on the samples.

I found two clean beakers and set them up on the bench. One, I filled with 100ml of water, a red sample from the

Helbreensfjord. The other, I filled with the same amount of water from a green Zodiac sample.

After a moment's thought, I found a third beaker and filled it with tap water, as a control. I sterilised a pipette and took three 10ml extracts from one of the Echo Bay samples. I squirted them out, one for each beaker, and stirred them up.

Another thought. I looked at the sample bags, thinking hard. The ones I'd used for the beakers were already half empty – if I did it again, there'd be none left for future experiments. I dithered for a moment. Using it all up felt like stealing from a dead man.

Hagger's gone, I told myself. If he was lucky, he'd get a small plaque in the mess, maybe a photograph on the wall with the other ghosts. The samples would get tipped down the sink if I didn't use them.

I emptied the two bags and repeated the experiment – three beakers, three samples, 10ml of Echo Bay water in each – but this time I cut three pieces off one of the pipes, and dropped them in. They bobbed about on the surface, like the last remnants of a shipwreck.

The voice over my shoulder made me jump. '*All staff, please report to the mess for an urgent briefing.*'

The gist of the meeting was that everyone's confined to base. Quam blamed the inevitable Health and Safety. It's fair to say the staff aren't happy: Eastman, in particular, gave Quam a hard time. I slouched in my seat and tried not to get blamed.

Afterwards, Eastman came to visit me. No particular reason; I wonder what he wanted to know. I don't trust him. If I had to pick anyone at Zodiac who I thought might be capable of murder, it would be him. Superficially, he's got that all-American charm: energetic, engaging and very good teeth. But if you look at the eyes, there's something dead, as if there's a small man inside his head pulling levers to operate the smile.

He asked how I was doing. It's getting tedious answering that question – I feel like an elderly aunt who's had a fall. I suppose I should be grateful for the sympathy. Then he asked about my work. Flipped through the notebook, which I didn't like, and found the sheet of paper that nearly killed me chasing after it in the wind. The one with the strange noughts, ones and twos.

'It's mine,' Eastman said.

That was news. But he didn't know any more than that; it's just some piece of radio garbage he picked up interfering with the instruments. Nothing to do with anything Hagger was working on.

'Nothing about DAR-X in the notebook?'

I told him that Hagger had taken some samples at Echo Bay.

'He ever do any work at Vitangelsk?'

'Not that I know of.'

'How about that key?'

Eastman's like that: always moving on. I'm sure when he was a kid they stuffed him full of Ritalin. I told him how I'd found the key at the crevasse, not mentioning Greta's theory that it came from Hagger's killer. He made a joke about Hagger's liquor cabinet, which I laughed at dutifully, but I didn't like the way he looked at the key. I'd have locked it away if I could – but, of course, I couldn't. Ironic. I hid it as best I could in a drawer full of lab equipment as soon as he'd gone. Then I took a sample from each of my beakers, strained them and stained them and put them under the microscope.

The green sample and tap water showed no change. But in the red sample – and especially the red sample with the piece of pipe – you could see even without counting that there were more bugs in the water than there were two hours ago.

I looked at the graph in Hagger's notebook again. Apparently, this should be just the beginning.

Forty-one

I'm writing this by torchlight, burrowed down in my sleeping bag like a boy reading past his bedtime. Except it's not kids' games any more. There's a storm raging outside so fierce it ripped off the anemometer; I think our communications dish has gone too. It sounds as though the whole Platform might blow away.

I'm not on the Platform. I've shut myself in the caboose they call Star Command. It sounds melodramatic, but I can't take any more risks.

Another gust of wind. The caboose is one of those round domes, like a diver's helmet; it's anchored into the ice, so it ought to be secure. But that wind . . . I can imagine it picking up the whole island and dropping us somewhere in Mongolia.

The key was gone this morning. I suspect Eastman, from the way he was looking at it yesterday. A horrible thought: what if it's his? What if he was the one who dropped it by the crevasse? Maybe he came back for it Monday afternoon, and hit me on the head while Annabel's back was turned?

I went to confront him, but I couldn't find him anywhere, even with everyone confined to base. I asked Quam, who said he hadn't seen him. He wouldn't meet my eye as he said it.

First the notebooks, now the key. Whatever Hagger was on to, someone at Zodiac is after it.

But they didn't touch the samples. I know, because I shut them in the fumes cupboard, with a strand of hair jammed in the door that would fall out if anyone opened it. Silly stuff I got from a spy novel. Hard to believe it's real life.

First thing this morning, I got out the beakers and examined them. Even without the microscope, the results were startling. In the green samples and the tap water, no change. But the red sample without the pipe was cloudy, and the one with the pipe in it looked like milk of magnesia.

I lifted out the pipe fragment with a pair of tweezers. The yellow plastic had turned brown, the smooth surface pitted and eroded. The sides were smeared with a translucent white sludge that, under the microscope, turned into a writhing mass of tiny worms, feasting on the pipe like maggots on old meat.

I put it back in the beaker so they could continue their meal in peace.

'Bon appétit,' I said to them.

'Talking to your experiments is the second sign of madness,' said Greta behind me. I jumped.

'What's the first?'

She snorted, as if it was obvious. 'Coming to Zodiac.'

She glanced at the row of beakers, but didn't ask what I was doing.

'I think I've made a breakthrough,' I told her.

She didn't look impressed.

'DAR-X were having a problem with corrosion on their pipes. Martin went to Echo Bay to take a look, as a favour.' I slipped the sample under the microscope and beckoned her over. 'See what he found?'

She bent over it stiffly, like someone peering over the edge of a cliff.

'Worms.'

'Micro-organisms, feeding on the pipes from the drill rig.

Methane was seeping out; that's why Fridge got abnormal readings. But Martin wasn't interested in the bugs. He wanted to know why they were growing there.'

She looked up from the microscope.

'Can bugs really eat plastic?'

I nodded. 'You've seen plastic burn? As a rule of thumb, anything that burns has energy in it, and plastic is incredibly rich. It's made from petroleum, after all. These bacteria can metabolise that into food energy.'

'Smart.'

'But there's something else in the water, something helping them reproduce.' I paused. 'Something that's making all the sea life on that coast explode, from plankton to polar bears.'

'So what is it?'

I deflated. 'I don't know. I don't even know where it came from. It just pops up in the Helbreensfjord, as if by magic, then floats away on the Stokke current.'

'The glacier?'

'That would be the obvious candidate. But Martin tested it from top to bottom and couldn't find a trace.' I thought of all the green-ringed X's on the map. 'That's what he was doing the day he died.'

'Did he know what it was?'

I spread the notebook open on the bench and turned through it. 'I think so. Look here.'

It was one of the last pages he'd written on. Another list of the samples (I know the references by heart, now) – with a set of numbers against each one.

'What does "ppm" mean?' Greta asked, reading one of the headings.

'Parts per million. It's a measurement of concentration.'

She pointed to the numbers. 'Is it a lot?'

'Depends on what it's referring to. If you're talking nitric acid, twenty-five parts per million is bad news. Something like ammonia, two or three hundred wouldn't do you much harm.'

(The values Hagger got fluctuate, but for the red samples they mostly sit in the high hundreds. In the green samples, next to nothing.)

'If he knew the measurements, he must have known what he was measuring.' I waved my hand around the room. 'The thing is, I can't work out how he did it. To test that many samples he'd have needed chemicals, titration equipment, maybe a mass spectrometer.' Even knowing what he used would give me a clue what he was looking for. 'There's nothing like that here.'

After a moment, I realised Greta had gone quiet. I mean, she's never exactly forthcoming, but this was a more deliberate silence. Provocative, almost.

'What?'

'I know where Martin kept his equipment.'

A shadow went through me when I saw the crucified Buzz Lightyear toy nailed over the door of the caboose they call Star Command. Luke has one just like it. But I forgot it the moment I stepped through the door.

There was a mattress on the floor, raised off the ground on a couple of pallets. Two sleeping bags zipped together on top of it. Most of the rest of the room was taken up with a table, and the three machines on it. They didn't look much different from desktop printers, or maybe a fancy water cooler. One was a mass spectrometer. One was a thermal cycler for replicating DNA. The third was a DNA sequencer. Hagger's usual mess filled in the gaps: test tubes, spare nozzles, used chemical hand warmers that looked like teabags, and half a dozen empty plastic bottles.

'Why didn't you tell me about this before?'

Greta gave me a hard look. I glanced at the mattress again,

with its double sleeping bag and twin pillows. The caboose would be a cold place to sleep; you'd freeze if you tried to undress. But maybe two people could warm it up a bit. If they wanted some privacy.

That wasn't my business. 'Do you know what Hagger was doing here? With the instruments?'

'We didn't talk much about work.'

It took an effort of will not to look at the bed again.

'That's a DNA sequencer,' I said, in the too loud voice of an embarrassed Englishman. 'He must have been trying to sequence that little worm he found eating DAR-X's pipes.'

Greta gave the sequencer a once-over, with the practical eye of a mechanic. I got the feeling she was wondering how it would come apart.

'I thought he was a chemist.'

'Biochemist,' I corrected. 'Sort of both.' I wondered how much she knew. 'Martin worked at the boundary of biology and chemistry. What he was interested in, what made him famous, was his work on the origins of life question.'

'OK.'

'Maybe you've heard of the idea that life evolved in the tropics, in nutrient-rich pools. You've heard the phrase "primordial soup"?'

If she had, she was giving nothing away.

'Martin didn't agree with that. He used to say that putting all the ingredients in the bowl doesn't make a soup. Someone has to stir it. He believed that the cycles of the Arctic sea ice, freezing and melting and freezing again, year after year, were what stirred up the soup and made the ingredients mix.'

If that sounds fluent, it's because I used to hear Hagger give the same spiel, time and again, when I was in his lab. And, almost always, get the same objection.

'There's no life in the Arctic.'

'That's not true. When the sea ice forms, the salt in the seawater gets left behind. Gradually, the water that remains gets saltier and saltier, until it's too salty to freeze. The ice forms a crystal lattice, with tiny holes in between where the supersaturated salt water stays liquid. And each of those holes is effectively a test tube, where any DNA particles in the water can combine and replicate to their hearts' content. When the lattice melts, the DNA's released into the wild, until the seawater freezes again. And each time, those strands of DNA get a little longer, until eventually they cross the threshold and become life.'

'It's a magical time,' said Greta.

'The point is, Martin found proof. Here, at Zodiac. The sea-ice samples he took a couple of years ago – when he analysed them he found that stray DNA in the water was mutating and recombining at an astonishing rate. Off the scale.'

Off the scale. Like the graph Hagger had drawn of those bugs.

'He took the samples back to Cambridge and ran some experiments. Basically, popping them in and out of the freezer a few hundred times and then seeing what was there. He'd nailed it: the longest strand of DNA ever observed naturally forming.'

I remembered reading the paper when it came out in *Nature*. I'd like to say I was happy for him, but that wasn't exactly true. I'd wondered what might have been if I'd stayed with him, not switched my supervisor all those years ago. Maybe it would have been my name on that paper as first author, my lab drowning in money from all the funding bodies dying to be associated with my research. Maybe even my wife toasting me with champagne, explaining to Luke what all the fuss was about.

And maybe it would have been me lying at the bottom of

that crevasse, said the bit of my brain that picks holes in everything.

The wind had risen and I'd forgotten my goggles. Walking back to the Platform from Star Command, I had to shield my face with my glove, eyes screwed almost shut against the ice that found its way inside my hood. The clouds were so low you could hardly see the far side of the fjord. I'd never imagined that perpetual daylight could get so dark. On the roof of the Platform, I could see some of the antennas bending like whips. A good day to be inside.

A folded piece of paper had landed on my desk. A mobile phone number with a +44 prefix, in handwriting so bad it could only be a doctor's. Underneath he'd written, *Burn after reading*. I assumed that was a joke.

I rang the number from the radio room. After a week in the Arctic, the homely brrrr-brrrr of the phone ringing sounded like a message from Mars.

K-Mart answered with a cheerful 'Yuh?' that became a guarded 'OK' when I told him who I was. I didn't expect any more. I'm the man who took his job.

'Is this about the compromise agreement?'

'Martin Hagger's dead.'

'Wow.' He sounded winded. 'That's . . . I had no idea. I've been on holiday. I *am* on holiday,' he corrected himself. 'Wow.'

'I'm trying to tie up a few loose ends in his work.' Like: *Why did it get him killed?*

'Right. Yeah. Of course.'

'He died before I got here, so I didn't get a chance to speak to him.'

'Uh-huh.'

'I wonder if you can tell me what exactly he expected me to do here.'

A long pause. 'You probably know more about that than me.'

'He didn't tell me anything.'

'Well he didn't tell me, for sure. Just told me to pack my bags.'

'Because of your tooth.'

His voice got less laid-back. 'There was no tooth. That was a story he and Doc put together. Something to do with funding, procedure, something like that. The truth is, he wanted to get rid of me because he thought you knew more than me.'

'I didn't . . .'

'I don't care,' he said, in the voice of someone who does. 'He was the worst supervisor, just gave me donkey work. Running around the island, collecting samples. Wouldn't even tell me about the enzyme.'

'What enzyme?'

Ignored. 'Look, I'm sorry he's dead and no hard feelings and all that. But you're the one who wanted the job. You figure it out.'

'I didn't want it,' I objected. But he'd hung up.

While I was there, I logged on to the computer to Skype Luke. It took so long to connect I gave up; then, just as I stood to go, he appeared on screen. He was wearing his Spiderman costume over his school uniform, and he looked sad. It made my heart break, in a minor way. Superheroes and children shouldn't look so unhappy.

'The lady said your plane crashed.'

I gave one of those artificial smiles you give children, and twisted my head one way, then the other. 'See? No damage.'

'When are you coming home?'

'I don't know,' I admitted. 'We have to wait for a new plane.'

'I miss you.'

'I miss you too.' But I was speaking to no one: the screen had gone blank. I thought the storm must have knocked out the Internet, but a few moments later a sentence appeared in the box next to the video window.

Are u there?
Still here. We're having a storm.
Is there lightening?

With the limited bandwidth, and Luke's typing, the letters stuttered across the screen. I found myself getting impatient with him, and then ashamed for being impatient. It wasn't his fault. Since it ended with Louise, I've been reliant on Luke for so much. It's too much weight to put on an eight-year-old.

Our conversation quickly collapsed into monosyllables. He must be getting impatient, too. I tried not to take it personally, though you always do, with your children.

The connection was so slow, I began leafing through Hagger's notebook while I waited. Only marginally less frustrating, but at least it was something to do.

What is X?

Maybe Anderson?

Absorbed, I didn't realise Luke was waiting for me to reply. I looked up to see a line of gibberish on the screen.

DGEBAPB

At first I thought the storm had mangled the transmission. Then I realised it was a riddle, a fad they had been going through at school when I left. Abbreviating sentences and making you guess what it stood for. The sort of unwinnable game schoolboys love.

I thought about it for a little bit, but I didn't have the

patience. Who knows what an eight-year-old's mind will come up with?

I give up

The reply took a good five minutes to come through. Maybe he'd wandered off, or started playing his Nintendo.

Don't Get Eaten By A Polar Bear

I thought of the bear I'd seen with Ash. I wished I'd taken a picture for Luke.

Love u Dad
Love you

The moment we disconnected, I wished I'd persevered, slow connection and all. I missed him terribly. I read over the last few sentences still up on the screen.

DGEBAPB

It made me think of a line from Quam's ludicrous form.
An acronym for a memorable sentence, suitably modified, would be advisable.
I looked down and saw Hagger's (mis)quote on the inside cover of the open notebook. *Some Say the World Began In Fire . . .*
Under no circumstances should you ever write your password down.

Hagger's computer took ages to boot, the way computers do when they haven't been used in a while. As if they've got lazy. I paced around the tiny room, staring out the window. The snow was so thick in the air you couldn't see anything; the closest to night there'd been since I woke up out of the coma.

Some Say the World Began In Fire, Some Say In Ice.

There was still some work to do to fit it to Quam's rules, and I couldn't afford too many wrong guesses. If the machine locked me out, I'd have a hell of a job explaining it to Quam. I played around with various combinations of capitals and lower case, possible substitutions of numbers for similar letters. A lot of options, lots of S's and I's that might turn into 5's and 1's.

I thought I remembered Hagger was born in 1955, so I replaced the two leading S's with 55. Tried it, heart in mouth, and nearly died when the computer rejected it. Tried it again, this time also replacing the S's of the second 'Some Say'.

Logging on . . .

Forty-two

I knew something wasn't right the moment the main screen appeared. Anyone's machine, you'd expect to see a clutter of icons, files and folders. Certainly, Hagger wasn't the sort of person to keep a tidy desktop.

This was empty.

I searched the hard drive. The file structure was still there – directories for experiments, for data, for papers – but each one was empty. Systematically stripped bare.

I could feel my heart accelerating. The wind moaned strange harmonies outside; loose ice rattled the roof so loud I thought it was in the room with me. I looked over my shoulder, but there was nothing there. *Nothing there.* That was the problem. As fast as I could recreate Hagger's experiments, someone was tearing them up. How long before they caught up with me?

One of the few programs left on the machine was the email client. I tried it, more in despair than hope, expecting another empty window. Instead – bingo. Whoever had wiped the hard drive – maybe he didn't have time, maybe he didn't care – hadn't deleted the old emails.

I scanned the subject headings, feeling more like a thief with every passing second. At least at Zodiac you don't get the routine admin stuff that kills so many office hours, and Hagger had kept his account pretty pure, work-wise.

Even so, the messages mount up when you've been dead for a week.

I could say, for dramatic effect, that I nearly missed it. That wouldn't be true. It's hard to miss a message headlined (all capitals) *URGENT* – NATURE – *RETRACTION*. I opened it at once.

> *Dear Martin,*
> *In view of our friendship, I'm writing to you in confidence. Whatever you've done, I want to offer you the chance to withdraw the paper voluntarily. If not, I will write to* Nature *and insist they retract it.*

It was from a colleague of Hagger's, at Cambridge. A scientist of the old school, he didn't mince his words. He'd reanalysed the samples Hagger had used for his famous experiment. He'd put them through a mass spectrometer.

> *You can imagine my surprise when I discovered that the water was saturated with enzymes (Pfu-87 polymerase, 457ppm), which inevitably created the conditions for the DNA propagation you observed. If this was the result of accidental contamination, then that is lamentably negligent lab work. But the samples have not been touched since they arrived in Cambridge, which leads me to suspect that you must have deliberately tampered with them before you conducted your landmark experiments.*

I should have turned on the light. My head hurt from the strain of reading in the dark; my eyes were spotty with tiredness. I felt sick, confused and scared.

If Hagger doped his samples . . . In a way, I felt the same as the day that Louise told me she was leaving. The world upended, as if gravity itself turned out to be a gigantic hoax that everyone else was in on, and no one had had the guts to tell me. After all, it was Hagger who drilled into me, in the dog days after my first, anticlimactic experiments, that there are no short cuts in science; Hagger who taught Introductory Ethics with missionary fire; Hagger whom I couldn't look in the eye after the Pharaoh scandal.

He was pushing sixty, and he hadn't had a hit in years, said that cruel part of my brain, the cockroach part that could survive a nuclear war. *He needed one more big grant to carry him over the line, earn his pension, or they'd have put him out to pasture.*

I still wasn't sure I believed it. In all the time I'd spent with his lab notebook, I hadn't seen anything that suggested a man with something to hide. More the opposite: a man who knew something was wrong but couldn't work out what it was.

But that wasn't the most important thing.

I printed off the message, in case whoever'd wiped the computer came back for the emails. Judging from the time-stamp, it must have been one of the last messages Hagger read. I didn't want it to be my last, too.

'Got anything interesting there?'

With the wind so high, I couldn't hear a thing. Certainly not Kennedy coming through the door. He has a knack, that man, of turning up when you least want him.

'It's blowing fit to wake the dead out there.' He smiled, and picked up the printout before I could grab it.

I would have snatched it out of his hands – but he'd already read it. His eyes widened. 'Here's a turn-up for the books.'

I had nothing to do except go along, and tell myself that if Kennedy wanted me out of the way, he could have made sure I never came out of the coma.

'It arrived the day Martin died,' I said.

'How did you get hold of it?'

'I guessed his password,' I admitted. 'I was after his data.'

If Kennedy understood the subtext – if, for instance, he'd been responsible for deleting Hagger's data – he didn't show it. He seemed more interested in the time.

'Eleven o'clock,' he murmured. 'And you're sure Martin saw it?'

'It was flagged as "read".'

I put out my hand to take it back. Kennedy ignored me.

'Let me show this to Eastman.'

'Don't do that.'

It came out sounding borderline hysterical. He leaned towards me, staring into my eyes as if checking me for signs of concussion. 'Are you all right?'

'It's private,' I mumbled.

A charming smile. 'That may be, but neither of us has a leg to stand on in that department, do we really? Reading a dead man's emails, I mean.'

And before I could do anything, he ambled off.

I logged off the computer and shut it down. Then I started getting my things together. Hagger's samples, the microscope and slides, my map with the X's marked. The beakers from my experiment I covered with cling film (not very scientific), and put in a cardboard box. The fragment of yellow pipe I'd put in the red sample yesterday morning was now almost completely gone, a sludgy residue at the bottom of the jar like old Weetabix.

The equipment filled three boxes and a backpack. No way I could carry all that through the storm in one go. I took it down to the boot room and got suited up. The wind gauge on the monitor said forty-seven knots, the temperature minus forty. The point at which Celsius and Fahrenheit read the same, I remembered from some ancient science lesson. I couldn't conceive of what it would be like outside, so I threw on pretty much everything I had.

Even that was hardly enough. Just holding on to the railings going down the steps, the wind nearly tore my arms out of their sockets. By the time I'd found one of the sledges, parked in the gloom under the Platform, I was trembling. Looking up, I could see lights shining from the windows like the portholes of an ocean liner. A shadow moved inside, probably one of the students watching the storm from the comfort of the mess, and I felt a pang as I imagined them there curled up on the sofas, laughing and joking and drinking hot chocolate. What was I doing out there?

I should go back. I staggered to the bottom of the stairs and gripped the rail. The wind was full-frontal now, blasting me back off the slippery steps. I looked up.

The door opened. Yellow light flooded out, only for a second, as two bundled-up figures emerged on to the steps. I shrank back under the stairs.

Sifted snow showered over me as they came down the steps. They stopped at the bottom and looked around. I cowered back into the shadows, though there wasn't much chance of them seeing me. Nor of me recognising them, but from their relative sizes I guessed Eastman and Kennedy. Were they going to the caboose?

They weren't heading that way. They seemed to be following the flag line for the mag hut. That would explain why they weren't carrying rifles. It must be nine o'clock.

I started up the stairs again, hauling myself into the teeth of the wind. Trying not to slip, or get blown away, I hardly looked beyond the next step. So I didn't see the door open again, or the figure coming out, or even feel the vibration of his footsteps.

It was too dark for shadows, too much chaos in the air to

catch any movement. But some deep sense, a survival instinct, made me look up. There he was, bearing down on me out of the blizzard.

With everything that's happened, I was probably never more vulnerable than in that moment. I began to lift a hand to fight him off, but the moment I loosened my grip on the rail I was almost blown off. I was defenceless. He could tip me down the stairs, break my neck, make it look like an accident. It had worked for Hagger. The only one they'd blame would be me, an idiot out of his depth in an Arctic storm. Someone who should never have come.

My senses were so heightened, I swear I could see each individual snowflake in the air as the figure lifted his arm . . .

. . . and beckoned me forward. I couldn't move. He beckoned again, more urgently, and almost lost his footing.

He wasn't going to kill me. Adrenalin had mashed my mind so much I could hardly process the thought. I squeezed myself to one side, and we manoeuvred around each other, like two sumo wrestlers trying to get through a door. Arms round each other for stability, close enough that I could see the name sewn on to his jacket. *Quam.* Close enough he could read the name on mine. We bobbed our heads at each other in a strange, almost ritualistic greeting. Like penguins.

He disappeared into the storm after Eastman and Kennedy, following the flag line. Battling the storm every step, I loaded up the sledge with Hagger's lab equipment. Last of all, I put a rifle on my shoulder, though I couldn't imagine how I'd fire it in those conditions.

I put the rope around my chest and just about managed to drag the sledge to Star Command. At least I had the wind at my back. I'd reached the door, when I saw Quam coming out of the storm with a bundle of safety poles in his arms. He passed like a ghost; I don't know if he saw me. Strange time to be rearranging the flag lines.

I turned on the light and the heater. No problem with the electricity, luckily. It was nearly 10 p.m., but there was no way I'd get to sleep with the wind howling around the caboose, and the adrenalin in my system. The power was still on. I unloaded Hagger's samples, and got to work.

Forty-three

I feel like I'm living a double life. All around me, Zodiac goes on as normal. Through the mess windows, I can see the students decorating for Thing Night; Fridge tramps around base breaking ice off his instruments; Greta's on the roof repairing storm damage. No doubt Danny's cooking in the kitchen, and Quam's flicking that executive toy on his desk. And me? I'm holed up in the Star Command caboose like a fugitive. I slept here last night, with a packing crate wedged against the door and a loaded rifle beside me. I wonder if anyone's noticed.

Even with the heater on, the temperature in Star Command is touching zero. I've got Hagger's samples in the fridge to keep them warm; I keep on expecting the thermal cycler and the mass spectrometer to pack up completely. I've had to insulate them with my jumpers so that I can get the samples hot enough to incubate. But I'm almost there.

The storm had died down this morning, but the wind was still rattling around the station. Even so, there was no mistaking the firm knock. I scraped frozen condensation off the porthole in the door and peered out. Greta stood there, in her pigtailed hat, holding a plate covered in foil.

'Waffle day,' she announced when I opened the door. 'I brought you one.'

'How did you know I was here?'

She uncovered the plate and handed me a fork from her pocket.

'I hope you like syrup.'

Even the short journey from the Platform to the caboose had chilled it down. The waffle was flaccid and rubbery. Even so, I was more grateful to her than I knew how to say.

I poked my fork into the Z stamped into the waffle's centre. 'It looks like the mark of Zorro,' I joked.

'Yeah.'

Maybe they don't have Zorro in Norway. She looked at the sleeping bag on the floor. I suppose she noticed the rifle, too.

'Working hard?'

I had to tell someone or I'd go mad. 'This is going to sound crazy, but I opened Martin's email last night. I found a message from a colleague in England, someone who'd reviewed his results from the big *Nature* paper last year. He claimed Martin doped his samples.' I explained about Pfu-87 polymerase. 'It's an enzyme to make the DNA in the water combine and evolve much faster than it would naturally.'

Greta shook her head. 'Martin wouldn't.'

'I don't think he did. He was as surprised as anyone. He knew there'd been trouble replicating his results. That's why he came back here to overwinter.'

I unrolled the map where I'd marked his samples. 'You can see what he was doing. All through the winter, collecting samples around Zodiac, trying and failing to replicate his own results. He didn't understand why it wouldn't work. That's why he was so down.'

I moved my finger up to Echo Bay. 'Then, in March, Quam sent him to help DAR-X with their leaky gas pipes. That was the breakthrough. Martin analysed the water there, and found it was bursting with these little organisms feeding on DAR-X's pipes. I'm guessing that made him wonder how they could have evolved so quickly, and reproduced in such numbers. So he reran his original experiment using water from Echo Bay. Bingo.'

'Are you sure?'

'Martin's original sample, for the *Nature* paper, came from a summer trip to Gemini.' A shadow crossed Greta's face. She must have been thinking how Hagger had kept warm at Gemini. 'He went down to the Helbreensfjord and got a sample. Pure chance. When he came back this winter, he stayed close to base.' She still looked sceptical. I pointed to the machine on the bench. 'I've analysed all his samples. All the ones from between the Helbreensfjord and Echo Bay – the red dots on the map – contain high doses of this enzyme.'

'OK,' she said.

'But that's not the crazy bit.'

'OK.'

'My PhD was on polymerase enzymes – specifically, on Pfu-87.'

'With Martin?'

'A guy called Richie Pharaoh. I switched PhD supervisors after my first year.' That was a story I didn't want to go into. 'The point is, Pfu is a naturally occurring enzyme. It was discovered in bacteria that live in volcanic vents on the ocean floor. But Pfu-87 is a synthetic variant, a version that's been genetically tweaked in a lab to work better. It doesn't occur in nature.'

I realised I'd begun to tremble.

'And that's the crazy bit? Because it's man-made?'

'The crazy bit' – the reason I was holed up in the caboose with a gun – 'is that I invented it. I made the modifications. That was my PhD, and the paper I published. Martin had a copy in his lab.' And I'd thought he was just checking my credentials. 'At least now I know why he brought me here.'

Greta thought about that. 'So one question.'

'Only one?'

'Why is the Helbreen pumping out this DNA chemical you invented?'

I wished I had a good answer.

'I have to go fix the satellite dish,' she announced. 'If we don't get the Internet back, people will start eating each other.'

Her question echoed in my mind a long time after she'd gone. *Why is the Helbreen pumping out this DNA chemical you invented?*

Answer: *It isn't.* I've tested all the samples Hagger took from the glacier three times over. No Pfu-87, from the top of the glacier down to the very front edge. Nothing until you get into the seawater below the ice. All green. As if it's just welling out of the seabed.

I was still thinking about it an hour later when Eastman came through the door. No knock, and I'd forgotten to jam it shut after Greta left. My rifle was on the other side of the room.

He smiled that brilliant smile, though it didn't have quite the same wattage. As if the bulb was going. His face was red, his eyes were bright and he spoke too quickly.

'What's going on?'

He was jumpy. Literally: he couldn't stay still. If I'd been stood near him on the platform at Cambridge station, I'd have assumed he was a drug addict.

As blandly as possible, I told him I was working on Hagger's old data.

'I heard they were bullshit.' Succinct as ever. I wished Kennedy hadn't shown him the email.

I explained why I thought Hagger was innocent, leaving out the Pfu-87. Eastman didn't seem to pay attention. His eyes were always moving, taking things in at a thousand frames a second.

319

'What are those?' he said, pointing to the machines.

I couldn't tell if this was just a prelude to an act of violence. I mean, I've seen enough films where the psychopath makes conversation about cheeseburgers or parking wardens and then suddenly smashes his victim's face in. I played along, and tried to edge around towards the rifle.

'Do they work?' he said.

'Perfectly.' I could almost reach the rifle, now. Eastman must have noticed. His arm suddenly shot out to block my way, thrusting a sheet of paper into my hands.

'I got another reading on that interference.' The paper was covered with noughts, ones and twos, the same as the one from Hagger's notebook. 'Looks like it's coming from near Vitangelsk. Up by Mine Eight.'

He leaned very close to me as he said it, as if I was a pretty girl at a party. Like the girl, I couldn't do anything except shrink against the wall, and wish I had my gun.

'If only we could *unlock* it.' Heavy emphasis; in case I missed it, he mimed turning a key with his hand. 'You know, with a key.'

It wasn't subtle. So I'd been right, the key must have been his – dropped where Hagger died. I tried not to show that I'd guessed. He'd kill me right there.

The sequencer beeped and broke the moment. The printer chattered, and a spool of paper came out. I tore it off and jammed it in my pocket before Eastman could get a look.

'Have you ever been to New York?' I asked, thinking of the bear on the key ring.

Thankfully, at that moment Kennedy came in and announced that Quam had gone to check one of the bear cameras. It must have meant something to Eastman. He left so quickly he forgot to take his paper.

★   ★   ★

As soon as he was out the door, I barricaded it with as many boxes as I could find. Which meant that when Greta arrived, five minutes later, I had to move them all over again. No waffles this time; she didn't even ask about the elaborate barricade. Her face was red, almost as if she'd been crying.

She fell against me. I just caught her, holding her to my chest like a hurt child. Her body convulsed with silent, tearless sobs. I didn't know what to do, except pat her on the back. Then, without thinking, I started to stroke her hair.

She pulled back from me as if I'd burned her.

'Don't—'

I held up my hands. 'I'm not . . . I wasn't . . .' Took a step back. Asked, ludicrously, 'Are you OK?'

She stalked across the room, head held so stiff you could have cracked bricks on it. Glanced at the readouts on the machines. She still looked as if she might burst into tears – or bite someone.

'It's nothing.'

'Really?'

'I had a bad experience.'

It's the sort of statement that ties me in knots. I want to help, but I'm petrified of being thought intrusive. A very English problem. I've always envied the people who can just throw their arms around complete strangers without analysing it from twenty different angles.

'Do you want to talk about it?' I tried.

'No.' She flexed her fingers, as if imagining closing them around someone's throat. 'You know why I came here? To Utgard?' I shook my head. 'To get away from all the assholes.'

Something on the workbench caught her eye. She picked up one of the plastic bottles lying there, spun it in her fingers, then threw it against the wall like a fielder shying at the stumps. '*Asshole.*'

I looked at the empty bottle. I'd thought they were solutes

for the machines, but now I read the label I saw it was something else. *Rhodamine B hydrological dye. Caution: Stains.*

There was only one person at Zodiac I knew who used that in her research – and Hagger was supposed to have broken it off with her months ago. No wonder Greta was furious.

Forty-four

You'd think, with two dozen people confined to a few hundred square metres of ice, it would be easy to find anyone you wanted at Zodiac. It took me the best part of an hour to track Annabel down; eventually, I found her on a pair of skis gliding around the perimeter. I wondered if we'd been chasing each other round in circles all morning, like Pooh and Piglet.

'I've been in the bang shop.' She waved her pole at one of the older, wooden huts, where they keep the explosives. 'Have you seen anyone go in there? Twenty kilos of det cord's gone missing.'

'Don't look at me.'

'No,' she agreed, in a way that seemed to imply I wouldn't be up to it. 'Probably one of the American students who doesn't understand the metric system.'

She pushed off and began to ski away. I followed.

'I want to ask you about Martin.'

She didn't slow down. I took the Rhodamine-B bottle out of my pocket and threw it in front of her. 'What was he doing with that?'

'You've just violated article nine of the Utgard Treaty,' she told me. 'Littering.' She stopped, bent down and picked it up.

'I found it in his lab. Half a dozen of them. I just want to know what you were doing there.'

'He must have taken them from my store. I haven't been in his lab in six months.'

'Greta thinks you have.'

Wrong thing to say. She started skiing again; I had to run to keep up.

'What was Martin doing with that dye? Did he come to you for help?' I was starting to sweat. Lithe and long-legged, Annabel seemed to glide effortlessly over the snow. 'You use Rhodamine to trace water in the ice, right? Was Hagger interested in something coming off the glacier in meltwater?'

She stopped and looked back. She wasn't even breathing hard. 'Be careful. Last time you and I went running around the ice together, you fell down a hole.'

'Did Martin ask you about the glacier? Please,' I added. A cramp was spreading through my side. I knelt down in the snow and pressed my hand on my knee. I probably looked ridiculous.

Annabel surveyed me, the Ice Queen looking down on her subject.

'Hagger asked me about the ionic profile of some water samples. That's all.'

'What did you find?'

'High sulphite levels.'

I struggled. Sulphite's a mineral, nothing to do with enzymes and proteins. Nothing really to do with biology at all.

But Annabel was holding something back. Waiting for me, behind her mirrored glasses.

'What do high sulphite levels mean?'

'Glaciers don't just push ice down to the sea. They're complex hydrological systems with their own chemistry. Ice is an insulator; it sits on top of the rock like a heavy blanket. Now, the rock has heat in it from the earth's core, and that heat can't escape, so it melts the bottom of the glacier. The whole thing's sitting on a water slide. As water flows through the channels, or over the rock, it gathers its own chemical signature. Chloride means it's come from melted snow; calcite means it's travelled under the glacier, in contact with the rock.'

'And sulphite?'

'Sulphite doesn't show up in meltwater much.'

'But you said—'

'There are only a few places in the world where it happens, so we don't have much data. But where there are mine workings that go *underneath* a glacier – and, as I said, that's not common – we've seen evidence that the mines can become part of the glacier's drainage system. Meltwater seeps into the tunnels, and then joins the glacier again and flows out at the bottom.'

'And sulphite ions are evidence of that.'

She nodded. 'Digging tunnels exposes the rock to air. The air oxidises the metals in the rock, which produces sulphite. Then water flows through and washes it out.'

I've got enough chemistry that I could follow that. 'So Martin showed you some of his samples.'

'Yes.'

'And the sample bags – do you remember if they had coloured dots on them? Red or green?'

'All the ones that tested positive for sulphite had red dots—'

'You're sure?'

In my eagerness, I'd jumped in too quickly and cut her off. She shot me a dirty look.

'I asked him about the dots. I thought he might be playing a joke on me. But he said all the red ones came from the Helbreensfjord, which makes sense. All the mines around Vitangelsk – the tunnels go on for kilometres. Some must go right through the mountain and under the Helbreen.'

'So Hagger's samples from the Helbreensfjord – the red

ones – contained water that had gone through these mine tunnels under the glacier and come out at the bottom.'

'The data's consistent with that hypothesis.'

'And Rhodamine B would prove it. I mean, if you poured some of that dye in at the top of the Helbreen, and found it coming out at the bottom full of sulphites, that would be the proof.'

'I've never put dye around there.'

'But Hagger asked you to.'

'It's not in my project. And unlike some people, I do what my funding body are paying me to do. That's why they keep funding me.'

I waved the dye bottle. 'So he tried it himself.'

She sniffed. 'Even if he did, he couldn't have interpreted the data. Finding Rhodamine in the outlet water, after it's travelled ten kilometres underground in who knows which direction, isn't an easy thing. Hagger couldn't even pour it straight. He had the dye all over his hands when he died.'

She pushed back a slender leg, then shot it forward to begin skiing away.

'Still does, unless anyone's cleaned him up.'

The cold store at Zodiac feels like a morgue at the best of times. Long racks filled with ice cores, steel boxes spiked with frost. The body at the end, wrapped in plastic sheeting, almost seemed natural. Almost.

I unwrapped the plastic and examined Hagger's body. It didn't bother me as much as I'd thought: the flesh was frozen so hard, I couldn't think of it as ever having been alive. As Annabel had said, a pinkish dye stained the hands, like a child who'd been overenthusiastic with the felt tips.

Was Hagger really so inept he spilled it all over himself?

I thought I heard a noise behind me and looked round. Nothing there, except the endless rows of ice cores.

The cores sample every snowfall that's ever happened on this glacier, one on top of the other. You can read them like tree rings.

Hagger had an ice core in his freezer, I remembered. I'd wondered, when I saw it, why a man who studied sea ice would care about the lifeless heart of a glacier. I'd also wondered how he came by it.

The whole thing's sitting on a water slide.

What if it wasn't what's *in* the ice that interested him?

I ran back to the Platform. Ignoring the party in the mess, I dived into Hagger's lab and opened the fridge. I'd forgotten the freezer compartment when I'd cleared out the samples, but it was still there: a stubby cylinder of ice that looked as if it had been chopped with an axe.

I took it back to the caboose and put it on the hot plate. Usually, you use the hot plate to break down DNA, but it worked pretty well as a stove. In a few minutes, the core was sinking into a puddle of its own meltwater. I poured it off into a beaker, prepared a solution and ran it through the mass spectrometer.

The graph matched the others perfectly. A bit weaker, but that was understandable: the contaminated water wasn't part of the glacier, but had flowed under it. The trace must be from residue that had stuck to the bottom.

The enzymes aren't *in* the glacier – they're *under* it.

I'm lying on my bed catching up my diary. So much work, but I've got almost all of it now. Time to lay it out for myself.

Meltwater → under the Helbreen → mine tunnels → Helbreensfjord → ocean current → Echo Bay
Contains Pfu-87 enzyme, turbocharging food chain along coast

- Algae $\rightarrow$ plankton$\rightarrow$ fish $\rightarrow$ seals $\rightarrow$ bears
- Accelerated evolution of *Gelidibacter incognita* bugs
- Contamination of Hagger's original samples

WHERE IS Pfu-87 COMING FROM?

$\rightarrow$ not from snow/ice accumulation – glacier samples negative
- MUST BE PICKED UP IN THE MINE TUNNELS

Eastman must know. All those loaded comments this morning about Vitangelsk, Mine 8. He was testing me to see how far I've got.

If he reads this, he'll kill me.

Still not clear why he gave me the paper with those numbers on it. Some sort of test? Connected with Pfu-87 enzymes?

If there were four numbers, it would make sense. Could be DNA sequence, $0 = G$, $1 = C$, etc. Be interesting to compare with DNA coded by enzymes.

Unless . . .

Pharaoh String! Is *that* why Hagger brought me here? Impossible.

Noise outside – someone coming.

I have to get to the Helbreen right now.

Forty-five

***USCGC* Terra Nova**

Franklin put down the journal as Santiago came in to his cabin. Kennedy was with him, leaning on a crutch. His bandages had come off.

'We took a look at the guys from the tent,' Santiago said. He looked angry about something. 'Tell the Captain what you told me.'

Kennedy licked his lips. 'The man you found out there – it's Tom Anderson.'

'I told him it can't be. Tom Anderson's got six inches and about eighty pounds on this guy.'

Kennedy looked irritated. 'I think you can trust me to recognise him.'

Franklin closed the book. 'Is he going to wake up so he can tell us himself?'

'Doc says fifty-fifty. He was out there a few days. The woman, Greta, she's in better shape. Doc thinks she arrived later, probably came to rescue him but ran out of gas. She must have let off the emergency beacon. Had it tucked up with her in the sleeping bag, to keep the batteries warm.'

A wistful look came over him. 'Be nice to have a chick to curl up in a sleeping bag with me out here.'

'Mrs Santiago would hate to hear you say that, Ops.'

'Mrs Santiago hates the cold.'

Franklin reopened the book. Santiago didn't take the hint.

'Something on your mind, Ops?'

'Just wondering, sir. If we do have Anderson, who the hell did we have before?'

Anderson's Journal – Tuesday (?)

I don't know where to start. Don't even know what day it is. After what's happened . . . If I can't make sense of it, how can I write it down?

At least I've got the rest of my life to think about it.

But that isn't long. In this cold, life expectancy's measured in hours. All that stands between me and the Arctic is a canvas wall. All that's heating the tent is my own body. I can already feel it failing.

I read a story, before I came, how a nineteenth-century ship sank near the Bering Strait. Months later, wreckage arrived off the coast of Greenland, carried thousands of miles by the ice. Maybe one day this journal will land in Canada or Alaska, and a cruise-ship tourist will pick it up off the beach. They'll wonder who I was, if this could possibly be true.

More likely, this flimsy piece of ice will spin off into open water and melt, until the ice gives and drowns the journal. Then all that'll be left of me is a few drops of DNA in the ocean.

I miss Luke. Dying doesn't frighten me on my own account – I'm not religious – but the thought of leaving him alone, and being without him, is making these last few hours a living hell. The best I can hope for, now, is that the ice holds long enough; that someone finds my body; that Luke can know the truth.

This is what happened.

I was on my bunk, staring at the sheet of paper with those noughts and ones and twos that I finally understood, when Greta came in.

'Thing Night,' she said. 'You're missing it.'

I swung myself off the bunk. 'I have to get up to the Helbreen. Right now.'

She tilted her head five degrees to one side. That was about as surprised as she ever gets.

'I know what Martin found up there.'

'OK.'

'We'll need climbing harnesses and head torches.'

'OK.'

We dressed for the cold. I could hear film music coming through the mess door, laughter and toasts, but they might as well have been on another planet. Greta fetched the climbing gear while I grabbed Hagger's lab book and the journal with my notes. Luke's Father Christmas letter peeked out of it, still undelivered.

I stood in the lab for the last time, and looked around. I had that feeling you get leaving for the airport, convinced there's some vital thing you've forgotten to pack. But I didn't dare wait any longer.

We left the Platform and headed for the snowmobile park. Just as we got there, a figure rose up from where he'd been crouching behind one of the machines. I was so keyed up, I almost shot him.

It was only Quam. He looked distracted; his hands were sticky, and he stank of petrol. Why he had chosen that moment for a spot of maintenance, I couldn't think.

'You're missing Thing Night.' He looked down, fiddling with his hands as if he'd spilled something on his glove. He sounded almost drunk.

'So are you.'

'Checking the fuel lines,' he muttered. Greta gave him a sharp look.

'Is something wrong?'

Quam shook his head. 'Just checking.'

I could tell she didn't believe him. I thought it was strange, too, but I had to be away. I grabbed her arm and tugged her towards the mag hut. 'The *reading*,' I said loudly.

Greta gave the snowmobiles one more unhappy look. She pointed to the flare pistol holstered on Quam's hip. 'Be careful with that thing.'

Quam covered it with his hand. 'Be careful,' he repeated.

He sounded dazed, like a zombie. If I'd only taken a moment to think about it, I might have put a few things together: the flare gun, the smell of petrol, the unlikely preoccupation with snowmobile maintenance. But the only exact science is hindsight.

'What now?' I asked, as soon as Quam was behind us.

'The Sno-Cat.'

'Won't Quam stop us?' Officially, we were still confined to base.

Greta shrugged. 'Maybe.'

The Sno-Cat was parked behind the machine shop. Greta unplugged the umbilical cord that kept the battery warm, and started the engine. The moment it roared into life, I knew we weren't going to get away unnoticed. The Sno-Cat's not made for subtlety, or for speed. Sure enough, as we crossed the flag line I looked out the back window and saw Quam running after us, arms and legs flailing like a puppet with a broken string. For a moment, I thought he might even catch us. But you can't run far in the Arctic. He pulled up suddenly, shouted something I couldn't hear, then turned away. My last view was of him trudging back towards the Platform, shoulders stooped and head down. I kept watching, waiting for him to reappear with a snowmobile, but he never came.

I pitied Quam, then. I hoped he wouldn't get into trouble on account of what Greta and I were doing. Of course, if I'd known what he was about to do, I would have turned the Sno-Cat around and put a bullet in his heart myself.

★　★　★

We crunched up the glacier and Zodiac disappeared behind us. In the tiny cab, there wasn't much between us: every time Greta changed gear, or turned the wheel, I felt the point of her elbow. At least we weren't cold, with the machine's heater built from an age before oil shocks and global warming. I unzipped my coat.

'Aren't you curious why we're doing this?'

She swerved the Sno-Cat around some obstacle I didn't see.

'Tell me.'

I explained my hypothesis, how the enzymes were running under the glacier and out into the sea through the mines.

'The mines are sealed with concrete,' she pointed out.

'Water can get in through microscopic cracks.'

'But how do *we* get in?'

'I think Hagger found a way. He used Annabel's Rhodamine dye to track the water flow under the glacier; he had it on his hands when he died. He must have followed the dye down one of the tunnels . . .'

'Moulins,' Greta corrected me.

'. . . and found where the enzymes were coming from.'

A pause. 'What's an enzyme?'

I'd spent the last three days thinking about nothing else; the question threw me. But of course, why should she know? I thought for a moment. The throwaway answer wouldn't do.

'How much do you know about DNA?'

'Some.'

Last year, Luke's school invited me to give a talk about genetics to his Year 3 class. I fell back on that and hoped I didn't sound patronising.

'Imagine the human genome like a tower made of Lego bricks. The bricks can only be one of four colours, and the tower is three billion bricks tall. The bricks are stacked in pairs – so six billion in total – but there are certain rules. A red brick always goes next to a white one, and green always next to blue.'

'OK.'

'Each pair of bricks is what we call a "base pair". In reality, the different coloured blocks are amino acids, four chemicals known by their initials G, C, T and A. To "read" the genome – sequence it – you just have to write down all those letters in the right order.'

I glanced across at her. 'Still with me?'

'Keeping up.'

'Now, DNA makes RNA, which is like a copy of that Lego tower but only one block wide. RNA makes molecules called proteins, and proteins – among other things – make enzymes. An enzyme is a tiny biological machine, made of proteins, that performs a specific task. Like a little mobile chemical lab. It can be as fundamental as making your muscles move, and as mundane as breaking down stains on your laundry. You probably have them in your washing powder.'

'I use non-bio.'

'If DNA is the operating system of life, enzymes are the apps. The enzyme Martin found coming off the Helbreen is one that's been created in a laboratory, for making DNA. Put it in a solution with the four bases, and it'll grab them one after the other and stitch them together.' I thought of Luke's bedroom at home. 'Remember my Lego analogy? Imagine you've got Lego bricks scattered all over the floor. The enzyme is like a little robot that can grab them one at a time, and snap them together in a preset order.'

Greta drove on. With the clouds low, it was dark enough that I could see the headlights roaming over the snow in front of us.

'That's why we're going to the glacier?'

'There's something else.' I got out the piece of paper

covered in numbers. 'Eastman intercepted these numbers being transmitted somewhere near Vitangelsk.'

She crunched into the next gear as if she was trying to decapitate it.

'I know what the numbers mean.'

She didn't look as impressed as I'd hoped. 'Is it the password to get into the mine?'

'It comes back to DNA. You see, the biggest problem with sequencing DNA isn't the technology, or the process. That hasn't changed much in thirty years, except to get quicker and cheaper. But each individual's DNA contains three billion base pairs – that's three billion pieces of information. And if you're going to make use of it, you have to store it accurately and be able to retrieve it. Even one mistake, out of three billion, could mean the difference between perfect health and an incurable disease.

'And the actual sequence makes mistakes too easy. In the genome, there are long stretches where the same base pairs, or pattern of bases, repeat themselves. Coming back to the tower, it's as if you're told to put 297 red bricks in a row. Very easy to miscount.

'The man I did my doctorate with – Richie Pharaoh – he was obsessed with this problem. Any time you sequence DNA, you're working with margins of error. You have to decide what you think's acceptable. When the original Human Genome Project announced to the world that they'd sequenced the whole human genome – the articles in *Nature* and *Time*, the TV fanfare, the ceremony with Bill Clinton – what they didn't say is that one in ten thousand of the base pairs was probably wrong. That was the margin of error they'd agreed on.

'Now, one in ten thousand probably sounds pretty good. But with three billion base pairs, that's still three hundred thousand mistakes – and it only takes one to ruin someone's life. And there are two ways errors can creep in. Either when you're reading the sequence, or when you're writing it down. Which, practically, means on a computer.

'So Richie Pharaoh devised a solution. Instead of standard binary code, the noughts and ones, where the same number always stands for the same base letter, he created a more advanced code where there are three numbers – zero, one and two – but each one records a different value depending on what went before it. Sort of like the Enigma machine in the Second World War, where the next letter changed depending on what letter you'd just typed.'

The system was pure Richie. Subtle and slippery, a solution to a problem most people, even leaders in the field, hadn't realised existed yet.

Greta looked mystified. 'Is this going to be on the test?'

'The point is, Pharaoh never published it and it never caught on. Scientists were happy with the fiction that they'd "done it", the software got better at correcting errors, and every time he tried to explain it to someone, their eyes glazed over. No one used it – except Richie Pharaoh. He always used it for his own experiments.'

'And now it's on Utgard.'

'I'm wondering . . .' I took a deep breath. What I was proposing was so ludicrous, my mind hit the buffers every time I tried to assemble the thought.

'I'm wondering if the reason Martin brought me here was because of Richie Pharaoh.'

Forty-six

'I should probably tell you some things about Pharaoh.'

We were up on the ice dome. A dream landscape of soft peaks and hard snow, and hidden fissures waiting to swallow you. A landscape like the past.

'At university, Richie Pharaoh was a racing driver in a world of traffic wardens.' Literally: his red NSX stood out a mile against the grey Volvos and Priuses in the car park. 'He was American, a New Yorker, smarter than everyone and arrogant as hell, but the arrogance only made you try harder to impress him. All the grad students wanted his attention. You knew if you made it in his lab, you could walk into any job in the country.

'But before he came, I'd started my PhD with Martin. That was where I met Louise. She was smart, pretty and ambitious. We worked hard, we played hard, we had a lot in common. Soon, we fell in love.'

Like a lot of stories, it sounds easy when you tell it back. I'd had a few girlfriends at university, but I still wasn't confident. Louise seemed so cool and unattainable. It felt like an eternity – really, it was only a few weeks – before I plucked up my courage and asked her out. Afterwards, she admitted she only said yes because she was so sure I hated her. Apparently, I look ferocious when I'm concentrating.

'I said we worked hard. Unfortunately, the work in Martin's

337

lab was tedious as hell. Endless cycles of heating and cooling, freezing and melting, measuring tiny fragments of amino acids to see if they'd grown at all. Martin had a great story to tell about how he was going to upend the scientific consensus, make us famous and answer the greatest mystery of all – the origins of life. That was why we came. The problem was, the science didn't agree with him. After a year, it looked as if I wouldn't have a single positive result to write up in my thesis. Which didn't have to be the end of the world: you can publish a thesis on negative results. But it won't get you a job afterwards.'

Even now, when I'm just the lab tech and it's someone else's career on the line, I still get that black hole in my stomach when an experiment doesn't turn out.

'Then Richie hit the department like a minor earthquake. This was 2003. The human genome had been mapped a couple of years earlier, the technology was improving every month, and all over the world scientists were doing things that had never been done before. A real frontier, while our careers were dying in a backwater. And Pharaoh was three steps ahead already. While everyone else was still trying to sequence genes and DNA, he was looking at how you could *make* it. Synthetic biology – artificial life. Martin wanted to know how life began once upon a time. Richie Pharaoh was going to make it happen here and now. He reasoned that if you stitched enough genes together in a machine, eventually your creation would cough into life. That was the theory, anyway.

'Louise went first. She was impatient for success, and she was falling out with Martin all the time on how slowly things were going. She looked at Pharaoh and saw everything she wanted for her career. I followed her a bit later. I didn't get any funding to do the degree – I borrowed the money – so I couldn't afford not to get a job at the end of it.'

It all happened pretty fast, June to September. By the time the undergrads came back in October, we were both settled in Pharaoh's lab. But in my memory, those months go on for ever, like the first summer you fall in love or work a job. Long hot afternoons (the fabled summer of 2003!) moping around the lab; long nights, Louise and me sitting out on the back step, drinking rum and Coke, sometimes until the sun came up. Me worrying, her cajoling. So much riding on it, everything at stake. These days, summer just means stressing about childcare.

'I felt bad for Martin. Losing a PhD student isn't good for an academic: it counts against you when things like promotion come up. But actually, I think it's the personal rejection that hurt Martin more. He'd treated us like his children, nurtured us and opened his mind to us – and we'd told him he wasn't good enough.'

I saw Greta's mouth tighten, and remembered she was on Martin's side.

'The first few months in Pharaoh's lab were a golden time. He had so much grant money coming in, he could do what he wanted. Hagger's lab was a scrapyard compared to the shiny new toys in Pharaoh's. Every time the manufacturers had a new machine, Richie was the first to get it, often before it came on the market. We went to Rome and Avignon and Prague for our lab meetings. And the data flowed so quickly we could hardly write it up fast enough.

'Of course, it came at a price. We thought we'd been working hard before: Pharaoh worked us twice as hard. The pressure to publish, to get papers into good journals, was immense. I think half the people in his lab ended up leaving with stress illnesses or chronic fatigue. We didn't play hard any more; we didn't play much at all. We were tired, we were busy and we got sloppy with a few things. That was how we ended up with Luke.'

339

When the test came up positive, Louise hit the roof. Left home for three days, wouldn't answer my calls or my texts. I almost reported her missing to the police. At that stage, I had no doubt she'd terminated the pregnancy. I just hoped she was alive.

I found out afterwards she'd been with Pharaoh. Strangely enough, he was the one who persuaded her to keep the baby. He told her creating life was the most powerful thing people could do. He said it was hypocritical to study life in a test tube but shy away from the real thing. He must have said other things, too; whatever it was, it did the trick. She came home, went straight online and started looking at nurseries and engagement rings. We never spoke about it again.

'From day one, Louise saw Luke only as an obstacle. Two weeks after he was born, she was back at work. We couldn't afford childcare, and we didn't have any relatives on hand. Louise's parents live in France, my dad lives alone and can hardly make himself a cup of tea, let alone look after a baby. Neither of us was willing to defer our PhDs. So we juggled. I took Luke during the day, while Louise worked, and at night I'd creep into the lab with the cleaning staff to try and eke out a few results.

'In retrospect, I suppose it was obvious the marriage would fail. We hardly saw each other, and we hadn't been married long enough to have much credit in the bank. We were exhausted the whole time, both felt we were running on a treadmill and couldn't keep up. I was failing as a scientist, failing as a husband and failing as a father. And I knew it. I didn't see Pharaoh any more, except when I dragged myself in for supervision meetings to be told how far behind I'd fallen. In Pharaoh's lab, there were no prizes for trying. If you were doing well, there was nothing he wouldn't give you. If you didn't meet expectations, you were dead meat. Natural selection, he called it, and he wasn't joking. There was no shortage of young carnivores waiting to take my place.'

I get shortness of breath thinking about it now. Back then, there were afternoons when I almost called 999 I was so sure I was having a heart attack.

'I said Louise and I were getting sloppy, and it wasn't just at home. Pharaoh drove us so hard, the only way to get results – publishable results – was by cutting corners. Everybody in the lab did it; the people who flourished were the ones who could do it most plausibly. Without any pangs of conscience.

'By that stage, I hardly knew what Louise was doing in the lab. One day, she came home at lunchtime. I remember it – she hardly ever got home before Luke's bedtime, and I was so happy she'd come to see us. We sat outside and I opened a bottle of wine. The moment she'd had a sip, she almost collapsed in tears. And Louise didn't do tears.

'She told me there was a problem. She'd forgotten to fill in an ethics form, and now the department had started to ask questions. At first I didn't see why that mattered: an ethics form is just bureaucracy. Forgetting it means a rap on the knuckles, but if you get a high-impact paper out of the research nobody remembers. As long as there aren't any complications.

'There *were* complications. For a start, it wasn't that she didn't have ethics approval for one experiment; they didn't have approval for any of it. Pharaoh was so paranoid about revealing his work, he simply ignored procedure. And it got worse. Louise had been working on artificially reconstructing a modified version of a coronavirus. If you think you've heard of that, it's because it hit the news about ten years ago as the cause of SARS. Now, we worked in a big building in the science park. One floor down were people working on genetic diseases, treatments for Parkinson's, leukaemia, you name it.

A big building, lots of test tubes shuttling around, lots of expensive trials – and one of her batches had gone missing.

'She went through forty-eight hours of hell wondering if some kid with cancer had been injected with her virus. She had to report it, of course. She was suspended and the whole building got locked down. The university threatened to cut off funding completely – not just for Pharaoh, but for everyone in the Institute.

'In the end, they found her samples sitting on a benchtop three doors down from her lab. Dyslexic delivery man misread the room number: no harm done. But I told you Pharaoh was arrogant. He'd made a lot of enemies higher up the totem pole, plenty of people who wanted to take him down a peg. If it came out he'd sanctioned his students synthesising the virus without any kind of approval or oversight, all the grants and publications in the world wouldn't save him. We both knew the only way he could protect himself was to cut her loose.'

I gazed out the window, staring at the white horizon.

'I took the blame myself. To protect Louise, of course, and Luke: rationally, I knew her career prospects were better than mine. But also to impress her. I knew, deep down, our marriage was pretty far gone, but I thought the grand gesture might win her back. And I hoped it would buy me some slack with Pharaoh. Louise was always his golden girl. It had to count for something.'

Without looking, I could tell Greta was rolling her eyes at me.

'You're right. Louise and Richie had already started their affair: I still don't know how they found the time. His marriage was breaking up. As soon as the scandal had died down, and his divorce came through, she told me she was leaving.'

All my memories of that time are darkness: winter afternoons, and endless nights of fights that only ended when

342

Luke woke up in tears and I had to go to settle him. I felt as though my whole life had been fed into a shredder; I didn't know if I could go on. A cold winter, but it never snowed.

'I got custody – Louise didn't contest it – and eventually finished my PhD at the Open University. I tried for a few postdoc jobs, but nobody wanted to hear from me. I ended up as an overqualified lab technician, wondering where my career had gone and doing the best I could by Luke. Just another single parent trying to squeeze through life.'

'And she died in a plane crash,' Greta remembered.

'A few years ago. Pharaoh was a keen pilot. They were working in Alaska, Pharaoh had been given big money, ten million dollars from the National Institutes of Health, to set up a lab there. One day, he and Louise took off for a sightseeing trip in the Brooks Range and never came back. Some people suggested suicide – there was talk the money had gone missing and the NIH were asking questions – but I didn't buy that. No one loved life more than Richie Pharaoh.'

'Must have been tough,' said Greta.

'To be honest, it was more like finding out some distant cousin had died. Sad, but not traumatic. I hadn't seen her in years, by then. Nor had Luke. I didn't think much about her, or Richie Pharaoh. Until Martin emailed me.'

That wasn't true. It never went away. I couldn't look at Luke without seeing Louise in him. Every day at work, watching the DNA unspool on our machines – the code of life – I'd think about how my life might have been different.

But I'd already told Greta more than I ever had anyone else. There are parts of that even my sister doesn't know.

'It probably sounds pathetic.'

Greta shrugged. 'Sometimes life is shitty.'

I couldn't argue with that.

★ ★ ★

Nothing had changed on the Helbreen. I got out of the cab, wincing as the cold hit my stiff joints.

'The crevasse was a dead end.' Unfortunate phrasing. 'He never went down there until he was pushed in.'

It wasn't hard to find the moulin. Since I'd been there, someone – maybe Annabel – had roped it off, to stop anyone else falling in. I removed the barrier, while Greta fastened our climbing lines to the Sno-Cat. There seemed to be an awful lot of rope.

'How far down are we going?'

'Maybe twenty metres. Maybe one hundred.'

She handed me a helmet.

'I wish I'd had this last time,' I said, though I wasn't really in the mood for joking. Revisiting the past had unsettled me, like when you wake from a dream just as it's reaching its climax. Even though you're awake, it won't let go of you.

I clipped into the harness and walked carefully to the edge of the hole. Whatever damage they'd done pulling me out, the wind and the snow had smoothed it over so cleanly only a tiny opening remained.

'I go first.' Greta kicked away loose snow to widen the hole, then pirouetted around and walked backwards into it.

I flicked on my head torch and followed.

Forty-seven

You expect ice to be clammy when you touch it. Your body heat goes to work and the surface gets slick. But not in the glacier. As I lowered myself in, bracing myself against the sides of the chute, the ice remained dry as dust. Against the vast cold of a glacier, a human body doesn't count for much.

The hole dropped a couple of metres, then angled away down a gentle slope. I crawled down after Greta, careful not to tangle myself on the rope. The tunnel was almost a perfect cylinder, as if it had been bored out by machine. Under my hands, the milky white walls swirled like marble.

The slope got steeper. Rather than waste energy, I sat down on my bottom and let myself slide, like being in a water pipe.

'*Stop!*' said Greta. The desperate voice you use to a child who's about to run into the street. I grabbed my rope and just stopped myself bumping into her.

She leaned to one side so I could see over her shoulder. My torch beam shone into almost perfect darkness, dropping away far beyond where the light could reach.

'Lucky you stopped where you did.'

I twisted my head to see more. Something flashed: a blade of light cutting the darkness in two. I brought the light back on to it and saw an icicle. Not the kind you get dripping from your gutters during a cold snap; this was taller than me and probably as broad at the top. At the bottom, it was as

345

sharp as a needle. And we were going to be descending right under it.

'Is that stable?'

Without answering, Greta went over the edge. Gripped the ledge, then became a glow of light slowly dimming. I didn't look down.

I don't know how long I waited there, eye to eye with the icicle. Whenever I moved my head, even a twitch, the light twisted so that the icicle seemed to wobble. Then I felt a tug on the rope. With a deep breath, I slipped over the edge. It wasn't so bad, actually. The hole was narrow enough I could keep one hand on the descender, paying myself out, and the other steadying myself on the wall. I was terrified of knocking that icicle.

And suddenly I was hanging in air. Instinctively, I flung out my arms, flapping and waving, but didn't touch a thing. With no hands on the rope, I fell backwards, was weightless for a moment, then jerked on the harness and see-sawed back up.

The rope swung and snagged. I heard an enormous crack above me. Whatever was holding the rope suddenly let go; I jerked down another metre, but something was falling faster. I actually felt the frigid air on my cheek as the icicle passed inches from my face.

'*Look out!*'

It shattered on the floor, while I hung in space, splayed out flat like a dead man in a swimming pool. Like Hagger at the bottom of the crevasse.

'Are you OK?' I called.

The wait almost killed me. Then Greta's voice came up from the depths.

'Alive.'

I kicked my legs and strained forward until I got hold of the rope. I almost tore my stomach muscles, and I was sweating like mad. As soon as my hands had stopped trembling, I found the figure-eight descender and started paying out the line again. It was a long time before my feet touched the ground. When I did, I could hardly stand up.

Greta turned on her torch – she'd been saving the battery – and emerged from the darkness. There was blood on her cheek, and water, where an icicle fragment must have hit her.

'I'm sorry,' I mumbled. An apology's rarely felt so inadequate. Greta's face made sure I knew it.

I shone my light around. We were at the bottom of a huge shaft, as high as a cathedral, which tapered at the top like a wine bottle. I couldn't see any way out, except a low crack just above the floor. Not even a tunnel, just a fissure in the ice.

'There's no way we can get through there.'

She pointed to scratches on the ice. 'Martin did.'

We took off our ropes and harnesses. I felt that odd feeling of weightlessness you get driving without a seat belt, but there was no other option. We only had a few metres of rope left.

And miles to go before I sleep.

I'm not claustrophobic, normally, but I nearly didn't make it. It was the narrowest space I've ever been in. My helmet scraped along the ceiling, and my chin almost touched the floor. I couldn't lift my head to look in front, couldn't even crawl. I lay on my belly, arms and legs out, squirming forward a few millimetres at a time. Each time I tried to breathe, my back touched the roof and I flinched with panic. All I could think of was a million tons of ice over my head, pushing down. How much would it take to pinch this tiny tunnel shut?

I heard Annabel's voice in my head. *Glaciers don't stand still. They're fluid. The ice is actually flowing very slowly, moving outwards under its own weight.* Back then, it had seemed academic.

Suddenly, I realised I could breathe again. The tunnel had opened up, not much, but enough that I could get off my stomach and look up.

As I raised my head, the torch beam glinted on a million points of light, a diamond-crusted ceiling like something out of 'Ali Baba'.

'Ice crystals,' said Greta.

Looking closer, I could see how perfect they were. Each was a mathematical miracle, the ice extruded almost paper-thin into a hexagonal spiral. When I touched one with the tip of my glove, it shattered into a hundred pieces. So fragile I wanted to cry.

I crawled on, trying not to hit my head on the crystals. Each time I did, tiny granules of ice shivered down the back of my neck like guilt.

And then they stopped falling, because the roof had taken off high over my head. The walls spread apart and became a round tunnel as wide as a sewer pipe. Grey ice walls rising out of crumbly rock, with a slick of cloudy white ice running down the centre like a stream.

I undid my helmet so I could take off my hat and neck-warmer. After a moment's thought, I took off one of my jumpers, too, and put my coat back on.

'Shit,' I swore.

'What?'

I showed Greta my dangling zipper. Somewhere, dragging myself over that ice, I'd broken it. Every time I tried to do it up, the coat just peeled apart again.

'I suppose I won't freeze.' To tell the truth, it didn't feel cold at all. The ice wasn't so dry here. When I rested my hand on it, I could feel the surface poised to melt.

Ice is an insulator; it sits on top of the rock like a heavy blanket. With a million tons of it over my head, that wasn't reassuring.

The look on Greta's face didn't reassure me either. 'A broken zipper's no good when we get out.'

I shrugged. 'We've got a lot of bridges before we have to cross that one.'

The tunnel looked wide enough to walk, after the interminable crawling. But Greta didn't do it the easy way. She braced her hands and feet against the edges of the passage, straddling the centre, and manoeuvred her way forward like a spider.

'Isn't there a faster way?'

'Not if you want to stay dry.' She nodded at the carpet of white ice in the middle of the floor. 'It's a stream. The top freezes, but the water flows under it.'

Curious, I smashed the ice with the heel of my boot. She was right. A small, steady stream ran underneath, unhindered by the ice. I took off my glove and dipped my hand in. The water was so cold it burned. When I wiped my hand on the lining of my hood, the water left a pink smear on the fur.

'We're on the right track.'

I copied Greta's awkward stance, straddling the stream and crabbing my way forward. It reminded me of one of those playground games, two logs set in a V and the goal is to walk forward with one foot on each until it gets too wide and you fall off. I remember doing it with Luke in the park near our house, dangling him over the gap (he was smaller, then) while my legs splayed further and further apart, until I looked like a gymnast or an eighties rocker. And then we collapsed in a heap of giggles and—

I should have concentrated. My foot hit a rock; my arms scrabbled on the glassy walls. I lost my balance and fell – straight through the ice.

The shock hit me like the electric chair. I went under and took a mouthful of water that almost stopped my

349

heart. I touched bottom – not deep – pushed up, and felt resistance. Something pushing me back down. I was under the ice, I was going to die, and the only thing crowding out the panic was wishing I could be with Luke one more time.

Then something caught me a glancing blow on the cheek. The ice cracked and my head popped up. Greta hauled me, dripping and screaming, from the stream. I leaned against the wall. I was soaked through. I could feel the cold crawling deep into me, worming into my bones so I'd freeze from the inside out. I coughed out a big gulp of water. I could taste it: filthy with sediment and chemicals from the rock. And who knows what else?

'You have to go back.'

'No.' I imagined myself squeezing through that fissure in my wet clothes. I'd freeze right into the ice, become part of the glacier. I couldn't go that way.

She didn't argue. Perhaps she saw the logic; more likely, she didn't want to waste time talking me out of my own funeral. 'Then you have to keep moving.'

Cold, miserable, I followed as fast as I could. I was shivering so violently, I struggled to keep myself upright. When I slipped, which was often, I didn't have the strength to brace myself; I just crashed through the ice again, back into the water, and had to wait for Greta to haul me out. I didn't feel it so much after the first time.

I thought of Martin. I remembered how his clothes had been frozen when we found them, and how I'd wondered about it then. He'd done this alone.

Was it worth it? I asked him through chattering teeth.

At that level of survival, the mind collapses and there's nothing but your body. I could feel every hair pricking up, every breath condensing in my lungs. The warmth in my blood and the cold in my bones battling for my soul.

Some say the world will end in fire,
Some say in ice.
From what I've tasted of desire,
I hold with those who favor fire.

Once the lines had come into my head, I couldn't shake them. They repeated themselves again and again, the way snatches of music sometimes do when I'm lying in bed and can't sleep. White noise – oblivion.

The passage ended in a jumble of ice and black rocks. I was almost too far gone to notice, but I did hear a noise. The trickle of invisible water, running down under the rocks into the stream.

'The mine,' said Greta, as if it was the most normal thing in the world.

We crawled through the hole, over rocks and ice still filthy with coal dust, into another world. More tunnels, nothing like what we'd been through. Straight and even, with cross-tunnels at right angles making a regular grid. More like being in the crawl space under a floor than how I ever imagined a mine.

It would have been easy to get lost in there. In places, wooden splints shored up the roof, chalked with still-legible Cyrillic letters. They must have meant something to someone, but not to me. Luckily, there was the stream to follow, running through a channel it had carved out of the rock floor. And I could hear a noise, a mechanical hum that got louder as we crawled on up the stream.

Ahead, something glowed ethereal white among the shadows and soot. I thought it was a trick, the torch beam blurring or burning my eyes, but no amount of blinking and shaking my head would move it.

It was a concrete wall. Water from a drainpipe splashed at

351

its base, the source of the stream. Above it bulged a round door, about three feet across, with a locking wheel like something salvaged from a submarine.

I tried the door. No joy, but I was so weak that didn't mean much. Greta added her hands to mine, and we heaved together.

The wheel turned. A seal hissed. The door moved inwards. Soft yellow light spilled through the crack.

'No locks on Utgard.' Certainly not here. A glacier, a mountain and an abandoned mine would be enough to deter most visitors. Not to mention the fact they'd killed the last man who found it.

Greta must have had the same thought. She got out her pistol and loaded a flare cartridge. In any normal world, that would have been my cue to leave: back to the Sno-Cat, back to Zodiac, all the way back to Cambridge and Luke.

But this was a long way from normal, and I was one degree off hypothermia. If I didn't keep moving, I'd freeze solid right there.

I pushed open the door and clambered through.

Forty-eight

I don't know if I was surprised; I had no expectations. I mean, what would be normal to find deep in an abandoned mine in the high Arctic? But even in the range of things you wouldn't expect to find, this was pretty far off the scale. It looked like a hospital, or a high-tech factory. Spotless white walls and floor; soft fluorescent work lights overhead. A large cylindrical tank stood in the centre of the room, filled with bluish liquid that bubbled and steamed. Half a dozen pipes fed it from the ceiling, and I could see a valve in the bottom that must drain through the pipe into the mine. A computer terminal beside it flashed its operating lights, controlling something.

I turned back to Greta, who was covering me with the flare pistol through the round door. 'It's—'

He must have been waiting for me. Somewhere in the shadows, knowing I'd come. I never saw him. Just a rustle behind me, then a blow to my back like being hit by a train. I fell hard. Rolled over, but before I could get up he'd pounced on top of me. He put his hands either side of my head and squeezed. God, he was strong. I thought my skull would pop. Through the pain and the door, I could see Greta screaming something. I screamed back, but with his fat hands muffling my ears I couldn't hear a thing. He pulled my head towards him as if to caress it, then slammed it back against the tiled floor. A

353

dark wave rolled through my skull and washed over my eyes. Greta dimmed. She still had the flare pistol, but with the target right on top of me she didn't dare use it.

She tried to get through the door. An awkward manoeuvre – you had to duck through. The man anticipated it. He leapt off me – very fast, for a man his size – and dived towards the door. Now Greta had a clear shot. She raised the pistol, but – too late. The man pushed her back, got hold of the door and slammed it in her face. The vibrations shuddered through the floor. He spun the wheel, then dropped an iron bolt to lock it.

He turned back to me. Behind him, the wheel on the door rattled and jerked, fractional movements as Greta tried to make it turn. But the bar held it.

The man came up and the door disappeared from view. Standing over me, he looked vast, a monstrous presence all in black.

He crouched down and his face came into the light. Flat cheeks, a high forehead and deep brown eyes that reminded me, strangely, of Luke's. Surprisingly gentle, for what he'd done to me. I tried to fight him off, but I didn't have the strength to even lift my arm.

A memory came back to me. Lying on the ice, head splitting. A silhouette, arm raised to smash my head in. Waiting for the blow.

'Who are you?' I whispered.

He lifted me, threw me over his shoulder and carried me away. I watched my reflection in the floor tiles. Past the steaming tank, bubbling quietly, through doors and rooms like a series of dreams. A world turned upside down, filled with strange and unspeakable things. One room like an operating theatre, steel cabinets and a steel table, and steel knives laid out on a tray. Another full of machines, dozens of DNA sequencers, like some sort of showroom, and for a mad second I thought I was back in Cambridge. A room piled floor to ceiling with tins of food.

Another door, and the picture changed again. A dimly lit room, filled with large specimen jars that skewed the light like distorting mirrors. Behind the reflections, I glimpsed monstrous things floating in blood-red fluid: fleshy shapes; ghastly deformities like limbs and heads; nightmares lurking behind the glass. I closed my eyes.

The last room was a stairwell with a flight of iron stairs. He carried me up – he never seemed to get tired – and through a final door.

This was the living space. It looked like some sort of trendy industrial conversion: concrete walls, a television mounted on one and a trio of David Hockney swimming pools opposite. A glass table covered in papers; plastic chairs, and an angular lamp that cast a soft yellow glow. A cup of tea sitting on the table was the only human touch.

A man and a woman stood by the table, like hosts whose guests are late for the party. He wore a neat steel-grey beard over a lined, weather-beaten face; she had blondish hair tied back in a ponytail. Both wore plaid shirts and thick corduroy trousers. They looked like a sturdy, retired couple – except that she wasn't any older than me. Five months younger, to be precise.

The man came forward as if to shake my hand. The woman stayed back, not quite meeting my eye, as if to say it wasn't her idea to invite me. The room spun as I was put down – quite gently – on to one of the chairs. I was upright, but it all seemed upside down again.

'You're supposed to be dead,' I said.

Forty-nine

Anderson's Journal

There were a million questions I needed to ask. I began with the obvious.

'What are you doing here?'

Louise stood next to the lamp. It hurt to look at her.

'I thought you died,' I added.

'You've been wrong about a great many things.' Pharaoh spoke for her. His voice sounded so familiar. An authoritative baritone, precise and pedantic, belying the speed of the thoughts beneath. 'There's no law that requires a person to prove he is alive.'

He turned to the man who'd brought me. 'Did he come alone?'

'There was a woman. I shut her in the mine tunnel.'

It was the first time I'd heard him speak. A soft voice, curiously flat, like someone who wasn't used to public speaking.

Pharaoh's face twitched. I'd seen it so often before, when you didn't give him the results he demanded. The anger, barely contained; the tone so sharp it made your confidence bleed.

'Then you'd better go find her.'

He might frighten grad students; maybe even fellow scientists, in thrall to his reputation. But the man behind me wasn't intimidated. I heard his weight shift menacingly.

Louise took a half-step forward, as if to stop a fight. She looked frightened – as well she might. God knows, the man was strong enough.

But Pharaoh stared him down, bulletproof confidence, as you would when breaking in a puppy. 'Now.'

'Let her go,' I said. 'She doesn't know anything.'

They ignored me. The moment the door closed, Louise relaxed, though it didn't do anything for me. I thought about Greta, and prayed to the God who doesn't exist that she'd get out before they caught her. Back to Zodiac, back for help. Though locked in that mountain, it was hard to believe in a rescue. Hard to believe anything, with Pharaoh and Louise standing there like ghosts.

They gave me dry clothes and a hot cup of tea. Then, like a grotesque replay of those nights in Cambridge when Pharaoh had us over for dinner (and what did they do when I was out of the room?), we sat at the table and talked.

'You asked what we're doing here,' said Pharaoh. 'You've had a look around. Surely you can hazard a guess.'

I tried not to think of the specimen jars. 'Making bugs that eat oil pipes?'

He chuckled. 'That was a somewhat amusing diversion. A synthetic micro-organism that can metabolise the polymers in the pipes. An act of sabotage. It would have impeded my plans if the exploration company brought too much attention to this island.'

'Why Utgard?'

'It's one of the few places in the world free from the tyranny of demotic morality.'

It was the way he loved to speak. 'No government,' I translated.

'No restraint on the pursuit of knowledge.'

'No ethics forms.'

I glanced at Louise, but she didn't react. It meant nothing to her any more – if it ever had.

Pharaoh leaned forward. 'Let's start from the beginning, Thomas.' He was the only person, except my mother, who called me Thomas. He picked a paperweight off the table and hefted it in his hand. A piece of polished jet: I actually recognised it. I bought it for Louise on a weekend in Whitby.

'Carbon. It's everything that matters. You, me, the birds and the bees and the flowers – every molecule in our body starts with a carbon atom. When God said, "Let there be life," what He actually said is, "Let there be carbon."'

It must be a lecture he'd given somewhere before, though I hadn't heard it. The phrases rolled out in that irresistible voice. When he said, 'Let there be life,' you could almost imagine the molecules jumping into line.

'But carbon's a promiscuous little element. Attaches itself to anything. With nitrogen, or hydrogen, it makes the stuff of life. But join it to a pair of oxygen atoms, CO_2, and you're in danger. You know what the more optimistic of the energy people call fossil fuels? Buried sunshine. It's the light that fell on the planet a hundred million years ago. Plants stored the energy as carbon. They lived, they died, were buried, and under pressure the matter was compressed until the carbon inside them turned to coal, or oil. When you burn it, the carbon is released and joins with the oxygen in the air, and all that ancient life is now a dangerous gas.

'Earth's going to change more in the next hundred years than it has in the last ten thousand. We've added six billion people in a century, and we're not slowing down. And the business model for our planet says they all have to buy automobiles, airplane travel, air conditioning and iPads, or the whole economy collapses. You want to talk about carbon? The last time there was this much carbon in the atmosphere, Greenland looked like Connecticut and Philly was seaside real estate. Even if you want to stop it there, we'd have to switch off every engine and power plant in the world tomorrow and not start them back up for fifty years. Instead, China's bringing a new coal-fired power station on stream every three days. I said coal is buried sunshine. If you count it that way, every year we dig up and release five hundred years' worth of sun into the atmosphere.'

'I never had you as a tree hugger.' As far as I remembered, the only science Pharaoh ever cared about was genetics. 'So what are you trying to invent here? Some kind of biofuel?'

'You're thinking too small, Thomas. That was always your limitation.' He glanced at Louise, who nodded her agreement. 'We've gone too far, the planet's not coming back. We've tipped the balance, and all we can do is adapt. That's my interest. The greatest endeavour of them all.'

He always had a good patter. I've seen him hypnotise audiences plenty of times, whether it was a prospective student, or a lecture hall, or the people who write the eight-figure cheques. But this was different. More assertive, more about showing off his own certainty than convincing you. *Evangelical* was the word that came to mind.

'You've heard the term "geo-engineering"? The hypothesis that the solution to the world's crisis is re-engineering the planet. Giant mirrors in space to reflect back sunlight, or saturating the oceans with iron to absorb more CO_2. Even if it were possible, the costs – and the risks . . .' He rippled his fingers into a fist, a classic Pharaoh gesture. 'I've chosen to approach the problem from the opposite direction.

'You're aware of the theory of Intelligent Design, I presume. Nonsense, of course, dreamed up by theists who are too timid to call their God by name. Their premise is flawed. If

359

they were scientists, they'd recognise there's neither intelligence nor design at work. Beauty, yes. Awe, most definitely.
But from the perspective of design, it's a mess. A billion years
of baggage. Wrong turns, dead ends and obsolescence. All
the dirty dishes our genome never got around to cleaning
up and putting away.'

He threw open his fist.

'You know why Paris is more beautiful than Los Angeles?
Paris was designed – redesigned, I should say – by a single
mind. Elegant, proportional; the old mess swept away. LA
just sprawled, millions of people all making their own self-
interested decisions.'

'I think they call it the wisdom of crowds.'

'The wisdom of crowds is what's brought us to the brink.
You know what happens when a creature's environment
changes faster than it can evolve?'

'Extinction,' said Louise. All the time he'd been giving his
lecture, she'd sat still beside him, twisting the wedding band
on her finger. She never wore one when we were married
– said it got in the way too much at the lab.

'I'm not arrogant. I don't even claim any special insight. I
just look at the data without prejudice. And I have the ability
to do this. To re-engineer mankind.'

I laughed out loud, and took some satisfaction from the
irritation that flashed across his face. The spell was broken.
Sitting at that table with Louise, prim and upright like the
couple in *American Gothic*, he suddenly looked absurd.

'Is that why you came here? To write science fiction?'

I was hoping I could get under his skin again. But he'd
got control of himself, and all I earned was a condescending
smile.

'Synthetic biology isn't fiction, Thomas. You ought to know
that.'

'You mean the Maryland group?' Pharaoh may be brilliant,

360

but even back when I worked for him he wasn't the only one pursuing synthetic biology. There's a group in Maryland who used the technique to create an artificial bacterium. It made the news a couple of years ago.

'The Maryland group's bacterium was a parlour trick. A two-piece jigsaw. I have the whole picture.'

'That's not possible.'

'Let me persuade you otherwise. You think I came here for the climate? Or the social scene? I mean, Maryland may be dull, my God, but . . .'

'The science you're talking about is fifty years off,' I said. 'If ever.'

'Look at World War Two. In six years, they invented radar, rockets, jet engines, the atomic bomb and nylon pantyhose to boot. Why? Because in wartime, nobody looks over his shoulder. That Maryland group? The science was simple – they could have done it ten years ago. The only thing that held them back was the paperwork. You know how long it takes to get ethical approval for creating new life? Think of stem cell research. So much potential, and it's been tied up with politicians and priests for thirty years.

'The irony is the hypocrisy. Any dumb kid with a hard-on can create life. And the government will subsidise that with welfare, tax credits, medical programs, no questions asked, even though that life will probably be – and I quote Thomas Hobbes – nasty, brutish and short. But try and do something in a lab that will benefit humanity, expand our potential . . .'

'Not possible,' I said, louder this time.

'Impossible is merely something no one has yet managed to do. And I have, Thomas. We've gone through every codon on the genome. We culled the junk, stripped out the weaknesses and the redundancies. Boosted positive attributes. Then we assembled the entire thing from scratch, all three billion base pairs. Smarter, tougher, more capable. Humanity 2.0, if you will.'

Heavy footsteps rang on the stairs. The door behind me opened. Pharaoh smiled.

'Well speak of the Devil.'

Fifty

He was alone; he hadn't got Greta. That was the first thing I saw, though the relief lasted just as long as it took me to think what else he might have done with her.

It was the first time I'd seen him properly. He wore black combat trousers and a tight black T-shirt that clung to his biceps – though any clothes would have been tight-fitting on that huge frame. Clean shaven, the sort of short-back-and-sides haircut that practical mothers give their sons. Snow crystals gleamed in his hair.

'Where is she?' asked Pharaoh.

He brushed a few stray bits of snow off his shoulder. 'Ice fall. I couldn't get through.'

I thought of the cracks I'd squeezed myself through, the creaking ice crushing the breath out of my lungs. I thought of Greta down there in the dark as a million tons of ice began to come down. I wanted to scream.

Pharaoh frowned. 'Did you find her body?'

He shook his head.

'She might have got through before it collapsed. Go take a snowmobile round to the Helbreen and check if she came out.'

The man didn't move. Just stared at me.

'Of course,' said Pharaoh. 'You haven't been introduced.' He held out his arms. 'Thomas, meet Thomas.'

I wasn't really listening, too lost in thoughts of Greta, and wondering if I knocked him down the stairs whether I'd manage to break his neck. It took me a second to realise what Pharaoh meant.

'He's called . . . ?'

'We named him after you.'

'It seemed appropriate,' said Louise.

'A second chance.'

'We're both still very fond of you.'

Now they had my attention. I stared at the man, this other Thomas, my mind filled with suspicion and wonder and doubt. I waited for him to come in, but he just stood in the doorway, like a child who's forbidden from the living room.

'What is he?' The words came out so quietly I had to say them again. '*What is he?*'

'You know what he is,' said Pharaoh.

Our eyes locked. I've been on the receiving end of that stare many times, never beaten it, but this felt different. He wanted me to believe him – needed it, perhaps. He'd laboured underground all these years, building his masterpiece, and now he deserved some recognition.

'You're welcome to genotype him,' Pharaoh offered. 'I have the equipment right here. You'll see things no one's ever seen before.'

Virtual-reality theorists have a phrase that describes the revulsion humans feel when we see an almost perfect simulation of a person: the *uncanny valley*, the point at which the illusion becomes too close for comfort, but not quite real enough. This was similar. The creature – I refused to think of him as Thomas – was perfectly real, almost familiar. Yet some deep animal sense in me recognised he wasn't real enough.

But it didn't add up. 'How old is he?'

'Eight hundred and sixty-eight days. Two years, four months.'

Pharaoh laughed at the look on my face. 'Quite the bouncing baby, isn't he?'

'Then how is he so . . . ?'

'Mature? An error.' A tightening at the corner of his mouth; I remembered how much he hated mistakes. 'One of the segments we snipped turned out to influence cell replication and development. He's aging at approximately twelve times the normal rate. We'll fix it next time.'

Something like fear crossed the creature's face. It really was a child's face: plump cheeks, skin unscuffed or worn. I couldn't help thinking of Luke, when he was a toddler.

'And the speech . . .'

'We've spent the last two years educating him. Genes for general intelligence, "G", are relatively easy to identify – that was the first area we improved. Married to his rapid development, it means he's quite the conversationalist. He also plays a mean game of chess.'

Looking at him, I started to see why I'd believed, intuitively, Pharaoh's impossible claims. Nothing obviously wrong: no bolt through the neck, or clumsy stitches up his cheeks. Not the sheer size, though if you'd met him on the street you'd certainly have stared. The arms, the legs, the nose and mouth were all correct. Even the eyes, the windows to the so-called soul. It was something greater, the way the whole package fitted together. Nature trains us in certain proportions: his were subtly different. I suppose Pharaoh would have said 'better'.

He was still waiting, staring at me as if he wanted something. More than wanted. *Coveted.*

'Go on,' Pharaoh said to him. 'Before she has a chance to get back to Zodiac.'

The creature – I couldn't think of him any other way – turned to go. There was no way I could stop him, but I tried anyway. For Greta's sake. All I got for my efforts was another bruise, and a scornful look from Pharaoh.

I sat down at the table, rubbing my arm. I tortured myself imagining Greta. Surviving the ice fall, dragging herself through the tunnels. Hauling herself up the rope towards that tiny circle of light. Coming out into the cold, thinking she'd made it. And then the monster's hands around her throat.

But even that was optimistic. More likely, she was buried in the ice.

I had to talk or I'd go mad. 'How did you do it?' I asked.

Pharaoh was happy to answer. To show off. 'The same way the Maryland group did it. Or, for that matter, what Roslin did with Dolly the sheep. We injected the synthesised genome into a human egg with its own genetic material removed, and then we implanted the egg in a host and brought it to term in vivo.'

In vivo. In life – in a human being. I looked at Louise.

'You gave birth to this . . . creature?'

'We prefer the term synthetic human,' Pharaoh said.

I thought of the specimen jars, the fleshy masses floating in the fluid. I remembered a phrase from the literature: *viable embryos*. Pharaoh had made it sound so routine, just shake and bake. But science is messier than we pretend; we never get it right first time. It took almost three hundred tries to make Dolly the sheep.

I had no sympathy.

'It's a shame you didn't give a damn about the son you already had. He still wakes up screaming in the night, by the way, because he thinks he doesn't have a mother.'

It's always a mistake to attack Louise. Hit her with a punch and the knife comes out. She put her hands flat on the table, shoulders tense, like a swimmer about to push into the deep end.

366

'You only cared for Luke because it was the one thing where you could compete with me.'

We'd had this argument before. This time, I wasn't going to play. Louise lapsed back into silence; I looked around the room. Once you got past the post-industrial concrete chic, you could see how primitive it was. There was a small kitchenette at the back, and a couple of doors that must be a bedroom and a bathroom. They'd obviously blown the budget on the lab space.

'Who pays for this?' I wondered.

'I had some grant money left over. Beyond that, a few discreet and far-sighted philanthropists keep us topped up. Our overheads are fairly minimal – just supplies, and a couple of support staff off-site.'

'Off-site?'

'UPS doesn't deliver here.' An ironic smile, permitting me to laugh. 'I pay the cook at Zodiac a small retainer to order in what we need, and leave it where we can fetch it.'

I rubbed my eyes. 'Danny's part of this?'

'He thinks he's supporting a global counter-terrorism conspiracy at the highest echelons. We also have a technician in Iceland. As you'll understand, to accomplish what we're doing takes vast computing resources. Computers need power, and power is in short supply up here. The number crunching is done on servers in Reykjavik – we appreciate their laws on data secrecy – and beamed to us here on Utgard. Your colleague Bob Eastman found our transceiver in Vitangelsk.'

'Is Eastman working for you, too?'

'Emphatically no.' He steepled his fingers, contemplating a problem. 'Eastman is a real danger to us, much more than the unfortunate Martin Hagger.'

'But Hagger found you out.'

'He came close.'

'So you killed him.' All the impotence and anger inside me suddenly found a point to fix on. 'You talk about the sanctity of life—'

'Life with a capital L.'

'You talk about building a better human. There are some pretty obvious upgrades you can make yourself.'

'I didn't kill Martin Hagger, Thomas.'

'He'd almost rumbled you.'

'And I had found a way to, ah, discourage him. Who do you think told the *Nature* editors to re-examine Hagger's sample? Who planted the idea in Francis Quam's head – discreetly, of course – that if Hagger stayed it would jeopardise his precious funding? Everything was in hand.'

'Evidently not.'

'Unforeseen circumstances.' Again the five fingers curled into a fist, like a flower closing its petals. 'For some time, we've allowed Thomas – our Thomas – the liberty of the island. We felt it was important to his development; also, we wanted to observe him in the wild. Obtain real-world data. Thomas is relatively impervious to extremes of heat and cold; he lived in an abandoned building in Vitangelsk. One day – last Saturday, to be precise – he came across Martin Hagger on our back doorstep.'

'He didn't know what he was doing,' Louise said. 'He was frightened.'

She looked too tired for someone so young. Bags under her eyes, a grey tint to her skin. I don't suppose she saw much sunlight, but it was more than that. It can't have been easy for her, alone with Pharaoh so long. He'd always needed fuel for his tremendous energy, I remembered, and he drew it from other people. That was why so many of his students burned out.

'Hagger provoked him. Thomas overreacted,' said Pharaoh

briskly. 'Thomas's emotional development has not kept pace with his physical and mental capacity.'

Again, I thought of Greta climbing towards the light.

'You mean he's got the body of a wrestler, Mensa-level intelligence and the moral compass of a two-year-old. There's a word for that kind of person in real life. We'd call him a psychopath.'

'There's an interesting debate to be had on the co-morbidity of certain desirable and undesirable behaviours. What's socially acceptable may not ensure the species' survival. How that plays out in Thomas's development is one of the major factors we'll be looking at over the next few years.'

'Did he sabotage the plane as well?'

'He couldn't bear to see you go.' That smile again, like someone speaking a foreign language, not sure you understand him. 'Thomas has developed a certain fascination with you. It was he, you see, who attacked you on the glacier when you went back there. He recognised you, then; he understood who you were. That's why he let you go.'

The figure from my dreams. The arm raised, the face staring down at me. Recognition.

'Why would Thomas care about me?'

'When we made Thomas, we didn't start with a blank sheet of paper. That would have taken too long. We took an existing human genome and edited the code. No point reinventing the wheel. Thomas is aware of that. He's fascinated by the idea that he has a twin brother.'

The words hit me like a bullet. 'You used my DNA? My DNA to create this . . .'

I caught Pharaoh smiling at me. I almost punched him – but I had to know.

'Not yours. You and he share only fifty per cent of your varying DNA. Before improvements.'

Louise was trying to look at me without catching my eye.

The way I used to watch her in the lab, sometimes. Pharaoh glanced at her.

'You'd better do this.'

Louise put out a hand to steady herself. The mug rattled on the glass tabletop.

'He's talking about Luke.'

Fifty-one

Emotions erupted I never knew I had. 'You used our son's DNA for *this*?'

It wasn't the most outlandish thing they'd told me that night. In fact, it made all the sense in the world, a piece that fitted perfectly. None of the rough edges that distinguish a lie. And for all that, it was the hardest thing I was being asked to believe.

She nodded.

'How?'

'The cord blood.'

Umbilical-cord blood is rich in stem cells; at birth, you can take a sample and freeze it. We did it for Luke when he was born – Louise insisted, though it cost a thousand pounds we didn't really have. *Imagine if he gets leukaemia, or needs a transplant, and those stem cells are the only thing that can save him*, she said. And of course, I agreed. For Luke's sake.

'That was for him.' I felt empty, as if the most precious thing I owned had been snatched from me and dashed to pieces. 'Not this . . .' I didn't shy away from saying it any more. '. . . this *monster*.'

I stood. Hurt and anger charged up inside me, years of accumulated friction ready to discharge like a bolt of lightning. I didn't mind if it killed me. As long as it took her too.

Remember Luke, I told myself. I had to get back to him.

371

For all the menace in the room, the strange unreality, I wasn't a threat to Pharaoh. He hadn't broken any laws – there weren't any on Utgard. If I revealed what he'd done, he'd be hailed as a genius, biology's Einstein. Or maybe Robert Oppenheimer. As long as I kept calm.

I forced myself to sit, gripping the sides of my chair.

'So what happens now?'

Pharaoh went to the kitchenette and got a bottle of whisky and a glass from a cupboard. He poured himself a generous measure. Didn't offer me one.

'We're not going to publish in *Nature*, if that's what you mean. We won't make ourselves popular if we announce to the world that seven billion humans have just become obsolete. My company is discreetly patenting some of the more advanced techniques we've developed. We'll feed them into the mainstream gradually, educate public understanding until this process feels as natural, as logical, as giving your kid his shots.'

It was a good spiel. Pharaoh had enough bombast that he almost carried it off – certainly, if I'd been an investor, I'd probably have opened my wallet. But coming from a man as sharp as Pharaoh, it all sounded rather vague. Some of the things he was describing might come to pass, and some might not, but there wasn't a master plan. He'd done this thing to prove he could. Because he was curious. Because he wanted the power.

'And me? Do I get pushed down a crevasse too?'

Another tic of irritation. 'I've already told you . . .'

'Or will you have your creature do your dirty work?'

'I'm not a murderer, Thomas. I'm in the business of *improving* life, not ending it.'

'What about *him*? Will you take him to New York, unveil him on Broadway? You'd make the cover of *Time*, no question.'

'I think *Life* would have been more fitting, don't you? If it was still with us.' Another chuckle. 'No. Thomas will stay here. The accelerated development you noticed means he probably only has a few years of life. We'll observe him, and apply those lessons to the next generation. In that respect, Utgard's perfect. A quarantine zone with no escape.'

'And Zodiac? Is he going to pick off the scientists one by one, if he doesn't like the way they look at him?' I had to laugh, though it sounded borderline hysterical. 'Like the fucking *Thing*.'

This time, I hadn't heard him coming. The door opened and the creature came back in, dressed to go out in a yellow parka and black ski trousers. For some reason, he had the DAR-X logo sewn on to the sleeve.

'I told you to go,' said Pharaoh. The icy voice of a parent who wants you to know his patience has limits.

The creature crossed to the television on the wall and turned it on. You could see his strangeness in every step he took, disproportioned limbs making disproportioned strides.

He's a machine, I reminded myself. Made of flesh and blood, but still a machine programmed by a computer.

'What are you doing?' Pharaoh demanded. His voice had risen, a note of worry puncturing the confidence, and I suddenly realised that the experiment was ongoing. He was making it up as he went along. Two years and four months. I remember when Luke was that age, how little I knew him compared to now.

The screen went white. At first, I didn't understand what we were seeing. The contrast was so high, almost monochrome, that everything looked alien and unworldly. White-speckled black, with a thick black mass churning at the bottom of the screen, flowing from a jagged white hole. Ice forming?

A shape at the top of the picture caught my eye. I recognised the familiar peaks that loomed over Zodiac. But then—

I was looking at Zodiac. But not as I'd left it, a few hours earlier. The Platform had been blown open. Black smoke poured out of it. The jagged edges I'd taken for a hole in the ice were pieces of metal, broken struts and bits of roof that had been hacked open like a tin can.

I looked at Pharaoh. He looked as confused as me.

'What—'

'I don't . . .'

He picked up a remote. He must have indexed the video; in a few seconds, he'd jumped to a different scene. The camera slightly straighter, the Platform intact. I could make out a cluster of snowmobiles in the foreground, a few of the huts further back. The time-stamp in the corner of the screen said 21:57.

Pharaoh restarted the video. After a second, two figures came into view from behind the Platform and headed towards the snowmobile park. Too far and indistinct to make out, but they must be me and Greta.

Greta. Even as a few distant pixels, it hurt to see her there. As we reached the snowmobiles, a third figure stood up among them. He'd been there all along, though I hadn't noticed him. Quam. I watched us chat for a couple of minutes, then Greta and I walked away. Quam went back to fiddling with the snowmobiles. After another few minutes, I saw a blob that must have been the Sno-Cat crawling up the Lucia glacier in the background.

Pharaoh hit the fast-forward button. The Sno-Cat climbed comically fast, up over the top of the glacier and out of sight.

And then it happened. The centre of the screen flared into a white starburst where the explosion overwhelmed the sensor, smoke leaking from its edges. A second later, the whole picture shook as the shock wave reached the camera and knocked it askew. More explosions, more starbursts. Smoking pieces of metal flew in every direction, cartwheeling over the snow.

The Platform's legs buckled, and the whole rear end collapsed in an eruption of flames and smoke.

'How . . . ?'

Pharaoh rewound the last few seconds and played it again at normal speed. The doomed Platform reassembled itself; the Sno-Cat hurried backwards down the glacier, reversed, and crawled back up and over the top. Quam came out from behind a hut and walked slowly towards the back of the Platform, under the mess windows. I thought of the others, all the Zodiac staff enjoying Thing Night.

Quam fiddled with something, then extended his right arm, pointing at something in the space. The arm looked wrong, too long for his body, but that was because he was holding something. A flare gun.

The camera was too far away to see him pull the trigger. Just the faintest flash, before the Platform exploded and engulfed Quam. It went up so fast, he must have packed oil drums or something underneath.

I rounded on Pharaoh. 'Is this something to do with you?'

One look at his face quashed that idea. He looked as if he'd been punched in the stomach.

I'm in the business of improving life, not ending it. I turned to the creature. 'You?'

The creature shook his head. Unlike the rest of us, he seemed immune to what we'd just played back. Wasn't even looking at the screen, but staring at one of the Hockneys as if thinking about something completely different. Perhaps he couldn't comprehend tragedy.

'I don't care what you've done,' I told Pharaoh. 'We need to get back there. If there are survivors . . .'

'Of course.' Pharaoh was still staring at the screen, hypnotised by the carnage. Beside him, Louise looked sick. She slipped her hand into his.

'Let's go.'

Fifty-two

My coat and trousers were hung on a hook in the stairwell, mostly dry, though the coat zipper was still broken. I Velcroed it shut the best I could. The hard edges of the notebook in the inside pocket pressed against my chest.

I noticed again the DAR-X logo stencilled on the creature's jacket. 'Where did he get that? Another "overreaction"?'

A tight look from Pharaoh told me I was on the money. 'An unfortunate encounter last September.'

They suited up, and led me down a long corridor lined with corrugated plastic to a heavy door in a concrete wall. Pharaoh unlocked it, stepped through some small sort of vestibule that smelled of sawdust, and out through another door. Daylight hit me, and I wondered what time it was. How many hours had passed in the tunnels, in the mine, listening to Pharaoh speak? It must be at least mid-morning. I'd gone through the night without sleep or food, and I felt it. I found my sunglasses in my coat pocket and put them on.

We were at the top of a narrow mountain valley, looking down at a cluster of tin-roofed buildings joined together by chutes and covered walkways.

'Vitangelsk?' I guessed. I'd only ever seen it on the map.

'Mine Eight.'

We skidded down the slope, following soft tracks in the snow. At the bottom of the complex we came to a large

376

building jacked up on stilts. It seemed to be the terminus for some sort of cable car or chairlift. In the space underneath, hidden behind sheets of rusting corrugated iron, Pharaoh pulled tarpaulins off two gleaming snowmobiles.

'Get on.'

All I remember about the ride is the cold. No spare helmet or goggles – they never expected guests – so I had to keep my head down and clench my eyes shut. With the zip broken, I could only Velcro my jacket shut and keep close to Pharaoh. He kept his rifle in a sort of holster attached to the saddle – I could probably have reached it, if I'd wanted. But what would have been the point? We were beyond that.

Any hope that the video might have been a fake, some warped practical joke, died ten miles from Zodiac. Pharaoh paused at the top of a rise; I opened my eyes, and saw a column of oily smoke polluting the sky. We went on; the wind cut my eyes and made me weep, but I couldn't stop looking at it. Wishing it would disappear.

We came down the Lucia glacier and saw the whole horror show. The Platform had blown open like a ruptured artery; several of the nearby huts had burned, and some of the further ones had been torn apart by shrapnel. You could see bare rock where the fire had melted away the ice around the Platform. The snow that survived was black and cratered with wreckage.

No chance to get into the Platform. Fires still burned inside; even as we dismounted the snowmobiles, another strut gave out and collapsed in a shower of sparks and screaming metal. We could feel the heat twenty metres away. No one could have survived.

Louise voiced the obvious question. '*Why?*'

I thought of the video, Quam taking the gun from his holster and calmly putting a flare into a pile of high explosives and oil drums. I remembered that night I met him in the corridor, the dead look in his eyes. *This island's trying to kill us.* Was it the pressure that had got to him? The endless funding threats; the egos and the sniping; something in his personal life?

I think it was this place. Surrounded by nothing, his mind had expanded so fast it shattered, like brittle ice drawn from a deep hole.

We wandered around the base, opening doors and checking the cabooses for survivors. *If only*, I kept saying to myself. If only Greta and I had stopped Quam when we had the chance. If only we'd guessed. If we hadn't rushed off to the Helbreen.

If we hadn't gone to the Helbreen, we'd have been on the Platform and we'd be dead. That's the truth.

The mag hut was far enough from the Platform that it had survived unscathed. I drifted towards it and peered in the door. The machines had stopped. All I smelled inside was dust and darkness.

But there was something else. A sound, a shadow, a sense of movement at the back of the room. It was too dark to see. I took off my sunglasses, but the contrast was so stark it made no difference. Could there be survivors? And if there were, did I want to give them away to Pharaoh? I hesitated on the threshold.

A shout spun me back around. Fifty metres away, Fridge stood in the open doorway of Star Command. His hair was wild and burnt away in patches; smoke smudged his cheeks. He leaned on a ski pole, but the pole was too short for his height so he listed like a drunk. His right leg hung bent at a painfully unnatural angle. I couldn't understand what he was shouting.

I still don't know if I heard the shot. If I did, I thought it was just another pop from the burning Platform. I'd started to run to Fridge. He'd seen me and turned, dragging himself towards me, still shouting. Then he suddenly fell backwards.

I thought he'd dropped his stick, or skidded on a patch of ice. It was only when I knelt beside him that I saw the hole in his jacket. Round as a ten-pence piece, straight over the heart, blood pumping out through the hole.

I took off my hat and pressed it over the hole, trying to staunch the bleeding. It wouldn't work. I tried anyway. Holding it in place, I looked up. The creature stood about ten metres away, rifle in hand. No emotion on his face.

'What have you done?'

Pharaoh looked as stricken as me. He ran over and grabbed the gun by its barrel, twisting it out of the creature's hands. He must have let it go. Pharaoh threw the gun on to the snow and stared up at his creation. There were tears in his eyes. They rolled down his cheeks and froze in his beard.

'What have you done?' he repeated.

Overshadowed by the creature, Pharaoh didn't look like the unstoppable tyrant I'd always known. He'd grown small, an old man whom time had caught up.

'Did I request thee, Maker, from my clay to mould me man?' said the creature.

Pharaoh squinted up at him. 'What?'

He said it again. Shreds of black smoke blew around his face.

'Where did you learn that?'

'Careful.' Louise had backed away. I didn't know who she was speaking to. 'Don't do anything—'

My hat was soaked through. I pulled off my neck-warmer and laid it on top. A drop of blood squeezed out from the hat and trickled down on to the Zodiac badge.

'I made you,' Pharaoh said. A trace of the old arrogance, holding out against a changing tide. 'You owe me everything. Every cell in your being.'

'And you? Does a father owe his son nothing, except the fact of his existence?'

Pharaoh took a step back. 'I'm not your father, Thomas.'

'What, then? A god?'

'Don't be ridiculous.'

'Why are you talking like this?' said Louise.

'My master? Am I your slave?'

'Of course not. You're—'

Whatever life might be, it goes in an instant. One moment, Pharaoh was living, a being of infinite capacities. The next – nothing. Those big, disproportionate arms he'd created reached out and clutched him in an embrace. One arm went around his head, the other held his shoulders fast. Almost as if he was trying to comfort him.

One arm moved; the other didn't. The neck cracked. Pharaoh slumped to the ground.

Louise screamed. I was too far away. Thomas picked up the rifle where Pharaoh had thrown it, aimed and fired. Blood sprayed from her neck and fell on the snow like rain as she twisted away and fell hard. Her body jerked as a second shot went into her.

I moved towards her, but a hand on my shoulder spun me back. He held me there, his fingers digging into my collarbone.

'Come with me.'

Fifty-three

Anderson's Journal

I struggled, of course, but I hadn't slept, hadn't eaten in hours, and he had the strength of the damned. It wasn't a fair fight. When I was down, he pulled open my jacket to take it off me – that really would have been the end. Then he saw the broken zip and thought better of it. He stuffed me in a sleeping bag, wound it up with rope, and tied me on the sled behind the snowmobile, packed in with the survival gear.

Strapped down, I could only twist my head and watch as he carried the bodies to the gulch and dropped them in. Pharaoh, Louise, Fridge; one, two, three. When he came to Fridge, the creature stripped off his yellow coat and put on Fridge's red Zodiac jacket. Fridge was big enough it just about fitted him.

He walked past and disappeared from my field of vision. The sledge rocked as he mounted the snowmobile. The engine coughed into life; I gagged as exhaust fumes blew over my face.

The smoking hulk of Zodiac Station slid by out of sight. I felt a see-saw bump as we crossed the shoreline. Then we headed out on to the ice.

I can't write much about the journey. While it was happening, it felt like one long moment stretching for eternity – and then when we stopped it seemed to have gone in a flash. Hours, I don't know how many, navigating the sea ice: bouncing over cracks and ridges, backing up when an obstacle blocked our way, trying again. Once I opened my eyes and saw dark water rushing beside us, as if we were taking a scenic drive along a lake. The snowmobile heeled over on the slope, and for a terrifying second I thought we'd tumble in. Mostly, I kept my eyes shut, my head burrowed in the sleeping bag to keep off the wind and the fumes. Pressing myself flat against the sledge to minimise myself. Dematerialise. Bumping and jarring as the sledge whiplashed on the rugged ice. The knots that seemed so tight weren't tight enough to stop me bouncing, bruising me deep into my bones. I waited for us to drop off the edge of the world.

And then we stopped. It felt sudden, though everything feels sudden when you have no control. The engine cut out and the silence hit me like a brick. Just wind and whiteness.

He dismounted, opened the engine cover and fiddled with the drive belt, the same way I'd seen Greta do it when we'd towed Hagger's snowmobile home. Then he went round to the back and pushed. The machine slid obediently over the snow, towards a break in the ice a few metres away. It splashed into the water, breaking the sugary crust that had already begun to form, and sank. Was I next?

He unloaded the sledge. The skis, the stove, the ration box and the tent. A strange replay of that first night with Greta, when we'd camped out and been found by DAR-X. *Except tonight, the role of Martin Hagger (deceased) will be played by Thomas Anderson.* The first of that name.

He put up the tent. He unstrapped me and carried me inside, like a bear bringing his meal back to the cave. I rubbed my arms inside the sleeping bag to get blood back where the cords had numbed them, while he melted ice over the stove. He thrust the metal cup against my lips, his clumsy hands spilling it over my face. The water was so hot I choked, but I forced it down. I had to get my strength back. The snowmobile was gone. The nearest settlement was probably Svalbard – or maybe Nord Station, on the tip of Greenland. Hundreds of kilometres.

'Why are you doing this?' I whispered.

'You are my salvation.'

He poured water into one of the orange meal packs and handed it to me. No spoon. I slurped it down. The pack said it was chicken with pesto, almost the most far-fetched thing I'd heard that day.

I swallowed it all and asked for another.

'Do you like it?' he asked. Genuinely curious, like a parent weaning a child.

'It's better than nothing.'

He squatted on the floor of the tent, watching me with those brown eyes that looked so much like Luke's.

He's fascinated by the idea that he has a biological twin.

I'll kill him, I promised myself. If I had to wrestle him into the water myself, drown us both under the ice, I'd find the strength.

'You keep a diary.' Not a question. 'I've watched you writing it. Through the windows.'

What else did he know about me? All the time I'd spent at Zodiac, searching everywhere for answers, and really it was me who'd been under the microscope. Writhing like a worm.

'I left it on the Platform,' I lied.

'You have a bulge under your coat, over your left breast.'

I undid the Velcro holding my coat together and extracted my journal. Damp, where I'd fallen in the underground stream, but the Gore-Tex had mostly kept it safe. I handed it over.

Play along, play along. I told myself my chance would come.

He gave me another meal while he read the first pages of the journal. When I'd swallowed it down, I asked, 'What's next?'

'There is a coastguard ship forty kilometres from here.'

'That's a long way without a snowmobile.'

'I am impassive to cold.'

He had a strange way of speaking, this outsize man-child. Stiff and earnest, like someone attempting a foreign language. With only Pharaoh and Louise to talk to all his life, he must have learned most of his English from books. Old ones, by the sound of it.

He went back to the journal. Inside the bag, I felt my pockets for any sort of weapon. A penknife, a screwdriver. Even a carabiner might do. I had nothing except a Bic pen.

Thomas looked up. 'Do you know what life is, Thomas? Is it the same as existing?'

'I'm not a philosopher.'

'Are you aware of endoliths? Single-celled organisms that inhabit the pores in between individual grains of rock, kilometres underground. They absorb nutrients from the rock itself; they obtain their energy from the heat of the earth. It requires all their resources simply to stay alive. Once every hundred years or so, they divide. One cell becomes two. And science says that is life.'

'Technically.'

He seemed to want more. 'You know you are alive. From the day you were born, you never doubted it. I lack that comfort. I feel I am alive, but all I know is what is inside me. How do you feel?'

'Pretty rubbish, to be honest.'

He didn't smile. I never saw him smile. Was that one of the untidy genes Pharaoh snipped out of his genome? Can you be human, if you can't smile?

'I think,' he said solemnly, 'life is taking your chances.'

★   ★   ★

384

He read. I lay there, waiting for my chance. But it's hard to launch yourself out of a sleeping bag. Every time I moved, he was on to me quick as a cat.

I tried to force myself to stay awake. I wondered about Greta. Did she get out, after all? Did she make it back to Zodiac? Did she come down the hill thinking she'd was safe, euphoric with success, only to find a smoking ruin? Would she die of cold or starvation before the rescue party came? If they came. Perhaps it was better to imagine she'd died in the cave, snuffed out in a second by a million tons of ice settling.

I thought about Luke. I imagined the creature escaping, making his way to Cambridge. Looking for his twin. I thought about finding him in my home, and what I would do to him then.

But even the imagination fails in the end. Robert Frost was wrong: desire, hatred, the hot-blooded emotions – they're no match for the cold. The world will end in ice. I began to drift. Each time my eyes opened, there he was, sitting beside me reading the journal. More than once, I saw him mouthing phrases, repeating them to himself as if studying for an exam. Sometimes he asked me questions. 'What is the Overlook Hotel? Who is Willard Price? What is a Dalek?'

And then I woke and he was gone. I scrambled out of the bag and crawled outside, just in time to see him clipping himself into the skis he'd taken from the emergency sled. He looked ridiculously large on them, like a circus elephant on a bike.

'I'm coming back,' he told me.

I didn't believe him. I threw myself at him, but he simply pushed off on his sticks and glided away into the fog. I couldn't chase; I didn't even have boots on.

I crawled back into the tent. He'd left me the journal, at least, and I had a pen in my pocket. I picked it up and started to write.

'Captain?'

Sitting at the chart table in the wheelhouse, Franklin closed the book and looked up. Nearly at the end, only a couple of paragraphs left.

'Ice is giving out,' Santiago reported. 'We should hit open water soon. Longyearbyen in seventeen hours.'

'Good.' Franklin pulled off his glasses and wiped them on his shirt. 'How about Anderson?'

'You mean the real Slim Shady?'

'The one who got away.'

'Nada. Pilot says if you want him flying bigger circles, he'll need more fuel. And overtime.' Santiago hesitated. 'He also said you should give him a quarter and take him to Foxwoods. You'll get better odds.'

Franklin rested his hands on the journal and stared out the window.

What the hell is out there?

'Call in the helo and wrap it up. No one can survive this place for long.'

'What about Anderson, sir? The one we do have.'

'What about him?'

'Do you think he'll live?'

A line from an old movie ran through Franklin's head. He had to smile.

'Who does?'

Anderson's Journal – Final Entry

Writing in a hurry, numb fingers clutching pen. All alone. Scribbling.

He's gone out, he may be some time. Said he'd bring help

– rescue – think he lied. Knows that much about being human.

He's gone to the ship. Thomas Anderson, sole survivor of Zodiac Station. They'll take him to England. Home. He'll have a life.

Life means taking your chances.

I thought I would have one. Maybe I did. Missed it.

Some say the world will end in fire, some say in ice . . .

On the rocks.

We took risks, we knew we took them. Things have come out against us, and therefore we have no cause for complaint.

I wish to register a complaint.

I love you, Luke.

Sounds from the ice. Groaning, throbbing, like a living thing. Breaking up? Almost like an engine. Footsteps. A bear?

Here I am. A speck of life adrift on the ocean, huddled for survival on my frozen raft. Clinging to hope, until the ice melts.

Acknowledgements

The Arctic can be a slippery place. For helping on my travels and keeping me out of crevasses, literal and figurative, my profound thanks go to Nick Cox of the UK Arctic Research Station at Ny-Ålesund, for sharing a fraction of his immense knowledge of Arctic science; Sara Wheeler, for telling me how to get to Svalbard; Doug Benn and Griet Scheldeman, for a crash course in glaciology and glacier caving, and an unforgettable night drinking whisky in Longyearbyen; Tom Foreman, who led the way through ice caves and abandoned mines; Stefano Poli and Yann Rashid of Poli Arctici, for three extraordinary days on the ice; the Kennedy family, for essential provisions; Karoline Baelum at the Svalbard Science Forum, who painted vivid pictures of science in the field; Jon Hawkins and Danny Davies, for lending me warm clothing; Sarah Hawkins, for introducing me to the right people; Miriam Iorwerth for sharing her amazing photographs; and James McIntosh, who miraculously knew everything I needed to know, and was always happy to help. Kevin Anderson gave me sedatives, antidepressants and head injuries whenever I wanted them. And an evening in the pub with Des Roberts-Clark provided me with more understanding of genetics than a month in the library, plus a fistful of plot ideas.

I'm grateful to everyone at Hodder for doing what they always do, which is running the best operation in publishing: Anne Perry, Kerry Hood, Jason Bartholomew and all their colleagues. Oliver Johnson steered the book with his usual ineffable genius; and Caroline Johnson scraped off the barnacles with a razor-sharp copy-edit. Jane Conway-Gordon watched my back and muttered dire warnings about polar bears.

For every day working on this book in the Arctic, I spent twenty at home. For those, and all the time in between, I'd like to thank my wife, Emma, for constantly supporting me despite some of my wilder scientific ideas (she has a professional interest in genetics); and my sons Owen and Matthew, for encouraging and distracting me in equal measure. One day, I promise, we'll go to the North Pole.

All the science in this book is based on actual research. In some cases I may have exaggerated or misappropriated the facts either to serve the story or to simplify complex ideas, or from sheer ignorance. In every case, those distortions are all mine, and no reflection on the real scientists who told me about their work.

For anyone who's curious, Utgard is located about halfway between Svalbard and Franz Josef Land, and further north, but you won't find it on any map. Likewise, Zodiac Station combines details of various Arctic and Antarctic bases, but the base, its personnel and its parent organisation are entirely fictional.